Censorshipped

A SMALL TOWN, BROTHER'S BEST FRIEND, SWEET ROMCON

SAVANNAH SCOTT

A gentle heads up for you

I love writing romcom.

The way I write this genre is very personal to me. I write characters who feel very, very real to me. Real people face real problems. You do. I do. We all do. My characters do.

This paragraph has possible spoilers as I tell you about content warnings:
Censorshipped has the following content that I think you might want to know about in advance: Parent with depression and death of a sibling (not on page).

If you find any other content in this story you think would warrant a content warning, please feel free to reach out to tell me.

And now, I hope you enjoy this sweet, heartfelt, beautiful love story ... and the humor and tenderness I sprinkled within these pages to make you laugh, smile, and maybe even tear up a time or two.

Happy Reading!
~ Savannah

Connect with Savannah Scott

You can connect with Savannah at her website
SavannahScottBooks.com

You can also follow Savannah on Amazon.

For freebies, book recommendations,
early sneak peeks at Savannah's writing,
and first notice of new releases,
sign up for Savannah's Romcom Readers email
at subscribepage.io/savannahscottromcom

For Jon
My personal comedian and forever faithful husband.
Thank you for giving me the best of you.

~

For everyone who ever laughed
at something I said or did.
Making you laugh makes my day.

A little thought ...

*Love is the one thing worth
risking everything else to have.*

Welcome to Bordeaux

Welcome to the quaint and quirky town of Bordeaux, Ohio.

If you've already visited Bordeaux through another *Getting Shipped* story, welcome back!

If you haven't been to our town yet, you're in for some fun times, heartfelt friendships, and sweet romances.

As Lexi said in *Friendshipped* ...

> *We're talking about Bordeaux, Ohio, not the port city along the coastal southwest of France.*
> *We don't pronounce our town name like our French sister city either. Some bright ancestor of mine who settled this valley in the 1800s pronounced our town name,* **bored ox.** *Yep. Like some bull standing out in a field wondering what to do with his day. And, believe me, we have plenty of fields with plenty of oxen who, from what I've seen, look pretty bored.*

So, welcome to Bordeaux ... where the oxen might be bored, but you never will be!

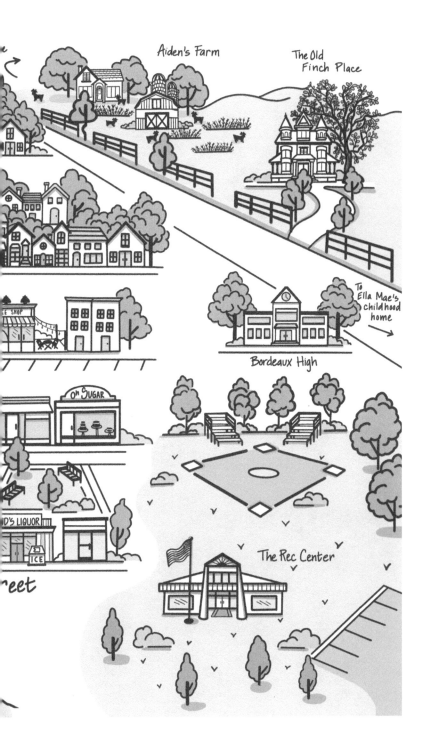

Aiden's Farm

The Old Finch Place

To Ella Mae's childhood home

Bordeaux High

Oh Sugar

D'S LIQUOR

ICE

The Rec Center

reet

ONE
Shannon

"And single, single, double. And single, single, double. That's right, now with attitude!"

I swivel my hips and pull my arms toward myself and push away in time to the music.

Glancing in the mirror, I stifle a giggle at the sight of the room full of senior women all attempting some version of pivoting their hips in time to the music. Half of them are beyond adorable. The other half border on terrifying.

"Shake it, don't break it, Mabel" Esther shouts over the music.

"I'm thinking I'll do both!" Mabel says, laughing.

The last beats of the song fade and I lead the group through a cool down. As I reach up and let my arms slowly fall to my sides with the final exhale, I see a pair of eyes I'd recognize anywhere peering through the tiny window in the door to our Rec Center dance studio.

Those eyes: green with brown flecks and this orange rim around the iris. Intense, yet playful. Never fully telling you what you want to know about the man behind them, but somehow still drawing you near because he's so irresistible. Trouble, your name is Duke.

He's here to coach little league. Which is outdoors in the ball

1

field, naturally, not right here in the hallway outside the dance studio. But, of course, in typical Duke style, he's scoping me out.

Not in that way.

Not in the way I want him to.

He's just my older brother's best friend, the most off-limits man on the planet. And he's checking in on me because he's always been like that. Flirty because it's his nature. And protective of me because–well I don't know why.

He waggles his eyebrows and winks.

I roll my eyes, which yes, I know, makes me seem like the sixteen year old version of myself instead of the twenty-six year old woman I am.

Several heads in the room have turned toward the door, following my gaze and catching on as to who is standing on the other side. I quickly shout out, "Don't forget! No class next Saturday because of the wedding!" But I think only one or two of the women are listening to me anymore now that Duke has arrived.

Esther, one of the seniors who comes regularly to my class, walks over and pulls the handle. "Oh, Duke! You just missed class. Shannon really had us doing all the gyrations and swivels like we were in our forties. You ought to come some time."

"I just might," Duke answers her, his eyes on me as he says the words.

Is that a threat or a promise? Or both?

"It's Senior Zumba," I mutter to myself. "Seniors only."

"We can bring guests," Esther's best friend, Mabel, says, apparently using her hearing aids today. "Remember when Bonnie Milgarden's grandkids were here for the holiday break? She brought 'em. Duke's just like one of our kids or grandkids."

Then she shouts across the room. "Aren't cha, Duke?"

"Far be it from me to argue with you, Mabel." Duke answers in his typical genial tone, flashing her a smile that always seems to get him what he wants.

I plaster on a grin and drop the subject. Maybe if I'm lucky,

Duke will forget Esther's invitation and all the seniors will forget it too. Though, their forgetfulness seems relegated to things like where they put their glasses or keys, never gossip, and they definitely will not forget asking Duke to come to my class.

While the women all flock to the door to socialize with Duke, I remove my headset, wipe my face with my hand towel, throw it in my duffle with my phone and bluetooth speaker, and then I stride toward the door.

Duke moves out of the way and props himself against the wall across the hallway, allowing everyone to pass through without his broad, muscular frame blocking the way.

He's got his arms crossed over his chest so his biceps pop just the slightest and his T-shirt strains across his chest just right. And he's smiling. Always smiling. His smile is the type that makes you wonder what he's been up to. It's the most unnerving thing in the world.

When the last of the women walks past me, I lock the door and turn to head out of the building.

"How's it going, Shannon?" Duke asks, pushing off the wall in one fluid movement to walk alongside me as I head down the hallway.

I smell the faint cinnamony spicy scent of Red Hots when he turns toward me. He's always sucking those things. It's the one junk food I think he allows himself to indulge in and for some reason, the smell of them makes me look up and momentarily study his mouth. I look away before he sees me.

"It's good," I say, forcing myself to keep my gaze aimed ahead of us.

It feels like he could read every thought I'm having about him if our eyes locked. And these thoughts are ones I wish I couldn't even interpret. I sure don't want Duke seeing them written across my face.

"Senior Zumba, huh?"

"Yep."

"I didn't know you were teaching. How long has it been?"

"A little over a month. Twice a week."

I can't keep the smile off my face. Dancing is my happy place. I never went as far with it as I wanted because of what happened to my sister when I was fourteen. But I never stopped loving dance–the freedom and discipline of training my body, and the gratifying way I push my limits as I lose myself in the music.

When my roommate Jayme mentioned that the Rec Center was looking for someone to start up Jazzercise for the seniors a couple times a week, I had to put a stop to that nonsense.

Jazzercise is so 1980. So Jane Fonda. So last century. I decided an intervention was needed, so I stepped in and brought the Beyoncé, Chris Brown, Charli D'Amelio vibe to our small town. And the women are eating it up.

"Mabel came into the shop to bring Pop a cherry pie the other day. She told Pop she's been coming here to–and I quote–shake what her mama gave her."

I giggle.

"She didn't."

"She actually did a little demonstration. I had to look away, but yes. Yes she did."

I glance up at Duke. He's beaming and chuckling and I don't think I can keep looking at him without reaching over and running my finger across his set of dimples peeking out from under the scruff along his jawline, or along those laugh lines near his eyes that should make him look old, but only serve to make him more attractive and boyish.

He softens his voice to the tone that gets to me the most, and says, "I'm glad you've got somewhere to dance, Shannon. And I think it's pretty awesome that you're doing this for them."

"Thanks," I squeak out. "I mean, thanks."

I say it with volume and steadiness the second time.

We reach the doors leading out to the parking lot. Duke leans on the metal push bar to press the door open. He waves me out.

"I'd better get to practice."

"Okay," I say. "Have a good one."

"It's always a good one."

It is when your whole being is made up of seventy-five percent sunshine and twenty-five percent I'm-here-for-the-party. I've never known Duke to have a bad day. And I've literally known him my whole life.

You know that saying "water off a duck's back"? That's Duke. Everything just rolls off him. He's perpetually flirting with life and every person he comes into contact with. He's as harmless as a puppy, except my heart feels like his chew toy, shredded from years of wishing he'd see me as something more than Chris' little sister.

I roll my shoulders as I walk toward my car. It's nothing new. But I'm getting too old to harbor a crush on Duke. I need to find a way to purge myself of this incessant attraction to the one man I can't ever have—the only man I ever really wanted.

TWO

Duke

I watch Shannon walk to her car. Then I force myself to turn and walk away, back down the hallway leading out toward the ball field behind the Rec Center.

She was wearing this criss-cross shirt that looks like it needs an instruction manual to put it on so a person avoids getting caught in the strings like a fly in a spider web. And yoga pants. I think they're yoga pants. All I know is I could see every curve of her figure without having to use an iota of my imagination—which is simultaneously convenient and inconvenient.

While I love looking at Shannon, I don't love other guys looking at her. And besides, looking at her in that outfit made me want to take her home and kiss her until our lips hum, and I can't do that—not now, or ever.

So yeah. Inconvenient.

Shannon just stared at me as if she were wearing a parka and ski pants instead of that dance outfit, which, to be clear, even if she were wearing snow clothes in the middle of summer, my urge to take her home and kiss her wouldn't diminish in the least.

If there's one thing I don't need, it's images of Shannon in that tight workout outfit running through my head. She's my best friend's little sister, and I promised Chris I'd keep an eye on her when he left to join the military.

Not that I think of her as a little sister. And that right there is the problem. Shannon is every bit a woman. Not just her figure or her beautiful smile, or her wavy hair that begs to be stroked, that pert nose and those rose-bud lips. Don't get me started on her lips. Full Shakespearean sonnets could be written about Shannon's lips. And yes, I may be a small-town mechanic, but I know my way around the bard.

Shannon's so much more than her looks. She's bright, funny, and interesting. Despite spending her free time reading tabloids, and basically living on junk food, she's not shallow–not at all.

I run my hand along the stubble on my jaw before pressing the push bar to open the door leading outside. I need to stop thinking about the million little qualities that make Shannon exceptional. Nothing will change the fact that she's forbidden to me.

Wanting Shannon is like sticking my tongue on an electrical socket. Which I did once, if you're wondering. Even I never did that twice. I can still feel the tightness and pervasive tingling to this day. A thrill that nearly killed me. That's what Shannon is.

And that's why I've been seeing Beth for the past year on and off. Beth knows it's not serious. I'd never lead a woman on. Seeing one another a few times a month merely provides a convenient way to pass the time and pretend we aren't both hopelessly single. But, that's gone on long enough too.

I'm not doing Beth any favors taking her out when she could be meeting a man who sincerely wants more with her. And, as much as I need to shake the feelings I have for Shannon, going out with women I will never want long term has proven to be one of the worst ideas I have ever had. And, I've had some pretty bad ideas over the years.

It's settled, I'm going to cut Beth loose on our next date. She deserves me telling her in person, or else I'd just pop her a text and call it a day.

I'm a hot mess, and I need to get a serious grip on myself, especially since Chris is due back home after he finally discharges from his military service in less than two months.

I have eight weeks to officially get over my best friend's sister.

"Coach D! Loooka this! I can throw it just the way you told me!" Mason calls out from the field a moment after the door to the Rec Center clanks shut behind me.

And just like that, I'm in coach mode.

I watch as Mason places his hand in the grip position we've been working on. I can see it from here, even though I'm still at least forty feet away from him. He pulls back and lets the ball fly. I watch for the twelve-to-six spin I want to see. The ball follows the pattern, spinning top to bottom and I let out a whoop of appreciation as it smacks into my assistant coach, Brooks' glove.

"That's how it's done!" I shout as I trot over and clap Mason on the shoulder. "That is how ... it's ... done, mini man. Keep that up and you'll be fighting off the scouts by high school!"

Mason grins up at me, his crooked smile taking over his face, and my day is officially made. Nothing beats the feeling of coaching these kids. I ruffle Mason's hair and send him toward the dugout where we'll gather the team before our official practice starts.

"He's getting way better," Brooks says, nodding toward the dugout.

"We still need to work on tunneling his pitches so they can't be read by batters, but yeah. Yeah he is."

"You do know he just turned eight, right?"

I chuckle. I can be a bit overzealous.

"Yeah. But Mason likes pushing himself. And there's no reason to let him develop bad habits he'll only have to correct later. He's got real potential."

"You say that about half the team."

"I call it like I see it. I never said Toby had potential. I just tell him he's got great team spirit, even if he couldn't hit a brick wall with a two-by-four at close range."

"True that," Brooks answers, shaking his head. "It's almost cruel of his parents to put him in little league."

"Nah. It's good for him. And good for the team. They need to learn to work together and compensate for one another. And to be respectful even when someone isn't a star player. I'll never let them pick on Toby. You see him smiling the whole practice. He loves it out here. It's not all about the win, Brooksy,"

I add a wink.

"I told you that nickname is only to be used by women. And I love how you of all people are telling me it's only a game, mister major leagues."

I chuckle and ruffle his hair like I do to the boys on my team. Brooks swats my hand away and runs his hand through his hair to fix it. The man has a thing about his hair.

Practice goes on for an hour. A few parents mingle in the bleachers. Some drop off, run errands and come back. We finish up practice and family members pour onto the field, kids running around, adults chatting with one another, gathering their kids, some coming over to talk to me or Brooks. Our team mom, Karina, walks around handing out the season's snack schedule like she's issuing detailed military tactics during a war. Snacks after games are serious business.

Cherry Blanchard comes running toward me. And nope. I did not stutter. Her name is Cherry. We live in the Midwest, which is the embarrassing stepchild of the south. Some of the names around here go miles beyond creative into downright "what were you thinking?" territory.

Anyway, Cherry went through a horrid divorce two years ago with Sparky Jones. Yep. Cherry and Sparky. Talk about a marriage doomed to end in flambé. She's got the look of a hungry hyena on her face. Not a good look on anyone, I assure you. And she's a hungry hyena wearing high heels and lipstick to match her name.

I busy myself collecting the empty water bottles we used to practice throwing techniques. I keep my head down toward the ground, eyes on the next clear plastic container in front of me.

"Duke! Oh, Duu-uke!"

Is temporary deafness a thing? I need to google that.

"Hey, Cherry," I say, without standing.

"How's my little superstar doing?"

Her little superstar is one of the most loveable kids on my team, Josh. And he's living proof that environment and heredity don't determine character. The kid's got a heart of gold and zero need to prove himself. I love him, plain and simple. He strikes out more than he connects for now, but we're working on it. I keep telling him we're all a work in progress. God knows I am.

"He's doing great. Always gives one hundred and ten percent."

"You're his hero," she purrs or coos or makes some animal noise that is obviously meant to get my engine humming to life. Instead I feel like installing a steering wheel lock and alarm system on every part of me around this woman.

"He's my hero," I say casually, keeping my eyes low while juggling the stack of bottles in my arms.

"Oh, look at me," Cherry exclaims. "Watching you clean up while I just hover here looking all cute and helpless."

And modest.

She bends over to start helping me, leaning in my direction in a very purposeful move so her top gapes, revealing more than I ever wanted to see of this woman. I pivot like the ex-ball player I am. Still quick on my feet when something's flying at me. I stand and mumble a thank you to Cherry over my shoulder on my way toward the recycle can next to the bleachers.

Brooks is laughing his head off when I approach.

"You got Cherried big time, man."

I crack a half-smile. "Hard to avoid it when she's zeroed in on every single guy in town like a heat seeking missile in a skirt."

"She's probably lonely."

"Not my problem."

"Definitely not," Brooks agrees. "But man, that was fun to watch."

"Glad to entertain. I'll be keeping my eyes peeled for when her radar hones in on you. It's only a matter of time. Hot fireman, eager single mom. It's a recipe for luh-uh-uh-uh-uhv."

"More like a recipe for disaster. But I'm hot, huh? Thanks, bro. You're hot too. Let's grab lunch sometime."

We both laugh. One of the kids calls out to Brooks, so he heads that way. Families filter off the field toward the parking lot, heading into the rest of whatever their Saturday has in store for them.

I talk to a few of the dads still lingering around, avoid the single moms—especially Cherry—and head to my bike. No, it's not a ten speed. Get real. I ride a Harley, like a man.

THREE

Shannon

When I open the door to the house I rent with Jayme, a bouquet of flowers on the dining table catches my eye. It's not unusual for us to have random flower arrangements in our house since Jayme works part-time at Ox Cart Flower Mart.

Our bulldog, Groucho walks over to me, or waddles. It's definitely more of a waddle. His nub of a tail moves way faster than he does.

"Hey, big boy. How's the man of the house?" I bend and scratch his head and he slobbers in appreciation. So like a man.

I walk toward the flowers and notice the telltale mini-envelope perched on a plastic stake among the hollyhocks, snapdragons, dahlias and hydrangeas. Okay. Not just random cast-off florist overstock. These were sent. Hmmmm. I open the card.

Shannon, you make life around here much more beautiful, just like this bouquet.

I blink, reread the card, and try to think who on earth would send this. My mind unhelpfully flashes to Duke. I send that thought to timeout. Nope. Not Duke. He's not a send-you-flowers kind of man. Besides, he's not, not, not the man I should want flowers from.

Unsigned card. A mystery man. Well, that's kinda fun. I should be a little more excited or intrigued.

I am. I'm so excited. And super intrigued. Really. I am. I just need to shower my post-Zumba sweat off and eat. And I need hot Cheetos. Then I'll feel the full thrilling impact of my not-from-Duke flowers.

Jayme comes strolling into the room wearing a shirt that says *My Favorite Dino Is The Thesaurus*. She's got her blond-brown hair piled high in a bun that screams messy hair, I don't care. Her arm cradles her laptop, and she's followed by one of our cats—the one who actually likes people, and pizza.

Oddball doesn't even know he's a cat. He thinks he's actually another bulldog—a bulldog who can lie on his back, do the splits and clean himself with the agility of a year-six ballerina, or leap onto the top of the fridge in a single bound. Like I said, Oddball. Little did we know how well his name would fit him when we picked it. His twin, Hairball also unfortunately lives up to his name.

"Hey," Jayme mumbles, obviously lost in thought. I'm used to her distant stare. Life with a writer means you learn to discern these "I'm concentrating" faces and steer clear. I'm ready to head upstairs for a shower without saying a word to Jayme when she turns back toward me.

"You got flowers."

"I saw. Who are they from?"

Jayme pauses and then a sly smile spreads across her face. "Nope. Florist code of honor. We never reveal the sender if the card is unsigned."

"You're a part-time florist, so doesn't that code only partly apply to you?"

"Nice try, apple pie. No amount of perspicacity will break me on this."

"Amount of what?"

"Perspicacity. You know, shrewdness, discerning thought. You make a point with that logic about me being part-time, but my lips are sealed like a vault. Like a vault below sea level, rusted and crusted shut."

"With lips like those, no wonder you're single," I tease.

"I'm single by choice. But, you, my magnificent friend, are not. And someone apparently wants to help you out of that little predicament. So go shower your stinky Zumba dancing self and let's eat."

I smile. Okay. Maybe I am a little intrigued.

The next morning I'm up bright and early thanks to my alarm. If it weren't for alarms, I'd sleep til nine or ten ... maybe I'd go all out and sleep til noon. I sigh just thinking of that possibility. The sigh turns into a yawn. Oh, I don't do mornings. But, I have to, so I spritz and fluff some dry shampoo into my hair and make my way downstairs. What? If the French approach to hair care is good enough for January Jones, it's good enough for me.

"Cute outfit, as usual," Jayme says around a bite of an English muffin.

I look down at my block print skirt and wedge sandals while I silently scheme of ways to coax the name of Mister Top-Secret-Flower-Arrangement out of Jayme. Last night I tried to blindside her with random questions in an effort to cajole the details out of her over our dinner of leftover fried chicken and canned fruit cocktail. She wouldn't budge.

"This really is the most excitement I've had in a while."

"English muffins for breakfast?" Jayme says with a little tilt of her lips. She passes a plate my way, the butter melting into all the crannies of the toast, and a dollop of jam on each circle of bread. With friends like her, who needs men?

"You're too good to me," I tell her.

"Oh, don't I know it," she says unapologetically.

"As wonderful as this plate of morning goodness is, I'm talking about the excitement over my mystery man," I say, attempting to get us back on track. I waggle my eyebrows for effect. "Any chance you want to throw me a bone–just a teensie weensie clue?"

"Nope. Not a chance. But, I have to say, I'm loving this new development in your life. I just might write this into a book."

Being a romance author means Jayme is constantly using that phrase: *I just might write that into a book.* Only her books are out of this world. Literally. She writes stories about extraterrestrial romances, vampire courtships or mythical creatures who find their fated mates.

I humor her. "An alien romance? Where the alien sends his earthling love interest exotic flowers from another planet?"

"I was thinking more of a shifter romance where the wolfman sends magical flowers to the woman he secretly loves and the flowers imbue some powers to her that she uses to escape when she is captured by his archenemy."

My second alarm goes off at full volume, the tune of *Gimme More* by Britney Spears blasting through the kitchen.

"Oh! Gotta run!"

"You and those alarms," Jayme teases.

I grab my purse off a chair and head to my father's accounting office. It's only five blocks from our house, in the old downtown section of Bordeaux. My work life could use a facelift rivaling the ones Sharon Osbourne gets, only with more resulting flexibility.

I've been my dad's receptionist since my senior year in high school. If you're doing the math, that's nine years at the front desk of St. James Common Cents Accounting Firm. Despite the unfortunate name, my dad is a sought-after financial advisor and accountant who has clients in Bordeaux and from many surrounding towns.

I'm not even full-time, though Dad intentionally overpays me despite my protests. I spend the other half of my workdays at the Dippity Do painting nails as a manicurist.

This patchwork job configuration worked for me when I was younger. At twenty-six, I'm starting to feel like the inspiration for the song, *Beauty School Dropout*, even though I didn't drop out since I never officially enrolled. I just built up a clientele and they couldn't care less if I'm licensed or not as long as I can detail their nails with a corn cob icon during Bordeaux Days or our Fourth of July, *Red, White, and Blue, and Corn Too* celebration.

Priorities, people. Priorities.

My 2012 Hyundai Accent hums to life when I turn the key. Okay. It's not so much a hum as a grumble or a sputter cough. But, it starts. And once it's going, it goes. I pull into a diagonal parking space in front of Dad's firm, which occupies a space that has been a dry cleaners, then a pet grooming salon, and finally, when I was in elementary school, a photography studio before my dad expanded from using our home as his office. Our backroom still has a myriad of supplies and equipment from each business transition.

I shut my car door, hoist my purse onto my shoulder, and walk toward another day of mediocrity. Neighbors and shop-keepers wave or shout out, "Good morning," and I wave back. We're nothing if we aren't friendly around here.

"Looks like rain," Esther says as she passes by me.

My eyes instinctively scan the cloud-dotted sky beyond the one and two-story brick businesses lining our street.

"Sure does," I agree.

"Well, we need it," Esther says.

We don't. We live in Ohio. It's always wet, either by way of rain, snow, or humidity. The entire landscape consists of varying shades of green. But, we always say we need the rain. I nod and wish Esther a good day as I duck into the office.

I'm only at my desk for less than a half hour when my dad calls me into his office. He has a few part-time accountants on staff, but they aren't here yet today, so it's just the two of us.

"Good morning, Shannon."

"Good morning, Mister St. James."

My father gives me a playful scowl. "That's Dad to you."

"We're at work. I've told you I want to be professional here."

"Okay, Bugaloo."

He's been calling me Bugaloo ever since I got the role as one of the children under the skirt of Mother Ginger in the Nutcracker when I was five. It has nothing to do with the play or the role I danced with my whole heart. He spontaneously called me Bugaloo that night, and it kind of stuck. I secretly love it. Just, not so much at work.

I roll my eyes, in the full spirit of professionalism, of course.

"Did you need something besides the opportunity to humiliate me before I've even had a Diet Dr Pepper?"

"Actually, yes."

I settle into one of the chairs dad has facing his desk for clients to sit in and open my phone to my notes app.

"Do you remember Jim Snyder?" Dad asks, tapping a pen on his desk-top blotter.

"Ummm, no?"

"He's a long-time client. We went to school together at Penn State. He's living in Cincinnati, but still consults with me for financial advice on occasion."

"Okay."

"He has a son your age."

"That's nice."

It's not nice. Whenever Dad's friends have a son my age, you can be sure of two things: one, the young man can't find a date without his parents getting in the mix. Two, I'm expected to solve that problem. When and how did I become the one stand-by answer to all undateable men in the greater Miami Valley?

"Yes. His son, Reginald, graduated from Miami University four years ago. He's working with his dad in the paper manufacturing business. I think he oversees some part of operations in their company."

"That's great, Dad. Welp. Good talk. I better get back out front to organize papers and sit by the phone and do the receptionist things you pay me for. Good talk. Like I said."

I stand, backing out of Dad's office like an explorer carefully retreating down a jungle path when he just turned a corner and came face to face with a wild beast who decided he looked like lunch. Only I'm lunch and Reginald–Reginald?–is my beast. Not my beast. A beast. A beast in thick glasses with irregular teeth, bad breath, no personality, and a desire to settle down and have me bear his brood of offspring. Did I mention I haven't had my morning Dr Pepper?

"Sit."

Dad spears me with that look he used when my teacher called him asking if he'd seen my report card–the card I had snatched from the mailbox and shoved between my mattress and the box spring to hide my D minus in P.E. What can I say? I don't like sweating unless I'm dancing.

I immediately halt my retreat from his office and return to the chair like the well-trained daughter I am. Why do I feel around twelve years old right now?

Dad clears his throat. "You aren't seeing anyone seriously, are you?"

"Um, well ..."

Dad smiles. He's got me. He knows it. And I love him. I'd do anything for him. Anything. But why does that anything involve a young man who inevitably has dandruff and halitosis, who lisps when he talks, or dribbles when he drinks? Why can't he find Matthew McConaughey's beautiful, long-lost, younger brother and fix me up with him?

"It's just dinner," Dad says, skipping the details and cutting right to the chase.

"Just dinner," I echo.

"He knows you have the wedding this weekend, so I told him you were free the following Friday and Saturday."

"What if I'm not?" I ask.

My mystery man pops into my head, followed by an image of Duke holding a bunch of wildflowers and driving up in front of my house on his motorcycle, looking all rugged and windblown and somehow hard and soft simultaneously. That man. Get out of my head, Duke Satterson. You aren't an option.

"Are you busy?" Dad asks, a knowing look taking over his face.

"You're so smug for a man your age. It's not becoming."

"Good," Dad says. "I'll tell Jim you're available and I'll give Reginald your phone number so he can text you."

"I need a burner phone," I mumble.

Dad laughs a good-natured laugh.

"You never know, Bugaloo. This just might turn into something. Reginald may end up being the man you've been waiting to meet."

I stand and walk toward my desk, and I swear I hear Dad mumble "unfortunate name for a young man," under his breath.

FOUR

Duke

T he sound of Aerosmith and Run-DMC belting out *Walk This Way* echoes through the garage, bouncing off the concrete walls, keeping me company while I work. Most of the town hasn't even started their work days, with the exception of the farmers who are usually up before the sun.

I've been under a truck for an hour, trying to figure out what is causing the brakes of Jimmy Shaller's Ford pickup to occasionally fail to engage even when he slams the pedal to the floor. I'm guessing it's the hydraulic pressure, so I'm bleeding the lines and checking the system.

My song is overpowered by someone blasting a twangy Rhett Akins country song through their car stereo out front. I personally take offense on behalf of Steven Tyler. A truck engine cuts off, followed by the undeniable and even twangier sound of Cooter Shartz' voice.

"Anyone home 'round here?"

"I'm here," I shout from under the pickup, rolling out and standing. "What can I do for you Cooter?"

"It's my alternator, I'm pretty sure. Or maybe it's the clutch. Could be a fuse, now that I'm thinking of it. The things runnin' all herky-jerky when it usually runs smoother than Vermont maple syrup."

I rub my hands on the towel hanging out of my front pocket. "Let me take a look at her and I'll let you know if any of your guesses hit the mark."

"Them ain't guesses, Duke. I'm tellin' ya from my years of experience. You and your pop ain't the only ones who knows cars around here."

"Yes, sir," I say, knowing better than to argue with Cooter, a man who uses the phrase herky-jerky to define a mechanical issue.

He gives me a side-eye, but doesn't say anything else.

"I've got Jimmy's truck up on the racks right now and then I'm doing an oil change. I'll get to your truck right after those jobs."

"Seems to me you could bump me up ahead of an oil change. Who's it fer?"

"Why does that matter?"

"'Cause it'll be dependin' on whether that person needs their car as bad as I need my truck."

"We take jobs in the order they arrive at the shop."

"That's sheer nonsense," Cooter says. "Who's got the oil job?"

I shake my head, walking toward the office off the side of the garage so I can write up a ticket and send Cooter on his way.

My pops is sitting at the desk drinking a cup of coffee from a mug I think I gave him for father's day when I was in second or third grade. And the coffee looks like the oil I let out when I do a change.

"Mornin' Walt," Cooter says as he follows me into the office.

Pops nods at Cooter and takes a convenient sip of his caffeinated sludge.

"I was just explaining to your son here how you'uns should organize your jobs."

Dad nods and opens a drawer, looking very interested in a

stapler, notepad and the dust lining the corners behind the office supplies.

"I'm sayin' you ought to put my truck ahead of an oil change, Walt. That's only sensible."

Pops looks at Cooter, doesn't say a word. Then he looks at me. Silence hangs in the room and I get the urge to laugh just because I shouldn't. I bite the inside of my cheek, and force myself to look at Pops instead of Cooter.

Pops glances back at Cooter. "We'll take care of ya' Cooter. Always have. Always will. Just give Duke your keys and sign the order. Do you need a lift anywhere?"

Cooter's face softens. "Well, now that you mention it, I could use a ride back home."

Pops nods again, and just like that, all's right in the world. At least in our world. Pops stands, stretches, downs the rest of that hideous drink, and grabs his keys off the hook.

"I'll be in the car. Sign the papers and meet me out front."

Pop's subtle, but always in control. And he barely looks his age. Sixty-eight. Most men would have retired by now in his position. He's starting the process of passing the business on to me. Says he's got two years before he trades in his wrench for a back-yard bench–his words.

I write up the order, attach Cooter's key to the clipboard, hang it on our jobs wall and watch him walk out the same bay door he came in.

The clock over the workbench says eight thirty. If I get through this brake job and the oil change, it'll be close to lunchtime. Then I can sneak out to meet with Principal Barnes at noon.

I've got an informational interview that no one knows about besides the two of us. I'm probably crazy, even entertaining this idea. But something about turning thirty in five months has me thinking about what I'm doing with my life.

I love my dad. And I'm good at working on cars. Tinkering with machines and fixing things has always come naturally to me.

But, you know what I love even more? The look on a kid's face when they finally work out a problem or learn something new.

And even more than that, I love coaching.

It's the one thing on earth that lights me up from the inside–that and watching Shannon dance. Not that I ought to watch her dance, or that it should light me up, but a man can't help when a woman affects him, at least I haven't found a way yet.

Principal Barnes wants me to take a position coaching the football and baseball teams at Bordeaux High School. To do that, I need to be employed as a teacher. I never thought I had any option but to take over the garage. It shocked me when Principal Barnes called me with this opportunity. I always figured most people in town saw me as a fun-loving guy with one toe over the line and a knack for auto repair. But, in one three minute phone call, he made me think I could be more.

Dad's looking to retire in a few years. He's always assumed I'd take on Satterson's Garage when he was ready to hand it over. I never questioned that destiny until Principal Barnes reached out to me. And now I feel like I'm being ripped in half. I'll have to choose one path over the other.

If I take on the garage, I'll always know I could have had more–my life could have been spent coaching and teaching. But, if I leave the garage ... well, I can't even start to think what that would do to Pops, or to Bordeaux.

Satterson's is the only gas and service station in town. People count on us. It's Pops' baby. His dad started the business back in 1950. Pops worked here from high-school on. And now it's my legacy. I've got four older sisters, but the garage lands squarely on my shoulders.

I'm still thinking about the meeting I had with Principal Barnes when Cooter comes by to pick up his truck. He only needed new spark plugs. A quick one hour fix, and no more herky-jerky. Of course, Cooter claimed he thought it was spark plugs all along. And, I didn't correct him.

Once Cooter drives away, I head to the Dippity Do for a haircut. My best friend Aiden's wedding is in six days and I want to turn heads for my role as one of the groomsmen. Not heads, actually. Just one head. She's a bridesmaid. And even though I can't do a thing about my attraction to her, I still want to watch the look on her face when she sees me in a tux.

As soon as I open the salon door, the sound of chatter fills my ears. I'm like a thorn among roses. Women sit under dryers, at mirrors, and with their heads tilted back in sinks getting their hair washed, but only one woman catches my attention through the hum of activity. Shannon's sitting by the front window at a little table. An elderly woman is seated directly across from her while Shannon paints her nails.

I stand still just inside the door for longer than I should, taking in Shannon's short skirt and those toned legs that seem to go on for days. She's got dancer's legs. And she's got heels on today. I'd love to see her get up and walk across a room in those.

The clearing of a throat draws my attention away from Shannon. Laura's got a knowing look on her face and her arms crossed across her chest as she smirks at me in a way that definitely says, "busted." I run a hand through my hair and ignore the look I'm getting. Laura got Shannon's attention too. She looks up from the manicure and our eyes connect.

"Hey, Duke," she says casually.

"Hey, Shannon," I say, giving her an equally easy-going smile.

Visions of Chris dance through my head. And they aren't like sugarplums. They're more like napalm bombs about to detonate for the thoughts I'm having about his younger sister. I shake my head and turn my focus to Laura.

She pats her chair. "Take a seat."

I obey and sit while she drapes one of those cape things over me. She doesn't even have to ask me how I want her to cut it.

She's the only person who's cut my hair in the past ten years. She knows what to do.

Shannon finishes with her customer, escorts her to the front of the shop and then comes back to her table. She leans toward the oversized purse on the floor next to her and pulls out a bag of sour patch kids and a soda like Mary Poppins producing a lamp and feather duster from her carpet bag.

"Dinner of champions," she says with a pointed look in my direction, daring me to comment.

"You wear it well," I say with a wink.

Shannon rolls her eyes.

"Get a room, you two," Laura says, spinning me so I face the mirror instead of Shannon. "The tension, I swear. Would you just finally admit you have a thing for one another and put the whole town out of their misery?"

Laura massages my scalp and I close my eyes and hum like a cat purring despite himself.

Shannon nearly shrieks. "What are you talking about?"

Laura shakes her head and looks up toward the ceiling.

"There's no tension," I say, thinking of Chris and refreshing my promise to him. A promise is a promise. And he's one of my two ride-or-die friends in life. I told him I'd keep Shannon safe from men. He'd literally kill me if he knew I had a thing for his sister. And he's been trained in tactics that could get the job done quickly or slowly, depending on what the situation calls for.

I hear Chris' voice asking me to promise him I'd keep an eye out for Shannon. I gave him my word. He told me specifically: *You know how guys around here can be. I just want her to be safe from all that. She needs someone worthy of her. Someone serious, not one of these guys who only wants her because she's connected to my dad. And not some player who can't settle down.*

He speared me with a look that either meant he trusted me, or he totally didn't because he thinks I'm one of those types—the ones who can't settle down. Maybe I am. I haven't settled down yet and I'm almost thirty.

People like to conjecture about me and Shannon, tease us, play matchmaker. And I've always tried to deny my feelings to myself and everyone else. Because, even if I were the kind of man who could commit to Shannon, she's never shown an ounce of interest in me.

"Shannon's like a little sister to me." I say to Laura, avoiding Shannon's eyes when I do.

I don't need to see Shannon's relief or confirmation. It's not her fault I've got an incurable attraction to her. I just need to keep resisting her.

She's nothing like a little sister to me, but that argument always seems to shut people down whenever they start speculating about me and Shannon. Living in a small town means people all have opinions and they share them whether you ask them to or not. We've been the subject of many conversations over the years. Shannon is always quick to say "not now or ever" or something equally definitive to let everyone know she's never thought of me in any way beyond being her second big brother. So, I play the "she's like a sister to me" card to perpetuate that idea.

"What he said," Shannon says. "Besides, you know I've got a date the weekend after the wedding."

She does?

"Oh. I know." Laura says. "Reginald, did you say his name was? Another son of one of your dad's friends?"

Shannon shoots Laura a look and I pretend not to notice.

"Reginald?" I ask on Chris' behalf. Not my business. Just looking out. "Now there's a name you don't hear very often–for men who aren't nearing retirement."

Laura coughs, just barely covering her laugh.

"Don't judge a book by its title," Shannon defends. "Reginald might have rugged good looks and a killer personality."

"Wait," I say, spinning toward Shannon so quickly the back of the chair knocks Laura off balance. "You've never met him?"

"Right. I haven't," Shannon says with a grin that is obviously meant to rile me up. "My dad knows his dad. And, honestly, with a name like Reginald, it's not like he's going to be a serial killer. Psychopathic murderers all have names like Charles, Ted, David, Jack, or Jeffrey."

"Or Harold," I add, not so helpfully. "Which sounds a lot like Reginald, now that I hear it out loud. Where is he taking you?"

"Oh no," Shannon says, wagging her pointer finger in the air. "You are never allowed to know the location of one of my dates again."

"Why not?" Laura asks, barely hiding the interest in her tone.

"Don't you remember when Duke stalked me all the way to Columbus for that date last fall? He sat a few tables away from us with the menu up to hide his face the entire meal. His beady little eyes kept peeking over at me when he thought I wasn't looking. And then he tailed us to the movies and sat two rows behind us, all slumped down like he could hide that big body of his."

Shannon waves a hand in my direction to highlight the fact that I am six foot two. I lightly clench my fists in an effort to pop my biceps for emphasis before I remember my arms are hidden under this cape-thing.

I mumble, "I don't have beady little eyes," as if that is any kind of defense for tailing her on a date.

Laura is busting up, holding her hand to her abdomen and gasping for breath. Other stylists and customers glance our way. Shannon has a half smile, which tells me she found my stalking amusing. And yes. I did all that. For Chris. He told me to keep an eye out. I take my commitment to him seriously—at least when it comes to other men, I do.

"So, when that guy walked me to my porch to drop me off, Duke was driving back and forth, up and down our street like Jesse out on patrol in his squad car! My date noticed the fact that we were being not-so-subtly spied on and shook my hand good-night. Shook. My. Hand. Then he hustled off my front porch like I had a communicable disease. All thanks to Duke."

Laura spurts out, "Stop! I can't breathe!"

"You can't even remember his name, can you?" I challenge Shannon.

"His name doesn't matter. The point is, you don't get to know where my dates are taking me. I'm twenty-six, not sixteen."

Believe me, I know.

Shannon pops a sour gummy candy into her mouth and bites it in half with a little more vigor than needed. She pulls the other half out past her lips in a movement that should be innocent. I watch her lips and then I turn my gaze back to Laura who has that knowing look aimed at me again.

I mouth "little sister" to Laura in the mirror.

She mouths, "riiiight," back to me. Apparently neither of us are convinced I'm neutral where Shannon's concerned.

FIVE

Shannon

After Duke leaves the salon, Laura pins me with a look.
"Why are you going out with this Reginald guy
anyway?"

"It's helpful to my dad."

"Filing papers and answering phones helps your dad. Dating
sub-par men doesn't help anyone."

"He might not be subpar. Just because his name is, doesn't
mean he has to be a dud. You never know. It could turn out great.
We may look back on this very conversation and remember the
day I started talking about my life-long love."

"Right. I'm sure that's what we'll be doing a year from now.
Reminiscing about you and Reg and how your mad love for one
another all began in the heat of early summer when your fathers
sent you out on a date to secure their business relationship."

Laura whisks the broom around under the styling chair and I
resist the urge to ask her if I can take Duke's clippings home with
me. That definitely crosses a line from crushing on my brother's
best friend into creepy territory, right?

I straighten my bottles of nail polish in the little display rack I
keep next to my manicure table, noting which colors are getting
low.

"I don't know. I guess I just hope against hope I'll finally meet someone interesting if I just go on enough dates. You know the whole, if you want to find your prince you have to kiss a bunch of frogs principle."

"That's ridiculous reasoning."

"Says the woman who dated her way through half the county trying to rid herself of her crush on her high-school sweetheart."

"Touché. All I'm asking is why you keep picking guys who will disappoint you. If I were a betting woman, I'd say you're trying to distract yourself from someone you really want. Someone tall, maybe a mechanic who rides a Harley, owns a restored Shelby, and has a flirtatious streak a mile long."

"Well, it's a good thing you aren't a betting woman, then. Because you'd lose. We've been over this line of thinking forever. Duke is Chris' best friend. And no. I don't let my brother dictate my life. But, it's obvious Duke sees me as a little sister. He said so himself today.

"And I don't have fantasies of us ending up in some romance fit for one of Jayme's books—only set on earth in daylight between real humans. Could you imagine the elusive, flirty Duke, settling for someone like me? And what if we broke up? It would wreck our whole friend group, not to mention what it would do to him and Chris."

"There's so much to unpack in that statement, we're going to need to get drinks after work to do it."

I turn my back to Laura so she can't see the truth written across my face as plain as the banner over State Street announcing Bordeaux Days.

Duke is the only man I want. He's the only man I ever really wanted. And he's the only man I can't have—for many reasons. Even though Laura is my best friend, I never have told her about my real feelings for Duke. Our town is just too small and that secret is far too vulnerable and pointless to share with her.

I don't want to be lonely the rest of my life. Dating men like Reginald may seem like a pitiful attempt at distraction to Laura.

But, deep down, I really am hoping to find a man who will measure up so I don't spend my life pathetically comparing every guy to Duke.

Duke can't be the only one.

He can't.

There have to be other funny, gorgeous, slightly-arrogant, playful men who hide a heart of gold under their devil-may-care exterior and who make my heart stop and my world come into focus whenever they are near.

Laura looks over at me and nods her head while crossing her arms over her chest.

"Mmhmm," she says. "You're thinking of whomever that guy is right now."

Even with my back mostly turned toward her, she knows me too well.

I swipe one more coat of mascara onto my lashes and give myself a once-over in the bathroom mirror. Tonight's the rehearsal dinner for our friends, Aiden and Em.

Duke's the best man.

I haven't gotten Duke off my mind all week. Thinking of him isn't unusual, but this week it's been more. Seeing him at the salon always throws me off. He sat half a room away from me, while Laura ran her hands across his scalp and I tried not to imagine what it would feel like for my fingers to comb through his sandy blond hair instead. Her legs naturally bumped his knees a few times as she maneuvered around his chair and I thought about getting my stylist's license just to have an excuse to be that close to him once a month.

I would run my hand slowly along the start of a beard he's letting grow in these days just to feel the way that coarse hair would give the soft skin of my palm a delicious, almost imperceptible abrasion. Then I'd bend in toward him, cupping his cheeks.

Maybe one or both of my hands would drift down to feel those biceps of his. Or I'd grip the front of his shirt just to steady myself. Our mouths would meet ...

I remember Duke's words—*Shannon's like a little sister to me*—and his declaration feels like a splash of cold water to my fantasy salon moment.

Duke's constantly reminding me and everyone else that I'm his sister from another mother. We're basically unofficial siblings as far as he's concerned, even if he's flirty and pushes limits. That's just Duke. Besides, he's been seeing that woman in Huber Heights for almost a year now. Granted, he never brings her here, but that doesn't mean he's not getting serious.

Maybe I'm right. Reginald will end up being gorgeous with a great personality. I shake my head at the thought. It's basically a law of the universe that a man with that name cannot be anything but what he is. A Reginald. Bless his heart. And bless mine while we're at it.

I grab my purse and walk downstairs to join Jayme who is already set to head out the door. She's sometimes flighty, and can run late, but my consistent lack of punctuality makes her look conscientious in comparison.

"I'll be on time tomorrow," I assure her. "This is just a dry run. I would never be late for the wedding itself. Besides, we're not late, late. Just fashionably tardy."

She puffs out a chuckle.

The wedding will be at Aiden's farm on the outskirts of town, even though his bride is from Boston. Em insisted that her life in Bordeaux feels more like home to her, and the friends she made here over the past year and a half feel like the closest ones she's ever had. That is with the exception of her best childhood friend, Gabriela, who, in my opinion, needs her own talk show, or reality show, or sitcom. The woman is a hoot!

Jayme pulls her car up along the gravel driveway toward the barn where the wedding will be held. It's hot and beyond humid—a typical Ohio summer evening. The buzz of bug zappers hanging high along the barn walls and the occasional bleating of goats serves as background noise behind the various conversations between all the members of the mingling wedding party.

"I told you we'd be the last ones here," Jayme stage whispers to me as we walk toward Em and the other bridesmaids. Em's wearing a knee-length cream sundress and holding a bouquet of sunflowers in one hand. Her red hair glistens in the evening sun beneath a small veil and I feel a flash of uncharacteristic jealousy. Em found her man and her life checks all the boxes.

Jayme leans into me and says, "Your turn will come."

Jayme may be a self-confirmed bachelorette and make a living juggling four part-time jobs, but she's sharp as a tack when it comes to reading people.

I nearly tear up at her words. So I shove her arm a little to make light of things. And then I say, "With Reginald, I'm sure."

We both laugh then.

Jayme's gets a strange look on her face and then she says, "Or with your mystery man." She still refuses to divulge his identity. "Just remember there are men out there who find you irresistible."

Another bouquet showed up this week with a note that said, *All I need is to see you smile.* Swoon.

All I need is to know who's sending me flowers.

"How are we supposed to end up together when I don't know who he is?"

"Patience young padawan."

Jayme grins with the smile of a woman keeping a juicy secret and I huff just a little. Still, the knowledge that someone has their eye on me buoys my spirits just a little.

Our girlfriends turn to greet us, all of us exchanging hugs, and then my eyes gravitate across the barn toward the men. It's like I've got a homing device implanted in me because everything blurs when I see Duke, throwing his head back in a laugh at something Aiden said.

Duke's Adam's apple bobs in his throat and his eyes sparkle.

He's got on a collared, white cotton shirt with the sleeves rolled part way up. I'm used to seeing him in mechanic's coveralls or a T-shirt and jeans. He cleans up well–very well. I shouldn't be surprised. And he's wearing the absolute heck out of a pair of dark jeans tonight to top off the attraction sundae.

Duke notices me and his eyes take on a heat I'd mistake as interest if I didn't know him better. I send him a wave with a wiggle of my fingers and turn back to my friends.

Gabriela looks at me and says, "You've got it bad."

"What? No. He's my brother's best friend," I explain. "We're like family to one another. My brother would be here, but he's in the Army. He, Aiden and Duke have been best friends since child-hood. That makes Duke completely off-limits and besides, he's dating someone else. Sorry to disappoint."

Gabriela just gives me a long look and adds a hum as if she knows something. Then she says, "I've never looked at my family members like that, chiquita."

Thankfully, Karina, Aiden's older sister, calls out that it's time to start the rehearsal. She insisted on coordinating the wedding instead of being one more bridesmaid, since we already have five women in the wedding party to Aiden's three men.

Karina's one of those efficient people who's been able to command a room since she could walk. She gets all our attention and sends the bridesmaids and Em to stand outside the barn doors while she lines the men up near the back wall inside the barn near an archway covered in wisteria and surrounded by hay bales that will serve as the altar.

Aiden's mom brings his adopted children out to where we're standing so they can practice their roles as ring bearer and flower girl.

Tomorrow there will be portable air conditioning units, but tonight the barn resembles a sauna–or a swamp. We take turns fanning ourselves and Em with our flattened hands. Not that it does any good. This summer the heat came early and the muggi-ness is nearly oppressive.

"I'm giving new meaning to being a glowing bride!" Em says. She's always able to roll with difficult circumstances in ways that amaze me.

"As long as the goats stay in their enclosure, your wedding will be far less memorable than mine," Lexi adds.

Karina calls over to us from the front of the barn, telling us to start the procession.

With a slight nudge from Aiden's mom, seven-year-old Paisley walks forward, holding an empty basket and concentrating hard while miming the tossing of petals. She's followed by her younger brother, Ty, who half runs and half skips up the aisle. No one corrects him, which makes me think that's how he'll do it tomorrow.

I watch Duke's eyes as they take in Ty. A grin splits his face. As if Duke needed more points in his favor, every time I see him with children, my heart sputters to a stop. He seems like the least likely candidate to be a responsible adult role model considering how he always walks the line between doing what's right and bending the rules. But, he's amazing with kids and obviously adores children.

Duke looks up from Ty and sends me a wink. My defiant knees buckle just the slightest. I straighten myself into first position–chin up, shoulders down, round relaxed elbows, legs straight, feet turned out. Ballet to the rescue.

Gabriela walks forward into the barn, followed a few moments later by Lexi, Laura, me and then Jayme. Once we're all up front in our places, Em enters the barn. Even though we're merely practicing, the look on Aiden's face says everything. A hush falls over the entire wedding party as the importance and sweetness of this moment sinks in.

Once Em is standing next to Aiden, he leans in and kisses her cheek with the softest of kisses. Then he whispers something in her ear that makes her grin and blush. They wordlessly link hands in this way that feels so natural and almost subconscious. I can't take my eyes off the spot where their fingers entwine–two lives joined together through thick and thin. They each found their person.

Gabriela wipes a tear. I'm feeling all sorts of schmoopsy watching a boy I grew up with and this woman who has become a good friend of mine practice for tomorrow when they will commit their lives and hearts to one another.

The pastor from one of our local churches goes through the motions: a sample of his sermonette, a cursory exchange of vows, and the kiss, which goes right through the G and PG ratings and seems headed toward PG-13 until it draws a long catcall and a whoop out of Duke, which sends everyone into a fit of laughter.

We run through the recessional, Duke escorting Gabriela, Trevor accompanying his wife, Lexi, and Rob giving his arm to his wife, Laura. Then Jayme and I walk side by side down the aisle and I can't help but wonder if I'll unwillingly live up to the old adage: *always a bridesmaid, never a bride.*

$\mathcal{D}uke$

Shannon: *Have you seen my shoes?*
Duke: *Why would I see your shoes?*
Shannon: *Gah! That was for Jayme.*

S hannon's always firing off funky texts to the wrong person or sending some typo that flusters her. It cracks me up and makes life way more interesting–like she always does. She has this way of bringing color into a room and turning up the volume by her mere presence.

Even though I'm known for being the life of the party and Shannon's a bit more reserved than I am, she's always been the one who grabbed my attention in any setting.

Duke: *(Laughing emoji) Good luck finding your shoes ...*
but, you could wear cowboy boots or any of your other shoes
and still look beautiful.

Did that sound too flirty? Forward? Nah. Chris would tell her the same thing. Only he wouldn't mean it like I do.

Shannon: *Fried them!*

Duke: *You fried your shoes?*
Shannon: *Ugh! no. That was for Jayme too. I found them. not fried them. Though, I should fry this phone. Stupid autocorrect.*
Duke: *I'm not saying user error, but ...*
Shannon: *Watch yourself, Satterson. I still know where you're ticklish.*

An image of Shannon lying on my bed or couch with me in a tickle fight that leads to more flashes across my brain faster than my will power can keep up with it.

We used to wrestle when we were kids. Back then our tussles were totally innocent. She was like a younger sister to me. And, yes. She knew how to get me to cry uncle by tickling my sides, armpits or that spot behind my knee.

Chris, and their other sister, Bridgette, always acted grumpy or pouty when Shannon and I wrestled like that, so it never lasted long. This time, if there ever were a this time, we wouldn't have Chris looming over us. Though, in reality, he's always looming over us even from hundreds of miles away.

Duke: *And I know the nickname your dad calls you.*
Shannon: *Dint you date!*
Duke: *What? Translation, please.*
Shannon: *Donut you dear.*
Duke: *???*
Shannon: *Gah! Don't you dare!*
Shannon: *Got tacos run.*
Shannon: *Ugh. *Gotta run* No tacos!! Not tacos! Jayme's calling me from downstairs. See you there.*
Duke: *See you, Hollywood. I'll be the incredibly sexy man standing next to the groom if you're looking for me.*

I started calling Shannon "Hollywood" when she was in junior high. That was when her obsession with celebrities and gossip really took off. She acts like she hates the nickname, but I promise you she likes it–way better than she likes when I call her Bugaloo.

Shannon: *(Rolling eyes emoji) Won't be looking for you. I'm here for the bride and groom. And then I'm off on my very hot date with Reginald next weekend.*

Reginald.

No way.

That's not happening.

I'm making it my personal mission to find out the location of that date. Right after I fulfill my obligation as Aiden's best man. Today, it's all about Aiden and Em.

And, unexpectedly, Memaw and Bill.

Two of our town's seniors who fell in love a few years ago have their part to play in today's ceremony. Not that it's planned. They've been dating, but still haven't tied the knot.

Bill apparently left his hearing aids at home today.

During the sermon, Pastor Mark makes a joke quoting "The Princess Bride" in an uncanny imitation of Peter Cook as the priest. "Mawwwage. Mawage is what bwings us togethah today ..."

While the guests erupt in laughter, Bill nearly shouts out to Memaw, "Who is Mal Wedge? I thought our bride went by Em now!" Bill's obviously unaware he's speaking so loudly.

Memaw, as we all affectionately call her, leans in toward Bill's good ear and yells, "Marriage, dear. Marriage."

Bill then says, "I know, I know. That's all you've been asking me about for the past year!"

That spurs my pops to shout out, "Make her an honest woman already, Bill. Marry the girl!"

And of course this leads to Pops' girlfriend, Mabel, turning to Pops and crossing her arms across her chest. "You're one to talk, Walt Satterson!"

As if that weren't enough, suddenly Bill drops to one knee. Well, it's not a drop for a man nearing eighty, it's more like a very slow descent, one he may need assistance to get up from.

Memaw gasps and covers her mouth.

"Virginia," Bill shouts from his spot near Memaw's lap. "You're the spunkiest, sweetest woman I know."

Memaw wipes a tear from her eye. I think we all do.

Bill continues yelling. "You kiss better than any other woman over sixty I ever met too." This earns a light swat in his direction and a playful scowl.

"And if you set aside the concoctions you call casseroles, you're near perfect." He shakes his head. "I've been a fool. Will you forgive me for making you wait so long and agree to be my wife? We can figure out whose house to move into later. And I'll get you a ring like a proper gentleman. I promise."

Memaw's sniffling.

Pastor Mark's mouth is gaping open, though he should be a little used to us by now, seeing that he took over his congregation here five years ago and he's already seen a herd of goats overrun a wedding in this same barn several years back.

"Yes, Bill, you old fool. I've been telling you I'd say yes if you ever got around to asking. I love you and I want to spend whatever days we have left on this earth as your wife. But you better stop knocking my cooking or you're going to have to start cooking for yourself."

This earns a few whoops from the younger women in the crowd.

Bill's smile says it all. He starts to attempt to stand up, and a few young men from around them rush over to help him to his feet. Memaw stands and the two of them kiss. The barn is filled with catcalls and whistles.

I'd like to tell you this type of disruption is totally out of character for our town. We all know it isn't.

Pastor Mark decides this is as good a time as any to grab a hold of the reins of this runaway ceremony and get things back under control. Memaw and Bill sit, the guests murmur and continue to turn and stare at them occasionally, but mostly, our attention is all drawn to one of my best friends and his bride for the rest of the ceremony.

It sounds cheesy to say the wedding was beautiful, aside from our unruly seniors. But, sometimes the simple ways of saying things are the truest. And that's what it was–beautiful.

Watching Aiden marry the unexpected love of his life gave me hope. We never thought he'd find someone–but he did. And if he did, I can. Maybe. And maybe I've found her–the one woman I really want–but the question remains whether I'll ever get the chance to make her mine.

Gabriela and I are dancing the second dance together while the other couples in the bridal party pair up around Aiden and Em. Gabriela's too perceptive for her own good.

"Your eyes keep drifting, big man."

"What? Oh. Sorry."

"I'm not taking it personally. Just interested in what's got your attention when a beautiful, single woman like me is in your arms."

I don't know what to say, and that's unlike me. I always know what to say.

Gabriela gives me a wink. "Don't worry. I'm not hitting on you. I've got my eye on a certain firefighter if I'm flirting with anyone west of the Hudson River on this trip."

"Brooks?"

My interest shifts from Shannon who is slow dancing with Jayme and twirling her right now, to the idea that I could match Brooks with Gabriela tonight.

"Mmhmm," Gabriela says. "He's interesting, and funny, and not too hard on the eyes. I met him a year ago at the surprise engagement bonfire."

"I can work with that," I tell her.

"Oh, sugar. I don't need you to work with anything. Have

you met me? I can do my own work. You seem to have plenty to keep you occupied. You leave the fireman to me."

I laugh. Brooks won't know what hit him. This should be fun.

"You have your eyes on a certain bridesmaid?"

"Uh. No. Nope. No."

"Well, that's convincing," Gabriela says, never missing a step in our dance. "I smell something fishy, and I know fish. I grew up near Boston harbor."

I chuckle. "I just keep an eye on her. She's my best friend's little sister."

Gabriela shakes her head. "Suit yourself. But, if you ask me, life's too short to want someone and not go for it. That's what I told Em a little over a year and a half ago, and look at us now—celebrating her wedding."

I instinctively glance at Shannon who is now being spun by Jayme who is shorter than her by at least six inches. She's ducking under Jayme's arm and laughing, but looking as graceful as she always does whenever dance is involved.

"Ask her to dance," Gabriela says. "I'm good at keeping secrets. Yours is safe with me. Just ask her to dance. Our bodies can speak with words the mouths are afraid to utter."

With that little nugget of wisdom, she turns and pats me on the chest, pushes away and walks toward the side of the barn where an unsuspecting Brooks is about to get blindsided in the best of ways. Gabriela should be the type of woman who makes me watch her walk away, and even makes me chase her down, but apparently I've got a very specific type.

The song changes to something upbeat, couples break apart and the bridal party mingles in with the other guests as the dance floor fills with people. Shannon and I end up next to one another in a circle made up of our friends. It's then I notice the song that's playing, *Marry You*, by Bruno Mars.

Shannon is doing this move with her hips while she shifts from foot to foot with the beat and raises her arms overhead. She's mouthing the words, *hey baby,* while she looks at me. Then the whole group belts out, *I think I wanna marry you!* Shannon's eyes meet mine while we're shouting the lyrics and a smile breaks across her face. I wink. It's the closest I've ever come to revealing the deepest longings of my heart out loud and I'm nearly trembling.

She misses the depth behind my gesture and simply laughs and keeps dancing.

We dance a few more fast songs and then she leans toward me and says, "I've got to get something to drink."

I shout over the music, "I'll come with you."

We make our way over to the bar at the back of the barn. Shannon grabs a cocktail napkin and dabs her forehead.

"You having fun?" I ask her.

"Of course! I love a wedding, and this one is amazing. I only wish Chris could be here."

"Yeah, me too."

We finish our drinks in silence, glancing at one another occasionally, but mostly people watching.

When the song turns slow, I angle toward Shannon and take her glass out of her hand.

"Dance with me," I say, not phrasing it as a question.

Shannon looks momentarily confused and hesitant, so I place the palm of my hand on her back and lead her toward the dance floor. Something about Gabriela's unexpected pep talk spurs me forward.

When we reach the edge of the square set out for dancing, I turn toward Shannon and grasp her hand. Then I place it up on my shoulder, ensuring we'll be closer than if she rested it on my arm or chest. Then I clasp her other hand and tuck my free hand behind her waist, pulling her in toward me. She leans into the space between us as Ed Sheeran's *Thinking Out Loud* ironically tells our story.

She may not hear it, but I do. These lyrics say everything I would say if I had the nerve. If we were in different circumstances.

If I hadn't promised her brother I'd protect her from men just like me.

Dancing with Shannon can't be described in words. Her body knows moves I never thought up, and though she lets me lead, she somehow spurs me to move in ways I hadn't planned, like spinning her out and drawing her back in until our chests land against one another, our eyes lock, the rest of the room fading away. The song ends and I hold her tight for one beat longer.

When she lightly pushes away, that same confused look is on her face. I wonder what my face looks like.

"That was ... fun," Shannon says.

"It was," I say softly. "Thanks."

"You're not a bad dancer," she says, placing her palm on my chest and hopefully missing the fact that my heart is trying to beat out of it at that exact moment.

"For a mechanic," she adds with a tease to her voice.

"Well, thanks, I think."

"No, seriously. You surprised me."

"I'm full of surprises," I tell her. And then before I say something I'd regret, or lean in and act on my instinct to kiss her, I tell her I'm going to get something to drink. I need to cool down and recover from the sensation of how right it felt holding Shannon in my arms.

SEVEN

Shannon

Reginald texted Wednesday to say we were going to "Out on Fifth" in Dayton. It's a weekly event where a city block of Fifth Street is cordoned off every Friday night so restaurants can expand patio seating into the streets and vendors have booths of all sorts. I have to admit, Reginald's choice of activity for our date has me a little hopeful.

I mean, a real Reginald, the one I unfortunately imagined him to be, wouldn't think of something so trendy for a first date, right?

Friday night at five o'clock Jayme answers the door while I linger upstairs. It's a thing with me. I like to have my blind dates screened by a friend, and I also enjoy making an entrance. So, Jayme answering the door serves two purposes.

We have a little code developed. Don't judge. It's important that I go into this night prepared for what I'm getting into.

If the guy's a straight-up ten, we're talking Chris Evans with or without the facial hair, or Jason Momoa early years or now in his more rugged, long-haired look ... Well, if that man comes to my door, Jayme will say, "Groucho, come meet Shannon's date."

Yes. We use the dog. Sue us.

If we're looking at an unknown variable, the guy might look

cute, but gives off a vibe that makes Jayme hesitate, or his looks are nothing to write home about, but he seems nice, Jayme says, "Let me put the dog away while I get Shannon for you."

And finally, if the guy should come with a warning label, Jayme says, "Just a second. Our cats just barfed in the laundry room. Could you wait out here on one of the porch chairs while I clean up the mess? Shannon will be right down." Then we assess whether I need an exit strategy, or I'm just going to follow through on one more bad night of dating.

I'm standing at the top of the stairs in my cuffed jeans and a kitschy print blouse like the one Elle Fanning was seen wearing around LA this past month. My outfit says fashionable and fun, but not "Oh yes, I do kiss on the first date."

I hear Jayme's voice from downstairs, "Let me put the dog away while I get Shannon for you."

Great. A solid five out of ten. At least he's not setting off any warning signals. I can do five out of ten. It's a fun Friday away from Bordeaux. A free meal. A favor to my dad. I square my shoulders and carefully walk down the stairs in my cork-heeled wedge sandals.

Reginald stands at the door watching me like he's enraptured. Jayme covers her mouth and coughs lightly as she looks from him to me and back again. He's frozen in place. I start to look down to make sure I pulled my zipper up and don't have toilet paper stuck under my shoe, but I know I'm good on all counts.

"Okayyy, then," Jayme says when I make it to the bottom stair. "You kids have fun!"

"Uh. Yeah. Thanks," Reginald says, looking at her like he just remembered she was in the room.

I have to say the way he's looking at me is an ego boost. I don't get out enough, and yes, men look at me, but there's something about the way Reginald is taking me in that says he thinks I'm way out of his league and he wants to make that up to me. It's sweet.

"I'm Shannon," I say, extending my hand.

"Uh, RJ," he says.

"RJ?"

"Yeah. It's a nickname based on my first and middle initials," he says with a light blush.

"Oh, well. I like it."

A look passes across his face and then he asks, "Don't tell me my dad told you my name was Reginald?"

"Maybe?" I say.

Reginald, or RJ, laughs. "I'll kill him. Or make him suffer. He knows better."

"To be fair, it was my dad who told me. Maybe your dad didn't have anything to do with it."

"Well, I'm not going to make your dad pay. After all, he set up this date." He smiles a really full smile, not a creepy clown smile like those ones in horror movies, just a really nice smile. It definitely bumps him from a five to a solid six.

"Shall we?" RJ asks.

He turns to open the screen door and I shoot Jayme a look that I hope says I'm not completely disappointed.

RJ might have potential. He's no Duke Satterson, but no one is. And Duke, get out of my date. Please.

The half-hour drive to Dayton is not horrible. RJ and I chat like old friends. I'm feeling exactly zero chemistry, but he's fun and kind and he can hold up his end of a conversation. And his choice in music is definitely bumping him up to a six point five. We sing along to Shawn Mendes, Harry Styles, and he even has a remixed version of an old Kool and the Gang song on his playlist.

The trouble is Duke.

He's always been trouble, but right now he won't exit my head long enough for me just to enjoy a perfectly nice six point five date. I keep thinking of Duke's eyes, Duke's jawline, Duke's sense of humor, Duke's way of boasting while still seeming self-deprecating.

I need a Dukesercism. It's like an exorcism, but instead of casting out some menacing spirit, I'd have Duke supernaturally removed from my thought life. Only I don't want to have my head spin around and pea soup to fly in a projectile from my mouth like the girl in that classic horror film. A woman has her limits, even when it comes to getting over a mega-crush.

We find parking and RJ holds my door open. He doesn't try to hold hands or touch the small of my back. He asks my opinion as to where we should grab a drink and where I want to eat dinner. We end up walking around with the drinks we buy at an outdoor stand and then grabbing a meal at Troll Pub which is just one street over.

We decide to split the Troll fries and chicken wings. I never split meals with a guy, but RJ makes me feel comfortable. It's like girls' night, but with a guy. That's probably not the most inspiring feeling to have on a date, but it's nice.

I'm stuffing a giant loaded Troll fry in my mouth, dripping with sour cream, bacon and cheese sauce when I have a full-blown hallucination.

Duke.

I see Duke.

He's over at a table in the corner across the room. And he's with a blond woman his age. Only, his mottled green eyes are trained over her shoulder directly at me.

I shake my head to snap out of my delirium. That only causes my imaginary Duke to stand up and start walking toward me. Correction: toward me and RJ. And, the closer he gets, the more clear it becomes that he's the real Duke. Right here. In the middle of yet another one of my dates. Only this time he's not playing Inspector Clouseau. This time, he's like a probation officer about to book me for violating parole.

He walks right up to us. No shame. Just walks up and stands between the two of our chairs.

"Shannon."

His eyes are latched onto mine with some sort of magnetic accuracy. He doesn't even acknowledge RJ.

"Duke." I answer like a belligerent child.

I don't know what it is about him that makes me act like I'm back in high school. It's unnerving. He's unnerving.

I gather my manners and say, "This is RJ."

"RJ?" Duke asks, losing his cool for a moment.

Yeah, buddy. That's what I thought too. He's not Reginald after all. So take that you date-stalker.

"Nice to meet you," RJ says, basically to Duke's back.

"Yep," Duke says, not even turning to look my date in the eye.

"Duke is my ..." I break off, inconveniently.

He's my what? Brother's best friend? My personal pain in the tush? My dream man who is currently taking up unpaid rental space in my head twenty-four, seven? My measuring stick for every other male on the planet?

"Uh. Are you two?" RJ asks. Naturally.

We both snap toward him simultaneously and nearly shout, "No!"

RJ flinches a little.

I turn to Duke. "Enough. You've ruined your quota of my dates. Besides ..." I point across the room toward the woman left stranded at the table where he had been sitting. "Your date looks lonely. Don't you need to go order, or eat, or take her home?"

"She's ..." he tries to explain but stops himself. "We were ..." He shakes his head, squints at me and runs a hand through his hair.

"Not my business. Just as my night out with RJ is none of yours. See you at home. In Bordeaux, I mean. Around town. Not my home. Or yours. Of course."

Duke chuckles. RJ looks shell shocked. I sigh and poke a fork at the plate of Troll fries.

"Yeah. I'll see you at home," Duke finally says. He seems to remember his manners, finally. He turns to RJ and says, "Nice to meet you. I'm Shannon's brother's best friend. I just ... keep an eye out for her. Anyway, Have a nice date."

RJ blows out a breath and tells Duke it was nice to meet him too. Duke retreats back to his table.

49

I try to go back to enjoying my meal with RJ. I really do. But, my eyes keep glancing over to Duke and that woman. She's definitely closer to his age than I am. She seems normal and pretty. I guess that's what he wants in a woman–normal and pretty. I must not be normal, because I do know I'm at least somewhat pretty. Why this bothers me so much, I don't know.

It's one thing to know Duke had a woman he was dating out of town. It's another to see him here with her. They aren't touching or sucking the same strand of spaghetti into their mouths at the same time like Lady and the Tramp. But, she is definitely his date. He's on a date. Well, I'm on a date. So there you have it.

"Are you okay?" RJ asks after a few awkward minutes.

"Yeah. Sorry about that."

"Oh, I get it. I have a younger sister. I only hope I can be that intimidating one day. She's twenty-two. Just graduated from college. She went to UCLA, but she's moving back to Ohio. I may have to practice being more like Duke."

All I can say is, "Please. Don't."

EIGHT

Duke

I messed up.
Big time.

Of all the places for Shannon to be out on her date, she picks Troll Pub. I tried to pop in on her dad this week, exchange small talk, then casually ask where Reginald was taking Shannon. I assured him I wanted to keep Shannon safe on a blind date, on Chris' behalf. He assured me Shannon was going out with a responsible young man.

Beth and I had planned to meet up so I could talk about us not seeing one another anymore. We like Out on Fifth, so it was a natural choice. She was completely on the same page when I told her we'd hit our expiration date.

It's not like I'm going to start dating Shannon now that I'm officially single, but I guess some relentlessly hopeful part of my heart thought I might. Even though I know I can't. And it's obvious more now than ever that she wouldn't want anything to do with me, even if I am free to ask her out.

Seeing her with that guy, RJ, looking relaxed and happy, did something to me. I didn't even tell Beth where I was going. I just pushed my chair back and stalked toward Shannon. All I could think of was the feel of Shannon in my arms at Aiden's wedding,

51

and then I pictured that guy with his arms around her after their date and I saw red.

She's not mine. And her date seemed decent enough. But he's not good enough for Shannon. Not that I'm good enough. No one is. At least no one I know. Still, I acted like a neanderthal or one of those bodybuilders who overdoes the creatine and ends up having roid rage. I owe her an apology and I plan to grovel if she'll let me.

So, I'm headed to the one place she can't kick me out of—senior Zumba. I'm wearing a pair of basketball shorts, a tank top and a pair of tennis shoes. I don't have dancing clothes. I don't even know what guys usually wear to dance in. Probably some tights or a leotard. Nothing I'd ever put on.

I'm driving my dad's truck over since we've got little league practice right after Shannon's dance class, and I need to haul the equipment with me.

I sit in the truck, waiting for enough of the class members to file into the Rec Center. I'm well aware Shannon won't shoot me down too badly in front of our seniors. She's got a heart for them and she'll want to save the drama for a time when we're alone. And then she'll let me have it. I know her well enough to know that. For some reason, the idea of Shannon all fired up and aiming her passionate outburst at me doesn't make me unhappy in the least.

I don't even know what I'm hoping for here. I just know I can't leave things the way they were between us at the restaurant last night.

I walk into the rec center and see the door to the dance studio wide open. Shannon is stretching up front and I try to sneak in without making a fuss, but I should know better.

"Duke! You came!" Esther shouts out from the front row.

Shannon's head whips around and she gives me a feisty look full of warning and something else I can't read.

I hold up both hands like the innocent man I am. "Just here

to dance—as a guest of Esther and Mabel—no harm no foul, Hollywood."

Her lips form a thin line and then her eyes turn to slits. She places her hands on her hips and stares me down.

In a way too formal tone, dripping with attitude, Shannon says, "Welcome to Zumba, Duke. I hope you're ready to sweat."

I crack my neck, stretch one of my arms straight across the front of my body while securing it with my free hand and say, "I'm ready. Bring it."

Shannon turns back to the front of the room, eyeing me in the mirror. I smile at her and pull my right arm over my head in a stretch that shows off the striations of my muscles. Then I switch and stretch my left arm. She watches and I see her checking me out. At least I think she is, until she turns to put on her headset and selects the first song.

"I'm sure glad you came," Mabel turns and says to me as the music for our warm up pulses through Shannon's bluetooth speaker.

"Me too," I say.

Mabel's been dating Pops for the past few years. They're pretty serious, though I don't know if Pops will ever put a ring on it. He lost Mom ten years ago, but still hasn't taken her clothes out of their bedroom closet. I can't imagine. I lost my mother. He lost his girl. But he and Mabel are cute together and she makes him happy.

I follow Shannon's movements, imitating each one while I check out my classmates. Every one of them is over sixty. Some of them are nearing eighty. All of them are smiling. And Shannon's smiling back at each one of them as her eyes meet theirs in the mirror. Until she meets my eyes. Then she gives me a look that could kill, or wound, or at least send the average man running from this dance studio. But, I'm not the average man.

She picks up the pace with the second song and we're doing spins and little hops. I spin the wrong way and bump into Esther. I catch her before she falls onto the floor.

"I'm fine. I'm fine," she assures me.

I get another death glare from Shannon.

By the end of the class, I'm sweating like I just ran five miles with Aiden. Dancing's no joke.

Shannon leads us through a cool down and then I'm swarmed by senior women telling me how cute I looked or how well I danced, even though I nearly sent one of them to the physical therapist.

"Come back anytime," Esther says as she and Mabel walk out the door, leaving me and Shannon alone in the room.

Shannon busies herself tossing things into her duffel and wiping her brow and neck with a hand towel. She's avoiding eye contact now that it's only the two of us, but I see when the shift comes over her. She takes a deep breath, widens her stance and looks up at me.

"Why did you come today?"

"I was invited."

"But why today? After last night?"

"I came because of last night. I wanted to apologize."

She hoists her bag up onto her shoulder and looks in my eyes like she's searching for something.

I just stay where I am, looking at her. She's beautiful, wearing a loose tank top over a sports bra and yoga pants, sweat running down the side of her temple toward her neck. I want to run my finger along that drop of sweat, push her hair back and cup her face. A flush grows across Shannon's cheeks. Does she feel this too?

"Well, go ahead," she says with her typical bravado.

It's always a cover for something less certain, and it makes me want to take care of her–not in the way Chris charged me to do, but in a much deeper way. I want to shield her from pain and make her relax. To let her know she can be herself and be safe in the world. I want to be the one she runs to when she's hurting, and the place she chooses to share her secrets.

I've never felt this kind of longing for anyone. It's foreign, but not unwelcome. Not when it's her.

"Are you just going to stand there staring at me, or are you going to apologize?"

Her lips turn up in a small smile. She's taunting me. And she loves it. If I'm honest, I do too. I love when she gives me flack. It's like a secret language we've shared for years. A way of connecting without breaking any rules.

"I'm going to grovel, starting right now. So buckle up, buttercup. You're about to experience an apology–from me."

She scoffs. "You're incorrigible."

"Oh, you know it." I chuckle.

Her eyes are dancing. Even her eyes dance.

I clear my throat. I truly am sorry, and as much as I love our banter, I need her to know I'm dead serious about this.

"I'm really sorry, Shannon. You're not a high school kid anymore. Not at all. And I'm well aware of the fact. I didn't plan to be where you were last night. I wasn't intentionally stalking you."

She huffs out a breath of disbelief and raises one eyebrow.

"Seriously. I didn't plan to follow you. I did stop by your dad's business on Wednesday to ask about the location of your date. He merely assured me you were going on a date with a responsible young man. He didn't give out details."

"I can't believe you went to my dad to gather details about my date. My dad didn't even know where we were going. Only Jayme knew."

"Do you think that's safe, only having one person know your whereabouts when you go out of town with a total stranger?"

She gives me a glare this time.

"I do. He was fine. And I was fine."

"Fine?" I grumble. "You deserve more than fine."

She looks up at me with a question written across her face. It's not one I'm answering today. I need to get through this apology and get out on the ball field where things are simple–not so muddled and tempting and full of lines I want to cross but can't.

"I just want you to know I'm sorry. I was at Troll Pub to talk with Beth, the woman I'd been casually dating for a while. We met there to call things off. I'd been dragging it on longer than I should just ... Anyway, I was there for my own reasons. Not to spy on you or ruin your night."

Shannon nods. Her face is inscrutable. I wish I knew what she was thinking.

"Why did you come over like that? You scared RJ at first. And you were so ... rude. It wasn't like you."

"I know."

I don't know what to tell her. I was jealous. Plain and simple. But I can't say that. Definitely not.

"I thought of a promise I made to Chris before he left. To watch over you."

"You did what?" she says, her one hand finding her hip in that defiant stance she gets when she's getting fired up about something. "Did you not just tell me I'm not in high school anymore? I'm twenty-six, Duke. Most of my best friends are married. Two of them have children. I'm pretty sure I can watch over myself. I'm going to wring Chris' neck when he gets home." She pauses. "Right after I hug him good and long. Then I'm going to kill him."

"Good plan," I say, smiling. I can't help but smile at her.

"Let's get this clear. I don't need you to be my watchdog. I'm a grown woman."

"That you are," I say, keeping my eyes on hers.

Do not look at what qualifies her to be a grown woman. Do not. My eyes drift down toward her lips. No further.

She huffs out a breath. I watch her lips go from pursed to puffing out on the exhale to relaxed and soft.

"I gave Chris my word," I say softly.

"And I get it. After what happened to Bridgette ... well, he's never gotten over it, even though he wasn't there."

"Maybe it's because he wasn't there. Guys are weird that way. We feel responsible for things–like we should have stopped something or solved it, even when there would have been nothing we could do."

Her face softens. Shannon barely ever mentions her sister Bridgette. The tragedy her family lived through twelve years ago changed them forever. I give her the space to direct our conversation. We're in tender territory. And, I know myself. I'm likely to joke us right out of seriousness when what she needs is compassion.

"I miss her," she says, her eyes getting dewey along the rims.

"Yeah. Me too. And Chris does too. Maybe that's partly why he went into the military. He's made for it, no doubt, but the Army allows him to feel like he's doing something. He can protect the people he loves while he serves his country. I think that's a big part of his motivation. But, leaving you here ... Well, he didn't want to come back and find out guys had taken advantage of you. It's a meathead philosophy, but he's your big brother. He'll always see you as the little girl he needs to look out for."

"I know," she says. "At some level I get it. And I even appreciate it a little. But don't you ever tell him that. Just please. Stop being his representative. You're not my big brother. I don't see you that way. I'm able to decide if a guy is worth my time."

I nod. I'm not sure how I'm supposed to honor her request and still keep my word to Chris, but that's not her problem. She's right in so many ways. She can handle herself. She doesn't need me hovering over her life. But, what if I want to? What if I want to block her from dating for my own reasons? I'm still such a hot mess. This woman turns me inside out and I'm not sure what to do about it.

"And RJ? Was he worth your time?"

I can't help but ask. Call me a glutton for punishment.

"He was nice. Easy to be with."

"Good."

Totally not good.

57

"But I'm not dating him. He felt more like a friend. And I had a nice night until some oaf decided to swing his weight around while I was in the middle of a euphoric moment with a plate of Troll Fries."

I laugh. "Euphoric moment, huh?"

"Have you had those fries?"

"I have."

"Euphoric."

"We good?" I ask her. Wanting more than I'm allowed. Always wanting more with her.

"We're good." She leans in and hugs me, her duffle banging against our hips, pushing us together awkwardly at first. I wrap my arms around her and give her a squeeze. She leans into me, her head resting on my chest, my heart pounding away, my fingers feeling her skin and aching to explore, to stroke through her hair and to cup her face. I rub her back with a light brush of my hands.

"Okay. Well. I'm off to coach my team." I gently push her away because my self-control only extends so far, and I'm pretty sure holding her while she's wearing her dance outfit is the limit.

"Smelling like that?" She wrinkles her nose.

"You should smell them." I say.

Shannon smiles at me and we walk out through the door together. She turns to lock the room and I head the opposite direction, out toward the field, away from her.

NINE

Shannon

I should exit the building, walk to my car, and go home. I could take a shower and then read a book or help Jayme with our Saturday chores. That's what I should do.

Instead, I watch Duke's back as he walks away from me to go coach his team. I've usually been known for my good judgment—except when it comes to Duke. And right now, I want to watch him coach.

I wait for the door to slam shut, that metallic sound clanging across the tiled floor of the hallway. For some reason, I count to thirty, giving him time to get beyond the grass that spans the space between the back door and the ball field. Hoisting my duffle onto my shoulder, I shore myself up and follow the path Duke just walked a few minutes ago. I carefully push the metal bar to open the door, then I grasp the door and hold it until it shuts behind me more softly than if I had let it slam.

I'm holding my breath. This is absurd. So what if I want to watch practice? It's a free country. It's a Saturday in the middle of summer. I can watch little league practice.

I walk toward the bleachers, not the ones in plain view of the field, but the old ones off to the side, where I might or might not be noticed by players, families or coaches. Especially coaches.

I make my way up to the top bench, as if I can conceal myself in the tree branches if I'm high enough. I'm a dork and I know it. But, now I'm committed, so I settle into this cockamamie plan and push a cluster of leaves out of my face so I can see more clearly.

Once I'm seated with my duffle next to me, I try to sort my thoughts. I picture the dance at Aiden and Em's wedding, the way it felt to be held by Duke. He said he knows I'm not a high school girl anymore. That night he made me feel like a woman–like he sees me as a woman, not just Chris' little sister. And Chris asked him to watch out for me. My mind swirls with details. And my heart thrums with longing.

Boys start to pile onto the field. Brooks and Duke are completely focused on each boy and on getting the practice underway. No one even looks in my direction–at least not up until now they haven't.

Brooks and Duke line the boys up, give a little speech, and start with some organized form of catch, walking from player to player, correcting their form or saying something to them. I can't hear much of what's said from here. But I see it all. See him. His muscles, his smile, the way he pours himself into this like it's the most important thing in the world–like each boy matters.

After they decide the team has practiced catching and throwing long enough, they divide the team into two groups and play a mock game. I restrain myself from cheering when someone makes a good play. No one has looked over this way. These bleachers are dilapidated and partly hidden beneath some old maple trees. They aren't anything like a hunting blind, but they're barely noticeable from the field because of the overgrowth from years of neglect.

One of the boys, Mason, hits the ball and it flies far. The outfielders run to catch it, but it goes past their heads and over their gloves. The boys on Mason's half of the team jump and holler while he runs all four bases, sliding home for show. When he pops up, Duke's right there, hunkered down, whispering something into Mason's ear that makes him grin big, and then leaning back for a high five.

Duke's wearing a ball cap. He must have put it on after he left dance class. While Mason runs past his teammates for a series of high fives, Duke lifts his ball cap off his head, runs his hand through his hair and puts the cap back on backwards.

No. He. Didn't.

Does he have any idea how completely sexy that is? And why is a backward ball cap so sexy? Maybe it serves as a display–kind of like a bird strutting around with his plume all fanned out when it's mating season. Or it's like the signage in the windows of every shop down Main Street: OPEN. Duke's wearing the equivalent of a ball cap welcome sign. And I want to go shopping. Yes. I. Do.

Between the way his hat sits on his head–making him an irresistible combination of rebel, yet all-American-boy–and the way his tank shifts showing off his arm muscles and his pecs, he's the picture of coaching hotness.

I could look away but why should I? I'm just going to sit here, pretending I'm a student of all things baseball. Maybe I'm highly interested in mentoring youth. I've definitely got team spirit by the buckets full.

Who am I kidding? I've got a raging crush on my brother's best friend. And now I know why it's called a crush. I'm being pulverized by my feelings for Duke. I was rightfully frustrated with him after last night with RJ, but when he made that apology–so sincere, and so very Duke–I couldn't hold onto my anger. Not even a little. If anything, his apology only made me want him more.

Just when my mind has fully drifted into all things Duke, Brooks glances up and over and I can tell the moment he sees me. He leans in toward Duke and says something, shrugging in my direction.

Duke looks up toward me and his face lights up with a smile that quickly turns into a smirk. Pompous. Arrogant. He's so full of himself. He knows I have no reason to be here, watching this practice, unless I'm here to watch him. And I'm so busted.

Duke doesn't leave my mortification at a manageable level. He wouldn't be Duke if he did. He says something to Brooks, who then turns to the boys and sends them into some sort of running drill. Then Duke strides over to me, taking the bleacher steps two at a time until he's standing one level below me, his figure towering over me and that irrepressible smirk still plastered to his face.

"So, you stayed to watch practice?"

"Mm hmm," I hum out, trying to get my bearings.

Oh, bearings! Where are you?

"And you decided to watch practice because ..."

"I love baseball."

"Hmmm," he hums, running a hand along his stubble as if he's considering the veracity of my statement.

He knows I'm full of it. I know I'm full of it.

"Yep. I love baseball," I say with a definitive nod of my head. "Love it. The snap of the ball against the bat, the way the batter runs from base to base. The catching of the ball. I love it all."

"Well, you sure outline the finer points of the game. I can tell you're a real fan."

"That I am," I say, lifting my chin a bit.

"Good. I like knowing how much you like baseball. I don't think I ever realized how much you liked it until now. As a matter of fact, I always wondered if you even cared that much about baseball. It's a good thing to know–how much you actually like it."

He winks.

Then he smiles a slow, seductive smile–like the wolf before he ate the little piggies and they never cried wee wee wee all the way home again. Or maybe that wasn't the same piggies.

"I think baseball has a thing for you too."

He says this with such a noncommittal tone that I almost miss the meaning. Is he saying what I think he's saying?

"I need to get going," I tell him, standing up so quickly I almost lose my balance. His hands dart out and catch my shoulders, steadying me. I'm pretty sure I'm shaking. I've had a crush on Duke for at least sixteen years. Ever since I realized he was a boy and I was a girl and he wasn't my brother. I never in a million years thought Duke might reciprocate my feelings.

Is that what he's really saying?

I think baseball has a thing for you too. What does that even mean?

"You doing okay there?" Duke asks, looking down into my eyes with compassion.

He's like a kaleidoscope, shifting from one aspect of himself to another within mere seconds. He went from arrogant to roguish to thoughtful in a matter of minutes right before my eyes.

"I'm good. Probably just need to get some protein after the workout."

"I'll help you down," he says, shifting his hands off my shoulders and extending one toward me as if I'm going to hold his hand while he walks me down the bleachers.

I bend and grab my duffel.

"I'm good. Thanks."

"That's good. Wouldn't want our devoted fans passing out and falling down the bleachers. Especially not so soon after their real feelings about baseball have come to light."

His back is toward me, but I can feel his smile.

I let out a long breath and walk behind him as he heads back down toward the field. When we're both on solid ground, he turns to me, reaches out and brushes a loose strand of hair behind my ear and says, "I'm glad you came to watch practice, Hollywood."

I gulp. Yep. I'm classy like that. But, my world seems to be rotating counter-clockwise right now. I need to get away and sort out what all this means—if it means anything.

"Thanks. It was fun. You're really good with them. I mean, you and Brooks. You're both good with your team."

"I'll tell Brooks you said so. And next time, you don't have to hide on the old bleachers. You've got a front row seat with your name on it anytime you want, Hollywood."

"Okie dokie. Thanks for that. I'll see you later," I say, backing away and turning to wave at Brooks who is waving my direction with a smirk that almost rivals the one Duke had when he first spotted me.

TEN

S he loves baseball!

Oh yeah. Shannon loves baseball. Which she totally doesn't love, or understand, or give two licks about. And that means, if I'm reading her right, the only reason Shannon Leigh St. James wanted to sit out in her sweaty workout clothes, hidden on the top seat of those splintering, rickety bleachers was because she wanted to watch me coach.

I'm invincible right now. Until the sobering thought of my last face-to-face conversation with Chris before he enlisted hits my inflated heart like a dart flying at a balloon. Whenever Shannon is right in front of me, it's easy to forget, but nothing has changed in terms of my promise to Chris.

Even though he didn't outright say it, I was obviously included in the list of men who should stay far away from his baby sister. Chris loves me like a brother, but he also knows me like a brother, and I'm not the kind of man he wants pursuing Shannon.

The night before Chris left, he was scared to death about the potential danger of his full-time assignment. I still hear his words to me when I drove him home from Aiden's and we were sitting in the front seat of my Shelby in his driveway.

Shannon's all I've got left, Duke. I don't know what I'd do if something happened to her. She's oblivious when it comes to how guys look at her. Half of them want to get close to her because my dad would be a good connection for them. The other half–I can't even allow myself to think of what they want with her. I'm a guy. I know what they're thinking.

You're like a brother to me. I've always looked out for you. This time, I want you to look out for me. Keep her safe. Keep an eye out and keep those guys away from her–the ones who would use her in any way, and the ones that don't deserve her. She needs to find a man who's worthy of her.

I don't think she even realizes how special she is. And if you ever tell her I said this, I'll hunt you down. But you know her like I do. She's special. I'm so afraid she'll settle–or worse, get her heart broken by some jerk who doesn't know how to treat her right.

I promised him. I even swore a vow on our friendship. I said I'd watch over her like she was my own sister. Chris let out the biggest sigh of relief. He thanked me repeatedly, telling me he could leave in peace knowing I had his back. All the while, I knew how I felt for her, but I knew what he was asking was more important than my feelings.

And he'll be home in six weeks. Home from serving his country. Home from sacrificing his entire young adulthood for my freedom. How should I thank him? By hitting on Shannon a few weeks before he returns? I told Chris I'd play unofficial bodyguard over his sister, and now I have to do that, even if it means the man I'm protecting her from is me.

Brooks has his eye on me as I walk back from where I said goodbye to Shannon. The team is packing up their mitts and parents are starting to show up to pick their boys up from practice.

"That was … interesting," Brooks says, looking up toward the spot where Shannon had been sitting.

"She just wanted to watch practice."

"Sounds logical. Hiding in the trees on the old bleachers to watch baseball practice alone in the middle of a hot summer day. Totally makes sense to me."

He doesn't roll his eyes, but he may as well.

"That's what she said," I say.

Brooks gives me a long look and then he stands and claps me on the back.

"Good luck with that," he says, walking over toward the dugout.

ELEVEN

Shannon

I'm showered and dressed, wearing a slouchy T-shirt and bike shorts with my hair in a messy bun, completely embracing the chill vibe that is Saturday afternoon. My laptop's open and Groucho's sprawled at my feet in front of the couch, snoring like only a bulldog can. He sounds like needs a C-Pap or a hefty nasal rinse.

And I'm not thinking about Duke at all. Not rehashing the way he stooped low to encourage the boy on his team who couldn't get his swing right. Not thinking of that backward ball cap and how the edges of his hair poked out just right, and I'm sure not thinking about how he said I had a seat reserved in my name anytime I wanted it.

He's a flirt. The king of flirts. He could give flirt lessons. Heck. He could even design an online course and become a world-famous flirtation instructor at the International Academy of Flirtation and Woo. Charm, charm, charm. That's all that was. Standard issue, run-of-the-mill charm from the sultan of sweet talkers.

And he made light of the reason I hung around to watch him. Like he was tickled by the knowledge that Chris' baby sister has a crush on him.

Infuriating.

Maddening.

Exasperating.

Still, I can't help the chill that runs through me when I think of him reaching out and tucking my hair behind my ear. I wish I felt one fraction of that sizzle around RJ–or any man besides Duke. My body shivers and a smile spreads across my face at the mere thought of that small gesture. I run my hand along the path his fingers took, remembering the feel of his gentle touch across my cheek and the shell of my ear.

The front door pops open and Jayme comes bounding in like the ray of sunshine she is, unencumbered by crushes and men who annoy women with their flirty, charmy backward-hatted ways. She's so blessed, and she doesn't even know it. I'd swear off men too, if I could.

"How's it poppin' sweet roomie?" she nearly sings.

"Fine."

"Fine is such a dull word. Try another adjective to give a more poignant description."

"It's Saturday. Don't I get a break from living with a walking lexicon for one day? Even God rested on the seventh day. I should think I get a break on the weekends."

"The brain is a muscle. Use it or lose it."

"My vote goes toward losing it. My brain has not been my friend lately."

Jayme looks over my shoulder at the tab I have open on my laptop. "What is that?"

"Oh, nothing," I say, tilting the lid shut a little to shield the screen from her.

"Nothing? It looked like a quiz. Was that another of your, *Which aging celebrity are you most likely to look like in ten years* thingies?"

"No. Nothing like that."

"Okayyyy. So, the closed laptop makes me think you don't want to share whatever this is with your favorite roommate. I can take a hint."

It's not that I don't want to share. And if I shared with anyone, it would absolutely be Jayme, Lexi or Laura. But I haven't talked about this with a soul and it feels a little vulnerable. Okay. A lot of vulnerable. Like standing on Main Street in my birthday suit while playing *Party in the U.S.A.* on a kazoo vulnerable.

I pop the laptop back open before I can chicken out.

"It's a quiz. But not a celebrity quiz. I'm taking a vocational interest inventory."

"Like for a job?"

Jayme plops onto the couch next to me, folding her legs under her, propping her elbows on her knees, and resting her chin on her palms. She's fully focused on me.

"Not a job per se. Just seeing what I'd want to do when I grow up. Even though I'm late to that game. I mean, do you ever feel like you're just trying to figure yourself out and you're supposed to have already gotten that dialed in years ago? I work two part-time jobs and neither of them thrill me. Of the two, I love doing manicures and pedicures, but I wouldn't want to do it all day every day."

"You're asking a woman who has four part-time jobs?"

I laugh.

"Yeah, but at least your jobs fit your passions. You freelance, write novels and come up with fortunes for fortune cookies. I think you even love working with flowers."

"I do. Mostly because they cheer people up. But, yeah. I love my cobbled little life. It's far more fulfilling than when I worked at the newspaper. I mean, I'd love it if my writing life took off and I were the next JK Rowling, only without having to wear a disguise to go out in public."

"But you do what you love every day."

"I do. And I'm wildly grateful for that. So, tell me, what does this all-knowing quiz reveal about you?"

"So far, nothing concrete."

Jayme reaches over, grabs the laptop and shuts the lid, setting it onto the coffee table.

"You don't need a quiz. You need a girlfriend. And maybe some of that strawberry lemonade I made. Hold that thought."

She bounds off the couch, heads into the kitchen humming some song I don't recognize and returns with two glasses of lemonade, handing me one.

"Now spill. Not the drink, your dreams. What would you do if you could do anything with your life? I mean, not even worrying about your finances. Let's say you got an anonymous donation and you never had to fret about making money."

"Wouldn't that be nice?"

I laugh, but Jayme doesn't. She sips her drink and stares at me with a look of deep interest from over the top of her glass.

"You know you're awesome. Right?" Jayme asks me. "I mean, who says you need to change a thing? Not me! You could be a part-time receptionist and manicurist until the day you die and I'd still look up to you and love you so much–through my trifocals and with my wrinkly hands and face."

"Awww. Well, right back at you. I'll love you even when you are a famous fantasy romance writer. Please never forget who cleaned the catbox all those days you didn't want to, and who vacated the house so you could have your creative space all to yourself to write masterpieces. Remember the little people when you make it big."

"I'd never forget the woman who scooped poop for me!" Jayme thrusts a fist in the air and we both laugh.

"But, seriously, what's your dream–if the world were your oyster ...?"

"Why do they say that anyway? What do oysters have to do with my life's ambition? If the world is my oyster, I'm surrounded by salty, stinky mush. No thanks."

Jayme tilts her head and looks at me through her lashes, her mouth twisted just the slightest.

"Stop stalling and tell me your dreams, girlfriend."

I sigh and lean back onto the couch. I know the answer. And

for some reason a tear comes to my eyes as I open my mouth to admit it.

"I'd dance."

"Of course you would! You were made for it. It's when you are most alive and most happy. And why the tears?"

Jayme pauses, and then softly says, "Oh. Your sister."

I wipe the stray tear that trailed down my cheek. I don't talk about Bridgette much, even though I think of her daily. Jayme knows what happened, even though she wasn't living in Bordeaux at the time.

Bridgette and I both danced. She was two years older than me. Our family was driving home from a competition in Columbus when we were sideswiped by another car during a fierce rainstorm. Bridgett was only sixteen years old. Our car swerved suddenly and tipped into a ditch, landing on the passenger side. My dad was driving. Mom was in the front seat next to him. Bridgette and I were in the back seat side by side. Chris had a football game, so he had stayed home.

I walked away with a concussion. Bridgette's seat belt didn't hold. She was rushed to the hospital in an ambulance. One lung was punctured by her broken rib. They took her into emergency surgery, but the trauma from the impact to her heart and other organs was too much.

She didn't survive the night.

Before the accident, dancing had always been my happy place. After we lost Bridgette, dancing seemed wrong. How could I dance when my sister never would again? The week after the crash, I threw out all my leotards, and my tap and ballet shoes. I came home from her funeral and tossed it all in our outside trash. I took my trophies and put them in a box which still sits on the top shelf of the closet in my childhood bedroom. I buried my dream with my sister.

And my mom has never been the same since. She battles chronic depression which comes and goes. Mostly it comes, and hangs around her like a relentless gray stormcloud. She's done everything to try to overcome it, and she has interludes where she's almost the woman she was before the accident, but then she slips back into a shell of the woman she was.

My parents took me to a therapist in Dayton six months after Bridgette passed away. At age fourteen I already lived on an emotional roller coaster. The loss of my sister served as an accelerator, fueling my angst. The counselor tried to help me see that I could honor my sister by carrying on our love of dance. I agreed, but some part of me refused to get on board with the idea.

Time passed and dance became a treasure behind glass—a memory in a shadowbox. I took up soccer in high-school just to quell all the people who constantly asked me when I would get back to dancing. I enjoyed soccer and I did well at it, but it wasn't dance.

I only started dancing again about four years ago—in my basement when no one was watching. One day I was doing laundry and a song came on—*"Come Get It Bae"* by Pharrell Williams. Before I knew what I was doing, my hips were swaying, my feet and arms tapping and moving in ways they hadn't in years. And once I felt the old feelings, the way I could get lost in a song and how my body could express itself through music, it was like something deep inside me woke up from a heavy slumber.

When the director at the Rec Center called me to ask if I would lead senior Zumba, I knew. I needed to take that volunteer position—mostly for the seniors, but also, for myself.

I look over at Jayme who is patiently sitting criss-cross applesauce, studying me. Oddball jumped in her lap a few moments ago, and he's sprawled upside down across her legs with his arms overhead and his hind quarters in a starfish position in the opposite direction. Jayme absentmindedly rubs his belly. His purr is almost loud enough to drown out Groucho's snoring.

I want to be a cat—eat, sleep, crawl into Duke's lap and let him rub my belly while I purr.

I shake my head.

"First of all, it's not like I'm going to make a career as a dancer.

I'm twenty-six. That ship has sailed. And I live in a town of two thousand five hundred people. Most of them think the local barn hoe-downs are the epitome of dancing."

Jayme's quiet. I sip my drink. An idea forms in my mind, but it feels too out of reach to even say out loud.

"You could teach," Jayme says, exposing my own secret thought without even realizing it.

"Maybe," I say. "But, it's Saturday and it's beautiful outside, and Em asked me to pop by the farm to check on things while they were away, so I'm going to table the adulting until Monday and go get my goat on."

I stand, taking my glass into the kitchen.

"Want some company?" Jayme shouts after me.

"If you want to come."

"Actually, on second thought, if you don't mind going alone, I should write. I have a deadline for this next draft of my novel and I also have to write thirty fortunes. But, I'll come if you want."

"Nah. I think I could use some solitude to sort myself out a bit. But thanks. I'll just head over to the MacIntyre Farm and be back in a few hours."

"Let's get pizza for dinner and watch a mindless romcom."

"That sounds so perfect. You're on. Oh! And I thought of a fortune!"

"Lay it on me."

"One side of the paper says, *Turn this paper over.* Then the other side says, *You just took directions from a cookie!*"

"I'm so using that!" Jayme beams. She's so easily pleased by the small things in life. I love that about her.

I pick up my laptop and head to my room upstairs. Halfway up, I turn and shout a thank you down to Jayme. I may never muster the courage to teach dance, or figure out how to make any of my unspoken dreams turn into reality, but talking with her loosened something up for me anyway.

TWELVE

Duke

What makes a sane man purchase a farm and then populate it with goats and a certifiably psycho llama? This is the question I'm pondering as I pull my Harley up the gravel driveway of Aiden's farm. He and Em have made a life for themselves out here. Their two adopted children complete the picture.

I'm not usually a man who envies others, but right now, thinking of Aiden's picture-perfect situation, I feel a pang of something like jealousy. Not that I'd want him to be robbed of any of this. I've wanted him to find a woman and settle down. Seeing him so content makes me happy.

But when I scan the horizon of my life, I can't see how I'll go from being an uncommitted grease-monkey to a man with a family and a job he wakes up excited to do.

Maybe I won't.

I kill the engine on the bike and walk up the rest of the driveway toward the goat enclosure. Aiden said he had a few of his neighbors from other farms coming in regularly to care for the animals. He just wants me to look around and make sure everything's okay. Which would sort of be like me asking him to watch over the garage while I'm gone.

Not happening, in case you were wondering. Aiden knows his way around a farm, but he couldn't tell an alternator from a kitchen whisk, so he needs to stay clear of my family business.

Billy Jean walks over toward the gate when she sees me. I'd never tell Aiden, but that lead goat of his freaks me out. She reminds me of the mean girls in high school, always flirting and seeming interested, but then turning on you when you least expect it. And the drama. His llama has all the drama, but Billy Jean is a close second when it comes to farm drama queens.

As if she can read my mind, Billy Jean walks over and makes a noise that sounds like *baaahhahhhahhh*, it reminds me of the wail of a dementor from Harry Potter.

"Hey, girl," I say from a good distance away.

She makes the noise again. Tilting her head back for emphasis.

"I'm just here to check on the farm for Aiden. Your man. You know?"

She answers me as if she understands me. Making another long bleating sound and walking toward me. She props herself up on her back paws, hooves, or whatever her feet are called, and aims her head toward the top of the gate.

"Um. No. I'm not letting you out. And I'm not petting you either. And why am I talking to a goat?"

She spits a little. Goats spit. I thought only the llama could spit, but now, I am covered with a light spray of some of the nastiest smelling stuff I've ever smelled. It smells like fermenting hay, or like Cooter after he's been out for a long night on a bender.

"Why *are* you talking to a goat?"

My head snaps up at the sound of Shannon's voice. I must be dreaming.

When I turn, I see her, laughing a little and walking toward me, no longer wearing her dance class outfit. Instead she's got on an old T-shirt and some bike shorts. And she looks incredibly sexy, all bare-faced and casual. I look over behind the house and see Shannon's car. How did I miss that when I pulled up?

"I'm just being friendly." I tell Shannon.

"I don't think she's impressed."

"Yeah. I got that idea–when she spit at me. What are you doing out here?"

"I came to check on things. Em asked me to look around and make sure everything was under control while they were gone. You?"

"Same. Aiden asked me."

We stand less than a yard away from one another, staring into each other's eyes. I've never felt awkward around Shannon before, but right now, my nerves feel like I've downed a pot of coffee.

"So ..." we both say at the same time.

Then we laugh a nervous laugh that reminds me of how I felt when I had crushes on girls in junior high and high school.

"What are your plans for the afternoon?" she asks.

"I thought I'd go for a ride after I check this place out. I need to clear my head a bit. How about you?"

I don't mention how I'm hoping a ride will help me sort through my inconvenient feelings for her in light of my loyalty to Chris.

"I actually thought I'd get some space alone to think while I was here," she says. "It's peaceful out here. You know?"

"It is," I say, looking across the pastures that spread beyond the barn. "What's got you so introspective on a Saturday afternoon?"

"Life. Goals. Decisions."

She gazes off at the barn like the answers could be written on the walls in invisible ink and somehow they are about to materialize if she stares long enough.

"Want to take a ride with me? Nothing clears my head like a ride on the open road. Might help. Can't hurt."

She looks me over from head to toe, taking her time to answer me. I feel like I'm holding my breath. I want her to say yes, but on the other hand, what was I thinking? Shannon on my bike means Shannon pressed up behind me, holding on and taking every dip and turn with me. I wanted to ride so I could sort myself out. With her nestled against me, I won't be sorting anything. I'll be lucky if I can think straight.

When her eyes meet mine she says, "Sure. Let me just text Jayme."

"Great," I say. "Follow me to my house and I'll grab my extra helmet."

I take another look around. Everything looks good, but I don't really know farming, so there could be something really out of place or a disaster about to happen and I wouldn't know what to look for. At least I kept my word to Aiden–and I got the bonus of seeing Shannon twice in one day–three times if you count me crashing Zumba class.

I mount my bike and pull down the driveway. Shannon follows me, and my thoughts take off like rabbits out of a thicket. Only my thoughts aren't so fluffy and cute.

I want that woman. And whenever she's near, all consideration of her brother becomes the farthest thing from my mind. Even now, with her a few car lengths behind me, I'm regaining a bit more clarity and resolve. But, whenever she's sharing the same air as me, all logic and loyalty fade like a mist.

I hop off my bike, grab my extra helmet from my garage, and stride back to where Shannon now stands in my driveway. I hold the helmet out to her. She straps it on like a pro, shifting it a little once the buckle is fastened.

"Ready?" I ask.

"Born ready," she says with a wink.

Okay then. I hop on and wait while Shannon braces her hands on my shoulders, throwing her leg over the back of the bike and wiggling to get situated. She wraps her arms around my torso and I take a breath, letting it out slowly. She gives me a squeeze and says, "Giddy up!"

I shout back, "Yes ma'am," as I push the gear to neutral with my foot, grip the clutch and push start. The smile on my face refuses to dim as we take off down my street. I weave through the neighborhood and out onto the road back past Aiden's farm and the other ranches out this way. Within ten minutes we're outside town, on the old road that leads to the reservoir.

Shannon holds onto me, her thighs gripping around mine, her arms comfortably around my waist, and her chest pressed to my back. I feel every shift she makes in position. She leans when I do and I'm hyper-aware of how well we move together. Sometimes, over the roar of my engine, I hear her carefree laughter. I'm either a genius or an idiot or some random combination of the two, because this is the best and worst idea I've ever had.

I shout over my shoulder, "You up for an adventure?"

"What?" she shouts back.

I turn my head and shout even louder, "Are you up for an adventure?"

"Always!" she says, and I can hear the mischief in her voice. She's the best kind of trouble.

"Okay!" I shout.

I turn the bike around and head toward the highway leading away from Bordeaux. We ride along in comfortable silence, the wind whipping around us, and Shannon tucked behind me. Twenty minutes later we're pulling down the road toward the Montgomery County Fairground.

"The fair! I can't go to the fair looking like this," Shannon says when I pull my bike to a stop and put my feet down to stabilize us.

Shannon hops off the bike, her body language betraying her protest. She wants to be here and I plan to show her a good time. I'm not sure what *Life, Goals, Decisions* meant to her, but it sounded heavy, and I'm just the man to lighten things up when they get too deep.

"Can't go looking like what? You look good to me," I tell her. It's a neutral statement, but nothing about me feels neutral when I say it.

"My hair's a mess, I'm wearing an old T-shirt and bike shorts."

"In the midwest in the summer. I guarantee you might even

be overdressed. You're in Ohio, Hollywood. Smack dab in the middle of a bunch of farmers and small-town people who wear their bathrobes to the grocery store on any given day."

She chuckles, knowing I'm only half right. We've got plenty of fully-dressed citizens. But we've got our fair share of *what was that?* going on around here too.

"But, if you want me to take you home, I will."

There's just enough challenge in my tone, I know I'll get her to give in. She always rises up when it comes to a dare, needing to prove herself like every younger sibling on the planet. And, she doesn't disappoint.

"If you can go in that. I can go in this."

She waves her hand up and down my body.

"This old thing?" I ask with a wink, pushing my chest out to make my old white T-shirt stretch a little. "I'm good."

I almost miss the blush rising up her neck. It's the second indication I've had today that Shannon just might be interested in me as more than a friend. I tuck that little tidbit away for now, not even sure what I'd do if she were.

"Okay, Hollywood. Let's go show these people how you do a fair."

THIRTEEN

Shannon

"... And cotton candy! Oh! And funnel cake. And chocolate covered bacon. And one of those deep-fried grilled cheese sandwiches. Or maybe fireman chili."

Duke laughs hard as I rattle off my list of foods I want to be sure to eat while we're here. His laugh is one of the best things about him. It's like every part of him gets in on the fun.

"Who's going to roll us out in a wheelbarrow after all that?" he asks, lifting his eyebrows and looking down at me with an adorable grin on his face.

"You'll feel like crap tomorrow, but in the best of ways!"

I'm like a kid right now, and I don't care. Usually I'm so caught up in hoping Duke sees me as a woman, but he was right. That motorcycle ride, and getting out of Bordeaux for a change of scenery lightened me up. Somehow, deciding the direction of the rest of my life doesn't feel as important right now.

I'm out on a Saturday night with Duke. It's not a date, but it's something, and I'm going to eat up every minute of it–while I also eat up my share of fair food.

I skip ahead of Duke, turning to send him a taunting look. "I dare you to ride that thing!"

I point up at a contraption that looks like a giant Q-Tip, only

81

you sit inside the round end and it spins while the whole center flips end over end.

"I'm a daredevil by nature," Duke says. "But I don't like putting my life on the line in a machine that was assembled by some carney three days ago, only to be taken apart next week. What if a screw's loose?"

I waggle my eyebrows at him. "So you won't ride a ride that boy just went on?"

I point to a child who can't be older than seven.

"I'll go on it, if you go on that," he tells me, pointing to the giant bungee. It's at least ten stories tall with two gigantic rubber bands dangling from the tops of the poles, coming down like a V toward the center seat that holds two people.

Basically, you are tilted back and shot into the air like a slingshot, then you boing around until you stop bouncing and they finally guide you back to the ground.

"Deal," I say, jutting my chin out just a little. "Better get on them before we eat our weight in junk food."

"Good call."

His grin spreads across his face like a sunrise, making those dimples pop. Two on the left, three on the right. It may sound excessive, but trust me, just as in everything, too much suits Duke just right.

He gives me one of his signature looks. Maybe he doesn't even know he's doing it, but every cell in my body hums a little like a stadium light warming up when the switch is flipped. There's this buzzing and then bright light floods everything. Only Duke has this effect on me, and right now I'm not complaining in the least.

We've never spent this kind of time alone before. There were nights when he'd show up to meet my brother for something and we'd talk in the living room before Chris came out of his room to leave with Duke.

Sometimes Duke and I would bump into one another around town and we'd stand chatting for a little while. But, usually we're surrounded by family and friends.

I can't remember another time when it was just Duke and me–definitely not one where we rode his motorcycle out of town to spend an afternoon and evening together.

Tonight I'm not Chris' little sister and Duke's not Chris' best friend. We're just two people out for a good time together, and it feels beyond right, even though I'd like it to be so much more.

I grab Duke's elbow and hook my arm through it. He seems completely oblivious to the effect touching him has on me, and I'm doing my best to hide the reaction my body has to being this near to him. I don't want to make this weird. I just want to savor this evening for whatever it is.

"Okay, Hollywood. Let's get dizzy together."

Famous last words.

We exit the Q-Tip from hell and I'm not quite sure which way is up. Duke, the same man who questioned this ride of doom, stands perfectly straight. At least the one Duke in front of me is standing straight. The other two Dukes to his left and right are swerving and bobbing.

"Stand still," I tell them.

He just chuckles that deep rumbling laugh. At my expense.

"I think I need to sit or find the off button," I say.

"I'm definitely not saying I told you so."

"Just wait. We still have the bungee cord. And the fun house." I remind him. "You may be the one weaving and bobbing after those."

"And the ferris wheel," he says with a lift of his brows.

"The only reason a guy wants to ride the ferris wheel is to get stuck at the top with a girl so he can make his move," I say without thinking.

Duke sends me a look I could only hope was real. It's a look that says he'd like to be stuck at the top of a ferris wheel with me. I turn and walk toward the bungee cord trying to clear my head of what I'd do to Duke at the top of a ferris wheel if I knew he'd really want me to. I'd take the memory of that ride to my grave.

Maybe Duke's a really bad kisser. Maybe he slobbers or his

lips go too firm or he breathes loudly through his nose. My eyes move to his lips, full and wide. I catalog his jaw and I know with infinite certainty he would be nothing but the best kiss of my life.

Duke's eyebrow raises. His eyes seem to heat as he notices me staring at him.

"Do I have a little something here?"

He runs the pad of his thumb over his bottom lip a little too slowly, letting it pop off at the end of the swipe. Dang.

"Uh. Nope. Ready to be a human sling bullet?"

"Is anyone ever ready for that?"

I look up at him through my lashes. "I'm ready."

I'm so ready. I only wish he knew how ready I was and what I'm ready for.

"You're a wild child, Hollywood."

We stand in the shortest line at the fair. Mostly surrounded by teenagers and young men who are probably four or five years younger than me.

"So you've got big life decisions on the brain?" Duke asks casually as we progress forward.

"Yeah. Trying to decide what I want to be when I grow up."

I try to match my tone to the lightness of his.

"I hear that," he mumbles almost imperceptibly.

"You know what you're going to be," I tease with a nudge of my elbow to his side. The solid wall of muscles I hit surprises me. "You're going to be the next proud owner of Satterson's. Must be nice to have your life laid out before you. No second-guessing. No regrets."

"Just because my life has been planned by other people doesn't mean I don't have regrets."

I study his face. His brow furrows for a moment. The look is gone so quickly I almost could have imagined it.

"I didn't mean to assume. I'm just having a mid-life crisis at twenty-six."

"You're young," he reminds me. "You've got time to figure all this out for yourself."

He starts singing really softly, but with a playful lilt to his voice. It's another one of the old songs he's always singing or playing on the radio in the garage. I know this one. It's by Cat Stevens about finding a girl and settling down and getting married. Only he puts the word "boy" in the lyrics. The song implies I've got time to figure out life. He's telling me everything he'd say in words by singing to me right here in the middle of a county fair.

Duke's voice has this resonance to it that makes me want to curl up and be held. When he sings, even playfully like this, you feel like you're remembering the best day of your life, or missing the one thing that matters most.

"I love your singing voice," I tell him when he tapers off and stops singing mid-verse.

"Aww shucks," he jokes as we reach the front of the line.

We're ushered onto the ride where I get to hear that same voice go up at least three octaves. Duke screams like a room full of teenage girls when he's scared. I spend the whole ride laughing so hard tears are spilling down my cheeks. The combination of his reaction and the thrill of the ride, and simply having his undivided attention has me buoyant when we walk off toward the food stands.

"The key to fair food is to pace yourself," I explain as we walk toward the first stand.

"And we start with funnel cakes?"

"You've heard the saying, save the best for last?"

He nods, obviously enjoying my antics.

"Well, with fair food, it's the opposite. You want to eat the deep-fried oreos and funnel cake first. You can have turkey legs and chili any day. Eat the food you never get to have first."

"And are we eating deep-fried oreos?"

"Twinkies," I correct him with a smile that won't quit. "The deep-fried Twinkies are a spiritual experience."

We get a funnel cake to split and walk to a nearby bench. I take a huge strawberry and whip cream topped bite once we're seated. Half of it seems to remain on my lips so I dart my tongue out to catch what's all over my mouth. Duke watches me, and I wish I could read his mind.

"Were you planning on sharing?" he asks with a chuckle.

"Maybe."

I twist so my back is partly toward him and take another bite. I let out an appreciative moan, licking my lips again. Duke's fork comes over my shoulder, his chest nearly pressed up against my back.

"Gimme a bite, St. James."

I don't know what comes over me, but I scoop a big forkful and turn, aiming it at his face. He opens for me and I pop the bite into his mouth. Our eyes lock as I drag the empty fork back out through his lips. I've kissed plenty of guys in my life. This moment tops them all. I don't think I've ever shared this much intimacy with a man.

Duke licks his lips slowly, his eyes not leaving mine. I feel the prickle of awareness and sheer want crawl up my spine and tingle across my scalp.

I want Duke. I've wanted him for so long I can't remember what it's like to live without this pang of emptiness inside me. It's a space only he could fill, and the way he's looking at me right now makes me wonder if he's feeling any of those same desires. He looks like a man preparing to kiss a woman–getting ready to kiss me.

"Duke! Is that you?" a woman's voice calls out, causing me to nearly drop the rest of the funnel cake.

Both our heads turn toward the sound of the voice calling Duke's name: Cherry Blanchard. Talk about putting a cherry on a crud sundae. I was inches away from a kiss I've waited years for, or at least I think I might have been, and now we've got Cherry to contend with.

"Hey, Cherry," Duke says.

His arm settles behind me on the bench. He's not putting it around my shoulders, exactly, but he has it draped lightly behind me in a very territorial stance. He doesn't seem to even notice he put it there. I scoot an inch closer to him. If he needs me to mark him as mine, I'll do a better job than Groucho on a walk around the block.

Cherry's eyes glance from Duke to me and back again. "Are you ... I ... well." She huffs. "I'm here with some friends. We took the boys out for a night at the fair. Who are you two here with?"

"Friends," Duke says quickly.

Too quickly.

Maybe I wasn't about to get the kiss of a lifetime.

"Well ..." Cherry looks back and forth between us, obviously trying to size up what we are to one another. "I guess I'll see you on the ball field, Duke."

"Sounds good," he says, giving that signature smile.

She smiles back and gives him a little wink and one of those coy waves where she wiggles all her fingers. It's so ... bold. When she turns, she pops each hip with so much sway she could knock out a small child as she walks back toward the group of Bordeaux people she came with.

Women throw themselves at Duke. I've always been a witness to this phenomenon. Between his unique blend of bad-boy and all-American hero, and the way he looks, it's inevitable. Top that off with the car he drives and his motorcycle, and then add in his unexpectedly tender heart, natural charisma, and his killer sense of humor. He's more tempting than a lifetime supply of Ghirardelli or an all-expense-paid shopping spree to Bloomingdale's.

Cherry's got to be at least five years older than Duke. That doesn't stop her from hitting on him–blatantly making it obvious she wants him regardless of what she thought I was to him.

Duke's quiet for a beat once Cherry's no longer around. The mood between us has shifted to something more detached, and I would do anything to rewind the clock and go back to the moment I pulled that fork out from between his lips.

FOURTEEN

Duke

Shannon left less than an hour ago. When she hugged me goodnight, I held onto her a moment longer than I should, but then I let her go and appreciated the view as she sauntered down my driveway and stepped off the curb toward the driver's side of her car, only turning once to wave goodnight before she climbed in and drove away.

Did I want to pull her in for a kiss? Does a goat spit? Like it or not, we both know the answer to that question now.

But ever since the virtual splash of cold water that came when Cherry interrupted us on that bench, I've been reminding myself of my promise to Chris and the reality of what I have to offer Shannon. I'm facing down two solid reasons I need to back off: loyalty and inadequacy. It's a bitter cocktail.

We ate our way through the rest of the night. I rode the mechanical bull and nearly lost every deep-fried, sugar coated, greasy item in my stomach while being thrown back and forth at increasing intervals on that crazy machine. But, it made Shannon laugh, so it was totally worth it.

Then we sat side-by-side on the ferris wheel, but I didn't make a move, as much as I had wanted to–maybe even planned to in some hopeful corner of my mind. It felt like Chris was sitting on my shoulder like one of those angels or devils, I couldn't tell which. Either way, I couldn't force myself to ignore him, despite the sweet peach and vanilla fragrance wafting off Shannon, or the fact that we did actually stall at the top, a view of the fairgrounds, the surrounding grassland and woods sprawled out in the darkness below us. Shannon's knee pressed against mine, her hair blew into my face. She looked up at me expectantly, and I looked away.

Loyalty can suck an egg right now.

As for inadequacy, I could be more. I'll never be enough for her, but maybe if I'm teaching and coaching instead of crawling around on a concrete floor and sticking my head under hoods all day. Maybe then I'd have more to offer her. I still wouldn't be half the man she deserves, but I'd be willing to strive to be that man.

I'd do anything to become that man.

And now I'm home alone, going stir crazy because I can't get the images of Shannon out of my mind. Her laughing. Her eating too big of a bite of that funnel cake and turning away from me so I couldn't get my fork into it. Her screaming on the HydroMax. Her gazing into my eyes with a look that felt like she would be right there with me if I made a move.

My phone rings and I say, "Hello"

No one answers, but I hear muffled voices on the other end.

I say "Hello?" again, but no one speaks.

Then I pull my phone back from my ear and study the number. It's Shannon.

She must have butt-dialed me. Typical. The woman almost ought not be allowed to own a phone between her typos and her accidental calls.

I should hang up. But then, I'm not really known for doing what I ought to–especially not when there's a chance I might have a little harmless fun.

"Soooo …" I hear Jayme's voice say. "A night out with Duke, huh?"

"Mm hmm," Shannon answers.

"And that was worth canceling pizza and a romcom with your fave roomie?"

Oof. They had plans. Well, Shannon didn't mention that, so I can't feel too badly.

"Sorry about that, Jayme. I just ..." Shannon takes a deep breath. I can hear it all the way over here in my spy lair, also known as my living room.

"I just never had this opportunity in all these years."

"And what opportunity might that be?"

"A chance to be alone–just the two of us. It's always been him and Chris, or him with me and my family, or us with a friend group. When he offered a ride on his bike, I thought it would help me clear my mind after all the heaviness thinking about goals and life and dance."

Dance? I wonder what she's thinking about dance.

I should hang up.

Nah.

I prop my arm behind my head and hold the phone to my ear, closing my eyes, like it will help me hear every word a little better.

"Well, that motorcycle ride definitely turned into more."

"Not enough of more, but yeah."

Wait. What? She wants more?

"Ooooh! I knew it!" Jayme's squealing at a level that should be used to alert people of an impending tornado. Dogs might start howling. Glassware may shatter.

"Gah!" Shannon has an outburst. "Ugh!" And another nonsensical expletive. "I mean ... argh blahh gah!" More frustrated gibberish. "You can't tell a soul."

Everything's quiet and for a moment, I think I lost the call. I lift the phone away from my face to see. The call is still live.

I really, really should hang up.

Not happening.

Not a chance.

Shannon wants more! I thought so at the ball field, and then on the bench with the funnel cake, but to hear the actual words from her mouth. That's something else entirely.

I feel like doing a fist pump and one of those celebration dances Ochocinco does after he makes a touchdown–the ones he always gets fined for because they are so over the top. I could dance around pretending I'm milking a cow, robbing a bank and changing a diaper all at once.

"Thank you," Shannon says. Jayme must have used some sort of body language to assure her of her secrecy.

"How long has this been going on?" Jayme asks, her excitement carries through the line.

"What? Nothing has been going on. That's the problem!" Shannon sounds as frustrated as I feel.

"I mean your crush, or feelings or whatever this is?"

"Seventh grade? I don't know."

What? Seventh grade? I do the math. I would have been in tenth grade. That would *not* have been happening. But now, her being twenty-six and me nearing thirty is barely a blip on the age-gap scale.

"And you've sat on these feelings for that long. All the times people conjectured and tried to ship you two, and you flatly denied having any interest in Duke. Even I had started to believe you didn't care about him. And I'm a hopeless romantic."

"I know. I just couldn't take the pressure. I mean, he's Chris' best friend. And he's a total flirt–a player in some ways. He's always got someone he's seeing out of town.

"Chris suspected I had a crush on Duke a few years back and he warned me against ever acting on my feelings. He said he loved Duke like a brother, but I deserve a guy who will commit to me and Duke's not a long-term type of man. Of course I denied my feelings to Chris. Anyway, none of that matters. Duke's not interested in me. At least that's what I thought."

I swallow the lump in my throat as quietly as I can, afraid any noise on my end will alert them to my totally inappropriate eavesdropping.

But, ouch. A player? I am a flirt, a harmless one. At least I've always thought it was harmless. It's sort of how I go through life. My friends have called me out on it before, but mostly in a *Duke always gets the girl. All he has to do is bat those eyelashes and give her a smolder and she's his* kind of way. They've never dissuaded me from being a flirt.

But I'm not a player. I've had some out of town girlfriends, if you even want to call them that, like Beth. But, I'm always clear about the parameters of what we're doing together.

I knew Chris was wary of guys who might pursue Shannon, but to hear that he specifically warned her off me, well, that's a lot to swallow.

I can't believe Shannon doesn't know the whole reason I'm uncommitted is because no one measures up to her. But, why would she know that? Should she even know that? With Chris coming home, the timing of me figuring this out couldn't be worse. And besides, maybe she's right. Doesn't she deserve someone more steady, less all over the map than me. But she wants me.

She. Wants. Me.

That truth feels like a shot of adrenaline to my heart, overriding my thoughts, my reasoning and everything else. I resist the urge to hop back on my bike and do something really, really foolish and impetuous.

"You thought he wasn't interested. That's past tense. What do you think now?"

"I don't know! Agh!"

I smile at the adorable outburst. And I want to go over there and wipe all that frustration and confusion away in one swift move on my part. You want to know how I feel? I'll be right over to show you.

"So you think he might be interested now?"

Yeah. Tell us, Shannon. Do you think I'm interested now?

I should fry for this invasion of privacy, but I wasn't the one who butt dialed. I know, I know. I'm the one listening when I should hang up. But you'd do the same thing. You know you would. Cut a man some slack here.

"I think ... maybe. Today he showed up in my dance class to apologize for last night when he acted all domineering and boorish during my date with RJ. Then, when he caught me watching baseball practice from the old bleachers ..."

Jayme cuts Shannon off. "Wait. Wait, wait, wait. You were at practice, hidden in the bleachers? Girl."

"Yes. Okay? Yes. I just wanted to watch him from afar, to see the way he is with those boys. To check him out in that backward ball cap. It was delicious torture, to be honest."

I'm wearing a backward ballcap every day of my life from now on. I'll be buried in one. People will ask me why I'm always wearing my hat and why it's perpetually backwards. This. This right here is why.

Delicious torture? I'm all over that. Consider it payback for watching her dance in that form-fitting outfit for an hour. I know all about delicious torture.

Jayme giggles.

"Anyway," Shannon continues. "After practice, well, after Duke saw me up on the bleachers ..."

Jayme cuts Shannon off again. "He saw you?"

"Yes. Let me tell you, okay? He saw me, then strode up the bleachers like it was his personal mission in life, and then he was all sexy-ballplayer, towering over me with a smirk I wanted to kiss right off that smug face of his."

Oh yes! Heck to the yeah!

She's not finished. She's like a fine-tuned engine when you tap the gas pedal just right. She's roaring to life, and I think I might need shackles to keep me restrained to my house tonight.

"Duke stood there all self-righteous and yet, still adorable, and he told me I have a place on the front row of the new bleachers with my name on it anytime I want it. And then, this afternoon, when I bumped into him at Aiden and Em's he invited me to ride on his bike. After we tooled around the back roads, he made a spur of the moment decision to take me to the fair. Where, I think he may have almost kissed me, except Cherry walked up and was all, 'Duke, oh Duuuke, oh, big man with the big guns. How are you?' while she batted her fake eyelashes and swished her hips like a trollop in an effort to make him drool."

"A trollop?" Jayme sputters out a laugh around the word.

"Whatever. You get the point," Shannon says on a huff. "After Cherry came on the scene it was like someone flipped a switch and Duke no longer seemed like anything but a friend, or just my brother's friend taking me out for a fun evening. So I don't know."

"Wow." Jayme says.

"Yeah."

There's so much in what she just said ... sexy ballplayer, oh heck yeah ... big guns, thank you for noticing ... jealous of Cherry, I can work with that ... but then the way she felt me pull away. She's not wrong. I sent mixed messages. Not intentionally, but I don't know my own mind. And now I'm messing her up because I feel like I'm a human yo-yo when it comes to Shannon.

"But, it sounds like he was interested," Jayme says with that typical hopeful note to her voice.

"Maybe. I don't know. I can't believe I'm spilling all this to you."

"I can't believe you haven't told Laura or me before this. Or Lexi. Or Em."

They're both quiet. I hold my breath.

"Seventh grade?" Jayme says with a note of disbelief in her voice.

"More or less," Shannon says with some sadness to her tone.

I want to hold her. Oh, don't get me wrong. I want to do so much more than hold her. But right now I just want to hold her and take away the note of discouragement coating her voice.

"The thing is," Shannon says. "If I told one of you, I'd have to tell all of you. And Laura is married to Rob. And Rob and Trevor are friends. And Em is married to Aiden. And Aiden is one of

Duke's best friends. And somehow, things leak in this town. People don't mean to, but secrets get out and before you know it, your private thoughts are common knowledge. I'd die if he ever knew how I felt."

I push "end" to cut the call off.

I wanted to stay on, but that last sentence felt like Jiminy Cricket chirping out a principled warning to my inner Pinnochio. My conscience couldn't take staying on the call if she doesn't want me to know how she feels about me.

But now I do know.

The question is: what am I going to do about it?

FIFTEEN

Shannon

"Don't come in here!" Jayme shouts from the kitchen as soon as I step into our house after a day of work.

Of course, I walk straight toward the kitchen.

"What happened?" I ask, suppressing a giggle as I look around at the mess.

"Not funny. Wipe that smile off your face. Wipe. It."

"There's no smile. This is my resting face."

"It's not your resting face. Your resting face looks like this."

Jayme makes a face that crosses between a concerned scowl and a faraway dreamy look.

"Good grief. I hope not. But back to you. And this."

I gesture around at what looks like a fight broke out in a pancake batter factory. If there were such a place. Is there? I mean, grocery stores do sell those little frozen pancakes in a cardboard box in the freezer section, which are woeful substitutes for the real thing if you ask me. By the time you thaw that puck of dough out, you could have whipped up some batter of your own.

"I got on the sourdough trend," Jayme says.

"Huh?"

"The sourdough trend. You know. I want to be self-sustaining. Garden, bake bread, grow herbs on the windowsill, maybe get some chickens down the road for eggs. And sourdough is good for your gut—all those little microbes wiggling their way through your intestines. It's healthy."

"I don't eat food that could blow up. And this ..." I gesture again. "Is a full blown microbe explosion."

"I didn't read the recipe right, so I overfed the starter. And then I put the lid on the jar ... So, I was writing away. I was in the zone, too. The alien, Khor, and the half-blood female were making such intense eye contact, she's in this virtual prison cell with light beams instead of bars, restrained by these ropes made of electrical force. And the alien who looks like a half-lion, half-man, with eagle wings, can't communicate with Violet, the half-blood earthling, since they have a language barrier, you know. So, she couldn't tell if he wanted to make her his lunch, or devour her in a totally other way ... Anyway, it was this moment of insane romantic tension and ... that's when it happened! Kablamo! I seriously thought someone was hunting deer in our backyard."

I'm giggling and then I can't help it. A laugh bursts out of me. Between the plot line and the disaster that used to be our kitchen, I lose it.

Jayme crosses her arms and looks mad for exactly a half-second and then she starts laughing too.

"You should have seen Oddball! He was by my shoulders on the back of the couch and when that thing blew, he jetted off the couch, used my lap like a springboard and shot through the room like a horse out of the gate on race day. He's still under the chair in the living room. Wouldn't even come out for tuna."

"Oh my gosh!" I snort.

Then we both bust up because I snort-laughed.

"What happened to Hairball?"

"He just stayed on the dining chair all chill, like, 'So something blew up. Um. Could we get a clean up in aisle six? Humans? Are there any humans around here?' And then he rolled onto his back and licked himself."

I shake my head.

"Let me set my stuff down and I'll help you clean up. And no more health food for you, missy. Trust me when I say, Fritos never blow up."

"No, they just kill you in your sleep."

"Um. Nice imagery. I thought you were the happy-go-lucky member of our dynamic duo."

"I'm happy-go-lucky, not brain dead," she says with a wink. "Oh, and I asked the girls over for girls' night. Now that Em is back from her honeymoon, I thought we'd all hang out. And ..." Jayme makes a little locking of the key motion near her lips. "Your lifelong crush is safely locked in the vault that is my soul."

"Okayyy," I say.

It's a relief having someone to share my feelings about Duke with, but what if Jayme does slip? Things have a way of leaking out around here. I grab the towel Jayme is holding out to me and wet it, then I start wiping little splats of batter off our walls and counters while she mops the floor.

An hour or so later, our three closest friends show up. Laura and Lexi, who have been two of my best friends since childhood, and Em, the newest addition to our friend group. She moved here from Boston over a year and a half ago.

Jayme miraculously managed to pull together a crock pot full of franks and beans and our friends line the kitchen counters with a salad and side dishes.

"It's a feast!" Laura announces. "Wow. Your kitchen is super-clean. You didn't have to clean for us, you know."

"Um, yes we did," Jayme says with a sly look in my direction.

We mill around chatting and filling our plates and then we take our dinner into the living room and pile onto the couches and chairs. Groucho tries to beg, but Jayme uses her bossy voice to get him to lie down again. Oddball is still under the chair until Lexi sits in it. He picks that moment to dart out like a flash of lightning, shooting straight up the stairs and out of sight.

"What's gotten into him?" Lexi asks.

"A little kitchen mishap. Cats. Am I right?" Jayme says.

"That's why I'm a dog person," Laura says. She winks at Groucho who takes that as a cue to stand and make the rounds begging one more time.

"So," Lexi starts in, "Tell us about the honeymoon, Em."

Em tells us all about the week she and Aiden spent in Puerto Rico, walking cobblestone streets in San Juan, snorkeling, kayaking the bioluminescent bays, and eating on the boardwalk in Ponce. The smile on her face says more than her words ever could.

"It sounds amazing," Lexi says with a dreamy look in her eyes. "It feels like ages since our honeymoon."

"Having a baby will do that to you," Laura says. "It feels like a while since ours too, though."

"Which I'm still mad about," Lexi says.

"Me too," I agree.

Laura and Rob eloped and had their honeymoon all in one trip. She always insisted that she was going to elope if she ever got married, but no one believed her.

"Maybe we'll renew our vows someday to include all of you. I just wanted to keep it simple."

"All's forgiven," Jayme easily says.

"Speak for yourself," I half-joke.

I'm dying to change the subject for some reason. It's not that I don't want to hear about Em's honeymoon, but our girlfriend nights used to be so much more about us. Now it's about husbands and babies and life after marriage. The chasm feels especially huge tonight between the two remaining single women and the three who are happily committed. And, since Jayme has chosen her singleness, I'm really the only one in the *pining away for the unattainable man* category.

"So." Laura turns her scrutiny on me. "How was your date with Reginald?"

Before I can answer, Jayme swallows so loudly the whole room turns toward her.

She gulps, picks up her lemonade, swallows three huge swigs in a row and then bursts into a coughing fit.

Laura gets this knowing look and fixes her eyes on me.

"What are you not telling me?"

"About my date? Not much. Duke showed up in the same restaurant. Funny coincidence. And he came over and introduced himself to RJ."

"RJ?"

"That's the name Reginald goes by."

"Whew. Well, that's much better than Reginald. So, Duke, huh?"

"Yep."

"Coincidence, huh?"

"Yep."

It's like a verbal ping-pong match started between me and Laura and our friends are the spectators, their heads bobbing as they glance from me to Laura to me, and back to Laura again.

"Anyhoo, he left us alone. The date was a solid six point five. No second date. I'm out."

I don't even dare glance at Jayme for fear of sending her into another fit of choking or worse. Plus, she seems like the clamp to her so-called vault needs a lock replacement. I'm not so sure my secret's safe right now.

"Not out," Lexi says with a plea in her voice. "Don't give up on dating or men."

I picture Duke. I don't want to give up on him, but I'm pretty sure I need to.

SIXTEEN

Shannon: *Hey, sweaty friend.*
Duke: *Hey.*
Shannon: *Did you still want to start a boob club? I think all the girls are down for it.*
Duke: *Um ... no? And I'm not even sure what that is, but I don't think you should either.*
Shannon*: BOOK! BOOK CLUB! oh my gosh. That was for Jayme – and I was calling her sweet friend. not sweaty.*
Shannon: *I'm relocating to another country. Nice knowing you. I'm moving to someplace obscure like Greenland. I'll buy a parka and an ice pick and learn to love flesh.*
Shannon: *FISH. I'll learn to love fish. Buh bye. No more texting for me!*
Duke: *...*
Duke: *Sorry it took a moment to answer. I couldn't breathe past my laughter. That text was something else. Even for you.*
Duke: *Don't worry. I won't tell anyone about your club. And you got half that text right. I am sweaty. Just finished a workout with Brooks. Firemen don't mess around about workouts.*

Shannon: *There is no club. It's a BOOK club. BOOKS. You know. Like what's between the covers.*
Duke: *Oh, I know what's between the covers.*
Duke: *Shannon?*
Duke: *Book club. Got it.*
Shannon: *Pretend this text steel navel happened.*
Duke: *Swear on my navel. (laughing emoji) This text never happened.*
Shannon: *Gah! Freaking auto cry ... auto cat recital ... Gah! Author correct. Ant crustacean.*
Shannon: *Forget it.*

"What's got you grinning like a goofball?" Brooks asks from across the weight room.

The Bordeaux fire station is so small and old, but they have a pretty decent set of machines and free weights in one room to keep the guys busy when it's their rotation. And, Brooks has to be overnight tonight, so I came in to keep him company. Or maybe I'm here to get out of my own head. Ever since I overheard Shannon's conversation with Jayme, I've been twisted up inside trying to decide what to do. Or not do.

"Just got another botched text from Shannon," I say, trying unsuccessfully to stifle my grin.

"I wish she had my number. I'd love to get at least one of her botched texts."

I look over at Brooks. A growly sound forms in the back of my throat.

"Oh, man. Wow." Brooks says, shaking his head.

"What? I'm here to make sure she doesn't end up with anyone her brother wouldn't approve of."

"And you're growling on his behalf–at me?"

"Exactly."

I wipe the towel across my forehead and neck. Then I give it a quick snap in Brooks' direction.

"Keep away from Shannon and we won't have any problem."

He nods, then smirks.

I send him a side eye. Then I tell him, "Thanks for letting me out-bench you."

"I'm nothing if I'm not hospitable."

"Oh, so that was you being a good host?"

"You know it," Brooks smiles big.

It's his charmer smile.

"Save that smile for someone like ... oh, I don't know ... maybe Em's friend Gabriela."

"She's something else."

"You think you can handle her?"

"And then some. If only she were local."

He smiles again. A different smile–like he's reminiscing or looking forward to Christmas.

I shake my head. Having someone local doesn't always simplify a situation. But I'm not about to share that wisdom with Brooks right now. I know who I need to talk to. And he just got back from his honeymoon.

"I'm out. Haven't seen Aiden since he got back from Puerto Rico. I need to catch up with him a bit."

"Send him all my love."

I chuckle. "Will do. Though you might want to save a little of that love for Cherry Blanchard."

"Nope. If it comes down to her or Aiden. It's all his."

I'm still laughing as I step out the door of the fire station, letting it clatter behind me. I've been riding the motorcycle around since it's warm out and most days it's not raining. But, I miss my girl–my sweet Shelby–when I don't drive her for a few days, so today I took her out for a spin.

My phone rings as I'm opening the car door.

"Hello, Principal Barnes."

"Please, Duke. I'm in my swim trunks by my pool. Call me Steven so I don't feel like I have to go dry off and put on a shirt and tie."

"Yes sir, Steven."

"We'll work on that. Anyway, do you have a minute?"

"Sure. Yes. What can I do for you?"

"Okay. Well, I've got a situation and it may work in your favor–depending on what you've decided about pursuing your teaching credential."

I'm silent, except for the sound of my heart beating out of my chest and the breath I'm trying to control.

"Mrs. Vasser called me this morning. Seems she went and got pregnant."

"She is married. These things do happen." I chuckle before I remember who I'm talking to.

Get it together, Duke.

And this right here might be why I'm better suited to be sticking my head under a hood all day instead of trying to mold the minds and hearts of America's youth.

But, to my surprise, Principal Barnes–Steven–laughs along with me.

"Yes. Yes they do happen. And as happy as I am for her and Wes, she's due in December. That means she wouldn't even finish out the first semester. She's asking to take the year off. Then she'll decide if she's coming back. So, I'm in a pinch, Duke. I need a history teacher, stat. You could help me out of that pinch. You see."

"I do. Only, like I told you when we met, I don't have my credential yet. I'm still looking into the link for the courses you sent me."

"Understood. But, we're a small town. People know you. I know you. I taught you in fourth grade for heaven's sake. We can bend things a bit and no one will complain. Besides, there's a protocol for situations like this, even in bigger cities. We can put you in under emergency circumstances. You'll have to take an exam to show your basic comprehension of the subject you'll be teaching. Then you'll start your coursework online and in the fall, we put you in the class while you simultaneously get credentialed.

And, more importantly, we get you on the field with our teams as our new head coach for football and baseball."

I'm stunned into silence. And you know me. It rarely happens that I don't have a quick comeback or at least a wink or playful look to distract people when the conversation hits a lull. Not at this moment. Right now I feel like a piece of taffy, being tugged to my limits.

"You with me, Duke?"

"Um. Yes sir, Steven. I mean. Yes. I am."

He chuckles. I do really like Principal Barnes. I also like my pops. A lot. And I owe Pops everything.

"Can I have some time to think about this?"

"Of course. Of course. I didn't expect you to answer me today. You take your time. And by *take your time*, I mean I don't want to be well into the end of July wondering if the next generation of Corn Cobs will be learning about the constitution or not."

"No. We wouldn't want that."

"Well, enjoy the rest of your day, Duke."

"You too, Steven."

"Hey! You got it. But, once August twenty-fifth hits, I'm back to being Principal Barnes. Got it?"

"Got it."

He hangs up, probably feeling all relaxed as he slides his sunglasses onto his face, sips his cold drink, and settles back into his lounger by the pool. Whereas I am feeling more squirelly than I did when Brooks joked about wanting Shannon's number.

I tuck my phone into my pocket and hop into my Shelby. Revving her engine, I aim toward the one place where I get my head set straight.

I park my car up the gravel driveway and see motion out in the goat enclosure. I recognize that dark head of hair–the one that belongs to my best friend. Not Chris, Aiden. The three of us are brothers from different mothers and we never had problems being a trio of friends. There's never been an odd man out or anything like that with us.

Maybe that's because I've been the one those two always had to conspire to keep out of trouble. It gave our relationship balance. I usually suggest something off the wall. They work together to keep me alive. But, when the chips are down, they each come to me privately for support or even advice. Deep down, they respect me despite shaking their heads in a *what are we going to do with Duke?* way.

"Hey, look who's back from the Caribbean Islands!"

Aiden looks up and gives me one of his smiles–the one that tells me he missed me, but it's plain he's happier than he's ever been. His skin is tan and he's got this glow to him like a man in love–in love with a woman he gets to call his own.

"There should be a law against being as happy as you are," I tease him as I walk toward the gate.

"And there should be a law against being such a charmer. What's got you down?"

Friends. They see through it all. I'm smiling. Joking. Driving my Shelby. But Aiden knows me.

"A woman. What else?"

He points to his smile. "A woman did this too. The right one makes it all fall into place."

"Yeah. Yeah. I hear you. I broke up with Beth." I open the gate to the enclosure and join Aiden.

"Good."

"Wow. You aren't messing around today."

"Nope. Not when it comes to you and your life choices. Then I'm serious."

I nod. "I'm serious too. Too serious for my own good these days."

We embrace with a bro hug and then I step back and hoist myself onto the stack of hay bales off to the side of the pen. We're silent while Aiden moves through his flock, checking for who knows what, and murmuring to the goats or himself as he goes.

"So?" he asks.

I inhale. Not recommended when you're at a farm among animals who intentionally pee on themselves, but I've already taken a deep breath by the time I remember this small detail.

"What would you do if you had a woman you really wanted, but she was off-limits for very good reason. You just found out she has feelings for you too. ... You know what? Never mind."

Aiden stands stock still, his hands on his hips, staring at me. His face looks pensive, lips pursed like he's trying to work through a math problem. Only, I'm the equation that refuses to be solved. I can't even start to ask him about the decision I'm facing about choosing between the garage and teaching. I probably shouldn't have even mentioned my predicament with Shannon, not if I don't want him to see right through me.

When he speaks, I nearly fall off the haystack.

"Shannon."

I look away, over his shoulder, trying to school my features, but my lack of an answer is an answer.

"Chris will murder you and he won't even do it in your sleep."

"I know. Trust me. I know. And I've been doing what's right by him. That night he left, he told me to keep her safe. He asked me, bro. Of all the people, he entrusted me to look out for her. And I have. Like a stalker at times, but I've kept an eye out for her and made sure no one took advantage of her. But, now I'm so twisted up over her."

"Because you can't have her?"

"Because I can't stop thinking about her, or finding ways to be near her. She's so fun and funny and vulnerable without being weak. Not to mention how she looks. It's like one day she grew up into this beautiful, captivating, bright, sassy creature. She's the girl I used to give wet willies. And now I want to give her wet willies in a whole other way."

I scrub my hand down my face and keep talking. It's like I can't stop now that I've started.

"What does she even put in her hair to make it shine and bounce like that? And she smells like the best dessert you never knew you wanted until you get a whiff of whatever shampoo or lotion she wears. But it's more than the product she uses. It's her. And she gives as well as she takes, never backing down, which, to be honest, is hot. Plus, she loves our seniors in such a quiet and faithful way. She's a loyal friend. And she gets me."

She really gets me. Maybe like no one else on earth. Why did it have to be her? Why couldn't it be some woman I met at a car show, or one of the granddaughters of the myriad of seniors who have tried to fix me up over the years. It had to be the one woman I can't have without wreaking havoc on my lifelong friendships and the delicate balance of our extended friend group.

I look back at Aiden, not realizing I had been staring somewhere far away, past the trees that line his property while I rattled on, finally letting all my thoughts about Shannon flow out now that Aiden uncorked the truth.

Aiden's mouth isn't exactly popped open, but he's got a flabbergasted look on his face.

I run my hands through my hair after pulling off the backward ball cap and replacing it on my head when I'm finished. What? I told you I'd be wearing it until I die.

"I'm a mess and it's only getting worse."

Aiden's face turns serious again. "What are your intentions?"

"Such a dad. When did you turn into a dad?"

"Maybe when I adopted two kids."

"Right. Well, I don't know. I never want to hurt Shannon—ever. But, you know me. Am I even capable of settling down with one person and making a life? And if I am, how would I be worthy of her? And how is this fair to Chris when he left thinking I was the one who had his back?"

"All good questions. Most of them are so far above my pay grade. I'm just a tech nerd with a hobby goat farm, I'm not some sort of relationship expert. You know that. When I hit the lowest point with Em, I came running to you. I wish I had something more I could say. You're really in a corner. That's for sure."

"I'm out here trying to get some answers. And, to be honest, I never planned on telling you. I don't want to put you in a position of holding a secret for me and keeping it from Chris."

"There's no secret to hold. You have feelings for Shannon, and she's off limits. Granted, I've never seen you feel anything like this for a woman. But, you haven't acted on your feelings, so I've got nothing to tell. If you were trying to start something with her, we'd have a different situation. But you aren't."

"No. I'm not."

But I might.

SEVENTEEN

Shannon

J ayme's sprawled on the couch when I get home from the Dippity Do, her phone in hand, laptop to her side, cat perched behind her, Groucho at her feet.

"Hey," she says absentmindedly.

"Hey," I say, kicking off my shoes and wiggling my toes. "Sometimes fashion just hurts. These shoes are awesome enough to enter a room before I do, but man. My toes may never recover from the pinching."

"That's why I spend ninety percent of my life barefoot."

"You can. You're working from home. I don't think my dad would appreciate a barefoot receptionist."

"Answer me this," Jayme says, finally looking up from her phone. "I'm confused. Are we supposed to plump our booties like the Kardashians, or do pilates to get a firm, tight butt? My instagram feed has alternating ads for each. First it's the booty-ful lift, now it's pictures of cellulite ridden tushies telling me I need to spend only ten minutes a day with a large rubber band to solve my problems. All this makes me want to do is eat a croissant from Oh! Sugar and watch reruns of *Schitt's Creek*."

I laugh. "This is what you spend your afternoons doing while I'm painting the toes of half the town?"

"It's not all I do. I also put ribs in the crock pot and did a load of laundry. Plus, I wrote another chapter in my book and completed my quota of fortunes for the day. Sometimes I work, sometimes I think about booties–especially when they're filling my feed. Why are booties on my feed anyway?"

"Probably because you are talking about booties and Siri's always listening. Just wait. You'll be getting twice the booty ads now that we had this little chat."

"Speaking of booties, have you seen that handsome mechanic you have a lifelong crush on?"

"We are not speaking of his booty."

"I know. I know. I was just trying to make a clever segue. He does have a fine booty, though."

"Oh my gosh. You did not just say that."

"I'm perpetually single. Doesn't mean I'm blind. The man was an athlete and he moves around at work all day. All I'm saying is that he has a Kardashian-approved rear."

I laugh. "You're horrible."

"And also, right."

"I can't complain about the view when he turns to walk away."

"Exactly."

I settle into the chair across from Jayme. "I've been thinking about our talk the other day."

"Which talk?"

"The one where I spilled the beans about how I feel about that certain mechanic."

"And?"

I take a breath and let out a long sigh. "Pursuing Duke would be the worst decision in the history of decisions."

"Are you sure?"

"Okay. You're right. Maybe it wouldn't be the worst decision. I mean there was the mullet coming back in style, and then there was the making of any sequel of Jaws. Of course there was the time Laura talked all us girls into jumping into the reservoir in our skivvies during March of our senior year. It wasn't even fifty degrees out and that water felt like ice. I couldn't even get dressed over my wet skin because we didn't bring towels for our pre-spring polar plunge, and then Officer Heinz rolled up and I jumped behind a bush, clinging my dry clothes to my chest ... anyway. Bad decision."

Jayme chuckles. "Or there was the time Esther, Agnes and Mabel decided to color their hair in the school colors of royal blue and yellow. They looked like a bunch of aging muppets!"

"All bad decisions. But, letting Duke know how I feel would be worse. Far worse."

And so much better.

No. Not better.

Worse.

"So, what are you going to do?" Jayme asks.

"I don't know. I've felt this way for so long. I can't imagine not obsessing over him, dreaming about being together. Wanting him whenever he's near. And it's only getting worse."

Jayme's silent for a beat. I can tell she's brainstorming, which probably isn't going to end well. She's studying the ceiling, and then her eyes snap toward me.

"I know what to do!"

"You do?"

"I'm a romance author. Trust me."

I give Jayme a look.

"It boils down to this. You want Duke because he represents certain qualities you think you need in a man. Once you list those qualities, you can search for them elsewhere. Find the man that checks those boxes—who isn't Duke, and voilà!"

It almost sounds logical.

Jayme sets her phone down and grabs her laptop.

"Okay. You start listing qualities. I'll take notes. We'll have the 'ideal man list' in no time. Then you can screen candidates."

"In Bordeaux?"

"We may have to do a county-wide search, granted. The point

is, you'll know what you want. And you know it can't be Duke, so your eyes will be open to other possibilities. You just need to quash this tunnel vision. He's not the only great man on the planet."

"True. Maybe there's hope with this mystery man who keeps sending me flowers."

Jayme smiles a small grin. I'm not thrilled about a man who won't simply come forward and ask me out. If he thinks I'm beautiful and bring sunshine everywhere I go and all the other things his notes have said, he ought to man up and ask me out. The charm of his mystery wore thin after bouquet number four.

If I had an inkling who he was, I'd send him a note telling him to put his money where his mouth is, or where his flower arrangement is. Whatever. You know what I mean.

Jayme has gotten more and more secretive about his identity, almost shrinking back when I ask. His first few bouquets came in rapid succession. But then there was a gap. And it's been a week since the last one.

Maybe Mister Mystery gave up–before anything even started. That makes it clear the flowers weren't from Duke. He may not see me as a potential love interest, but he's no coward. If he wants a woman, I'm pretty sure he'll just go get her.

Jayme cracks her knuckles and poises her hands over her laptop keyboard. Something about making a list of ideal man qualities brings up this unexpected urge to cry. Maybe I don't want to let go of my feelings for Duke. But do I really have a choice? I'm twenty-six. Pining away for an unattainable man needs to stop.

I straighten my posture, give my hands a light clap and say, "He needs to be funny. A man has to have a sense of humor. One that comes naturally. Nothing forced."

"Got it."

"Arrogant, but simultaneously self-effacing."

"Mm hmm."

"Gorgeous."

"Definitely. Should I add, nice butt?"

I roll my eyes.

"Adding it."

"You don't need to add it."

"You don't want a man with a nice butt?"

"I don't want it on my ideal qualities list."

"Okay. Flabby butts and flat butts acceptable," she rattles off while typing.

"We can just leave the butt specifications off the list."

"Your choice," Jayme says with a light smile and a shake of her head. "Does he need to be blond?"

"Preferably."

"Got it."

"Kind hearted. Loves children. Athletic, but not overly so."

"Like not a body-builder?"

"Exactly. I don't want some guy who's always talking about supplements and reps."

"Agreed. Plus those bulging veins everywhere. In an alien, that's a quality most women want. Not so much in a human."

I laugh.

"A guy who makes my skin tingle, cracks me up, takes care of me, always seems to know what I need. Someone who gets me. Like, he takes the time to notice me or goes out of his way to make sure I'm safe and okay."

"Like stalking your dates?" She winks.

"Not a stalker. More of a guardian."

"Mmm yeah. That's one of Duke's strong points. But, of course, I mean, being a guardian. That trait in any man. Any not-Duke man."

"Exactly. Any not-Duke man."

I sigh. Then I close my eyes and all I can see is Duke laughing with me at the fair, him bent over a kid on his baseball team, him showing up to Zumba, the way he looks at me with a half smirk that's so darn flirty and yet open like he's got nothing to hide.

"You know what? It's been a long day. I think we'll table the list for a bit."

"Because your list is basically all about Duke?"

Jayme has a softness to her eyes as she sets aside the laptop.

"It can't be Duke. He's not ideal. He's the opposite of ideal. He's my brother's best friend. He casually dates out-of-town women, and he's never been serious about anyone whose name wasn't Shelby or Harley."

"As in his car and his motorcycle."

"Exactly."

That last line wasn't completely true and I know it. Duke is loyal if he's anything. He's supported his dad all these years in their business, and he gives his all to those little league kids. He puts his friends first. Still, he never has been in a committed relationship that seemed to matter. What if serious relationships just aren't his style? And even if he would get serious, who's to say I'm the one he'd choose?

"Let's give men a rest for now," Jayme says with a sympathetic smile. "We've got a crock full of ribs with our names all over it, and I saw *Love Actually* was on Netflix."

"I think I'd rather watch *Guardians of the Galaxy*."

So I can watch something blow up besides my overly-romantic heart and my dreams of a future with Duke.

EIGHTEEN

Shannon

The little league team has moved into their official summer game rotation. The big season for baseball is spring, but we have a summer team so the boys can keep their skills honed, and probably so the parents can keep from going bonkers while their kids are out of school all day, every day. Summer ball is more casual, but we still have games with teams from surrounding towns.

Despite my better judgment to put some distance between me and the object of my obsession, my friends unknowingly decided we all ought to meet at the ball field to support Duke and Brooks as they coach their team this afternoon in the first home game against the Corn Corners Cattlemen. Duke let his players name our team this year. We're the Mighty Fireflies. Because fireflies are oh-so mighty.

Karina, the team mom, even made an outfit for the team mascot with a little glowing pouch on the backside. I think our friend Rob, who is also our resident science geek, rigged that up for her. Karina's daughter, Ashley, is running around buzzing and flapping her arms in the costume and shouting "Mighty!" then pointing at us in the bleachers so we'll shout, "Fireflies!"

Jayme leans over toward me and whispers. "Oh, sweet slice of

Kardashian pilates heaven. Do you see your man in a pair of baseball pants?"

I give her a friendly glower and whisper, "A. He's not my man. And B, please stop talking about his butt or any part of him."

Jayme fans herself and whispers in a perfect impersonation of Will.I.Am the rapper, "Sorry, sorry. It's just, daaang, girl. Someone needs to lock that down."

Laura is sitting on the bleacher bench below us. She turns back and says, "What's all the commotion about back there you two?"

Jayme and I both nearly shout, "Nothing!" in unison.

Laura points at me and then Jayme and then back at me. "*Sooo* not nothing. And I will get to the bottom of whatever it is."

Jayme makes the motion of zipping her lips. I stare at the field and shout "Fireflies!" even though Ashley hasn't bopped—or buzzed—our way to shout "Mighty!" And, to make matters worse, my blurting about nocturnal insects with glowing booties gets the attention of one hot coach in baseball pants that are far more awesome on him than I'd admit to Jayme—or anyone.

He lifts his ball cap, looks at me, rakes his hand through his hair, and pops the hat back on his head. Then he winks at me. Thankfully, Laura's distracted by Trevor and Lexi showing up with their baby, Poppy, when Jayme leans in and asks, "Are you sure he's not interested?"

"I'm sure. He's just a hopeless flirt."

"Such a shame."

"Yeah."

I don't have time to mope and wallow in my not-ever-gonna-get-Duke blues because three of our seniors step onto the field to slaughter—I mean sing—a spirited, yet off-key rendition of the national anthem. Then the game begins and we all eat hot dogs off the cart brought in by Mad River Burgers and shout til we're hoarse throughout all nine innings.

Our boys win. I could barely have told you the score or most game details, though, because I was so focused watching Duke in action—especially when Toby struck out and Duke squatted down to give him a pep talk and then ruffled his hair before sending him off to the dugout.

The sight of Duke being all paternal caused my ovaries to send off fireworks to rival those over Main Street during Red, White, and Blue, and Corn Too. The rockets red blare had nothing on my urge to jump through the stands and wrap my star spangled self around Duke and show him my flag was still there. But, I obviously do not embrace living in the land of the free and the home of the brave, because my cowardly rear stayed planted in the stands.

Probably for the best.

As people file off the bleachers and mingle after the game, Duke makes his way over to me.

"Good game, Satterson."

"Thanks for coming out," he says.

A small bead of sweat drips down the side of his face from being in the hot sun, geared up and moving around coaching. It would help if Duke smelled like a men's locker room, or a dead fish, or at least like most guys when he sweats. But, no, as fate would have it, he smells … amazing. Like a spicy, musky, clean man.

How does a guy sweat and work as hard as Duke and end up smelling clean? It's like a dryer sheet had a tryst with red hot cinnamon candy. Which, I admit, sounds beyond weird, but Duke smells like fresh laundry and red hots. And being near him makes my tongue tingle the same way it does when I suck on that cinnamon candy—which I needed to stop thinking about and pronto. Duke and my tongue are not to be thought of at the same time.

I barely realize I'm licking my lips until Duke's eyes zip down to my mouth. As if he would ever be interested in anything to do with my mouth besides putting some sort of duct tape over it so I never ended up actually kissing anyone— ever. It really isn't fair. If I can't have him, why can't I find another man to date and eventually fall in love with? But, it seems that Duke is out to ruin me in more than one way. I'm ruined like the Aztec civilization, only with way fewer priceless artifacts and exactly zero men traveling from around the globe to discover my hidden riches.

Without realizing what I'm doing, I reach out and touch Duke on the arm. There was a reason I started touching him— besides the fact that I can't not when he's this near. What was that reason again? Hmmm. I forgot.

I look down. My hand rests on Duke's forearm, his hairs tickling my palm. It's more like his warm skin could set my hand on fire. Not literal fire, obviously. It's a heat that moves through me like when the sun hits a parched leaf just right and consumes a dry grove of trees in the summer. I'm consumed by a mere touch.

I glance up and meet Duke's puzzled expression. He raises his eyebrows and gives me that lopsided, smirky look that drives all logical thought not only right out of my head, but completely out of town.

"What are you looking at me like that for?" I ask, indignantly.

People talk and laugh all around us. Kids run past us chasing one another. But it feels like we're in a temporary bubble of our own.

Duke doesn't answer me. His eyes track down my shoulder, to my bicep, then my elbow and finally land on my hand. My hand! The hand that hasn't left his forearm and is now brushing little strokes across his skin. I snap my hand back like I touched a hot stove, only I touched a hot mechanic and my face looks like I've been burned from the sheer heat of our connection.

"You were petting me." Duke says in that typical older-brother teasing voice.

"I wasn't petting you," I say. "I was ... "

He cocks his head to the side, looking like he has all the time in the world for me to explain why my hand was mapping his arm like a child learning braille. "I was comforting you."

"Comforting me?" He asks with an amused look on his face.

I'm not comforting him. No one is comforting anyone here. And I'm so far from comfortable.

"Yes. You know. Comfort? What friends do for one another when they are feeling sorry for each other."

"And you were comforting me because ..."

Yes. Why am I "comforting" him, anyway?

"Ummm. Because Toby kept missing the ball today. And I know as a coach you invest in those kids."

"Sure do," Duke agrees.

"So. Comfort." I say with a nod of my head.

"Well, thanks, Shannon. I feel much better about that strike out now that I got comforted."

He says the word with a resonance and scrumptious grit to his voice that I feel in every molecule of my being. The look in Duke's eyes makes me want to take him away from here and comfort him, alright.

"Feel free to show up and comfort me anytime," Duke says with a chuckle.

He's mocking me. It's the teasing voice he's always used with me—the one that instantly reminds me I'm Chris' little sister where Duke's concerned.

Granted, I did just pet the man's arm like some lovesick teen.

"I mean it," Duke says sincerely, snapping me out of my almost-swirl into self-pity land. "You always make me feel better, Shannon."

Well now. That I can work with.

NINETEEN

Duke

I never intended to learn to play guitar. My family's not all that musical, and I was so into sports that I didn't have a lot of free time to consider hobbies. We all thought I might end up going into the major leagues before I hurt my elbow in my Junior year, so music was the farthest thing from my mind.

I don't think I'm actually angsty enough to be a good musician anyway. But, when Chris and Aiden decided to start a garage band in high-school, they dragged me along. Chris on bass, Aiden on drums, and I took up the guitar.

And I can thank the guitar for paving the way into the hearts of several high school girls back in the day. I had such a crush on this one girl, Sandy. She's long since moved away and gotten married. My feelings for her died a few months after they started anyway, as adolescent infatuations are prone to do.

Sandy had always looked right through me as though I were invisible–until the day she saw me playing guitar. I couldn't believe how quickly I went from being a nobody to seeming instantly attractive and desirable. Being the lead member of the band apparently imbued me with some sort of elusive "it" factor. I would have taken my guitar with me to class every day if my teachers were cool with it. They weren't.

Needless to say, I started taking lessons once I saw the power of the guitar. Now, my beloved acoustic sits in the corner of my living room like an old friend. I rarely play it for anyone, but it has become a way of working through restless thoughts and emotions.

And tonight I've got plenty of both.

I started playing around with some chords, and those turned into a melody. And now I'm adding words off the top of my head. Music expresses my heart—saying what I would if I could.

I let my mind run when it's dark
I think of what I'd like to be
Your name is painted on my heart
But for you it's hard to read

I have built myself a castle
I put my sweat into these walls
But you break down my ego
I've begun to lose it all

All my life I've had only options
But with you I've had no chance
The thing I seem to want the most
Is just to have your hand

And when you dance
All my troubles melt away
When you dance
I can barely say my name
They way you drift across the floor
It leaves me begging you for more
So will you dance
Will you dance

My imagination taunts me

Showing me what could be real
And the hope it starts to haunt me
I need tell you how I feel

Just the thought of you excites me
I'm in love with all you do
You'll always be my favorite dancer
I love to watch you move

And when you dance
All my troubles melt away
When you dance
I can barely say my name
They way you drift across the floor
It leaves me begging you for more
So will you dance
Will you dance

Maybe someday I'll tell you
That you deserve the world
You'll always be my picture perfect
Imaginary girl

The front door is open, allowing the night air to breeze in as I sing, losing myself in the words and images of Shannon. I can almost feel the ghost of her touch today and I'm picturing what I'd do with her if I could.

I'm lost in my own world and in my music—so lost I don't hear anyone approach the house and pull the door open. I look up and Aiden's standing in my doorway with his arms crossed across his chest and a smug smile on his face. It's the smile of a man seeing right through his best friend. I'd like to wipe that smile right off his face.

"You've still got that well-rounded voice when you sing. It's gotten deeper with age, but it's still so soothing. What I'd do to be able to sing like you."

"Would you croon to your llama?"

"She'd probably make some ungodly noise at me if I did. Billy Jean might dig it, though."

"How long have you been standing there?" I ask, setting the guitar down next to me so the back of it rests against the couch.

"Long enough."

"Want a drink?"

"I'll take what you're having."

"After you intruded on my privacy, that would be an IPA."

"Door was open," Aiden says with that same know-it-all tone.

"For the night air, not for nosy friends who pop by and rub their happy post-honeymoon selves in my face."

"I'll make you a deal," he says, following me into the kitchen. "When you go on your honeymoon, which you will someday, I'll let you be sickeningly happy and rub it in my face so badly when you're home."

"I don't know if I'll ever have a honeymoon," I say in far too pouty of a voice.

Aiden shakes his head like I'm pathetic.

"I'm hot when I'm wallowing in self-pity, admit it."

"You are not my type, but if I were into beefy mechanics with an ego the size of Clarke County, I'd be all into you, my friend—pity party or not."

I pop the top off a bottle and hand him his drink.

He gives me this look that tells me he's about to get serious and then he says, "I'm glad you aren't going after the placeholder anymore."

"You mean breaking things off with Beth?"

"Yeah. That. And I haven't heard of any replacement, so that's big for you. Until you have her out of your system, you need to abstain."

"Out of my system? Shannon or Beth?"

"Beth never was in your system. Our best friend's little sister.

Until you get over not being able to have her, yet wanting her so badly, you probably just need to be alone. Let the idea of her run its course. To be honest, I'm not sure writing songs about her is the way to do that. You probably need another approach."

"And what approach would that be?"

"Like I said, abstinence."

"Have you ever tried to fall out of love with someone?" I ask, getting a little louder than I intended.

"Love? Are you sure that's what this is?"

I stare at Aiden. Unsure how to answer him.

"That's a big word," Aiden continues. "We all love Shannon. But it feels like you're talking about something a whole lot bigger than what we feel for one another in our friend group."

"I am," I say too quickly. "Or, maybe I am. I don't know. I've never been in love before. As lame as that sounds, it's true. With her, it's different."

"I don't know what to tell you."

"I didn't think you would. It's a messed up situation. But, I'll get through it. Don't worry about me. You've got enough on your plate from day to day."

"I do. And I just added another helping."

"What's that supposed to mean?" I ask.

He looks at me, tilts the neck of his bottle to mine and says, "We think Em's pregnant."

I let out a whoop and literally do a jump in my kitchen. It's one of the jumps I used to do when holding an electric guitar during a gig—where I'd land doing this half splits thing, one knee bent, the other leg straight out in front of me. It drove the girls crazy and I could land that thing like a boss, jump back up and keep playing. It was one of my signature moves. "Was" being the operative word right about now.

There's the distinct sound of ripping fabric as I land.

Aiden instantly collapses at the waist in a fit of hysterics, spraying a mouthful of beer across my kitchen.

I struggle to stand from the position, losing all my cool and looking like a newborn foal. My chances of bearing offspring probably just decreased by half after that maneuver. We're laughing hard which makes it doubly difficult to stand. I grab the side of the island and pull myself up. Then I run a hand down the front of my jeans and tilt back against the counter.

"Let me see," Aiden says between gasps of laughter.

"See what?" I ask, grabbing my beer and crossing my other arm across my chest.

"Your backside. I have to see the rip!"

"You haven't even taken me to dinner. No one sees the backside without at least buying me a meal first."

Aiden chuckles and I do a little spin for him with a bow at the end.

"You totally ripped your jeans," he says laughing and then taking another sip of beer. "Man, that was awesome! I wish I had a heads up. I would pay anything to have gotten that on film!"

"Worth it," I say. "You are going to be a dad. I can't think of a better way to celebrate than busting through my Levi's."

"Technically, I am a dad already."

"Yeah. Of course. Ty and Paisley. No. Right. You're right. This is just ... well it's more. And I'm so happy for you. You're gonna fill that farm with adorable red-headed babies, aren't you?"

"I don't know about filling it, but yeah. We're pretty over the moon about this. Don't tell anyone. I want Em to be the one to tell the girls. I haven't even told Trevor yet. Lexi would kill me if he heard before she did."

I'm replacing a fuel injector when my phone buzzes on the tool shelf. I wipe my hands and grab my cell. Usually, I wait for a break between jobs to check calls and texts, but something tells me to check who's texting.

When I look at the screen a cartoon image of a unicorn with

tears of laughter streaming down its face stares back at me. I chuckle. Then a text pops up:

Shannon: *Yikes! I don't know where that random unicorn came from. I wasn't even trying to text anyone.*

Duke: *You need a phone chaperone.*

Shannon: *I'm not that mad*

Shannon **BAD. Not that bad.*

Duke: *Case in point. But, don't go changin'…*

Shannon: *I love that song.*

Duke: *Maybe I'll sing it for you sometime.*

Shannon: *I love when you swing*

Shannon **SING*

Duke: *(Laughing emoji)*

Shannon: *(Gritting teeth emoji)*

Duke: *(Unicorn emoji) (Heart emoji) (Laughing emoji)*

Shannon: *(crossing arms emoji)*

Shannon: *Are you going to Aiden and Em's for the bonfire tonight?*

Duke: *Can't. Sissy's coming into town with the kids. Pops is having everyone over.*

I'm the youngest of the five children in my family. Here's the Reader's Digest version of things. My parents married right out of high school. They had a marriage I'd want to carbon copy, if I thought I were the type who could actually settle down and make one woman happy.

Mom and Pops were twenty-five when they had Amy, the typical bossy older sister who could run a small army and solve almost every problem from finding my missing baseball cleat to helping any of my sisters when they broke up with yet another boyfriend.

My parents had a daughter every two years after Amy's birth for the next six years. Liz–the free spirit, Julie–the athletic entrepreneur, and Sissy–the gentle, introverted intellect.

Julie's the most like me, and she ended up divorced. Take notes here. If she could have held onto her marriage, I would be more hopeful about myself in that department. Not that it was her fault that her dufus of an ex couldn't appreciate her for the amazing person she is. But, I digress. Let's get to my birth.

Dad wanted a boy so badly, so they kept trying even though it appeared they could only make girls.

Eight long years after my sister, Sissy, was born, I came along as a total surprise. Dad, who jokingly called himself Abraham and Mom, Sarai, was so overwhelmed at my appearance that local legend has it that he gave away free gas at the station from sunrise to sundown the day I was born.

Amy and Liz live in town–both married. Julie is divorced–as I said–and living her best life in New York City. At least that's what she says, and knowing her, she's making the best of whatever life she's living. Sissy lives in Columbus. Also married.

So, I grew up with four older sisters who all thought they were my surrogate mothers, and then I also had my actual mom. I don't remember any day of my life when I didn't have someone trying to tie my shoe, wipe my nose, or tell me what to do. Ahh the perils of an only baby boy in a house full of women.

Maybe being surrounded by females taught me how to charm women, and maybe it's why I'm a little gun shy when it comes to imagining voluntarily committing to sharing a house with any woman ever again.

Except Shannon.

I can easily imagine coming home and taking the weight of her day off her shoulders. I'd sit on the couch, pulling her legs into my lap so I could rub her feet after our kids were in bed. She could tell me about whatever was on her mind. And I'd just listen and stare at her, unable to believe she was mine. Every day I'd have to pinch myself if it ever came to pass. We'd sit together, talking and laughing until I leaned in to kiss her, and then we'd take things to the bedroom ...

I have to stop thinking about a future that obviously can't happen. I look down at my phone and resume the unexpected text exchange with Shannon.

Duke: *Are you going to the bonfire?*
Shannon: *I was. But, I've got plans.*
Duke: *What kind of plans?*
Shannon: *Gotta run. I'll text later.*
Duke: *What kind of plans?*
Duke: *Shannon?*
Duke: *Shannon?*
What is she doing tonight?

My fingers itch to text her again, but she's obviously intent on driving me crazy with curiosity since she didn't answer my last question.

I have half a mind to cancel going to Pops' so I can spy on Shannon. Not spy, spy. Just check up. For Chris. On his behalf.

As if he has osmosis, my phone buzzes with a text from Chris. Right when I'm thinking of what I'd be doing to his sister if she were my wife. Excellent.

Chris: *Hey.*
Duke: *Hey. How's it going?*
Chris: *Great. Just turned in my ETS.*
Duke: *Extra Turkey Sandwich?*
Duke: *Eight Toad Stools?*
Duke: *Explosive Turd Slingers?*
Chris: *How old are you again? It's End Term of Service. Turning in my supplies to the Army. It's part of getting ready for discharge.*
Duke: *Ahh. And I'm the same age as you, old man. Almost thirty.*
Chris: *And yet ...*
Duke: *Don't go getting all serious on me. You know you love me.*
Chris: *We don't say love in the Army.*
Duke: *Well, I love you, man. I do. So, what has you texting me on a weekend? Shouldn't you be out wearing your uniform, slaying the ladies with your awesomeness like the decorated officer you are?*
Chris: *That's me. Lady slayer. I'm actually calling to check on*

Shannon. I talked to Dad yesterday and he mentioned she's going out dancing tonight. She told him she's going out with Angie from the salon and Angie's boyfriend and some other guy.

Dancing? I thought she might be going on a date. This sounds a lot like a double date.

Shannon's got a date–with a stranger.

After telling Jayme she likes me.

Why does this bug me so much? I know we can't make anything happen between us. Still, the idea of her going out with another McLoser and dancing with him sends my skin crawling.

Or worse. What if the guy is her type?

Nope. He's not.

No one is.

I realize I'm pacing the garage now, running my grease-stained hands through my hair at the idea of Shannon out with some other guy. I shoot off another text to Chris.

Duke: *What do you need from me?*

Chris: *Just keep an eye out. Dad says Shannon seems restless these days. She could use a friend. Someone to watch over her. Distract her. Vet this guy for me if there's more than one date.*

Duke: *You got it.*

Chris: *I knew I could count on you. I gotta run. The guys in my company are heading out to some bar and they insist I come. I'm going for morale.*

Duke: *Is that what the kids are calling it these days?*

Chris: *Ha. Yep. Thanks again. For watching out for Shannon.*

Duke: *Always. Have fun "morale building."*

Chris: *(rolling eye emoji) Later.*

Duke: *(kissy face emoji) Later.*

I consider walking into the office and telling Pops I can't make it to family night, but the last time we all were together was over three months ago, so he won't go for it.

We don't have places to go dancing here in town, so Shannon's got to be going to a town nearby. Maybe I can get away from Pops' early and figure out where Shannon went.

But then what?

TWENTY

Duke

One thing I'm really good at, besides restoring old cars and coaching ball, is being Uncle Duke. I've got nieces and nephews ranging from fifteen years old down to seven. All of them are at Pop's tonight–and it's raining, on Shannon's date. I can't help but smile as I get out of my Shelby. With each drop of water that hits me, I think of her date getting rained out and I feel a strange sense of victory, like the powers that be are on my side.

The noise level in my childhood home never was anything near what you'd call "quiet." We always had neighbor kids in or friends from school over. Even though I barely remember Amy and Liz living at home since they both were gone by the time I was six, the three younger Satterson siblings still managed to keep the chaos rolling. And Mom never seemed to mind. Our home was "the house" on the street.

Tonight, with all my nieces and nephews, and my sisters and their husbands here, it feels like old times. The house is properly full of life.

"Hey! The party can start now. I'm here!" I say, raising the bag of drinks in my left hand and doing a little dance.

My seven-year-old nephew, Bryson, shouts out to me as I pass by, "Isn't it true, Uncle Duke?"

"What, buddy?"

"That cow farts are causing global warming. Cow. Farts."

"I'm not a scientist. I'll have to ask my friend, Rob."

"Your farts are causing my death," Bryson's sister, Ariel, shouts at him.

I stifle a chuckle.

"My teacher said cow farts are ruining the air we breathe and melting polar ice caps," Bryson continues after almost ignoring his sister.

He did stick his tongue out and lurch for her under the coffee table where he apparently thought no adult would notice.

"Well, I can't say much about cow farts," I say. "I know they smell bad enough to ruin a lot of things and maybe even melt something."

Bryson breaks into a fit of giggles, proving he's less of an environmentalist and more interested in saying *cow farts* and getting adults to say it too. I can't help but chuckle. I'm a guy, after all.

My sister Sissy, who is Bryson's mom, rolls her eyes at me and mouths, "Thanks a lot."

I mouth back, "Anytime," and then I turn toward the back of the house. At the kitchen doorway, I freeze. Mabel is wearing Mom's old apron and Pops is sitting at the kitchenette table watching her prep supper with a smile on his face–the same smile he used to reserve for my mother. Amy's prepping the salad at the other counter as if all's well in the world.

"Hey, son. Good to see you," Pops says as if we didn't just see one another an hour ago at the garage.

"Hey. Can I help with anything?"

I set the bag of drinks I brought onto the island and tuck my hands in my pockets.

Instead of Pops answering me, Mabel says, "Oh, Duke. That's so nice of you to offer. Amy and I've got this."

I force a smile onto my face. Giving myself a little pep talk, I head back into the living room, hoping to lose myself in conversations about cow farts.

Ten years. Mom's been gone ten years. And if any man deserves companionship, it's Pops. Maybe it's just all the stuff swirling in my head about Shannon's date tonight. I don't feel like sharing her. But, she's not mine to share. I'd do well to remember that.

Amy shows up at my side as I'm leaning on the arm of the sofa. She bends toward me so only I can hear her.

"Let's go out on the back porch and watch the rain roll in before supper's ready."

"Sounds good."

I follow my sister out the back door, breathing in the moist, soddy smell that comes with a good rain.

"You'd never know we live in the same town as little as we see one another," Amy says, leaning back on the wall of the house and staring across the yard, watching the branches sway with the warm breeze and falling rain.

"I'm sorry. I should stop by more often."

"It's not just you," she says. "I let life get too full sometimes. I thought it would ease up with the kids hitting their teen years, but they still need me just as much, only in different ways now."

"You're a good mom. Mom would be proud."

"I know. I wish she could see the kids grow up, and they could walk over here after school to sit in the kitchen, soaking up her love and wisdom, eating her homemade cookies while she made supper."

We're both quiet, letting the rhythm of the downpour fill the space between us.

"I like Mabel for Pops," Amy finally says.

"She's a character," I say. "But, yeah. He deserves the companionship, and she seems to make him happy."

"Deliriously happy. He's like a schoolboy with a crush. It's so unlike him. He's so straightforward and down to brass tacks. But with her, he's almost giddy."

I nod.

Amy studies me.

"Pops isn't the only one who deserves companionship, you know."

"Ahhh. Is that why we're out here?"

"Sort of. I heard you called it off with your out-of-town fling."

I grunt. This town has no secrets.

"I'd almost think you were holding out for someone special," she teases. "That would be if I didn't know you as well as I do."

"What if I am?" I blurt defensively before I have a chance to think better of it.

Seems like I'm unable to keep a poker face around Aiden or my meddling sister.

"If you are, then you ought to do some business or get off the pot."

"What did you just say?" I chuckle, staring wide-eyed at my older sister. She never uses foul language. Probably the whole cow fart conversation would have drawn some semi-stern glances from her to me and Bryson if she'd been in the living room to hear it. Saying something about getting off the pot is as good as swearing for Amy.

"Do something about it. If you have feelings for someone, don't hold back. Caution never was your style. You're a risk-taker by nature. Even Julie would tell you to go for it. She told me last week that she doesn't regret marrying Mike. She said she learned a lot. Going through the divorce has been the hardest year of her life, but she wouldn't trade the good times they had or the lessons she learned. She'd definitely tell you to take a risk."

I rest my hands on the railing of the back porch, pushing up some chipping paint and cracking it apart in my fingers while I consider Amy's words.

Sissy sticks her head out the door. "Dinner's just about on. Please, come in and help rally the troops. We need you, Ames. No one is listening to me at all."

"I'll be right there," Amy tells Sissy.

I look over at Amy. My next words come out almost as a whisper. "What if I don't have what it takes?"

She's unaffected, as usual. "To what?"

"To be the man she needs me to be."

"The fact that you're asking that question means you probably have all it takes and then some."

Amy pushes off the wall and comes to stand next to me, wrapping her arm around my back and giving me a side hug.

"Marriage is messy. It's harder than you can imagine at times."

"Not exactly the pep talk I'm looking for here."

Amy smiles up at me. "With the right person ..." Her eyes hold mine. "It's the greatest blessing. Having a partner, someone to raise kids with, to laugh with, to cry with, to grow old with ... there aren't words."

I let out a breath I didn't know I was holding. I feel exposed, but also seen.

"And you'll be the best," Amy says with a squeeze. "What woman wouldn't want all this?"

She waves her free hand up and down in front of me.

"Got that right," I joke.

Amy smiles softly.

Her husband, Jonah, comes to the back door. The sound of a cacophony of voices carries from behind him. "Amy, it's madness in here. Your skills as a drill sergeant and chaos coordinator are desperately needed."

The look that passes between them must convey some secret language they share because Jonah smiles and turns back into the house.

When Jonah lets the door drop behind him, Amy turns to me and gives me one of her motherly hugs. I'm not ashamed to say I melt into her embrace–in a very alpha, sexy-guy, totally super-masculine way.

"You've got this," Amy says as she turns and walks into the house.

Dinner with the family at two tables distracts me for a while.

We laugh and eat, and I feel like I'm a part of something special. But, as soon as dinner dishes are being cleared, I make my excuse to leave.

Pops sends me a surprised look. "You only came for dinner? Can't you stick around?"

I inadvertently look toward Amy.

"He's got something he needs to do for me," she says without missing a beat. "Something we were talking about earlier. It's important."

"Ooooh, a mystery!" Mabel exclaims.

"No mystery. Just an errand," Amy says calmly.

I hug all my sisters, nieces and nephews and then I drive home to get my head on straight. I'm tempted to start hunting Shannon down in the surrounding towns–to what? Fall on one knee and confess my undying love to her in front of one of the town hair-stylists and two guys I don't even know?

Even in my mildly ruffled state I know it would be a futile waste of time to try to find her. The likelihood of me ending up where she went is slim to none.

So, drawing from the few shreds of sanity I have left, I head home, brush my teeth, put on some clean boxers and climb into bed.

I can't sleep.

My mind keeps wandering to what Shannon's doing. I picture her shimmying against some random guy while loud music blares from speakers at a club, and my blood nearly boils.

I get up, grab my guitar and start to play, but my fingers won't hit the chords. Then I try to watch a movie, but I keep losing track of the plot.

What did she wear?

Is that guy hitting on her?

Is she interested in him?

I march back to my room, throw on jeans, a T-shirt and my jacket, and then I walk out to my driveway. The rain has stopped and the sky is full of clouds rimmed in white from the moonlight.

The air has that distinct smell that comes after a good storm. I lift the tarp off my bike and hop on, knowing exactly where I'm going. It's ten thirty. She could be home by now. She should be home by now.

"Okay, Dad," I mutter to myself.

"I'm not her dad," I mutter back to myself. "Absolutely not her dad. I'm not even her brother. And thank God for that."

My neighbor's out in her yard wearing a robe over her pajamas, righting planters the wind must have blown over onto the lawn. She looks over at me with a concerned look on her face.

"Evening Mrs. Greenleaf. Do you need a hand with that?"

"Evening, Duke. No, I've got this. I'll get the rest in the morning. Be safe out there."

I nod toward Mrs. Greenleaf and take off for Shannon's block. Not her house, just her block. I circle around the neighborhood. Her car isn't parked out front or in the driveway. She should be home by now.

I drive past her house and keep going. I'm not stalking or spying. I'm out on a nighttime ride because I can't sleep.

I circle back around the block.

What?

It's a free country.

I can ride anywhere I want. I always liked this block with the quaint craftsman homes. It's one of the older streets in town and the houses feel like a step back in time. That's why I'm here. I'm doing a late night historical tour of Bordeaux. After all, I'm in the process of deciding whether I'll accept the opportunity to be the town's history teacher. Maybe I need to buff up on all things historic.

I circle my bike around again, you know, to get a full appreciation of the local architecture as I cruise back down Shannon's street.

Her lights are still off. The house is dark, her car hasn't miraculously parked in the driveway over the past three to five minutes.

I kill the engine and straddle my bike next to the curb across the street from her home like some stalker ... or neighborhood security in a leather jacket. Yes. Security. That's what Chris wanted. I'm just looking out for Shannon. From a distance. Okay. A distance of thirty yards or less, but I'm only here to see she makes it safely home. Then I'll be able to sleep knowing she's in her house–alone.

Car lights turn down her street and I jump. The car drives past me and I start breathing again.

What the heck?

I shouldn't be here.

What would I have said if that had been her?

"Oh, hey, Shannon, I was just out for a ride *down your street* when I decided to stop to take in the night air *in front of your house.*"

She'd never buy that.

I stick my key in the ignition as another car rounds the corner. It's worse than rush hour. Which, we don't even have, unless you count a three car backup behind an Amish cart out on County Line Road.

I'm about to kick the starter when lights flash behind me. I turn and am greeted by the blare of halogen.

Jesse.

Just my luck.

Our local law enforcement. Or as close as we get to having law enforcement.

Jesse rolls up next to me. "Is there a problem, Satterson?"

"Why would there be a problem, Jesse?"

"You're sitting here on a residential street seven blocks from your home in the middle of the night, after town curfew. I got a call."

He got a call?

Sheesh. This town.

"I thought curfew only applied to minors," I say.

"It does, but still. No one needs to be sitting on a residential street staring at the houses after ten."

"Before ten it's okay?" I ask.

Jesse makes his serious cop face. He's like the policeman in the Lego movie. His voice even takes on that tone. I grew up with Jesse. His dad got all my respect. Somehow it's harder to take Jesse quite as seriously when it always feels like he's playing cops and robbers–minus the robbers.

Tonight I don't have the bandwidth to mess with him, so I just say, "I was just checking in on Shannon for Chris."

Jesse nods. "Chris sent you here?"

"He did."

I mean, he may not have specifically asked me to set up a stake-out outside his little sister's home, and he for sure would not approve of ninety-nine percent of the thoughts I'm having about his little sister, but aside from that, he did ask me to look out for her.

Jesse's got mad respect for Chris. I guess it's the whole law enforcement and military thing.

Whatever it is, Jesse grins and nods and then says, "You're a good friend," in his very official cop-voice, not his day-to-day voice.

If Jesse knew how badly I'm fighting the urge to walk up to Shannon when she gets home, pull her toward me and finally kiss her, he wouldn't be saying that right now.

I just nod.

No sooner has Jesse driven off, then Shannon shows up– alone. I let out a breath when I see her drive up in her car and park. She doesn't seem to see me.

I'm holding my breath as I watch her walk toward the front steps.

Just when I'm putting my hand on the ignition, sure she's going to open the door, go in and leave me to drive away unseen, I hear her shout over her shoulder. "Do you want to come in, Satterson?"

It takes me a moment to realize she's seen me and she's shouting to me.

"I better not," I shout back.

"Okay, suit yourself," she shouts, opening the door and stepping across the threshold.

The door shuts behind her and a wave of emotions washes over me.

Then my cell rings. If this is Chris, I'm going to know for sure he has surveillance here in town.

I look at the screen. It's Shannon.

"Hey," I answer.

"Hey. I'm not even going to ask what you are doing outside my home, or how long you've been there, or why."

"Great. Good call on all of that. Did you have a good time?"

I settle onto my seat, everything in me relaxing now that I know she's home, alone, and safe. Just hearing her voice feels like a sedative and a stimulant were simultaneously shot into my bloodstream.

"Honestly?" she says with that adorable huff in her tone.

"Yes. Was it a fun night?" I ask.

It dawns on me that I want her to have had a good time. Not a good time with some yutz who thinks he's good enough for her, but for her night to have been fun for her. In an *I'll never see that guy again, but I liked going out dancing* sort of way.

"Not really. It's not my scene. Everyone was trying to either attract attention or pick someone up."

She sighs, sounding weary.

"Did guys hit on you?"

I can almost hear her roll her eyes.

"Are you rolling your eyes?" I ask.

"It's a club. Guys hit on girls. It happens. I was there with friends. Angie and her boyfriend and this guy Collin."

"Collin? What kind of name is that? Is he British? Because this whole *British guys are sexy* thing is overrated. They're just guys. Usually uptight guys. Guys who don't know how to kiss."

She's laughing and I love the sound of it.

"This goes for the whole continent of Great Britain?" she clarifies. "And how many British guys have you kissed, Duke, in the process of determining their skill level?"

"Where you're concerned, it's the whole continent. I don't have to kiss a Brit to know what I'm talking about here."

"You're infuriating," she says with no heat in the words.

"Back at you, Hollywood."

"I should get to bed. I feel a little run down and tired."

"Okay. Well, I'm glad you had a decent night out with zero snogging of British guys who are too uppity for you and not able to treat you the way you need to be treated."

"He wasn't British."

"But he may as well be because he's not the one."

"No," she says with some sort of wistful tone to her voice. "He's not."

I want to scream that I'm the one. But I can't make her promises. Even though I overheard her talk with Jayme two weeks ago, and despite my sister basically sending me on a mission to take action tonight, I can't. Chris' face flashes across my mind and right now I wonder if a promise to a friend is worth this level of torture.

I know one thing. I can't keep living like this.

TWENTY-ONE

Shannon

A truck is sitting on my head. A truck full of rocks and racoons banging pans. Not literally, but it may as well be. I lift my head and the throbbing makes me lie back down. I feel hot and sticky but then a cold chill runs through me.

Great.

I'm sick.

Pulling my covers back up over myself, I curl into the mattress with the hopes it might swallow me whole. I let out a groan, which must have been louder than it seemed, because Jayme shows up in my doorway a moment later.

"Hey, girl! It's Saturday! Rise and shine little miss Zumba instructor. I've got a fresh smoothie with your name on it."

"No smoothie," I rasp out.

At the thought of a smoothie, my gut threatens to expel everything I ever ate including that hefty swallow of glue in kindergarten and those nasty kale smoothies from the phase during high school when we went on our one and only health food kick as a friend group.

I moan again.

"Are you okay?" Jayme asks, still in my doorway.

"Noooo. Not okay."

"Are you sick?"

"So sick," I half groan, half speak.

"Aww. Poor baby. Okay. Change of plans. I'll make broth and toast when you're ready. And tea. And that fizzy Vitamin C drink. We'll get you well in no time."

"Sounds like a plan," I say in my half-volume voice.

A cough overtakes me, followed by a sniffle.

Do I have the stomach flu and a cold? Well, don't say I'm an underachiever. Apparently I've gotten sick with more than one illness all at once. Great.

"Zumba!" I say with as much energy as I can muster. "I have to cancel."

"Leave it to me," Jayme sweetly offers.

"You don't know all the people who attend the class."

"Who does?"

My blurry mind scans the options. I don't really trust any of the seniors to call everyone. Some of them hold age-old grudges against one another and they'd skip informing that old rival out of spite. I know for a fact some of them are still angry over another woman dating the guy they crushed on in high school. Certain townspeople are notorious for these outrageous barely-hidden, fifty-year-old resentments. They put the Hatfields and the McCoys to shame.

Duke knows who's in my class. He came twice. That man. I keep trying to rid myself of thoughts and feelings for him, and he keeps popping up like a whack-a-mole game. A sexy, thoughtful, funny, bad-boy whack-a-mole.

"Give me my phone," I say, sticking my arm out from under the covers while the rest of me hides from the world.

Jayme plops my cell in my outstretched hand.

I roll over and push myself up to sitting, but promptly collapse.

"I'll text for you. Or should you call?"

"I'll call. Can you hit Duke's number?" I ask, another coughing fit following my words.

Duke's deep voice comes through after the second ring. "You've reached Duke. Please leave a message after the beep."

I decide to leave a message.

"Hey, Duke, it's Shannon." I cough and sniffle. "I'm sick. Probably good you didn't come in last night."

Jayme shoots me a look full of question marks. I ignore her.

"I need to call my Zumba students to tell them class is canceled."

My phone rings with an incoming call while I'm leaving the message. It's Duke. I hang up on the message and answer him. "Hey," I say and then cough. "I need someone to call my Zumba students to tell them class is canceled." I break into another coughing spell.

When I stop coughing, I add, "I'm sick," as if it weren't obvious.

"If you weren't out so late in the rain with that Collin guy, you wouldn't be sick."

More coughing.

"Hey, take it easy," Duke says. "You really are sick. What can I do?"

"Not tell me who to date, for one thing. I've got one big brother. You're not it."

"Gotcha. Do you need anything else?"

"Can you call my students and tell them class is canceled?"

"I'll do one better than that."

"Uh oh." I groan.

"No. This is good." He pauses for effect and then announces, "I'll sub for you."

"Duke," I moan. "You can't teach Zumba."

"I've been in your class. Mabel and Esther can help me. What's so hard? We're just going to dance to music. It'll be fun."

"I won't be able to talk you out of this, will I?" I ask in my raspy voice.

"Nope. I want to do this—for you."

For me. Why does he have to say things like that? My brain

145

can't think clearly. I'm woozy and weak. I feel like telling him all the things he could do for me if he were willing. So, I hurry and end the call.

"Okay. But no one better get hurt."

"We'll have a blast. Don't fret. Just rest and drink lots of fluids. I'll check in with you later."

"Okay." I sigh. Despite my sickness, a smile takes over my face thinking of Duke and the seniors dancing this morning. "Thanks, Duke."

"Anytime, Hollywood."

He hangs up and Jayme's standing over me, no longer offering panaceas for my illness. She obviously wants details.

I close my eyes, extend my phone to her and say, "We'll talk. Later. I just need sleep."

~

I roll over feeling like I'm waking from a coma, or starring in a sci-fi movie where aliens invade the planet and slow time so that everything feels rubbery and cottoney all at once. That's what I get for living with a fantasy romance author.

Slowly, the room comes into focus.

I squint at the clock on my dresser. Three forty-two. Three forty-two? It's afternoon and I slept the day away. I do feel a bit better. I take a test run of trying to lift my head and it works. After I pad into the restroom, put on a pair of fluffy socks and a sweatshirt–yes, in the middle of June in the midwest–I make my way downstairs.

"Well, if it's not Sleeping Beauty in the flesh. You're making me hot just looking at you. Why the winter wardrobe? I think it's ninety outside."

"I'm chilly."

"Oh, yes. That's the fever. I'm glad to see you up from the dead, though it would have been so much better if Prince

Charming would have dropped by to kiss you and wake you from your accursed slumber."

"It's Prince Phillip. Prince Phillip kisses Sleeping Beauty."

"Right. Right. You're right. Prince Charming is the one who has a shoe fetish. Gotcha."

I chuckle and then sputter cough as I make my way to the sofa. "You should know your princes," I chide Jayme. "You're the romance author. Besides, it would be beyond embarrassing if Duke saw me like this. Let alone kissed me."

I sit on the couch across from Jayme who has her laptop set up on a tray table in front of the cushy chair she's taken over and turned into her writing station today. She owns a desk but rarely uses it.

"It's about time some men kissed the frogs instead of always leaving that dreadful task up to the women," Jayme declares. "Don't you think?"

"And I'm the frog in this scenario? I went from Princess to frog pretty quickly."

"You are definitely a princess, but there's no doubt you'd kiss like a frog—or some amphibian with reptile breath—right now."

"Can't argue that."

"What can I get you?"

"Aww. Are you playing nurse today?"

"Nurse with ulterior motives," Jayme says, standing up and pointing in my direction. "I'll make you soup or toast or whatever hot drink you want, and you'll spill about last night and especially about that comment you probably hope I'd forgotten about Duke coming inside our home last night. You need remedies and I need details. It's a fair trade."

I lean back on the throw pillow behind my back, pull my feet up onto the couch and groan.

"Alright," I agree. "Soup and tea, and then I'll spill."

Jayme goes into the kitchen and I hear her shuffling around and humming. By the time she comes back into the living room,

I'm dozing again. When she sets the tray of soup and tea on the coffee table, I wake.

"Sleeping Beauty," she coos. "You really are too beautiful. If I were a jealous woman, I'd be green. You even look gorgeous while you're sick."

"Oh yeah. I look gorgeous."

I duck my head into my sweatshirt like a turtle.

"You do. Not in a *take me down the red carpet because I've been primping all my life for this moment* way, but in a natural-beauty way. Like you're sick, but you just can't look bad, even on your worst day."

"That might be the sweetest compliment I've ever received."

"Well, that's just wrong. Because the sweetest compliments should always be about what's inside the package."

"True."

"Enough compliments. Give me all the juicy details about your night out dancing, and especially about Duke."

"Dancing was fine."

"Three words I'd never expect to hear from you. *Dancing* and *fine* never coexist in your world. It must have been awful."

"It wasn't awful. I think this guy Collin thought we were on a blind date."

I take a sip of my tea. "Mmm. This is good. Thanks."

"No problem. And, of course he thought it was a blind date. You go out as a single woman and a single man with a couple. That's the definition of a blind date."

"I had told Angela I didn't want to be set up. But she failed to pass the memo to Collin."

"Collin. Is he British?"

"That's what Duke asked. And, no. Sadly. No. He's just a guy from Dayton who works at a bank. Nice enough. Not the best dancer."

"What kind of dancer was he?"

"The kind who looks like a marionette–a hesitant, self-conscious marionette, all jerky and awkward."

"Poor guy," Jayme says, shaking her head and laughing a little. "Was he cute?"

"I guess. But, again. I wasn't there for a date. I just thought I'd give myself a chance to get out of Bordeaux and go dancing. Angie's a single mom, so I thought she'd need to get home early enough that I'd have an easy out. I drove myself in case anything crazy happened. My plan seemed fool proof."

"Famous last words."

"Tell me about it."

"So what was this about Duke not coming inside last night? Did he stalk you all the way to the club?"

"I wouldn't put it past him, but no. He was parked across the street on his motorcycle when I drove up at the end of the night. I asked him in, more to show him he was busted for spying on me. He declined and drove home. Nothing much to tell–as usual where we're concerned."

"I'm pretty sure he likes you. Why else would he stand in the rain stalking your date?"

"It wasn't raining by the time I got home, but the simple one word answer is: Chris. It's Chris. I can tell he's behind all this stalking. It's got his signature all over it."

"How would Chris know about your date?"

"He has his ways. He's been trained in tactical operations. I'm not even a complicated mark to follow. I'm sure he's got some mole in town feeding him details."

"That's just creepy. Makes me happy I'm an only child."

"Tell me about it."

"But, it's also sweet in its own way."

"Tell yourself that. It's mostly creepy and then it's annoying. I have yet to see the sweetness."

"You think he's taking time out from his life as a platoon leader to scout out your dating life?" Jayme sounds incredulous, but she doesn't know my brother.

Still, I consider her words. Chris does have more important

things than scouting out my dating life. Maybe I'm being over-sensitive.

"Yeah. You're right," I admit. "That's crazy. Though, I wouldn't put it past him. He's beyond protective of me. It's irrational. But, under it all, I know he means well."

"So, that brings us back to the fact that Duke was standing in the residual rain watching to see that you got home safely from your night out with another man." Jayme sighs. "I'm definitely writing that into a book."

"You do that."

"Maybe a vampire romance. He stands outside her home in the dark ..."

"Vahnting to suck her bluuuhd," I say in my best vampire impersonation and then I bust out in a coughing fit. I grab for my tea while Jayme laughs.

I think about Jayme's take on things. If Duke is stalking me without Chris' prompting, I'm at a loss as to why he'd be doing that. A feeling of warmth spreads through me. And it's not the fever.

TWENTY-TWO

Duke

Senior Zumba was a little avant-garde this morning. But, Shannon never has to know. I did the Macarena, the Chicken Dance, and some Boot Scootin' Boogie along with a classic–the Hustle–which all the seniors knew. Everything was great until that song. Then Bonnie spun left and Esther spun right and both of them were committed, I'll give them that. The collision seemed to happen in slow motion.

Thankfully, no one broke a hip, or any other bone. So, all's well. I'm just hoping with all the hope I can muster that Shannon never hears the complete details of my subbing for her. Though, I doubt that's likely since about halfway through the class, Aiden and Trevor showed up. How they knew I was teaching is beyond me.

This town could be appropriately renamed Lookie Loo, Ohio. We're so very nosy. Am I nosy? Darn straight I am. But, my nosiness is justified. I only step in where I should–as in times when Shannon disappears on a blind double date.

As if my friends showing up to Zumba weren't enough, a few minutes later, our town's biggest gossip and self-proclaimed internet sensation, Ella Mae, showed up with her bestie, Meg. They filmed part of the class on their phones until I insisted they put them away. After all that, I'd be crazy to think the details of the class won't get back to Shannon.

I've texted Shannon twice since class let out with no answer yet. I'm getting antsy. She sounded pretty bad off this morning, barely getting a sentence out before she launched into a coughing fit.

I know she has Jayme there to help her.

She's fine.

I don't need to worry or check on her.

Forget it. I'm going over.

But, not empty handed.

I stop at the Kroger's to pick up some soup, throat lozenges, cough syrup, vitamin C, and zinc. At the checkout counter I see a big bouquet of sunflowers, so I throw those in the cart too. Shannon loves sunflowers. I remember her telling me that when we were little. I hope she still loves them.

A small voice in my head asks what I think I'm doing. And the bigger voice tells that small voice to head to time out. I'm considering being a teacher. I may as well practice my discipline. Though, I'm ninety-nine percent sure time out isn't used in high school. Maybe I'll revive the practice.

I park my car and take the porch steps in two strides. My palms are sweaty, which is absurd. This is just Shannon and it's just me bringing her some get-well supplies. And flowers. Get-well flowers. Friendly flowers.

Jayme opens the door.

"Were you planning on knocking, or were you just going to stand here waiting for us to notice you in all your awesomeness?"

"A knock was in the works." I spread my arms–one holding the grocery bag and the other the bouquet. "My hands are full. But, you did notice my awesomeness, so ..."

Jayme smirks. "Well, come on in."

I walk past Jayme and toward the kitchen, looking for Shannon. A pile of blankets is lumped on the couch, but she's not down here.

"I brought some stuff for Shannon–to help her get better."

"That was super thoughtful of you, Duke."

"Yeah, well, Chris would want to know someone's taking care of her. Not that you aren't. I'm sure you are. But, I'm here on his behalf."

Jayme eyes me, crossing her arms over her chest. "As his stand in?"

"Exactly." I nod.

"Like a second big brother," she pushes.

"Yep. Like that."

Jayme's eyes narrow just the slightest and her brow raises over one eye. Side note: I always wanted to be able to do that, but I'm not very good at it. I can smolder like a sexy campfire, but I can't do that thing she's doing. Jayme's awesome at the one eyebrow lift.

"Okaayyyy," she finally says. "Well, Shannon just went up to use the restroom. She should be back down in a minute if you want to wait for her. Unless you were just doing a drop and run."

I tell Jayme I'll wait. She picks the flowers I brought off the kitchen counter, makes quick work of trimming the stems, asks me to grab down a vase and arranges them so they look even better than they did in the plastic wrap.

I follow her into the living room and watch her place the flowers on the coffee table. It's then I notice the other bouquet on the dining table. With a little white card. Did someone else send Shannon flowers? Or are those for Jayme? And how do I ask without seeming like the jealous and hopelessly obsessed man I am.

"Looks like I'm not the first to bring flowers," I say as casually as I can.

Up, up, up goes that eyebrow.

I ignore the eyebrow. I need to get to the bottom of this. "Who are those from?"

"Oh, those? They're from a secret admirer."

I can feel my face scowl. And Jayme smiles a satisfied grin.

"Your secret admirer, or Shannon's?"

"Not mine," is all she says.

Shannon has a secret admirer.

That's it.

Something in me snaps. I can almost feel it, like a rubber band stretched too thin for too long.

Chris is going to need to find a new bodyguard for his baby sister–or whatever I have been doing for him–and I'm probably going to need to find a new best friend because I'm not going to sit on the sidelines anymore as if I'm not falling for Shannon.

Maybe Amy's right. The potty analogy isn't working for me, but I do need to do some business. I just need to figure out how, but I'm not sitting around waiting to see if Shannon could be mine anymore. I already know how she feels. I just need to man up and show her I feel the same.

Now that I've got that settled, I remember there's one more thing I wanted to ask Jayme.

"I was going to ask you a favor."

"Me?"

"Yeah. And it has to be confidential. Just between the two of us."

"Okay. I think I can promise that, depending on what you're going to ask."

"I'm considering taking on a job at the high school. Well, I don't honestly know what I'm doing. Pops needs me at the garage. But, Principal Barnes reached out to ask me about coaching and in order to coach, I need to teach. Then the history teacher got pregnant, so that means I could be teaching history. All contingent on me passing a test to qualify. Nothing's firm. It's all just possibilities. But I need a tutor to help me prep for the exam."

"Why me?"

"You're the smartest person I know and you work from home. I figure we can find time to study around your other jobs. I'll pay you, of course. I just need the help."

"Rob might be smarter than me. But, I'm honored you'd think of me. I'd be glad to. Text me some times that could work for you and we'll get on this. I think it's awesome that you could be the school coach. It's like that job was made for you. And I could totally see you teaching history."

"You could?"

Huh. I figured everyone in town would be in stunned shock and disbelief, doubting me as much as I doubt myself.

"And you can't mention this to anyone," I repeat. "I still don't know what I'm going to do about my responsibilities at the garage if I say yes. Honestly, I don't even know if I can say yes. But I figure I may as well prepare for the teaching position either way. It can't hurt to see where this goes. If I fail the exam, that's my answer."

"I doubt you'd fail even without my help."

I study her. Did she hear what she just said?

"You're smart, Duke. I'm sure you could pass this test in your sleep if you just study. But, sometimes a tutor is useful for more than facilitating comprehension. You might just need me to help you build your confidence."

"Yeah. Well, thanks."

I don't blush. I'm not blushing. It's a little hot in here. That's all that is. I'm a man who is so cool with needing help and having someone see through me and encourage me. And no matter how much I needed to hear what she said, I'm not going to tear up over Jayme's words either, so get over yourself.

"Thanks for what?" Shannon asks as she comes down the stairs, looking drained, but still so beautiful. It's a different kind of beauty. Her temporary weakness draws out something in my baser nature. I want to take care of her–for the rest of our lives.

"How are you feeling?" I ask her in a soft voice, sidestepping her curiosity about my conversation with Jayme.

"Better. I slept all day after calling you. I haven't done that in years."

She walks toward the couch and I follow her, lifting her blankets while she settles in. I tuck the blankets around her without even thinking about how this appears to her or Jayme. I glance at her face and see a look that can only be described as wonder. Well, Shannon, get used to it. I plan to be the one tucking you in until you're old and gray. You'll see. And soon.

When I straighten, both women are staring at me like I grew two extra legs and just offered to pull a cart around town selling balloon animals.

"I brought you some cough drops and stuff. It's all in the kitchen." I say, like some schoolboy who brought a crumpled bunch of wildflowers to his mom from his rough-and-tumble walk home.

"And flowers," she says, eyeing the bouquet on the coffee table.

"Yeah. And flowers. I thought you liked sunflowers. You used to anyway."

Take that, secret admirer who doesn't know what flowers she really likes. Roses and whatever else fill that bouquet on the dining table are amateur hour. These sunflowers say *I know you, and I'm the one.*

Jayme's sitting in one of their stuffed chairs smiling like the Cheshire Cat who ate the canary.

Shannon looks up at me. "Thanks for all that."

"Well, let me know if you need anything else." I hook a thumb toward the door. "I'd better get going. Feel better."

I head out the door before I wind up blurting all my feelings to Shannon. I need a plan, and I need to get a grip. But I also need to get the girl. And I will.

I'm pulling into my driveway when my cell pings with a text:

Shannon: *I didn't get to ask you. How was Simba?*
Duke: *Zumba?*
Shannon: *(rolling eyes emoji) Yes. Zumba.*
Duke: *It was good. No Lion King characters were harmed during our dance.*

Shannon: *Har har. Seriously, though. Tugs you. You're Maxine.*

Duke: *??? I'm not Maxine. I'm more of a Max. A very masculine Max. Like Mad Max, you know?*

Shannon: *I meant, THANK you. You're AMAZING.*

Duke: *I am, aren't I?*

Shannon: *And Andre gang*

Shannon: *Gah! ARROGANT. Not Andre. No gang!*

Duke: *I'm not arrogant. Just realistic. Have you seen me? With this ball cap on backward and a little stubble on my jaw. I'm a walking dream. Admit it.*

Shannon: *You're something alright*

Duke: *Now you're talking*

Shannon: *(Rolling eyes emoji)*

Duke: *Admit it. I'm the most Maxine. ;)*

TWENTY-THREE

Shannon

Shannon: *Know what I'm craving?*
Duke: *What?*
Shannon: *You noodles*
Duke: *My noodles?*
Shannon: *Ugh! Pho. Pho noodles.*
Duke: *Because you can call me noodles anytime (winking emoji)*
Shannon: *What does that even mean?*
Duke: *Are you seriously asking ME what I mean in a text? Why don't I take you to Pho? I know a place in Dayton.*
Shannon: *You'd so Rhys?*
Duke: *What?*
Shannon: *Joy do rat?*
Duke: *Ummm ???*
Shannon: *Ugh. I mean: You'd do that?*
Duke: *Oh! Yes. Anything for you, Hollywood.*
Shannon: *And I was texting Laura, not you.*
Duke: *Well, I'm guessing she wouldn't take you to Dayton for Pho.*
Shannon: *No. You've got that right.*

Duke: *So it's a good thing you texted me. Plus, I'm way better looking than Laura.*
Shannon: *I don't know about that.*
Duke: *You know. Admit it and quit denying.*
Shannon: *You're incorrigible, Satterson.*
Duke: *If, by incorrigible you mean adorable, yeah. So I've been told. I can be there in about twenty minutes. See you then, Hollywood (winking emoji)*
Shannon: *(Eyeroll emoji)*
Duke: *(Arm muscle emoji)*
Shannon: *(Face palm emoji)*
Duke: *(Noodle bowl emoji)*
Shannon: *(Heart emoji)*

I hop off my bed where I've been leaning back casually like I don't have a care in the world and start running around my room like it's on fire–or I am.

Duke's taking me to pho. It's not a date.

Not. A. Date.

My brain sends back this message that goes something like, "Does not compute." And then some small voice in my head that sounds like the entire cheer squad of Bordeaux High starts chanting "Date! Date! Date! Date!" like a fight song being screamed at fourth and ten in a tied game. Only, there aren't pom-poms involved. It's more like an announcer saying "This is a broadcast of the emergency alert system: YOU'VE GOT A DATE!"

I'm slamming drawers. Which, obviously means I'm opening them, then I slam them. Then I open them again. I can't seem to make sense of what's in the drawers. Nothing good. I need something good.

"Gah!" I scream.

Jayme appears in the doorway a minute later.

In a perfect imitation of Lurch in the Addams Family, she says, "Youuuu ranggg?"

"No! Yes! No! Oh my gosh! Wally willickers! I have to get pickles and prickles! I'm snickered! There's no way I can do this."

I may be hyperventilating. I need oxygen. And a new address. He'll be here any minute and he can't see me like this.

"He who?"

I look at Jayme with a baffled look on my face. "Did I say that out loud?"

"Which part? You said so much. You sound like a Lewis Carroll poem on crack. Calm down."

Jayme walks over to me, places her palms on my shoulders. Like the paragon of peace that she is in this moment, she walks me backward until the backs of my legs hit the bed.

"Sit," she commands, in the same voice she uses with Groucho.

I obey way better than he does, it should be noted.

"Now," Jayme says in her preschool teacher voice. Not that she is a preschool teacher, but she has the voice to qualify as one. "Let's start from the top. What do you need besides pickles and a change of address?"

I take a big breath. "Duke is coming to take me to pho."

"That's pho-nomenal," Jayme says and then she laughs at her own joke.

I glare at her. I'd like to think it's a friendly glare. It really isn't.

"Sorry," she says. "So is this a date, or are you going as pho-rends?"

"Oh, stop with the pho jokes!"

"I think they're pho-nny," she says, ducking as I whip one of my fluffy decorative pillows at her.

"Okay. Okay. I'll make this my grand pho-nale of pho jokes."

"Not a date," I say, trying to get us on track again. "I think it's not. Maybe it is. I don't know."

Jayme sits next to me on the bed. "Okay. So you're planning on changing from the very stay-at-home look we have going on here ..."

She waves up and down from my mussed hair which has been

washed once since I got well–two days ago–and dry shampooed yesterday, all the way to my fluffy slippers. I'm wearing sweats. Old sweats. Comfy sweats. Not date sweats, if there are such a thing.

"Yes! And he'll be here any minute."

As if I summoned him with my words, there's a knock on the door downstairs and I scream like the woman in the nineteen-fifties horror movie, *The Creature of the Black Lagoon*.

Jayme bursts out in laughter.

I not only need a new address, I need a new housemate.

"Calm down, Shelley Duvall. This isn't *The Shining*. It's just Duke. Now, pick out a cute outfit, comb your hair and I'll distract him until you're dressed."

She leans over and takes a big whiff.

"What are you doing?" I ask.

"Just giving you a sniff check. You're good."

"Oh my gosh. You did not just do that."

"Friends don't let friends go to pho with stinky pits. It's a thing. But, like I said, you're good."

She stands from my bed. Then she turns and puts one hand on my shoulder.

"This is Duke. The man who brought you get-well groceries, and sunflowers. The man who stood in the rain making sure you got home safely from that blind date that wasn't a blind date. He's the man who voluntarily covered your Zumba class–which I wish I could have seen in person. That man doesn't care what you wear. He's here because he cares about you–as a friend or as so much more. So relax. Okay?"

I nod. "Thanks, Jayme."

"No problem."

There's another knock.

Jayme tilts her head toward the stairs. "I'd better go get that."

I shout after her. "Don't give him the sniff check!" and then I take a solidifying breath and walk toward my closet.

About five minutes later I'm descending the stairs in faded

jeans and a boho blouse with some strappy white sandals. I'm no Bella Hadid, but I think I look good. I quickly did this blowout thing I saw on YouTube so my hair looks fresh. Then I put on a bit of lipstick and mascara.

Duke whistles as my foot hits the living room floor. "I didn't know we were dressing up."

"Oh this?" I say casually. "I just hadn't put on real-people clothes since I was sick, so I thought I'd actually get dressed."

"You look great," he says, clearing his throat.

Jayme's eyes look like a tree frog. They're bugging out of her head right now and I want to find the button to pop them back in place before Duke notices.

She wags her eyebrows as he turns to open the door for us to step outside.

I shake my head incredulously.

Romance authors. What are you going to do with them? Still, I owe her big time for calming me down and for keeping Duke occupied while I got ready.

"You kids have pho-un" she says with a light laugh.

"Good one!" Duke exclaims.

"Oh, she'll be here all night," I deadpan.

"That I will," Jayme says with a smile. "See you when you get back."

"I'll bring you some to-go pho," I offer.

Jayme shuts the door and Duke puts his hand on the small of my back as he opens the door to his Shelby to let me slide in. It's a very date-like move. The sensation of his hand on me feels electrifying. I smile and control my breathing while I settle into the passenger seat.

"So, the Shelby, huh?"

"It was that or my bike, and since you've been sick, I didn't want to have you out in that wind too long."

"That was thoughtful."

"Always thinking of you, Shannon."

Not even Hollywood. And, he's always thinking of me? What does that even mean?

TWENTY-FOUR

Shannon

W e ride without saying much for a while. The corn fields and ranches drifting past outside the windows. I think of Jayme's books, how she always talks about companionable silence. We have that, but a different kind of quiet settles between me and Duke. This silence feels pregnant with something important. I just wish I knew what.

"So," Duke finally says as we reach the highway and merge onto it. "You mentioned you were wrestling with goals when we were at the fair. Anything crystalize for you since then?"

"I wish," I confess. "I have some ideas, but they all seem so lofty. It's not like I'm unhappy. I just feel myself getting older, and it's like a deadline is looming over my head. I don't want to miss my chance to choose well while I'm young."

"I hear that," he says, his eyes wandering across the horizon, then glancing at me with a seriousness that isn't typical of him. "I had fun at the fair, by the way."

"Yeah? Me too."

"And I never knew you were such a daredevil. How did I miss this fact about you?" he teases.

"I'm a multifaceted woman."

"That you are," he says in a voice that makes my skin hum. So often I feel like he still sees me as an annoying adolescent, but right now he's making me feel very much like a woman.

"Do you have a bucket list of daring things you want to do in life?" he asks casually.

If you only knew. I'd reach over and run my hand over your day-old scruff, especially tracing the corners of your jaw where they jut out in that chiseled way making your face seem so masculine and rugged. Then I'd rest my hand on your thigh while we drive. And when you parked, I'd lean over and finally kiss you. I'd kiss you with a kiss we'd both never forget.

"Shannon?"

"Um. Yeah. Right. I'd go skydiving. I want to go up in a hot air balloon too. I know that's not super thrilling, but the idea of floating near the clouds with nothing separating you from a fall to your death but a wicker basket thrills me. I think hot air balloons are romantic too."

Really? *Romantic*?

I basically just threw that word out there like a castaway lighting an S.O.S. signal on fire in his remote lagoon. Next thing you know, I'll adopt a volleyball as my best friend and start talking to inanimate objects. I do not need to be bringing the concept of romance into this night with Duke.

"Hot air ballooning, huh?"

He says it like he never heard me burn my island to the ground with the R word. Thanks be.

"Yeah. Have you ever been?"

"Nope. But I'd love to go sometime."

"Maybe I'll take you," Duke says easily. He adds a signature wag of his eyebrows.

"That usually works for you, doesn't it?"

"What?"

"That whole flirty thing you do with your eyebrows."

He does it again. "This?"

"Yes. That."

"I'm not interested in usually, Hollywood. You know me well enough to know when I'm playing and when I'm dead serious."

But do I? I don't think I do. He seems to turn the charm on like a sprinkler system, and everyone in his radius gets hit. He charms the seniors, the children and the women. He even charms his friends and his customers in a very Duke-ish way.

And he charms me.

I'm not immune.

Not in the least.

Thankfully, we arrive at the restaurant without any more talk of romance or flirting.

Pho hits the spot. And pho with Duke is ten times better. We laugh. We talk. He circles back around to my dreams and goals. I'm surprised. I didn't think he paid that close attention. Literally no one else, except maybe Jayme, asks me about my goals.

Letting Duke take me to pho is definitely the most relaxing, enjoyable night out I've had in so long–well, since the fair, actually. And that's a bad, bad thing. I need to protect my heart. And that means I should be keeping my distance, not texting him about my cravings, dressing like I'm going on a date, and then spilling my heart out to him over a bowl of hot noodle soup.

It could be a quick and slippery slope from letting Duke be my emotional support animal to wanting him to be my everything. He can only ever be my friend, and even then, he'll always be Chris' friend first.

I respect Duke's loyalty. I also know better than to let Duke's obligation to my brother be my excuse for getting special time alone with him, especially when my feelings for him go so much further than his ever will for me.

Duke drops me off in front of our home, jumping out of his side of the car before I can say, "Don't worry. You don't have to walk me to the door."

This isn't a date, I remind the cheerleading squad in my head. They sit on the bench looking as dejected as they should when their team didn't win, their pom poms sagging and their shoulders slumped.

Duke opens my car door. "I had a good night. Thanks for inviting me."

"I didn't invite you, exactly," I say as I climb out.

"No? I recall you texting me to tell me you were craving pho."

"And you offered to take me."

"That's right. I did, didn't I?"

"Yep."

I take off toward my front door, feeling like I've got to get these inner cheerleaders away from the playing field as soon as possible.

Duke catches up with me in three long strides. "What's the hurry? Did I say something wrong?"

"No. You're fine. I really appreciate you taking me to pho. I had a great time."

"Can I get a hug?"

"A hug?" I gulp in the G sound at the end of that word and almost choke. He wants me to touch him–to hold him–right now.

A couple cheerleaders look up. I send them a look. Girls. We lost the game. Stay right on that bench.

I might be going crazy. Can a woman go crazy with longing? If so, I am. Officially, certifiably crazy.

Duke steps forward, his arms outstretched and I melt into his embrace, lifting my arms from my sides to wrap around his waist. I lean my cheek to his chest and he holds me.

He murmurs something into my hair. I can't make it out.

"What?" I ask, not lifting my face.

"Nothing," he says. And then he pushes away with a smile and a wink.

"I'll see you soon, Hollywood. Call me with your cravings anytime."

I shake my head at him and walk the rest of the way up the walkway and into my house.

When I shut the door behind me, Jayme hops down from the couch where she had been kneeling backward, looking out the front window. She jumps so quickly it elicits a rare bark from Groucho. He settles as soon as he sees it's only me.

"You were spying!"

"Oh, you know it! Nice hug."

"It was," I say. "A friendly hug. An oh-so pho-rendly hug."

I try to laugh at my own joke, but my laugh turns into this pitiful sigh of resignation. I set the take-out bag we brought home for Jayme on the coffee table and glance toward the door where I just hugged Duke goodbye.

"You aren't going to get over him, are you?" Jayme asks.

I'm sure it's a rhetorical question, but I answer anyway. "It doesn't seem like I can."

"Okay ... change in strategy!"

"We had a strategy?"

"Sort-of. You did the whole friend thing, and then the letting him care for you thing. Now we need to get out the big guns."

"I'm not sure I like where this is going."

"You will. Trust the romance author."

"I'd trust you with werewolves. I'm not sure human love affairs are your specialty, to be honest."

"Pfft. It's all the same. Love is love. Do you not even feel the least bit curious as to what my strategy is?"

"I'm curious. You've got me there."

"Sit down."

I plop into one of the living room chairs.

"I know he's got feelings for you. You should have seen his face when he nearly sniffed your hair off your head during that hug. He's got feelings. You just have to make him admit those to himself and then he's going to pursue you like a kid chasing the ice cream truck on allowance day."

"How do you suppose I do that?" I ask for the sake of argument.

"Easy and obvious. You make him jealous."

"What? How?"

"You get someone to play as if they are into you, and you make Duke believe you are so over any crush he might suspect you have on him. You show him you are ready to date, date, date."

"I don't think so. He's already seen me date. He just stalks me and interferes and gets all broody and domineering."

"Hmmm. And those are signs of what?"

"Signs of loyalty to my overprotective brother."

"No. No. No," Jayme says, wagging her pointer finger for emphasis. "Those, my beautiful friend, are signs of a man who doesn't want to see you dating. And why doesn't he want that? Because he wants *you*."

I ponder Jayme's words. It feels like the first time my parents handed me a lit sparkler on the Fourth of July. I couldn't believe I got to hold that bit of fire on the end of a stick. It was simultaneously beautiful and terrifying. If I accept what Jayme is saying ... I don't know. Mostly, I think I'll drop the sparkler and burn myself. Badly.

"Listen," Jayme goes on. "If you don't want to make him jealous. Then you ought to flaunt what he's missing. Work it, girlfriend. You've got everything any man would die to have. And he's a man."

"I'm not going to just throw myself at him."

"Of course you aren't. That's tacky. You're not going to throw yourself at him. You're going to be like a rainbow trout. He's the fisherman at shore. He doesn't think there are any catchable fish in the water until ... Bam! ... You jump up and grab his attention in all your rainbow-y glory. Then he scrabbles to throw out a line so he can catch you. And, of course, you let him."

"So you're saying I should chase Duke until he catches me?"

"I couldn't have said it better myself."

TWENTY-FIVE

Duke

Shannon walks into my garage, her hips swaying slightly in a way that comes natural to her. She looks like a fantasy–my fantasy–come to life. The midday sun shines behind her, illuminating her figure, even giving a hint of the lines of her legs through the skirt she's wearing.

She walks, placing one foot in front of the other, like the world is her catwalk. Her dancer body always has this easy posture, straight, but unforced. And those shoes. I never thought I had a foot fetish until today. The way those strappy, heeled sandals wrap around her feet, and draw attention up her legs makes me want to drop and do fifty.

It's not the feet or the sandals–it's her.

Some women put on that kind of swagger to try to drag a man's attention to them. That's never been Shannon. She has this undeniable sexiness to her without even making the slightest effort or being aware of how completely intoxicating she is. She's so poised and effortless–her every movement graceful, and yet something about her makes me want to ruffle her up.

I clear my throat–which does nothing to clear my head.

"What do you think you're wearing?" I ask before I think better of what's coming out of my mouth.

That dress could literally kill me if I keep looking at her. Death by female in dress. I think it's a thing.

But, I sound so much like a big brother I almost cringe at my own words.

"This old thing?" Shannon answers, her obvious irritation barely cloaked by her sarcastic tone and the taunting tilt of her lips.

Shannon waves her hand up and down the light cotton sundress and shimmies a little, making the bottom edge flare and twirl slightly before it settles again across her bare, tan legs. I swallow the lump in my throat.

She puts on a fake southern accent and says, "Why Duke, are you concerned some local man might take a shinin' to me?"

Then she bats her lashes in an exaggerated fashion and gives another twist of her hips, completely oblivious to what she's doing to me.

Some other man.

Over my dead body.

She is trying to kill me. It's official.

"I just don't think Chris would approve of you gallivanting around town in a skirt that short."

Really?

What am I saying?

This has nothing to do with Chris and everything to do with me. Shannon can wear whatever she wants. I just want to be the only one seeing her dressed like that, only I haven't figured out how to spring that truth on her.

"Galavanting. Such vocabulary. Jayme would be impressed. And, if you hadn't noticed, my brother is out of town."

I nearly growl as I scrub my hand down my face. What has gotten into her? The last time I saw Shannon was when we went to pho. We left things a little awkwardly, I'll admit. She seemed to retreat into herself when I dropped her off, but then she gave me that hug I haven't been able to stop thinking about since. I thought we were good.

"I'm sorry," I say.

It's all I can think to say. I already overstepped my boundaries with her. I decide to keep my mouth shut to avoid saying anything else that might make her angry, or that would permanently lock me into the big-brother-once-removed category.

I pick up my wrench and get back to work, asking her from under the hood what she's here for in the first place.

"You and your way with words," she mumbles, probably to herself, but with Shannon, I never know. Half the time I think she's trying to drive me crazy–to push me until I come unglued and do something about the pulsing electric current always just beneath the surface between us.

She doesn't give me any more time to ponder what it would be like to finally break through all the barriers and lose myself in a confession—one that would betray my best friend to the core. A confession followed by a kiss that would show her everything I've been dying to say for years.

"I'm here to talk about a welcome home party for Chris."

I pull my head out from under the hood.

"A welcome home party?"

"Yes. I thought it would be nice to put something formal together. With mom being ... well, you know. And dad being immersed in the demands of his business, I figured it would fall on me to put it together. I thought you might like to help."

"I'd love to help."

I'm about to say more, but the phone on the wall rings. Pops is out today, so it's just me.

I hold up a finger to Shannon and walk over to answer the call. "Satterson's. How may I help you?"

It's Jed White. He tells me one of their hands backed the tractor into a ditch while the plow was attached. He needs me to come provide a tow. I end the call and turn to Shannon.

"That was Jed White. He's got a tractor in need of a tow. Want to tag along? We can talk about this party on the way."

"Sure. If you don't think I'd be in the way."

"You're never in the way. Hop up in the tow truck. I'll just scrub my hands and then we can head over there."

I watch Shannon walk toward my tow truck. She looks like the co-star in some small town movie where her boyfriend runs the towing company and she's far too good for him or their town, and yet, she's his. Maybe it's not a movie. Maybe it's more like a pipe dream.

The radio in the tow truck comes on as soon as I turn the key. *Lady* by Styx comes through the speakers I upgraded a few years back. I reach over to hit the power button. I don't need a love ballad filling this space between us. Shannon grips my wrist. I turn my head toward her and our eyes lock.

"Don't. I want to hear it," she says. "You're such a classic rocker."

I back out of the lot and we drive toward the outskirts of town toward the White's farm. As the song fills the cab of the tow truck, I absentmindedly sing along. I can feel Shannon staring at the side of my face. I can't look at her and sing these words. Each phrase expresses my heart in ways I haven't figured out how to yet–even the line about being a child who grew up. It's her. All her.

"I love your voice," Shannon says shyly. She said it at the fair, but this time it feels different.

I smile, keeping my eyes dead ahead. "Thanks. I like yours too."

She giggles. "My singing voice? When did you hear me sing?"

"I haven't in a long time. Why don't you refresh me?"

She surprises me by singing along. We spend the rest of the ride serenading one another to *Lady*, and then *Bohemian Rhapsody* by Queen comes on and we rock out. Shannon gets super dramatic, putting her hand to her heart whenever Freddy Mercury sings, "Mama." When the snare hits in the song, she fakes hitting an invisible drum set on my dash. I consider driving right past the White's and taking this show on the road. I don't want to end this moment we're having.

But, duty calls.

I pull into the driveway of the White's farm. Jed and a few of his hired guys are standing around the ditch staring at the tractor.

When I hop out, Shannon stays in the truck. Jed glances over at her, his features never revealing an ounce of curiosity or surprise. While farmers out here tend to keep to themselves, having so much of their own lives to tend to, I don't put it past him to possibly spread the word in a very unassuming way. All Jed'll have to do is mention to his wife something like, "So, Shannon St. James was in the truck with Duke when he came to pull the tractor out of the ditch today." Oooweee that's gonna spread like butter on warm toast.

The ditch is just to the left of the main driveway– a V-shaped depression that runs an entire section of the fence line, about five feet wide and three feet deep. I step closer to see what we're up against. The whole time I'm out here, a small voice in my head keeps asking me who's going to do this kind of work for our town if I decide to take the teaching job. I come up blank.

The tractor's back wheels are both down into the ditch and the plow attachment is half in the ditch and half protruding out the other side. The ground is muddy from the summer rain we had.

"We was gonna lay some pipe out here for irrigation before the harvest or the winter freeze," Jed explains. "Dug the trench, but haven't gotten around to layin' the pipe and fillin' it. Well, sir. That's what you get for percrastinatin'."

"It could happen to anyone, Jed. You work hard. Don't knock yourself."

"Well, if I don't knock myself, I'd be knockin' my hired boy. He's still wet behind the ears for a farm worker. Can't blame him for not knowin' how to drive a tractor. Most of you uns have been drivin' 'em since you was twelve or so. Am I right?"

"You aren't wrong," I agree.

It's the way we do things out here. We all get our turns at the tractor to help out, or just for fun. By the time we reach the legal age where we're supposed to get behind the wheel of an automobile, we've learned how to maneuver farm equipment like a pro. A car on a flat, paved road is nothing–except in a snowstorm or one of our serious rains.

Jed gets a call on his cell. He has to tend to something in the barn. "Will you be alright out here without me for a quick minute? I'll be right back."

"I've got this, Jed. You go on and take care of business."

Speaking of taking care of business has me thinking of Amy and her nudge to do something about these feelings for Shannon. Everything reminds me of that lately.

I pop open the driver door of the tow truck. "You okay in here?"

"It's a little hot," Shannon says. "I think I'll get out."

"In that?" I ask, looking at her outfit.

Someone should be taking her to an out-of-town restaurant or concert dressed like that. She's way overdressed for watching a local boy drag farm equipment out of a muddy ditch.

"It's fine," she says with a snap to her voice.

"All I mean is that you look too good to be out in the mud."

There. That's better.

"Oh, I do, do I?"

"Mmhmm."

I turn before I get myself into trouble. I've got a job to do and then I need to get on the back of my bike and ride some open roads so I can figure myself out and make a plan. Being near Shannon has me inside out and upside down–a lot like Jed's plow. I'm stuck and I need a tow up and out of this situation.

I get the tractor hitched to the truck. After telling Shannon to stay clear, I hop in the cab and press the accelerator slowly. We budge, but not enough. Might have to detach the plow, but pulling both out separately would be a far more complicated job. It's better if they can remain attached.

I walk toward the tractor, wondering if I need to lay something down for traction under the front tires. When I step down to get a better look at the wheels, my foot hits a slippery patch of mud, and I go down, landing in a massive mud puddle.

"Oh my gosh!" Shannon shouts, her laughter erupting immediately. "Are you okay?"

She's too amused to be fully concerned.

"I'm okay," I say, looking down at my mud-encrusted hands. I wipe them on my shirt, but it's coated too.

"I've got another shirt in the back of the cab. Can you help me lift this off?"

I start to pull on my shirt, but I'm getting mud everywhere.

"Was this intentional?" Shannon asks, propping one hand on a hip and staring at me with her eyebrows raised.

"Falling in the mud?"

"Yeah, so you could show off your ... you know" she gestures at my chest. "And be all *I'm so tempting*."

"Tempting? Do you think I'm tempting, Hollywood?" I give her a look full of promise and questions.

She rolls her eyes and huffs, but the light blush creeping up her neck tells me everything she won't.

I stand and take my time removing my shirt.

"It was my nefarious plan," I say with a wink. "To fall into a pile of mud, because, what woman can resist a man coated in muck?"

The blush climbs higher and Shannon looks away, crossing her arms.

"You aren't going to help me?" I ask in a tone of complete innocence. "How else will you see my six pack and the definition of my pecs?"

"I think I'll manage."

She glances at me, but turns as if she's walking back to the truck.

"Wait, Shannon. I really do need your help."

"Promise to behave yourself."

"Hmmm," I say, acting like I need to deliberate while I lift my shirt a little higher, exposing everything up to my rib cage. Her eyes drop, shamelessly cataloging my torso.

I inch the shirt up higher and her gaze follows the movement. I'm delirious from her attention, and she seems momentarily unaware of her blatant perusal. I feel her. She may as well be running a hand up my skin. Everywhere her eyes land heats. I lift the shirt in one movement and throw it off me. Her mouth drops open. She turns quickly and walks toward the truck, slamming the door behind herself.

That was either a really smart move on my part or the dumbest thing I've ever done.

TWENTY-SIX

Shannon

I wanted Duke to be my first kiss ever since he helped me tie my skates at the ice rink while Chris skated off after his crush at the time, Jessica White. I may have been twelve. Who knows. All I knew was Duke's heart was as gorgeous as his face–and that's one gorgeous face.

Unfortunately, my first kiss was with Gilbert Milgarden. Don't ask. It was all braces and teeth and lips and hands–more like a sloppy game of twister than an actual romantic experience.

First kisses aside, now that I've seen Duke without a shirt, my life will never be the same. I'll be picturing half-naked Duke until I die. I'm sitting in the cab of the truck, my hands slightly trembling from adrenaline while I wait for him to make his muddy way over here to get a new shirt. I can't even look him in the eye. He saw me. He watched the way I reacted to his body and now he's coming toward this truck.

I pull out my phone and start to text Jayme. Normally I'd call Laura for all major freak-outs. She's my oldest and closest friend. But, Jayme is the only one who knows about Duke and she's done a stellar job keeping my secret safe.

It's all I can do to keep myself from turning my head when he reaches the door and opens it, still shirtless and smirking.

Okay. Okay. I looked.

For the sake of science. Or on behalf of women everywhere. Or something.

I mean, when else am I going to see this side of Duke? At the reservoir when we're swimming with all our friends, yes. But for some reason, those times I've seen him in swim trunks never hit me like this–him clad in muddy jeans and work boots with his ball cap on backward and no shirt.

Lawd. It's too much.

Apparently the sight of him is bringing out an inner southern girl in me.

Maybe I should sit on my hands, just in case they go rogue and reach out to touch him. I grip my phone like it's about to jump away from me.

"You okay?" Duke asks all casually and not like a half-dressed hottie who definitely is toying with me right now.

"I'm great. I'm not the one in a solo mud-wrestling competition."

"We could change that," he winks.

Darn him.

"If you're feeling left out, there's plenty of mud to go around."

"I'm good," I say, unable to stop the smile that creeps across my face at the thought of me and Duke in the mud together.

What? No.

No mud. No Duke in the mud. No wrestling Duke in the mud until our lips meet and we finally kiss.

"Get a shirt on and get back to work, Satterson."

"Yes ma'am," he says with that boyish grin, dimples popping and biceps popping and pecs popping. So much popping. Orville Redenbacher would be jealous.

Duke grabs a shirt from the back seat and slowly lifts his arms, letting it fall down inch by torturous inch. His head is hidden from me, so I indulge myself in the view, actually licking my lips. I didn't mean to. It just happened.

I can't even say how glad I am Duke's face was covered while I mortified myself with unrestrained want over this man who drives me crazy in every way imaginable.

After he gives the final tug to the hem of his shirt, he picks up that naughty, disturbing ball cap from the front seat, pulls it onto his head–backwards, of course–and gives me this taunting look before he turns and says, "This shouldn't take too long. Roll down the windows so you don't get too overheated."

Well, we all know it's way too late for that warning.

～

With all that shirtlessness and the impromptu sing-alongs both to and from the White's farm, combined with my confused, love-struck brain, we never did discuss Chris' party. I spent the rest of the afternoon dancing in my basement since I didn't have any appointments booked at the Dippity Do.

Dancing helped. It always does.

After I've showered and had a bite to eat, I decide to drive over to Duke's.

For party planning.

Just that.

Everyone knows planning a party in person is better.

I knock on Duke's screen door since the inside door is wide open. Duke shouts, "Come in!" His voice echoes through from somewhere toward the back of the house.

I open the door and step over the threshold, and it's a good thing my hand is still on the knob when Duke appears in the front room.

He's not wearing a shirt. Again. And I lose all capacity to hold myself upright. You'd think I'd have gotten my fill of shirtless Duke earlier this afternoon. You'd be wrong–so very, very wrong. As a matter of fact, I think I've found my new goal in life. Seeing Duke shirtless as often as possible seems like a worthy use of my days.

Some people pursue anthropology, an admittedly obscure life calling. If I remember correctly, anthropology is the study of human biological and physiological characteristics. I'd like to be an anthropologist of Duke. I'd study the heck out of his physiological characteristics, devoting myself to my work.

I never understood when people said someone made them weak in the knees until now. My grip on Duke's front door seems to be the only thing standing between me and a collapse into a pool of wobbly Jell-O on his entryway floor.

He's sweaty and toned, his muscles more defined than earlier. Was he working out? Not a speck of mud remains on him, instead, he glows with a sheen of perspiration. And dear sweet mercy me, I can count a one, two, three, four, five, six ... yep an honest-to-goodness six-pack, with two baby muscles that almost make it an eight-pack. Though, no one would dare say "baby" about what's displayed in front of me right now. Unless they were going to say "Ohhh, baby!"

Duke looks like a blond Zac Efron in that spread he did for *People*. Zac flipping Efron, friends. Only better. Zac Efron never made my heart race like the energizer bunny with a fresh battery. The hotness of Duke Satterson would make the last day of August feel like eating a popsicle on a visit to the North Pole while tiny elves dropped ice cubes down your shirt.

I manage to move my eyes up Duke's torso, not a hardship, mind you. That is, until I meet his gaze. He's fully smirking at me —that playful, knowing, boyish grin. Only nothing beneath Duke's neckline looks at all boyish.

Eyes up, Shannon. Don't let him see you stare—or sweat.

"Um, hi," I say in the typical dorkiness I often fall into whenever Duke's around—especially, apparently, shirtless Duke.

"Um, hi," he echoes slowly with another smoldery smirk.

"Yeah, so, well ... I'm just here to go over details about the party, since we didn't get to talk much in the truck."

"Sorry," he says, gesturing to his shirtless upper body. "I was just doing pull-ups. I thought you were Aiden."

"I'm not."

"Obviously."

That sly smile creeps across Duke's face. His eyes dip toward my mouth. Is he looking at my mouth, really? I think he is. Wait. Why would Duke be looking at my mouth with a look like that? It almost looks like he's thinking of ... no. He wouldn't be.

I close my mouth and run my tongue over my gums. Maybe I had lettuce between my teeth. The perils of salad being the only healthy food I enjoy means there's a ninety-nine percent chance of me walking around with something green in my smile at least once a week.

"Come on in," he says, turning to give me a full view of his uncovered back.

It's equally impressive. All those lines and ridges.

I'm here for party planning.

Party. Planning.

Plan the party, Shannon. For your brother. Who would freak out and probably kill someone if he saw you staring at his best friend's back while thinking of climbing him like a tree.

Right. Right. Good.

Party planning. Check.

By the time we're in the kitchen, I'm all business. Party business. Not Duke's business, to be clear.

"Do you want something to drink?"

"Do you want to get dressed?"

He chuckles as he casually runs a hand up his torso, across his chest and then through his mussed hair.

"Is it bothering you that I'm shirtless?"

"Bothering me? No. Of course not. What would make you think I'm bothered? I'm twenty-six. It's not like I haven't seen a man shirtless before? Or you–since you seem intent on disrobing in front of me today."

Okayyy. Not the best line to end on. But, it's out there now.

Duke hums and smiles a half smile as he turns toward the fridge, which I'm pretty sure is not where he keeps clean T-shirts.

"Orange juice, soda, beer, or flavored sparkling water?"

I'm disarmed enough that it takes a second to realize he's offering drink options.

"Um, just water is fine."

Shirtless Duke grabs a glass from the cabinet. Triceps, hello. Shirtless Duke fills the glass with ice and then water from the fridge dispenser. Lats, come to mama. Shirtless Duke walks toward me like a male model in an ice water commercial. He could totally sell ice water—even though it's free.

I take the glass from him, down the contents and slam it onto the island in one motion, like an Irishman at a pub the day Notre Dame wins the bowl game.

Duke chuckles and crosses his naked arms over his bare chest. I will not survive this visit.

"Thirsty?" he asks, wagging his brows and chuckling.

He has no idea. Or maybe he does.

The way he's smirking at me makes me think he totally does.

Over the years I've developed a little smirk guidebook covering all the smirks of Duke Satterson. It's not written down, but I've cataloged each one and their hidden meaning. It's the kind of thing a woman does when she's forced to live in a small town with a man she wants more than her next paycheck or an all-expense paid vacation with the Hemsworth brothers. It's a smirk-saurus, or a smirktionary, if you will.

One of my favorites is his smoldering smirk when he's confidently flaunting every bit of his hotness. This comes with a lift of the eyebrow.

Yeah. Yeah. I've seen Disney's *Tangled*, and no. That man, Flynn Ryder, was child's play compared to Duke's smolder. Duke's smolder could set me on fire, it's so incendiary.

Next you have the playful smirk where Duke's boyish side comes out. He pulls this one out to cheer people up, or when he's ribbing his friends. He'll say something ridiculous and use the playful smirk as a final punctuation mark.

The bad boy smirk speaks for itself. Duke's always been one

to push the limits. He gets this devilish look in his eyes whenever he's up to something that's bound to be trouble. It's nearly impossible to resist him in all his James Dean glory. It's a fact. The bad boy is like a free pint of Ben and Jerry's at that time of the month. Irresistible even though we know we'll pay for it later.

Duke's knowing smirk is reserved for times when he watches someone mess up or back themselves into a corner. He gets this look that says he sees you. It's conspiratorial and always makes me squirm, but that knowing smirk says whatever he picked up on will stay just between the two of us.

Growing up, I'd see one other smirk only on a few rare occasions. It made an appearance when he resolutely focused on winning a ball game. I've seen it when he spotted a classic car in mint condition. It's a smirk of sheer want and appreciation.

And that all-consuming smirk is the one he's aiming at me right now. Duke's a predator and he's on the hunt. His pupils are dilated, his tongue darts out, and his focus narrows on his goal. Hunger is written in every twitch of his lips, and every bat of those unfairly long lashes. I should do something to stop this, but I can't say I really want to.

TWENTY-SEVEN

Duke

Yes. I'm flirting with Shannon. I can't help it. Every time I turn, she's watching me like she's never seen a man with his shirt off before. I'm male, human, and fully attracted to her. What do you expect from me?

She chugged that water like she was in a contest at the county fair. Her throat bobbing with every swallow, eyes closed. I'm torturing myself as much as I seem to be torturing her. But that's about to end. I'm putting both of us out of this misery.

We'll enter a new kind of torture as soon as I cross this line, but I can't take resisting her one more minute.

She's not in that infuriating dress she wore earlier. Instead, she's in cut-off shorts and a loose tank top with a sports bra under it. She's got her hair up in some poofy bun thing that exposes her neck and shoulders. I want to kiss my way up and down that silky skin and then pull the tie out of her hair so that it spills down around me like a satin curtain.

I'm not known for my restraint, which is ironic since I've lived my adult life keeping this secret longing for Shannon under lock and key, holding myself on a short leash where she's concerned.

Usually, I'm the guy who says what everyone else is thinking when they're afraid to say it. I call people out in a playful way, using my charm to speak the truth.

I'm getting tired of watching Shannon–wanting her with this chronic ache–doing the honorable thing by her brother while I suffer.

Yes. Chris is sacrificing for our country, and by natural extension that's for me. He's been on the front line as my defense. And I've always had his back. Always will if he lets me.

But I'm not some sleazy guy trying to take advantage of his baby sister. I'm a man who wants to take care of her in every way possible. I'm sick of being a stand-in big brother. Tonight my patience has worn thin.

Shannon's eyes go wider as she watches me move closer to her. I should ask her if she wants this, but I'm afraid that would engage some thinking part of her brain or mine and right now every non-verbal message she's sending says, "Yes. Yes. Yes."

I can't tell if I moved those last few inches toward her, or she leaned toward me, eliminating the distance between us. All I know is that the tips of my fingers are holding the soft skin of her cheeks and our lips have come together in a kiss that says, "finally," and "more," and "you, only and always, you." She tastes like sugar and warm, juicy summer fruit straight off the tree.

I turn her on the barstool so her body faces mine more fully, and I step between those dancer's legs, tilting her head up toward me. She arches in like a cat, letting out this small mewling noise and I know I never want to kiss another woman for the rest of my life.

I kiss her deeply and then softly. My lips tease hers, brushing lightly, leaving my skin tingling from the contact. Shannon gasps, but the hand resting on my bicep clenches as if to hold me there. I'm not going anywhere. Maybe I'll never go anywhere ever again.

A bomb could be set off under my feet and I'd spend my last moments on earth kissing Shannon. I lean in. This time, allowing my lips to linger on hers while my hand on her back secures her to me. My other hand is running through her hair. I must have undone that tie at some point. The silky softness of her hair runs through my fingertips.

Shannon starts playing with the hair at the nape of my neck. Then she's stroking the stubble on my jaw with both her hands, cupping my face like she's worshiping it. Her lips match the movements of my mouth. I lose myself in the sensations of our connection. Lose myself in her.

Shannon

D UKE'S KISSING ME!

Shannon

O h. My. Gosh.
Duke is kissing me. We're kissing and it's the most passionate, tender, hungry, intensely sweet kiss I've ever had. He's leaning into me, holding me steady, stroking my hair like it's his job. And if I were giving out performance evaluations, he'd be getting a raise and a promotion. Goodness this man knows how to kiss.

When he pulls back, my eyes do not open. I don't open them because I don't know if what just happened between us was actually real, and I need it to be real with every fiber of my being.

And if it wasn't real, or he looks at all like he's about to apologize or bring up my brother's name, I don't know what I'll do. I don't regret one second of that kiss.

Speaking of seconds, I want more. A second helping of Duke's kisses. But I'm frozen here, unwilling to open my eyes and face my doom. I must look ridiculous, and the more time that passes, the more I'm sure Duke doesn't know what to do with me. Maybe he's planning his exit speech. Or my exit speech, since I'm in his house, after all.

"Shannon," Duke's gravelly, post-kiss voice breaks into my

mental tailspin. Then he says it again, "Shannon." This time with a softness laced with a hint of concern.

"Mmhmm," I answer, with my eyes still shut.

I wonder if I could maneuver my way out of here keeping my eyes closed without bumping into anything major. I would very much like to avoid seeing the reaction Duke is having to that kiss. I know he regrets it. Obviously, it built up between us with all the play-flirting, and the shirtlessness, and with us both being single young adults. It was bound to happen.

And now it did.

And I'll face it–face him–just not right now.

"Shannon," Duke says again.

I feel his hand cup my cheek.

"What's going on in that pretty head of yours?"

His other hand smooths down my hair. It feels so nice. I get why Oddball likes his tummy rubbed. This is beyond nice. I'm just going to sit here and let Duke pet me in his guilty state while he wrestles with the reality that he just broke the bro code.

Then I'll go, and we'll get things back on track. Solid plan. He's still stroking my hair, softly, steadily. His other hand hasn't left my cheek. I lean into it. If this is happening, I may as well soak it up for all it's worth.

"Talk to me," Duke's deep voice sounds so laced with affection that I almost open my eyes.

Instead I squeeze them shut to make sure they stay that way.

"Did I mess up?" he asks. "I need you to talk to me. You're freaking me out just a little bit here."

I'm freaking *him* out?

"What was that?" I finally say, my face still tilted into his hand, his other palm stroking down my back so sweetly I could cry.

"That. Was a kiss," he says. And I don't have to see him to hear the smirky smirkiness that's obviously plastered across his smirkish face.

"I know it was a kiss," I say, opening one eye.

He smiles.

"There she is," he says, like he coaxed a rabid, stray, mama racoon out of her little hole under the porch.

I reluctantly lift my head off his hand and shrug my shoulders so his other hand falls away. I square my posture and look Duke straight in the face.

"What I'm saying is, what did that kiss mean? Do we regret it? Was it a mistake? I get it if it was a mistake. I mean, you've been caring for me. I've seen your amazing torso up close today, and we're both single. It happens."

Duke places his hands on either side of his hips. It's a nice look on him, as you can imagine.

"Let me take those questions one by one," he offers. "What the kiss meant was that I am seriously attracted to you, and not just physically. And I have been for a while. It meant you are too, if I was accurately reading all those soft sounds and the way you cupped my face and kissed me like I was the air you needed to breathe."

He pauses to make an infuriatingly smug expression. Then he continues before I can say a word. "Do we regret it? I will never regret that kiss. If your brother comes home and sets an entire sniper team on me for touching you, I will still not regret that kiss. Whether you regret it is something you'll have to tell me.

"It was not a mistake. And if it was, I plan on making many, many mistakes in the days and weeks to come, if you'll let me. Finally, yes. We both are single, which is highly convenient when it comes to me continuing to kiss you in the near and distant future. And I do have an amazing torso. Thanks for noticing, and for gripping onto it and for rubbing your hand across it while you kissed me like I've never been kissed before."

"Oh."

That's all I'm able to say when he finishes. I sit staring at him like he's a mirage. All these years of wanting him and hiding my feelings, all the times I convinced myself he was just a flirt, not flirting with me specifically. Could it be all that time he wanted me too?

"You've wanted me?"

I have to ask.

"I should win a Nobel prize for self-restraint. I have wanted you so badly, Shannon."

"Since you and Beth broke up?"

He laughs. His six pack does this sexy clenching thing and my eyes gravitate toward his midsection to stare. He sees me watching him and the energy between us shifts. Duke steps toward me. He takes my palm and places it on his abs. On. His. Abs. I'm touching the six-pack! Then he tilts my chin up toward him.

In an almost inaudible voice, deep, gritty and full of sincerity, he says, "I've wanted you for years, Shannon. For years."

Then he leans in and he kisses me again. I reach up and tug his head toward me and hold him in place. My hand hasn't left his abs. I move my fingers just a little and he lets out this groan into my mouth that I feel down to my toes.

Before I know what's happening, I'm being swept up into his arms and carried. He's still kissing me while he's stalking through the kitchen toward the front room and then placing me on the couch.

I laugh when I plop down out of his arms.

He sits next to me and puts his arm around behind me, rubbing his thumb across the exposed skin on my shoulder. Yay me for wearing a tank top!

"Do we need to talk about this?" he asks.

"About kissing?"

He chuckles again. How is he so calm and sure right now? I feel like we need to contact a geological society to make sure the earth hasn't shifted completely off its axis and we're not hurling toward the sun as a result. Nothing feels the same. I can't find my center. But it's so, so good. If this is the end of the world as I know it, I'll be fine. And now that song is looping through my brain.

"Man. What I'd pay for a ticket on the ride that is your thought process right now," Duke teases.

He looks into my eyes, searching them, and somehow conveying this strength and calm I don't feel in the least. But I'm starting to settle the longer I sit here with him–watching him watching me.

"I meant, do we need to talk about what it means that we're kissing?" he asks.

"Are we kissing for tonight only, or ..." I shake my head in disbelief. "Wait. You said you plan to keep kissing me?"

"Are you in shock?" He laughs again, a gentle look in his eyes.

That look sends me back into my memories–back to the year when I was learning to ride my bike. I still had training wheels. Aiden, Duke and Chris were pros at riding. They could even go no-handed, or pop a wheelie. Bridgette could ride with them, though she usually didn't want to. I pedaled as fast as my legs would go to keep up with those three boys.

Then, the day came to take my training wheels off. Chris wasn't as protective at age ten as he became later. He just wanted time with his friends without his pesky six-year-old sister in the mix. I can't blame him. Dad took me out front and I wobbled, toppled, got back up, and kept at it.

Duke stopped in front of our house and told Aiden and Chris to go on without him on their ride around the block. He dropped his bike on our front lawn and sat on the lower three steps at the end of the walkway leading to our porch and watched me.

He'd cheer when I got something right and he'd go silent when I fell, until I brushed myself off and then he'd shout something encouraging like, "You've got this, Shannon!"

He had this same look in his eyes back then, soft, caring, and all for me.

"I think I am in shock," I say. "It feels too good to be true."

"Ah. That's what they all say," Duke says with a flex of his bicep, adding a kiss to it to cap off the cocky display. Goofball.

"Could you *please* put on a shirt? For the love."

"That's not what I'm used to hearing from the ladies, Hollywood."

He's teasing me. And I see through it. He knows I'm nervous and he's giving me a dose of his best antics to help me along. And I love him for it. Not love, love. Just, you know, really appreciate in an extra-fond, I-want-to-have-your-babies kind of way.

"Well, get used to things being different," I tease back.

"I could definitely get used to that," he says with a wink.

He stands. "I'll put you out of your misery. Make yourself at home."

He stretches his arms overhead and flexes, intentionally. Then he sends me another wink.

"I'll be right back."

He's almost out of the room when he turns to ask, "Hey, did you eat?"

"Uh. No. I didn't. I mean. I had a salad, but I could eat."

"Worked up an appetite, huh?" He chuckles.

"You've got a way to go before you get me to work up an appetite, Satterson."

Oh. That did not sound the way I meant it to.

He shakes his head and walks around the corner, obviously going to get a T-shirt, which I both appreciate and regret him doing.

I hear him shout from his room, "I'll order Chinese or we can get Mad River Burgers. What sounds good?"

I shout back, "Either is fine."

And then I sink back into the couch and make myself at home. In Duke's house–where he just kissed me.

As soon as that thought hits, I pick up one of the throw pillows, bury my face in it and let out a muffled squeal of joy.

Duke kissed me!

And that changes everything.

THIRTY

Duke

I hear Shannon scream even though I can tell she's trying to cover it up. I chuckle to myself as I grab a T-shirt out of my dresser and pull it on. Then I do a fist pump in the air and let out my own quiet whoop. I don't do that rock star jump. Learned my lesson there.

I make a pit stop in my bathroom to scrub up quickly and put on deodorant. Poor woman had to deal with my post-workout sweat. She didn't seem to be complaining, but now that I have her here, I don't want to scare her off by smelling like a locker room.

I grab two to-go menus from the drawer in the kitchen on my way back to the living room. My heart settles when I see Shannon's still here. She was so freaked out and skittish after that kiss, I wouldn't put it past her to bolt. But, she's sticking around for now, and if I have anything to say about it, she'll be here a lot more often from here on out.

We need to discuss things, like how we'll handle our friends, Chris, our families, and this whole nosy town. But, for tonight, I want to preserve this little bubble we're in as long as I can. We're just going to cozy up with a movie and some chow mein, then we'll kiss some more. And some more. And then, before she's too drowsy, we'll quickly consider the outside world. Just to get our heads on straight and mostly so Shannon knows we've got this—together.

I'm not looking forward to that conversation, or the reality it represents, but I'm tucking everything that's not about me and her out of the way for now so I can go enjoy what I've been waiting for years to experience: Shannon in my arms.

We order take-out Chinese, and I make a call to the pizza guy to have him go out of his way to pick our meal up for us.

There's this awkward moment when Decker knocks and says, "Pizza's here!" through the closed door.

While he's correcting himself to say, "I mean, er, Chinese food!" I get up off the couch to open the door.

Shannon unexpectedly darts off to the kitchen—in a crouched position like she's playing paintball. Maybe she was in a hurry to get drinks to go with the meal, but I'm pretty sure she's hiding from the delivery guy.

My suspicions are confirmed when I come into the kitchen with our food and she's hunkered down behind my small island.

"He's gone," I say, shaking my head and smiling because she's adorable right now. She always is.

"Sorry." She laughs nervously. "I just didn't want to grease the rumor mill."

"Good thinking, actually. So, plates or take out boxes with two forks?"

"Take out boxes, of course."

"Okay then."

I grab the bag while Shannon carries our drinks and we spread the containers of orange chicken, Kung Pao beef, honey walnut shrimp, chow mein, steamed veggies, and egg rolls across the coffee table. I pick up one box, Shannon picks up another and we start digging in.

"This is so good," she says around a bite of noodles.

"Yeah? Let me take a bite."

Instead of turning like she did with our fair food, she takes a forkful of noodles and holds it out to me. I open and let her feed me. Noodles dangle out of my mouth while I try to suck them in and we're both laughing at the mess I make of myself.

This is hands-down the most fun I've had in years. And it's so easy. Being with Shannon always has been effortless. Somehow I thought adding romance to the picture would complicate our natural comfort with one another. The look on her face tells me she's feeling as relaxed with me as I am with her.

We pick a movie–a classic romcom called *My Best Friend's Wedding* with Julia Roberts.

Shannon leans over to check her phone while I'm getting the movie cued. "Agh. My phone died. Do you have a charger?"

"In the kitchen."

She plugs her phone in and then picks up another take-out container before settling back next to me on the couch.

"I'm not touching that stuff. It's all yours," she says, pointing to the container of steamed veggies.

"You and your vegetables," I say laughing.

It strikes me how different this is from anything I've ever done. I'm not used to knowing the little idiosyncrasies of the women I date. I keep things distant on purpose. With Shannon, I already know her more than I know most other people, even my best friends.

We settle in for the movie. Whenever a new actor comes onto the screen, Shannon shares behind-the-scenes trivia about them. We finish our Chinese. Take-out boxes litter my coffee table, and Shannon is tucked into my side.

I shift around a little so my leg extends down the couch and Shannon repositions herself so she's leaning back on me and her legs stretch out between mine.

I never have women over to my home unless you count my sisters. I guess I've been waiting for Shannon to be the one I do all of this with–ordering take out, watching movies while we nestle together, talking, or not needing to talk.

It's her. I've been waiting for her.

Shannon's engrossed in this scene where Julia Roberts is

explaining how the groom actually wants Jell-O–and by Jell-O, Julia means he wants her, not the crème brûlée bride he's planning to marry.

"You're here," I murmur into the top of Shannon's head, sliding my hand down her arm in a soft stroke.

She tilts her head back over her shoulder to look at me and her smile takes my breath away. It's relaxed and it spreads all the way to her eyes. It's as though her whole body is smiling at me.

I kiss her forehead and leave my lips lingering there. She hums this quiet hum and her eyes flutter shut.

Then she flips over so she's straddling my legs and her hands are in my hair, cradling my head while she looks at me like she's in awe. We're sitting here staring at one another, my hands on her hips, her hands in my hair, and our eyes saying so many things to one another.

Then, Shannon slowly leans in and kisses me. It's the sexiest thing I've ever experienced in my life the way she takes charge and moves toward my mouth without ever taking her eyes off mine. She cups my jaw, and then her hands come to rest on my shoulders. We move like a couple who have been together for years, learning the nuances of what it means to fit with another person just right.

This kiss feels like memories and home, temptation and bliss, and I want to devour her, one soft sigh at a time. She's everything I imagined she'd be, but more. She's simultaneously familiar and new. And I'm at her mercy. Nothing matters but this kiss and her.

When we break apart, her eyelids are at half-mast and she's grinning at me with a smile I want to put on her face every day for the rest of our lives. I'm still holding her, unwilling to take my hands away from her waist and hip.

Shannon ruffles my hair playfully, and then exclaims, "We missed the best part of the movie!"

"And you're complaining?"

She wriggles off my lap, grabbing the remote so she can rewind to the part she wants to see. I watch her, unable to act cool or unaffected. She's got me wrapped around her little finger and we both know it.

"Come 'ere," I say, once she hits play.

She scoots over and leans her head toward my chest while I drape my arm around her. She watches the movie. I watch her. It's a win-win.

Before too long, I hear her breathing go shallow. Her head sinks into me a bit. She shifts around to get cozier, probably without even realizing she's doing it, and then she's out.

I let her sleep. Her head is right under my chin. I dip down just the slightest and inhale. She smells like a garden of flowers in spring—like she slept in a pollen shower while fairies dusted her temples with honeysuckle.

What is the matter with me? My brain is officially short-circuiting from her nearness.

Pollen shower? Fairies? Really?

The credits finally roll and I don't move or try to wake her. What happened between us tonight solidified something that had always felt elusive, but there's a thin fragility about everything between us too, as if the slightest wrong touch could shatter what we've just started to explore. I want to hold her to me as long as I'm allowed.

It took us too long to get here.

What if this doesn't last? What if I blow it?

A noise outside makes me turn to look out my front window. Shannon wakes, groggy and disoriented. She looks around and I can see the awareness of everything dawn on her face. Like, *I'm at Duke's? Duke is here. We kissed. I fell asleep on him*. She gives me a sleep-sated smile and stretches.

"What time is it?"

I look at the clock next to the T.V. "It's almost eleven."

"What? Oh my gosh! How long did I sleep?"

"I honestly don't know. You dozed off on me and I liked holding you, so I just let you sleep."

"What would you have done if I hadn't just woken up?"

199

"Stayed here."

"All night?"

"Maybe."

She looks at me with a slight squint in her eyes, but her mouth is turned up in a grin.

"I better go home. I have work tomorrow at eight."

"I'll get your phone."

Shannon uses my restroom and I hand her cell to her when she walks back into the living room.

"Gah!" she says looking down at the screen. "Jayme texted me eight times and I have five missed calls."

Shannon hits Jayme's contact info and leans back onto the arm of my side chair while she calls. She's looking into my eyes, but she's preparing to talk to her roommate.

I only hear Shannon's side of the call, and a few bits of what Jayme says.

"Hey." ... "I'm fine. Sorry I made you worry. My phone died." ... "I'm at Duke's."

Shannon looks at me, raising her eyebrows and pinching her lips together.

"I came over to plan Chris' party."

Not a lie.

She shrugs her shoulders and raises her eyebrows.

"Well, we ended up getting Chinese and watching a movie. I dozed off on his couch."

All true.

She wags her eyebrows at me.

Yeah. I remember what we did too. I'll never forget it.

"Okay. Well, I'm just going to get my stuff together and I'll be home." ... "Okay. And thanks for caring about me. You're the best." ... "Okay. Bye."

She ends the call and looks at me with her business face. "We should probably talk about where things stand before I go."

Her shoulders are squared off as if the talk with Jayme reminded her there's a world out there, outside of this little island of Shaduke ... or Dunnon ... Yeah. Not naming our relationship like the trendy people do. Those are both ridiculous names. Shaduke sounds like one of those nonsensical words in a nineteen-fifties song. Shaaa-duke, shawada wada. Shaaaa-duke. Nope. And Dunnon sounds like yogurt.

"What do you think?" Shannon asks.

"Sorry. I was thinking of our relationship name."

"What?"

"Nevermind. Yeah. We need to talk about us."

"Okay," Shannon says, crossing her arms over her chest. Business mode. Right. Okay.

"May I say something first?" I ask her.

"Sure."

I'm standing between the front door and Shannon. I want us both to move to the couch, but I can tell she's feeling uptight, so I stay where I am.

In a soothing voice, with as much sincerity as I feel, I start to share my heart with her.

"I want you to trust me. I've finally got you. I'm not letting you go. We obviously need to talk about what we tell people about this ..."

"Or *if* we tell them," she says.

"Do you not want to tell them?"

"I do." She pauses and looks past me toward my front yard. "I just wonder if we should wait. This is all so new. As soon as people know, they'll be talking, and we'll be like Prince Harry and Meghan Markle. They had to make a Megxit from being royal because of the insanity of being under the magnifying glass at all times. Their every move was under public scrutiny."

I shake my head. She earns her nickname. Such a tabloid connoisseur. Still, she has a point. As soon as anyone hears of us spending extra time together, let alone pursuing anything romantic, there will be no rest for either of us.

"So, you want to keep this quiet?" I ask.

"Well, what if word gets back to Chris and neither of us were the ones to tell him?"

She looks wounded by the mere thought of what it would do to Chris. The expression on her face mirrors my feelings. It would kill me if Chris found out some backward way. I want to man up and talk to him, and I need the chance to do that before word spreads to him–which it would before the sun comes up if we're not careful.

"We should be the ones to tell him," Shannon says. "And I don't think we should text or call. He needs to hear this in person. He's trying to focus on ending his career in the military right now. We need to give him that much."

I nod. I totally agree. But, the reality of our options is sinking in like a giant boulder in my gut. I finally have Shannon, and now I have to slurk around as if she's my dirty secret instead of parading her around like I want to do.

I want to hold her hand at the movies, to take her out to eat, to have her jump up into my arms when my team wins a game. I want to hang out as a couple with our friends who are couples. I want the whole picture.

I don't want to keep us in the shadows. But, we don't have much choice.

"I think we should tell Chris in person," Shannon continues. "If this is going to be a thing. I mean, more than a few weeks of a thing."

"Oh. It's a thing." I give her a serious look.

How does she still not realize it?

She's all I want. And I definitely want her.

I'm going to convince her how much I've wanted her and will always want her–whatever that takes.

"Okay. Then we need to tell Chris in person," Shannon says with a single nod of her head. "We should let him come home, settle in, and then we'll take him somewhere and break the news to him."

"Somewhere secluded? And is he sedated in this scenario?"

She giggles.

"You laugh, but you're not the one he is going to possibly kill. And that's not a euphemism."

"He won't kill you." Shannon rolls her eyes.

"Right. Maim. That's so much better."

"Back to the plan."

"The plan that ends in my death or dismemberment?"

She rolls her eyes again.

"I'm only half joking," I say. "Or a quarter joking. Whatever. You're worth it. A few weeks with you and I'll be ready to die."

"What did you just say?"

"That came out wrong. I mean, I'd rather have a few weeks with you and face the wrath of Chris St. James than not have you."

"Awww."

Shannon gets up, walks over to me, and stands on her tiptoes. She gently kisses me on the cheek.

"That was sweet, Duke."

"Oh, I can be very, very sweet. Wanna practice? I'll be sweet and you kiss me every time I'm sweet. It'll be fun." I wag my eyebrows.

She yawns.

"Next time," I tell her, putting my arm around her shoulders. "We'll play *Duke's the Sweetest* next time you're here. Tonight, let's get you home safely. We won't let anyone know we're together for now. It's going to be hard. But I believe in us."

"You do?" She tilts her head and looks up at me, the question written all over her face.

"I do."

"Okay. Well ..." Shannon shifts her weight from foot to foot.

"We've got this. I've got you. Keeping things under wraps is temporary. And you were smart and thoughtful to think of what could happen. I've been in a total Shannon haze over here and I would have made a mess of this. But, I've got you now."

"A Shannon haze?" she asks, giving me a seductive grin.

"Delirious over you, Hollywood. You've got me upside down and inside out in the best of ways."

I turn toward her and pull her in for a hug, but she moves in for a kiss when I do, and I'm not complaining–not in the least. I hold her to me after the kiss, memorizing the feel of her in my arms.

I want to ask her when I'll see her again, which is cheesy as all get out, so I don't. We live in the same town. We'll see each other.

"We still need to plan Chris' party," she reminds me.

"That we do, considering how much we accomplished tonight."

"I think we accomplished the most important thing," she says. This time she winks at me, and I'm done for.

Shannon grabs her purse. I put my hand on her back and hold the door open for her. We walk toward her car in silence. It takes me a beat before I realize I can't have my hand on her back right now in case Mrs. Greenleaf is watching.

Remember that character, Roz, in Monsters Inc.? She'd always say "I'm watching you," in this nasally, menacing voice. I feel like our whole town is silently saying that line right now. They're watching us. Always watching.

THIRTY-ONE

Shannon

I'm flying around the house like a madwoman this morning. I slept like a rock when I got home, a blissed-out, dreamy, well-kissed rock. Thankfully, Jayme was already asleep. But, she's not sleeping now. Not at all.

"So, you and Duke planned Chris' party last night?"

"Mmhmm."

I stick my head in the fridge pretending to look for something to eat, even though I rarely eat breakfast. If Jayme sees my face, she'll read me like a book. A romance novel, to be exact.

She'll be like, "Aha! You were kissed–well kissed–last night!" Then I'll have to tell her everything, which in one way would be great, and a huge relief. But, in another, very important way, would be tempting fate too far. It's one thing for Jayme to know I have a crush on Duke. It's another to know he and I are ... whatever we are.

I smile big. I mean, big like a first-grader on picture day. You know. The smiles where every tooth shows and the smile almost takes over their whole face? That's me, head in the fridge and a grin that would win elections right now. A first-grader for president! Whatever. It's early. I'm in luh ... like ... lots and lots of like

... and I don't think I'm going to be very good at this secret-keeping thing.

I think of Chris and my smile fades. I have to be strong for him. He deserves to be the first to know. I keep thinking of Chris, and not Duke, that six pack, our couch snuggles, feeding him Chinese ... Nope. Just Chris. Serious, stern, overprotective, pain-in-my-tush Chris.

"Are you trying to cool the house by way of the fridge?" Jayme asks from behind me. "I already made you a smoothie and I'm not quite sure what else you could be looking for in there."

"You made me a smoothie?"

"I already told you that when you descended the stairs with that quixotic look on your face."

"Oh no. No you don't. I went to bed late. I have to work. I'm out of soda. I don't want to translate. Please, please speak English."

She just chuckles. "Sorry. If you were normal and drank coffee like the rest of the human race, I'd make you a pot every morning. I'd even froth milk. But, alas. You drink a concoction of chemicals."

"Which makes me nice. I'm nice when I drink chemicals. And awake. Coffee is gross."

I pick up my smoothie from the counter and take a sip.

"This smoothie is delicious, though. And you are amazing. I wish you wanted a relationship, because any man would be lucky to have you."

"I had a man, if you'll remember. The man who thought red-headed strangers with big ... nevermind. I have men. Dozens of them."

"I'm not talking about your aliens and vampires or the fae who loved me." I make air quotes around that last phrase.

"That fae was smokin' and the epitome of a cinnamon roll hero."

I suppress a smile.

"No doubt. But, you know he's not real, right?"

"Sort-of. He's real enough. Real enough that I'm happy. No man could live up to my book boyfriends. And I have you and the kids and so much more. I'm happily done with men. Human men, that is."

She calls the cats and Groucho her kids. I'm fine with it. It's cute, really. And, hmmm. Maybe this explains why all her romances are with fantasy creatures and not real men. I'd like to get a hold of the man who broke her heart. I'm not violent, but my legs are strong and I could do some damage. He'd heal, but not before he remembered how badly he hurt one of the sweetest people on earth.

"You do have me. And you always will."

"Not if your secret admirer takes action." She lightly shakes her head after saying that as if she's not a fan of his anymore.

"Or Duke," she adds quietly.

I'd almost forgotten the secret admirer. Flowers kept trickling in for a while, they've slowed recently. Jayme kept her lips sealed about his identity. Now I'm in a bit of a pickle. I don't want anyone but Duke. I never did, but now I really don't. Well, this guy, whomever he is, hasn't come forward, so it's not even an issue right now.

I decide to fully ignore the Duke comment since she barely said it.

"Anyway," Jayme says. "Sip your smoothie while I tell you that quixotic basically means idealistic, head-in-the-clouds. That was you this morning. You practically floated down the stairs. Then you nearly bumped into the dining table. And I've never seen you bump into anything. You're a dancer. You glide through life. So, what gives?"

She's too observant for her own good. I refuse to lie. I'll hide, which, I guess technically is a little like lying, but it's a sin of omission, not commission. And I tend to think it's staying on a side of the line that works under certain circumstances. Protecting Chris' heart is one of those times when a little omission is justified. I'll skirt the truth, but I'm not going to start making up whoppers.

"I'm tired. It was a late night."

Truth.

The best late night of my life. But she doesn't have to know that.

"And the floating, all ethereal and starry-eyed?"

"Don't know what to tell you."

Man, if that isn't the truth!

"So, what did you and Duke work out about the party? You were there for a long time."

"Mostly we watched a movie and ate Chinese. We still have a lot of details to hammer out. I'll let you know."

Gimme More blares through my phone. Saved by Britney. #FreeShannon. Whew. That was close.

"I gotta run. Let's see if the girls want to come over tonight. It's Friday and I feel like a girls' night."

What did I just say? For one thing, I want to see Duke. A lot. Like, every waking moment.

For another, if skirting the truth around Jayme was hard, what will it be like when the two women who've known me since elementary school are here, cornering me? And Em will be here too. She's sharp, even though she hasn't known me as long.

We do girls' night regularly. It's less often now that three of the five of us are married, but that makes it all the more special. I wasn't thinking. It just came out. Of course I'd want a girls' night. Only now, I'm going to be on pins and needles the whole night.

I'm about to shut down my computer at my desk and head over to the Dippity Do for my afternoon appointments when I see a man walking down the sidewalk toward our office.

He's stunning. A little rough around the edges, but that makes him all the more perfect. And when his eyes meet mine, a flurry of tingly flutters erupts in my stomach. Are those butterflies? This man is giving me my first case of actual butterflies.

He pauses outside the window and simply stares at me with that predatorial smirk–the one he gave me last night before he kissed me and the world slipped off its axis.

I can't look away, especially when he licks that lower lip of his and runs his hand across his jawline.

I finally manage to look away, shaking my head lightly, glancing down at my desk, aware of the blush rising up my neck toward my face. He's a rogue. And now he's my rogue. At least, I think he is.

When I look back at him, he's still staring. He's mouthing, "I want you."

I giggle nervously. This feels so fun and a little dangerous. Just like him. Dangerous, but also, ironically, so very safe.

"Are you okay out here?" Dad says as he walks into the reception area.

He must have heard me giggle.

Duke steps away from the window and toward the door. Well. This will be interesting. Or a disaster.

"I'm fine," I assure my dad. "I just thought of something funny from last night. I'm wrapping up here. Do you need anything else for today?"

"No. I'm fine. Have a good weekend, dear. And if you have time, stop in on your mom. No pressure, but she always brightens up when she sees you."

"Oh, Duke. Good afternoon," Dad shifts his focus from me to the interloper who is trying to push every limit for some unknown reason. Oh, except, he's Duke. Pushing limits is his specialty.

I feel like my face has been painted with the words, "We kissed! Oh, how we kissed!" I look down at my desk and hunt for my purse–which is right in front of me. Well, lookie there.

"Good afternoon, Mister St. James. I thought I'd pop by to talk about a financial decision I'm trying to make. Sorry I didn't make an appointment."

"I'm not busy, Duke. Small town on a Friday. You know how

it goes. Though, I imagine you have people popping in with last minute repairs all day on Friday."

"It gets busy, that's a fact. People want to bring their issues in at the end of the week, hoping we'll work some magic and keep them from being out of an automobile over a weekend."

Duke hasn't given me the time of day since he crossed the threshold, which is for the best. But also unnerving.

"Oh, hello, Shannon," he finally says. "You look beautiful today."

"Thanks," I say, giving him a death glare while my dad turns to walk back to his office.

"I'll be right in here, Duke. Come on back after you chat with my beautiful daughter for a minute or two."

Not good.

"Will do, sir."

"Living up to my reputation as a flirt isn't hard today," Duke says in a low whisper that does things to me. "You make it easy, Hollywood."

Duke winks a lot. Some guys who wink are being smarmy or presumptuous. Some just look like they need a bottle of eye drops. Not Duke. When he winks at me it's like we've got a little secret. And it feels delicious. And, hooo buddy, do we have a secret.

"Did you really think it was good to come here like this?" I ask him in a stage whisper.

"Better to hide in plain sight," he says. "Besides, I couldn't wait to see you again. And now I have. But I messed up, because I thought seeing you would be enough. It's not even close. I just want more. What have you done to me, Hollywood?"

Oh my gosh. This man.

I don't even have words.

I'm blushing, and my skin is all tingly and warm. I just want to hug him or kiss him, or both. Lots of both. And I've felt that way for so long. But, now I can do all those things–and yet I can't.

He showed up at my work, knowing we'd both be stuck doing

nothing about what we feel for one another. Well, the least I can do is give him a little of his own medicine. Besides, it will serve as a prelude to whenever we are alone together again. Which won't be tonight, thanks to me and my big mouth.

I lick my lips oh so slowly, looking up at Duke through my lashes as I do. He shifts his weight just a little. Mmhmm. He feels it.

Then I tuck my bottom lip in with my teeth and when I let it pop out, I say in a slightly husky voice, "Mister St. James is waiting for you, Mister Satterson. I have to get to my job at the salon. Have a good day."

I turn and walk toward the door, knowing full well I'm being watched.

THIRTY-TWO

Duke

Shannon is a minx.

I had no idea. She's been taunting me for years, but it never seemed intentional. Today, she turned the tables on me at her dad's office, and I loved every torturous second of it.

I want to see her tonight. I need to see her. But, I also don't want to freak her out by being all needy and smothering. This preoccupation isn't like me. I'm not being prideful when I say I'm usually the one being pursued while trying to keep things light. I've never felt this unhinged and eager for time with another person.

I don't have the strongest track record with committed relationships, but now I see that's because I was always on the wrong track.

As soon as I'm out of my very legitimate meeting with Shannon's dad, I send her a text. I'm not even to my car when I start typing.

Duke: *I like that thing you did with your lips.*
Shannon: *Talking?*
Duke: *Nope. You know the thing.*
Shannon: *Smiling?*

Duke: *I do love your smile. But, nope.*
Shannon: *Eating?*
Duke: *The way you licked your lips and bit down on your bottom lip. ... Am I allowed to text about that?*
Shannon: *You just did. And, I'm glad you liked it.*
Duke: *I'd like a repeat performance in private.*
Shannon: *Would you now?*
Duke: *I'm a very appreciative audience.*
Shannon: *Sounds fun. And, sadly, I have girls' night tonight.*
Duke: *Til when?*
Shannon: *We don't set a timer and call it quits when the buzzer sounds. I really don't know.*
Duke: *Let's see. Three married women, one with a toddler. One with two elementary school-aged kids. I'm thinking eight-thirty. Nine if you all go wild and crazy.*
Shannon: *You're not making a good argument for marriage and kids.*
Duke: *I make a great argument for both marriage and kids under the right circumstances. My point is. You're free after nine.*
Shannon: *Hypothetically.*
Duke: *Then let's hypothetically plan for you to meet me outside your house so I can hypothetically drive you some-where away from prying eyes and get a repeat performance of that lip thing. I'd like a front row seat. In a seat very, very close to you.*
Shannon: *I'm blushing now, and Laura is looking at me with a some mucus grin.*
Shannon: *Soup is us*
Shannon: *Super bus*
Shannon: *Suspicious. Gah! Suspicious grin!*
Shannon: *If I can slip out, I'll text you. If not, let's plan something tomorrow.*
Duke: *Just look up at Laura and say, "Duke's making me*

laugh. We're planning Chris' party."... Can you stay after
Zumba tomorrow and watch the game?
Shannon: *I told Laura you were making me laugh. She*
shook her head like she knows you and your antics. I think I
can stay after Zumba.
Duke: *Good. Then we can "party plan" after the game.*
Shannon: *Why is that in quotes? We really do need to*
party plan.
Duke: *I love when we party plan.*
Shannon: *You're incorrigible.*
Duke: *Always have been. Moreso where you're concerned.*
Shannon: *My one o'clock is here. Gotta run.*
Duke: *See you tonight. When you sneak out.*

She doesn't answer. Her appointment obviously arrived. I've
been leaning on the door of my car, staring at my phone and grinning like a lovesick fool. When I look up, Aiden's standing a few
feet away on the sidewalk studying me.

"What's got you smiling like that?" he asks as he walks
toward me.

"Nothing much. I'm a smiley guy."

"A woman, huh? I thought you were abstaining after Beth.
Getting Shannon out of your system."

Yeah. Well. That plan sort of took an unexpected turn when
Shannon ran her hand up my bicep and pulled lightly on the back
of my hair while we kissed like teenagers in my kitchen yesterday.

I wish I could say that out loud to Aiden. Well, not that,
exactly. But, something about Shannon and how we finally made
our way to one another, and I will never want or try to get her out
of my system ever again.

"Yeah. It's not some woman." I tell Aiden.

Truth-ish. It's technically not some woman. Can I say how
much I hate keeping details from my closest friends? I'm not a liar
and I don't like feeling like I have to cover up something so
amazing with half-truths.

"What brings you into town?" I ask.

"Just picking up feed and running a few errands for Em."

"Don't tell me she has cravings already."

"Shhh," he says, even though no one is near us. He lowers his voice and says, "No cravings yet. She just needed some odds and ends, so I'm her man for the job."

An image of Shannon waiting at home for me someday while I run and get her things at a store flashes across my brain. I like that image so much I can't contain my smile.

"There's that smile again. And it's a lot like the smile of a man in love. What gives?"

"Just happy for you. Hoping for my own happily ever after one day. That's all."

Aiden eyes me suspiciously. "Yeah. I'm living the dream. Running errands."

We both chuckle.

Then he asks, "Are you coming out to the Res tomorrow evening? Rob and Laura said they're going and Trev and Lex will be there. Em's going to girls' night at Jayme and Shannon's tonight. She said she's going to ask them while she's there."

"Yeah. I'll come. I've got a game at noon."

"We'll be there–at the game."

"Good. You gotta get Ty around the sport so he gets a feel for it. I'll be recruiting him next year."

"You're dedicated. I'll give you that."

I think of the coaching offer I'm mulling over. I can't tell Aiden about Shannon, but maybe I should ask him about my opportunity with the high school.

"You got a minute to grab a bite or a drink somewhere? I need to bounce something off you. We can always talk later if not. I've only got an hour til I have to get back to the garage."

"I've always got time for you. Let me text Em and I'll meet you at Bean There Done That in a few minutes."

I pocket my phone and hop in the Shelby, running my hands over the dash and appreciating her more than ever. I lucked into this car, restored her from scratch. Do I love her? A little.

"Love ya' Shelb," I say. Then I crack up at myself.

I turn the key and shoot over to Bean There Done That and park in one of the spaces out front. The lunch crowd has dissipated. Tables are wide open aside from a few stragglers.

I walk to the counter and order a bagel with cream cheese and a black coffee. The coffee here is the type Pops ought to be drinking instead of that sludgy stuff he makes in that ancient pot in the office. I need to get him a new coffee maker for Christmas, and maybe a subscription to one of those coffee-of-the-month clubs.

Aiden walks in behind me and places his order. I walk to a booth in the front corner, away from the counter and any occupied tables.

"So, what's up?" Aiden asks as he slides into the bench across from me.

"Something big," I admit.

Saying it out loud makes it real. Asking Jayme to help was one thing. I'm only agreeing to taking the exam for now. Doesn't mean I'll do anything about it if I pass.

"I'm all ears," Aiden says.

He's got such an ease about him when it comes to helping others. It's like he was born to bear other people's burdens. It rarely weighs him down, and he tends to have solid wisdom most of the time.

I clear my throat. "Well, Principal Barnes called me a little over a month ago. He wants me to coach the baseball and football teams for the high school."

"That's awesome! You were made for that. I always figured you'd end up coaching somehow. Back in the day we all thought you might go pro. But, no one plays forever. I don't know why, but I imagined you'd come back here and settle down when you retired from the majors. And then you'd coach."

"Really?"

I'm struck dumb. I stare at Aiden like he's a stranger.

"You thought about my future?"

"Well, yeah. I thought about you and Chris—all of us—what was going to happen, where we'd live, who we'd marry. That was when I was with Millie, so I figured she and I would settle down together. I didn't know who you or Chris would end up with. I saw the military for him a while before he decided on it. He's made for that kind of thing."

I shake my head, studying Aiden.

"I don't think I ever thought about your future once, except to tease you about needing to get off the farm to find a woman, and I was dead wrong about that. I'm a crap friend."

"You're a great friend. You make me laugh and you're there when I need my head straightened out. You've always had my back. I'm just different than you. I think about people—study them—consider what's next for them. It's kind of like a game."

"I could see that. Like guessing where they're headed and then watching to see if you were right or not."

"Exactly. What else are we supposed to do for fun around here?"

We both laugh. It's a known fact we find plenty to do. But there's a season in every life of a person living in a small town where you feel like this bored kid on a hot summer day with nothing to do. You whine to everyone who'll give you the time of day about how small and boring this podunk town is. You itch to shake the dust off your boots and go where the action is.

Later you get over it. Or you don't. Those who don't usually move on. The rest of us find the good in the simple things like bonfires and festivals, barn dancing and nights around the lake.

Most of all, it's the people. We may drive one another nuts, but we wouldn't know what to do without one another. That's the best part of a small town—the people.

Aiden's sitting quietly, giving me time to think while he sips his coffee and breaks off a bit of the pastry he bought. I notice a bag to the right of him. Good man. Bought his wife a treat while he was in town.

I thought I was going to the majors years ago too. What would have happened to Pops and the garage then? I didn't even give that one thought in my teens. Mom was alive and it seemed like I could pursue anything I wanted. Ball was it. But then she died, I got injured, and everything changed. And I got stuck—or I took my rightful place. I'm not sure which.

"I put all those dreams somewhere far out of reach years ago," I admit to Aiden.

"That happens. But, now you've got this opportunity."

I nod. "But I have to think of Pops and the garage and this town."

"That's a lot for you to be responsible for. Anyone else you want to add to that list? Maybe you could add Pluto. No one's looking out for Pluto since it got kicked out of our solar system."

I chuckle, shaking my head lightly.

"Point taken. Kind of ironic coming from the man who takes on others' needs in his sleep."

"I've grown a lot since last year."

"I know you have."

"What I'm saying is you aren't responsible for over two thousand cars and the people who own them. Your pops just wants you to be happy. I know that's true. Sure. What man hasn't looked at his son and hoped he'd follow in his footsteps, only do more and better? It's a thing with us dads."

"You dads. When did this happen? My best friend is a dad. It's pretty mind blowing."

"And it's the best thing that ever happened to me. Em and the kids are my world."

"And here I thought I was the best thing that ever happened to you."

"I'll always love you, snookums."

He blows me a kiss for good measure.

I pretend to catch his kiss and then I puff my chest out. "It comes with being me. People love me. They can't help themselves. I've tried to get used to it."

Aiden shakes his head, but he's smiling.

"All I'm saying is you don't owe this town or your dad to keep Satterson's alive and running. And, buckle up, this next thought might level you. Maybe someone else will fill your shoes at the garage."

"And who would that be? Bubba White? Decker? Cooter?"

"I'm not saying just anyone could step in. We all know you're exceptional at what you do. But, you never know who might step in. Maybe someone will move here. Either way, don't shut out the possibility of following your dream solely based on some unspoken obligation you feel to your pops or this town."

I nod again. It's a lot to take in all that Aiden is saying. I take a sip of my coffee. My bagel sits on the plate untouched.

"What does Pops say about all this?"

"I haven't mentioned it to him."

Aiden looks at me with his eyebrows up and his mouth twisted to the side. "I see."

"I know what you're going to say. I need to talk to him. And you're probably right. But, I don't want to burden him with this. He'll probably say I should do this thing–go coach and teach. He'd never tell me how much I'm letting him down. But it would be there in his eyes, and it would haunt me."

"If he feels disappointed and doesn't tell you, then that's his business. If he wants you to stay at the garage and doesn't say anything about that to you, well, his loss. I know that's hard to swallow. But, it's not up to you to run ahead of him, figure out what he needs, and make sure those needs are met. He's a grown man. If he doesn't tell you his real thoughts, that's on him."

"How did you get so smart?"

"Hanging out with you."

I laugh.

Aiden's eyes lock on mine. I can't find a trace of humor in his expression.

"You'll be a great coach," he says. "You already are. You've got a way with kids, and you see through people like no one I know."

"I don't know what to say."

"And, if you want to take on Satterson's and grow old being the third generation to pump gas and fix cars, do that. Make it yours. Own that shop with pride. And never look back."

I give him a slow clap, which turns some heads. I'm half-joking, but also deeply moved. When it came to making lifelong friends, I hit the jackpot.

"Man, you should run for mayor! That speech was awesome."

Aiden laughs hard. "Weren't you the one to tell me to cut back on responsibilities just last year?"

"You would make a great mayor, though. Admit it."

"Yeah. Maybe. You never know. I better get back to being king in the meantime."

"King?"

"Of my castle," he says as he stands and grabs his plate and cup. "Oh yeah, man. You know I'm the ruler of all I survey."

We both laugh hard.

"You know Billy Jean rules that farm," I say, referring to his lead goat.

"You got me there."

We set our plates on the counter. The worker asks me if I want my bagel to go. Aiden stands with me while I wait for her to bag it up.

"Thanks. Really. I needed this."

"Anytime. You know that. Oh! And I heard you and Shannon are collaborating to put together a welcome home party for Chris. Let me know if you need anything for that."

"How did you hear that?"

"Bordeaux."

That's a complete answer. Our town.

It's a good reminder that nothing stays private or hidden for long. Shannon and I might be deceiving ourselves if we think we're controlling the narrative about our relationship.

THIRTY-THREE

Shannon

"Grab that tray of appetizers and bring it out to the living room," Jayme says.

She's had writer's block all day, which translates into her cooking up a blue streak. We have puff pastries filled with artichoke hearts, ricotta and pesto, bacon wrapped dates, homemade hummus with crackers, and a charcuterie board with fruit, nuts, meats, cheeses and pickled veggies. She also made homemade lemonade in three flavors: blueberry, strawberry and pure lemonade.

"Are you okay?" I ask Jayme, picking up the tray.

"I'm fine. Just fine. Really, really fine."

She's flitting from spot to spot in the kitchen, checking things, putting items from baking sheets onto platters, stirring, wiping, spreading.

She reminds me of one of those cartoons where the character zips from one spot to the next. She's the culinary version of Speedy Gonzales.

"Arriba, arriba ... andale, andale!" I shout as I make my way into the living room.

There's a knock at the door and Jayme lets out this anxious squeal from the kitchen.

"Laura and Lexi are here!" I shout over my shoulder.

I open the door and let them in. Groucho makes his way over to greet Laura. He's got a dog-crush on her. She dotes on him more than most people, so she's earned his excessive devotion. He makes some embarrassing grunting noises while she bends to pet him.

"Make yourselves at home. I'm just going to see if Jayme needs anything." Like mouth to mouth, or a strong sedative.

I walk back to the kitchen.

Jayme's pacing with her hands in her hair.

"Hey," I say.

She keeps tugging on the strands and looking around.

"I can't remember where I put the baked Brie," she says with a note of panic to her tone.

"Oven?" I ask.

She looks at me like I just solved a Rubix cube in under fifteen seconds. Then she grabs oven mitts and opens the oven door. "Oh my gosh! How did I not set a timer?"

I walk over, take the oven mitts out of her hands, point to our kitchenette table and say, "Sit. Now."

Jayme looks at me with a stunned expression, but then she pulls out one of the four chairs and plops down.

"Talk to me, Jayme. You have cooked enough food to cater a small wedding. You're scurrying around like your tail feathers are on fire. What is going on?"

I pull the brie out and pop the oven door shut with my hip.

Jayme buries her face in her hands.

"I got an email today," she mumbles into her palms. "From my agent."

"A good email or a bad email?"

"There's this publisher that wants my vampire series."

"That's great!"

She looks like she could cry.

"It's not great?"

"It's great, but it's so scary."

"Vampires, duh?" I joke.

She rolls her eyes, but a small smile breaks through.

"I mean it's scary for me. Like, what if this really happens? What if I get picked up by this publishing house, and then I have to write on demand? But I can't write good books anymore because I'm mentally blocked by all the pressure, and then I fail miserably. And I don't merely bomb in my little obscure invisible corner of the writing world, but I flop on a big stage while people are all watching me?"

I set the Brie in the empty spot among the variety of crackers on the board Jayme had set out. Then I slide into the seat across from her at the table.

"Breathe," I tell her.

She does.

"That's better. I'm pretty sure every writer goes through this. But, you'll do great. They wouldn't be asking you for these books if they didn't already know how good they are. So what. You couldn't write today. You'll occasionally have days like that. I had days when I couldn't land a jump or turn. But you'll have way more days where the words flow and you're in the zone."

She looks up at me, her shoulders relaxing just a little.

"I hope you're right."

"I know I'm right. And if you flop on the big stage, at least you will have taken the chance. You'll never reach your dreams if you don't take a few risks along the way."

Jayme smiles and nods.

"Can we celebrate? With the girls? Or do you want to keep this a secret?"

"It's just an email from my agent. The first of many."

"Let's celebrate ... Here's to the email!"

I pick up my glass of lemonade and raise it high. Jayme doesn't have lemonade yet, so she raises her empty hand. I say "clink" before I drink a sip.

"Mmm good. You make the best lemonade. And the best

fortunes for Chinese cookies, and amazing flower arrangements. And you write really great romances between non-humans!"

"What's gotten into you?"

"What do you mean?"

"You're just so ... happy."

Duke.

I want to say his name. To shout it. To sing it. To make up an interpretive dance in honor of him.

Instead I say, "I'm happy for you. Now come on, let's go share this news with the girls."

We stand and hug and then we each grab more of the food and walk into the living room. Em has arrived since I went to check on Jayme.

The five of us grab seats on the couch and living room chairs and settle into our usual easy conversation. No matter how long we go between girls' nights, we fall right back in where we left off whenever we get back together.

After I announce Jayme's big news, and we properly embarrass her with a toast and cheers, Lexi shares that Poppy's starting to say words.

"She's calling Trevor Dada and won't say mama yet."

"It's not fair," Laura laments. "The mom does so much and then the babies go and say 'dada' first."

"You've seen how she looks at Trevor," Lexi says with a warm smile. "He's her world."

"Such a daddy's girl," Laura says.

"I hate to see when she starts dating. He's going to be something else," I say.

"Oh my gosh! I know," Lexi says. "He already told me she's not allowed to date until she's twenty-five."

We all laugh.

Em shares about the kids and the farm. Laura talks about a trip she and Rob will be taking to Hollywood for his contract out there with the studios.

I have the strongest urge to tell my closest friends all about

Duke. I'm finally dating him and I can't say a thing about it. Not yet.

As if she's reading my thoughts, Laura says, "So, I hear you and Duke are planning a homecoming party for Chris."

"Yep."

"Just the two of you?" Lexi asks.

It's an innocent enough question, but I blush.

Jayme catches my eye from across the room. I smile at her and look away before she reads my expression and figures out more than I want anyone to know right now.

"We're just starting to plan. We'll get everyone involved once we have the details worked out."

"Mrs. McIntyre told me you were doing some planning at Duke's last night." Lexi says with a coy grin.

Laura wags her eyebrows and Jayme looks like her wheels are spinning far too close to the truth.

I choke on the bacon wrapped date I just popped into my mouth. All I can do is nod while my eyes water and I get my breath back under control.

When my voice comes back, I say, "We were planning at his house. I stopped by there after work."

I look at Jayme and she gives me a questioning glance.

"Convenient," Laura says with a wink. "Anything we should know about? Did you two make out?"

Of course she asks this. She's too blunt for her own good.

I straighten. "We talked about the party a little, then we watched a movie and ordered Chinese. Like I said, we'll share details when we're ready."

And I mean it.

As much as the details of my night with Duke feel like water boiling right up to the edge of a pot, I can't spill anything.

"You two would make the cutest couple," Em says, oblivious to the history this town has of trying to endlessly matchmake us ever since Chris left for the military. She wasn't here all those years.

"Wouldn't they?" Laura adds, unhelpfully.

Lexi chimes in, "Too bad they're like siblings." She wags her eyebrows toward me.

Laura laughs, "Siblings my fanny. That's some high-voltage chemistry. There's nothing sibling about it."

"We're talking about Duke here," I remind them. "He's a flirt. He doesn't settle down. He's got chemistry with anything on legs."

As much as I'm throwing out a diversion, I hear my own words and the grain of truth in them feels more like a bowling ball to the gut.

Duke is a flirt. And he doesn't settle down. What makes me any different? Have I fallen under his spell? Is he just having a good time? He says what we're doing is unlike anything he ever had with anyone else. But is it?

"Unfortunate," Em says. "But, then again, I think for the right woman, any man will settle down. Or at least any good man, and Duke's a good man."

"He really is," Jayme says.

I hope they're right.

Thankfully, Em brings up the plans to go to the reservoir tomorrow evening and then the conversation shifts to the Fourth of July, and all talk of me and Duke seems to be forgotten—at least by everyone in the room but me.

THIRTY-FOUR

Shannon

I hate to say Duke was right, but he was so right. By eight-thirty, Lexi starts making comments that she should get back to Poppy. Then Em says she should get back to the farm. It's not even nine when our three guests are filing out the front door toward their cars, each of them carrying a plastic grocery bag full of homemade finger foods.

I'm standing next to Jayme in the kitchen as we wash the dishes and clean up from her cooking frenzy. I don't know how I'll manage to get out to meet Duke. I probably should text him to tell him we'll have to take a rain check.

I'm about to go grab my cell when Jayme says, "I'm exhausted."

"I imagine," I say, looking around at the stack of dishes drying in the rack and the rest of the leftovers we packed into containers. "You basically hosted a one-woman version of *MasterChef* or *Beat Bobby Flay* in here."

She laughs, shaking her head at herself. "I think I'll head up to bed as soon as I pop these containers in the fridge,"

"Good call. Actually, let me do that. You just go on up and get ready for bed. I'll see you in the morning before I leave for Zumba."

"You sure?"

"Very."

My heart starts beating a bit faster. Maybe I will be able to sneak out to meet Duke.

Jayme trudges upstairs. I make quick work of stashing the tupperware in the fridge, turn off the kitchen light, and then I grab my cell.

Shannon: *Coast is clear. Do you still want to hang out tonight?*

I wait a bit. Duke doesn't answer. Maybe he's asleep. It's only nine-thirty, though. He could have given up on me or changed his mind. My thoughts start to spiral, and then my phone buzzes with a notification.

Duke: *Sorry. I thought my phone was next to me. It was in the kitchen. Why would you even ask if I still want to hang out? I've been sitting here waiting for your text since eight.*
Shannon: *You have?*
Duke: *In a totally cool, manly way. Just being there for you. Not in a dying to see you and completely coming unglued, uncool way. Just to be clear.*
Shannon: *Oh, we're totally clear.*

My face nearly splits open with a grin. He's been waiting by the phone for me. For me.

Duke: *I'm already at my truck.*
Shannon: *That fast? And your truck? When did you get a truck?*
Duke: *It's technically the garage truck. But, I drove it home in the event you'd be available. I'll park across the street from your house unless you think I should park further down.*

Shannon: *Across the street should be fine.*
Duke: *On my way. See you in a few minutes.*

I grab my purse off the side table and pop my phone into it. Then I slowly open the front door and guide it to click softly behind me. I pad across the porch barefooted, carrying my sandals in my hand. When the reality of what we're doing becomes clear, I shake my head at myself. We're two grown adults sneaking around like we're teenagers.

I see the lights of the pickup come down the street toward me and my heart rate clips into a gallop. Duke cuts the lights and slows the truck without killing the engine. I open the door and hop up, and before I'm even buckled, he starts to roll down the street.

I burst into a nervous laugh.

"Pretty fun, huh?" Duke says, winking across the cab of the truck at me.

"Pretty crazy."

"Scoot over here," he commands.

"Bossy."

"I can be very bossy when needed. I haven't touched you all day, I'm in the cab of a pickup. I want you sitting next to me."

"Okay then, Satterson."

I unbuckle and move to the center of the seat. Duke puts his hand on my knee like he's been doing it for years.

Then he says, "That's more like it."

I don't argue because that is more like it.

Way more like it.

I let out a breath I didn't know I was holding.

"Did you ever sneak out as a teen?" he asks.

"Maybe. I mean, of course Laura had us all doing crazy things like hijacking tractors and jumping into the Res at night."

"With a guy though? Did you ever sneak out to meet a guy?"

"Do you really want the answer to that?"

"Yeah. Maybe not," he chuckles. "I'd just like to be your first."

"You're my first," I tell him.

"And I hope I'm the last," he says with ease, like it's normal for him to declare some sort of life-long commitment when we've only been together a little over twenty-four hours.

I don't say my next thought out loud.

I hope he's the last too. With everything I am, I hope so.

Duke gives my knee a little squeeze and says, "I thought we'd drive out by the Clawson's place."

"Now you know good and well the only reason a boy takes a girl out to the Clawson's is so they can make out."

"Is it now?" Duke asks, his voice dripping with his personal brand of mischief.

"Always has been."

"Hmmm."

He doesn't deny it and I feel the thrum of anticipation vibrate through me. Duke's profile is muddled in the dark of the truck, but still pronounced enough for me to see a pensive look pass across his features.

"Are you okay?" I ask.

"You're here."

"What's that mean?"

"I'm more than okay. You're here. That makes everything okay. I was just thinking how much I'd like to take you out to dinner. I want to walk through town holding hands. I want to sit like we did on my couch, but at the fireworks show or at one of Aiden's bonfires–with you nestled between my legs, leaning back on me like I'm your own handsome, doting lawnchair."

"You make a heck of a lawn chair."

"Right?"

He's quiet again.

"I know what you're saying. I felt like I was coming unglued sitting with the girls and not telling them a thing about us. It felt almost dishonest and that made me all sorts of antsy. It's not natural. I usually tell them everything."

Duke nods. "I hear you."

"We will do all that," I assure him–probably trying to convince myself at the same time. "This isn't forever. It's only a few weeks until Chris is home and then we'll give him a week or two and we'll tell him–once the newness of being home wears off."

Duke nods again–just a single bob of his head. "You're right. Okay. Enough of that. I didn't ask you out after dark to mope about having to keep us under wraps."

"Besides," I tell him. "We can make this fun. Once everyone knows about us, we won't be sneaking around anymore. Let's enjoy this as much as we can. We've waited too long not to enjoy it."

"Well, now that you put it that way ..."

His grin crinkles at the corner of his eyes and then his mouth joins the smile. When his tongue darts out and licks his bottom lip, I sigh. He's irresistible and I'm in trouble.

Duke pulls up the dirt road along the outside of the Clawson's property. They live outside town on a huge acreage that's partly farmed, and partly left wild. They have an old barn that probably should be shored up or condemned.

If those walls could talk, most of the high-schoolers in town would probably have been grounded at one point or another. I know Laura and Rob used to sneak out here when we were all teens. It was their place.

I'm pretty sure Mr. and Mrs. Clawson are well aware of the way people sneak out here. It's just one of those things. No one's doing anything illegal, so they let it slide as long as we leave them be.

Duke puts the truck in park in a clearing just off the dirt road. Then he hops out of the truck and comes around to open my door.

He gives me his hand and I grab it, hopping down and shutting the door behind me. When I turn, he pulls me toward him. I think he's going in for a kiss, but instead, he tucks my head under his chin and holds me close.

"I'm so glad you texted," he says.

"Me too."

"I thought you might not."

"Why would you think that?"

"Maybe the girls wouldn't leave, or Jayme would stay up and you couldn't get out." His voice goes quiet. "Or, you could have changed your mind."

"I wasn't going to change my mind," I say with a squeeze around his waist. "Not a chance. Thankfully, you were spot on about the girls dropping like flies before nine. And Jayme baked herself into a frenzy today, so she went to bed early."

Duke wordlessly takes my chin between his thumb and fore-finger and tilts my head so I'm looking up at him. The moon is nearly full, and the stars fill the summer night above him.

"I've never felt like this," he says, sounding so uncharacteristi-cally small and vulnerable.

"Me either," I confess.

Then his lips are on mine and he's backing me up against the truck holding my head while his other hand clasps my back and drags me toward him. I run my hand through his hair and soak in the feeling of being in his arms.

Laura's words float through my head. *Siblings my fanny.* I start laughing against Duke's lips and I can't stop. Duke pulls back and looks at me with a grin across his face.

"Never had a woman give me that reaction to a kiss before. Am I losing my game?"

"No. It's just something Laura said tonight."

"What'd she say?"

He keeps his arms looped around me. I'm still leaning back against the truck. There's this ease between us that's always been there, but now it's so much more.

"The girls brought up how you and I are party planning for Chris. Of course everyone heard about it already. Trevor and Aiden's mom even knew I was at your home last night. Lexi made some smart comment about it being too bad that you and I are basically siblings and Laura said, 'Siblings my fanny.'"

Duke chuckles. "That woman's too perceptive for her own good."

"She's my best friend. Jayme and I have grown so close since we've been living together. But, Laura's been my bestie since elementary school. It's so hard not telling her everything."

"We will. She'll have the last laugh."

"She'll love that," I say. "It's one of her favorite things in life."

"Being right?"

"Basically."

"Come on," Duke says, "I've got something to show you."

He takes my hand and leads me around to the back of the truck. When he releases the hatch, I catch a glimpse of a pile of blankets and pillows.

"Presume much?" I ask, poking him in the ribs.

"Ow. And no. I thought we'd cozy up back here and watch the stars. Chat a bit. Cuddle. You could do the lip thing. It's all totally innocent."

"You and the word innocent rarely belong in the same sentence."

He claps a hand to his chest like he's been shot. "You wound me, Hollywood."

I laugh, and then before I know what's happening, Duke's hands are on either side of my hips and he's lifting me up into the truck bed. I've been lifted by guys before. Always in ballet. Not a single one of those experiences ever made me suck in a breath and feel so weightless.

Once I'm settled in the back of the truck, Duke hops up to join me. He turns with his back to the truck bed and hoists himself up with his arms, landing on his butt in a move that's sheer masculinity at its finest. Then he rolls over onto his hands and knees and prowls toward me on all fours. I instinctively scoot backwards in a gawky sort of crab crawl until I hit the back wall of the truck bed.

"I'm not gonna bite." He chuckles. "Unless you want me to. I might nibble, though."

"Gah. You're insane. You know that?"

"Crazy for you, Hollywood."

Duke makes quick work of spreading out some thicker blankets to cushion the truck bed and then he props the pillows up along the back so we can lean on them.

"You're way too good at this. Must be from years of practice taking girls out in a truck to have your way with them."

I don't know what made me say that, and I feel the way it killed the spark simmering between us as soon as the words are out of my mouth.

Duke isn't phased. He pauses for the briefest moment and then he takes my hand and laces our fingers together, rubbing gently across my knuckles with his thumb.

"I'm not gonna pretend I've been a monk, Shannon. You know me better than that. But, what's behind us, including dates with men named Reginald, is behind us. Ask me anything you want to know if it's keeping you from moving forward here. Otherwise, I'd rather spend the night holding you and making the most of this time together."

"Sorry," I say.

And I am. I don't need to be insecure. Duke's given me no reason to think he's trying to divide his time between me and someone else–or more than one someone else. He's been nothing but attentive and eager since we kissed in his kitchen. It may just take a while for the reality of his feelings for me to sink in.

"I think I'd rather make the most of our time together."

"Nice choice," he says, brushing a thumb along my chin and making a ding-ding-ding sound like I won a prize on *The Price Is Right*.

Our mood shifts from playful to serious in a heartbeat. It happens every time he touches me. I feel hungry for him. His hand moves from stroking my chin to cupping my cheek and I lean in for more.

Duke doesn't rush our connection this time. He purposely slows us down, using his hands to steady me, his arms drop and his fingertips dig gently into my hips as he pulls me near. His kiss is soft, leisurely, and searching, as if we have all the time in the world to explore one another and express the feelings we've been holding back for so long.

He teases my lips with his, leaving a tingling sensation across the sensitive skin where his stubble brushes against my mouth. His pace and the way he commands our movements unravels me bit by bit. I feel myself collapse into him. He hums and I giggle. His answering chuckle vibrates against me. I move my hands to knock that ball cap off his head so I can run my fingers through his hair.

We kiss for a while. I don't know how long. The heat between us builds and Duke pulls back, breathing heavily and then resting his forehead on mine.

"You will be my undoing," he mutters. "Not that I'm complaining."

I cup his jaw and smile up into his eyes.

"Is this real?" I ask him, still unable to believe we're here, kissing and holding one another.

"It's more real than anything I've experienced before," he says. It's the second time he's said something like that and I let the reality seep in a little more deeply.

We're actually doing this.

THIRTY-FIVE

Duke

I can't wipe the smile off my face. Shannon's curled in against me while my back is up against the rear of the truck bed. Two nights of holding her in my arms and I already know I'll never get my fill.

She kissed me like no woman has ever kissed me before. Maybe it's the combination of our familiarity and the tension of waiting so long. Maybe it's just her.

"Look!" She points at the sky as a shooting star zips overhead.

"Did you know the ancients saw shooting stars as portents?"

"Did you just say portents?" she asks, laughing softly, her head brushing against my chest with the movement of her laughter.

"I did indeed. I'm not just a dumb jock with a butt that could inspire poets."

"Oh my gosh!" she yells, laughing and smacking my chest. "You are too much."

"That I am," I agree. "It's my brand. Seriously, though. The ancients said that a shooting star meant something great was about to happen, either good or horrible, but something of magnitude."

"That sounds like one of the fortunes Jayme writes. You will see a shooting star and something magnificent will happen."

Shannon makes this eerie oooo-weee-oooo-ooo sound.

"Well, I think something magnificent is already happening," I tell her.

"Me too."

She snuggles back into my chest and I reposition my arm around her shoulders again.

"So," I ask. "If you could do anything in the coming five to ten years, what would it be?"

"Sit in this truck and watch the stars with you."

I smile.

"Done. What about during daytime hours? What would you do with your work life? Do you want to keep painting nails and supporting your dad's business?"

Shannon goes quiet, so I wait. I really want to hear her dreams. Now that we're together I want to know what she really wants in life. It may be too early, but it feels like we're running behind schedule–like we should have started dating years ago and already be engaged or married. I want to make up for lost time. I want to dream together–and I want to help her make her dreams come true.

Shannon pushes off my chest and says, "I'd teach–dance. You already know why I had to give up dancing. As crazy as it sounds, teaching the Zumba class has made me realize how much I love teaching dance. Almost as much as I love dancing."

She searches my eyes like whatever I say next will make or break her belief in this dream.

"Why don't you teach then–more often than once a week?" I ask. "You're a great teacher. Way better than me. Though, I'm a close second. Just ask Esther."

Shannon laughs. "I wish I could have seen you teaching Zumba."

"Probably best that you didn't."

She sighs heavily. "There's no studio here in town. It's not practical. I'd have to drive somewhere else to teach."

"Corn Corners is twenty or thirty minutes away. There's Huber Heights."

Her spine stiffens and she looks away.

"What just happened?"

"Nothing." Her voice is suddenly tight and her words clipped.

"When I said Huber Heights, your whole body went rigid." I study her. "Wait. Are you jealous?

"Of Huber Heights?"

"Of Beth."

I hate to bring up another woman when we already said we wanted to move forward, but her reaction feels so much like jealousy to me. And I want to clear the air if that's what's needed.

"No!"

"Do you know that Aiden gave her a nickname?" I ask.

"No. And I'm not sure I want to hear it."

"Because you totally aren't jealous."

"Exactly."

"Know what I think?"

"Nope."

"I think jealousy looks hot on you."

She smiles a reluctant half-smile, and then she forces her lips back into a thin line.

"You never have to work for anything," she says. "You just turn on the charm and women flock, doors open, potholes in the road even fill themselves."

"Yeah. That's my life to a T. Especially the potholes. If you're not jealous, what bothered you about Huber Heights."

"I'm not jealous."

"Well, good. Because you have no reason to be. Aiden called Beth *The Placeholder*. He saw that she was just someone I hung out with to fill a space in my life. He knew I was head over heels for someone I couldn't have. That's all I told him for years. And he would tease me about my out of town friendships. Called them 'substitutes,' or 'girl-of-the-month,' but, since Beth and I kept seeing one another for a year, he gave her her own nickname."

"I'm not sure I want to think about all those *out-of-town friends*, as you call them."

I hear the hardness covering the fragility in her voice.

I should drop this, but it feels too important to shove it down. It will just hang around like a living thing between us if we don't address it.

I want Shannon to know me for what I was, but also see for what I am. I'm not a perfect man. I'm so imperfect, it's almost comical. But I'm sincere, and she owns my heart. She really always has.

"They weren't you, is my point."

I let that truth fill the cool night air between us. Shannon crosses her arms in front of her and her bottom lip sticks out just the slightest. So many memories of her in this exact stance flood my mind. I keep them to myself.

"I didn't think you wanted me," I tell her. "And I didn't think I could have you. So I sometimes took other women out because I was lonely. And I was trying to find someone who might prove to me that I could live without you. No one did that. No one."

"And you found Beth."

"And I left Beth."

She nods and leaves her head dipped downward. Man, I did not plan on this night going in this direction.

This childhood chant goes through my mind about going on a lion hunt. We'd clap our hands to a rhythm and tell this story of a hunter going on a lion hunt. In the song, each time he hit an obstacle, we'd chant, *you can't go around it, can't go under it, can't go over it. Gotta go through it*. Shannon and I gotta go through this. I'm sure of it.

I place my hand under her chin and hold it gently so I can tilt her head up. I want her to see my eyes while I explain this to her.

"I'd prefer avoiding talking about my past with you. The last thing I want to do is hurt you. I want to protect you, to care for you, to keep you safe. Maybe I shouldn't be going into it with you. But I want you to know I've never been serious with anyone. I've never stuck with anyone past six months. Beth and I went out longer because we were lazy and we enjoyed each other's company. But we both knew we weren't one another's end game."

She nods. I'm still holding her chin, but my hand slides to cup her face. Then I bring it to rest on her shoulder.

"It's way too soon to be talking like this," I say. "But, since we already got into murky waters with this topic, I'll tell it to you straight.

"You are my end game. No one else. No one else ever was or ever will be. I know that's a big bomb to drop on you before we've even told our friends or families about us. But, we're not starting from scratch here. I've known you for as long as I can remember. And I know what I know. You're it for me."

A tear slides down her cheek and I brush it away. Years. So many years we lived around one another. I'd go back and erase so much. But, I can't, and I refuse to let the past clog our future. If Shannon needs time to reconcile all of this, she can have all the time she needs.

I lean in, testing her reaction. She tilts her face up toward me. I kiss the spot on her face where the tear landed. Then I kiss her forehead, her eyelids. I brush her hair over her shoulder. I lean toward her ear and whisper low and soft, "You. Only you."

Then I kiss my way up her neck to this spot under her ear that I discover should have a map with an X marks the spot on it because she lets out a soft sound and pulls me toward her like I flicked a switch. She takes over and forces my lips to meet her mouth. Then she's on my lap and we're all hands and lips and sighs and sweetness.

She pulls back to look at me. And the next words out of her mouth bring tears to my eyes. Manly tears. Guy tears. Maybe I'm just sweating through my eyes with a testosterone-laden reaction. I've still got my man card, that's all I know.

"You're my end game too," she says softly.

Tears fall. It's cool. I'm crying and I earned every drop. This woman. She's been out of reach, completely unattainable–forbidden, even–and now she's telling me I'm it for her.

I lean into her, making sure she sees me. "I kinda figured I was by the way you just tried to eat my face." I chuckle, pulling her close.

She smacks my bicep, but I'm smiling so big, and she is too.

I pull her in and she rests her head under my chin. I rub my hand up and down her back.

"I really don't want to take you back to your house tonight."

"I know."

"Let's elope." I mumble into her hair. "Chris won't be so inclined to kill me if I'm your husband."

She jerks back. "You're crazy! Are you serious right now?"

"Only half. But, not really. I'll take you out to eat first. That's the way these things go. You take the girl of your dreams to dinner. Wine and dine her. Then you marry her."

"Much better plan," She says. "Much better."

It was two in the morning when I dropped Shannon off at her house. I waited in the truck and watched her make it inside, and then I rolled down the street with the truck lights off until I was five or six houses away.

When I woke up in my bed with the faint rays of predawn sun streaming in the window four hours later, I felt invincible.

Okay. I'm yawning. But I'd trade a good night's sleep for time with Shannon every day if she'd let me. I won't. But I would.

I'm on my way to drop the truck back off at the garage, so I can't text. Otherwise I'd be messaging Shannon to remind her of some highlights from last night and to say I can't wait to see her at the game this afternoon–just to make sure she's thinking of me as much as I'm thinking of her. If there's such a thing as more than non-stop, that's how often thoughts of Shannon's kisses, her laugh, and the feel of her in my arms are flicking through my brain.

I can't believe I told her she's my end game–less than thirty-six hours after our first kiss. And she told me I'm hers. When Chris hears about us, it'll be an end game, alright. More like Marvel End Game, where half the population is wiped out by the rage of one man. Maybe I should take a trip to see him. Nah. Shannon's right. He deserves to finish out his term of service without our budding romance distracting him.

I need to call Principal Barnes, aka Summer Steven. I chuckle to myself picturing a scene where Clark Kent turns into Superman, only it's Principal Barnes in his tropical swim trunks and goggles dashing into a phone booth and exiting wearing a suit and tie.

It's a bird! It's a plane! It's the man whose office you never want to be sent to!

The phone rings once and then his relaxed, cheerful voice comes through. "Duke! Good to hear from you. Are you calling with good news?"

"I guess you could call it that. I'm scheduled to take the exam. I've got Jayme Culhane helping me study. If I pass, I'll take the position."

"I have no doubt you'll pass, especially if you study. This is great news. Call me when your results are in. I'll be in Aruba for fourteen days. We leave next week. I'm taking Mrs. Barnes on a little Caribbean holiday before we have to get back to real life."

"Well, have a great trip."

"We will. We will. We're going swimming with stingrays and getting our hair braided in cornrows. Just imagine the school spirit that will inspire!"

Cornrows. Wow. And this man is my new boss. Maybe.

"I'll talk to you when we're back, Duke. I can't tell you how pleased I am about this decision."

My stomach feels shaky all of a sudden when he says that last word. Decision. It makes everything seem so ... final.

"Um, Principal Barnes?"

"Steven."

"Right. Steven. Could you not spread news of this decision yet–until I pass the exam and we make things official. I still need to finalize some things with Pops about the garage, and I want to get that all worked out before this becomes common knowledge."

"Oh, I totally understand, Duke. You have my word on it. My lips are sealed. Anyway, my lips will be on an island somewhere south of Florida along with the rest of me for the coming two weeks. No chance of me spreading any news there."

"What news?" I hear Mrs. Barnes ask in the background.

Great.

"Nothing, dear. Work-related stuff."

"It's summer, Steven, dear. And it's Saturday. You don't need to discuss work until late August. Come let me put sunscreen on your nose. It looks a little red." Mrs. Barnes' voice sounds so clear she must be standing right next to Principal Barnes.

"Yes, dear. I'll be off this call in a jiffy." Principal Barnes says with the speaker muffled. Then he turns back to the phone and says, "Gotta run, Duke."

"Sounds good. I'll call you after I get my test results."

"Go Corn Cobs!" Principal Barnes shouts a little too loudly into the phone.

"Go Corn Cobs." I say with as much gusto as I can. It feels like it's important to echo our school chant, even though I can't tell you how glad I am to be alone in the cab of the truck right now. I hope he doesn't expect me to shout that phrase randomly and regularly.

What's with me and team names? I currently coach the Mighty Fireflies, and I'm potentially being hired to lead the Corn Cobs to victory. My coaching resume reads like a Saturday morning children's show line up.

THIRTY-SIX

Shannon

Zumba class feels more purposeful for me today after telling Duke I want to teach and him responding with two simple words, "Why not?"

I'm focusing more on how I lead. I'm watching the seniors follow. Yes, they're darling, sometimes klutzy, and always a hoot. But, they're here, and they follow everything I tell them to do. And I see them benefitting from dancing. I'm making a difference.

Maybe I won't teach dance full time, but I could take up another class here. I have free time. Although, I want to spend every spare minute with Duke. The man does work. I could do this as a hobby–maybe host three classes a week. Not only for seniors. Young moms could come midday. My mind starts to swell with possibilities. All because Duke believed in my dream.

The man has way too much power over me. I'm not sure how I feel about that. When I look at my face in the mirror, I know how I feel. I'm glowing, and not just from physical exertion.

Duke makes me happy.

Speak of the local hot mechanic who puts a different smile on my face than I've seen in years ... I glance up as I'm toweling off and saying goodbye to my students and he's standing there in the doorway looking like a model for Coach magazine. Not the Coach that sells purses, but the baseball coach who makes me want to run my hands up and down his chest and into his hair right now.

"Well, hello, ladies," Duke says to the seniors leaving as they pass him.

Duke is pure charisma and magnetism personified. I'm not kidding about potholes filling up as he approaches. I'm pretty sure each of these women feels like they are forty years younger when he looks at them with his signature roguish grin and winks.

When his focus shifts toward me, I suck in a breath and steady myself. It's overwhelming to be the object of this much intensity. Before two days ago, I'd have told you this is just Duke. He's a flirt. But right now, his eyes say, "Shannon, I want *you*."

And all the molecules in my body are turning and pointing toward him like little metal shavings being drawn into the lure of an irresistible attraction.

When no one is looking, he mouths, "Good morning, sunshine."

I roll my eyes at him.

It's that or run at him in a jump straddle and wrap my legs around him like a baby koala. That wouldn't exactly keep our relationship under wraps, so I'm going for the *Get over yourself, Satterson* approach.

He walks toward me as the room continues to clear, his cleats making that subtle clacking noise on the tile. He's wearing his cap backwards which seems to be his thing lately. I'm not complaining.

Come to mama, big boy.

Nope. No. Don't come to mama. And what was that thought? Stay away from mama. Because I'm ninety-nine percent sure if he gets any closer I'll lose all my self-control and throw myself at him.

I hoist my bag onto my shoulder and grip the strap with one hand. That leaves one hand free for something it ought not do.

The room is clear. Duke is less than a foot away from me. My heartbeat sounds like a street drummer with buckets overturned. My breath comes in pants like a leaf blower being turned on and off. Oh yeah. I'm sexy like that.

"We're in public," I remind him—and myself.

"Alone," he says, reaching out and wiping a sweaty lock of hair off the side of my face.

"With an open door to a hallway where anyone could see us."

"Two old friends—practically siblings—saying good morning before the ball game."

"Riiiight."

Duke leans in close and I forget that I'm sweaty and gross and probably smell like someone's sneakers.

He puts his mouth on the shell of my ear and says, "Good morning, Hollywood."

I shiver. My eyes flutter shut. I lose the capacity to speak. I wobble. Duke's hand cups my elbow.

He said that same sentence last night, when he dropped me off. He kissed me in the cab of his work truck before I hopped out. It was around two a.m. and he looked at me with hooded eyes and said, "Good morning, Hollywood," and I giggled like a schoolgirl.

I step back a tiny bit, just to recalibrate. He steps forward and places the softest kiss on my cheek. "I couldn't wait to see you. You're consuming my thoughts and I don't really know how to live like this. What are you doing to me, Shannon?"

He honestly looks baffled, like no one has ever impacted him like this.

"It's just me," I tell him.

"Just you," he echoes, but there's this look of wonder in his eyes like he's trying to reconcile the me he's known his whole life with the me he's been kissing senseless for two days straight. Or not even that long. Time is a rubbery, goopy thing right now.

"I better go. I think I smell like the ape house at the Columbus Zoo," I tell him.

"Nope. You smell like dessert."

"You are officially crazy."

"Vanilla," he says as if I didn't just question his sanity. "And caramel or butterscotch. Butterscotch. You're like an ice cream sundae, Hollywood. Sometimes you smell like peaches, but today you've got the butterscotch sundae thing going for you."

Of all the compliments I've ever received in my life, this one may be the one I remember until my dying day. The look in his eyes, the sound of his voice, the way he looks like a rugged man and a playful boy all wrapped up in one scrumptious package. It's so him.

"Okay, well. If I'm going to make it back for the game, I'd better run. And we are meeting for party planning after the game, right?"

"Party planning," he sends me a salute followed by a devious wink.

"No. Real party planning. Let's meet out somewhere to make sure you behave."

"You think taking me in public will make me behave?"

"Good point. Come to my place. That way Jayme can be the Duke-blocker."

"You're killing me, Hollywood. But, if you're serious, I'll come to your place around two-thirty."

"I'm serious. If we spend every party planning meeting making out, we'll never end up with a welcome home for my brother."

Duke's face darkens for a moment at the mention of Chris. But, the look passes as quickly as it came.

"Okay. You win. I'll be a well-behaved version of myself at two-thirty in your home with our unsuspecting chaperone, Jayme, watching our every interaction."

And now I'm wondering if it's such a hot idea to have Duke over to my home.

∼

The Fireflies won again, proving that they are indeed mighty. I drive home and start tidying the living room right after the game. I didn't want to stay around after congratulating Duke, watching single mom after single mom approach him to give him a warm thank you. Warm as in cozy by the fireplace in a small, fur-fringed nightie warm. Also as in get your hands off my man. Only no one knows he's my man.

I'm going to have to get used to his pheromones or whatever it is that draws women like flies to honey if I'm going to stay with him—which I have every intention of doing. He was cordial. He never led one of them on.

Duke even looked like he was running from Cherry. It was a brisk walk, eyes averted, but it came awfully close to a run at one point. Brooks and I made eye contact and shared a laugh at that one. As funny as that moment was, seeing the way women touch Duke's arm while talking to him, or tilt their heads, or bend just a little to try to give him a show. It unnerved me and I had to skedaddle.

Now I'm channeling my hopefully unwarranted jealousy into cleaning and straightening our front room. Jayme walks through. "Wow. Go you, Mrs. Clean. This place looks amazing. What's the occasion?"

"No occasion. I just felt like cleaning."

"Since when?" she chuckles.

I shoot her a fake wounded look and laugh.

"I mean. Have you seen your bedroom? I'm just curious why the sudden urge to be so domestic."

Of course it's at that moment that Duke knocks on the front door. I answer it, and Jayme's eyebrows shoot up, and then she nods once.

"Duke's here to party plan. We can go in the kitchen if we'll be in your way."

"And give up the chance to show off our newly-spiffed-up living room? No. I wouldn't dream of that. I'll just write in my room."

Jayme turns and walks upstairs.

When she's out of earshot, Duke asks, "What was that about?"

"She was teasing me about cleaning up."

"You didn't clean for me, did you?"

"So full of yourself."

"Have you seen me?" he asks, pursing his lips so they're even fuller than usual, clenching his fists so his triceps pop, and looking down at me through his obnoxiously long lashes.

I roll my eyes.

"Sit down, Satterson. We need to get this party planned."

"Yes ma'am."

I sit on the couch and Duke settles in right next to me. I'm in the corner, so I can't scoot away from him. He smells like body wash and something that's just him. Like a wooded glen filled with cinnamon rolls. I have this urge to dance through those woods in my tutu while eating baked goods dripping with frosting.

Duke puts his hand on my knee.

I pick his hand up and place it on his leg.

He wags his eyebrows at me.

I mouth, "Behave" to him, because even though Jayme is sequestered upstairs, and her brain is probably in that writing zone where she barely hears anything outside the roar of her own creative thoughts, she'll for sure hear him putting his hand on my knee, or any untoward words we say to one another. Just thinking of Jayme makes me use words like untoward. Geesh.

Duke lifts his hand up off his thigh and runs it down my hair so slowly. In a way too gritty and deep voice, he says, "So, what did you have in mind?"

I'm relatively sure he means for the party, but right now, with the feel of his palm caressing my back, I've got a lot of things in mind, and Chris coming home is the least of them.

I reach around, pull his hand off me, give him a stern teacher-face, even though I'm not a teacher, and say, "Do you think we should rent the Community Center, or see if Aiden will let us use the barn?"

"I think we should do whatever makes you happy," Duke says with a temptingly mischievous look in his eye and a brush of his hand down my forearm. He's totally not talking about the party right now.

"Gah!" I say.

I shake my head. And I can't help but smile. He's incorrigible. But haven't I always known that? It's part of what I love about him. Love, in a very, *not giving my whole heart to you yet* kind of way.

I stand and relocate to one of the side chairs. Duke collapses back onto the couch, but with a smug look on his face. He laces his fingers behind his head so his arm muscles are on display. I've dreamed of moments like this–for *years*. But right now we need to keep things hush-hush, and we need to prepare for my potentially angry, annoying, overbearing, but devoted and occasionally sweet older brother to come home from his honorable service to the people who love him, even though he's a turdball.

And I'm going to make that happen.

"Okay," Duke says, leaning forward, so his elbows rest on his knees and putting on a serious expression. "We ask Aiden for the barn. It's still going to be hot, so we'll use any money we'd have allocated for renting a space to rent the A/C units we used for Aiden's wedding. Then we'll ask around at Mad River Burgers and Pop's Pizza for donations or discounts on food for the celebration.

"You can ask your Zumba class to provide side dishes. They'll turn it into a contest trying to outdo one another. It gives them something to do so they don't meddle in details we want them to steer clear of. I'll get Bubba to DJ. He's been doing that here and there and he's not bad.

"We should have one meeting with all Chris' closest friends to get them to contribute some money and time to help cover costs and set up. You can ask your dad for some money too. We can divide responsibilities at that meeting.

"So I'll go to Pop's and Mad River this week. And I'll talk to Aiden. You cover the seniors, your dad and the friend group. We'll reconvene after that's all done."

He takes a breath and I just stare at him.

"What?" he asks.

"You just planned the whole event in under thirty seconds."

"I can be efficient when I'm motivated. I brought the bike. Let's go on a ride."

He stands and I set down the pad and paper, absentmindedly shouting up to Jayme, "Duke and I are going out for an errand. I'll be back in just a bit!"

She shouts back, "Okie dokie. Be safe, kids!"

I'm still shaking my head a little when Duke hands me the helmet. I thought I knew every side of this man. I love that he's full of surprises.

THIRTY-SEVEN

Shannon

D uke drives us through the neighborhoods, then down country lanes, past the ranches on the outskirts of town. He turns onto remote roads between Bordeaux and our neighboring towns. We ride and ride, my arms around his waist, the wind whipping my hair back, and nothing but the sound of the engine as our soundtrack.

We're on a backroad I've never traveled when Duke unexpectedly pulls to the shoulder and kills the engine. He dismounts and then turns around. Before I know what he's doing, he's on the seat, facing me. He lifts my legs and settles them on top of his.

Then he unclips my helmet and says, "I can't go another mile with your arms around me without kissing you."

I'm feeling sassy, so I say, "Took you long enough."

That statement has the effect of throwing lighter fluid onto a flame. The way he kisses me–whew. He grips my cheeks and draws my face toward his and then his hand comes behind my neck so he can tilt my head just right.

His kiss is wild and free, fitting the scenery and this moment on his motorcycle, in the middle of cornfields and dirt roads. Eventually, our kisses slow, his lips softening to something achingly tender and full of emotion before he pulls back. He wipes the back of his hand over his mouth like he just drank a frothy mug of beer. His eyes never leave mine while he rebuckles my helmet. His face has such an affectionate expression of disbelief. Then, as if he's done what he aimed to do, he wordlessly hops off the bike, turns so he's facing forward, and drives us toward home.

About ten minutes outside town, I see this old brick building I've never seen before. I tap Duke on the thigh and shout to let him know I want to stop. Mostly we can't hear one another over the engine and the wind, but the combination of my shouting and tapping gets his attention.

When he pulls over, I point to the building. "What's that?" I ask.

"You've never been out this way?"

"Not that I remember. It's not like there's anything out here that would draw me in this direction. I mostly take County Line Road past the ranches to the north or go south out State Street if I'm leaving town."

"Makes sense. That's an old elementary school. At one point there were more working farms out this way, so those kids would come here instead of going all the way into Bordeaux for school-ing. When things were smaller, that's how it was. It's sort-of the middle ground between the one-room schoolhouse and the bigger school buildings we have now."

The embossed stone over the entryway says, Richard F. Outcault Elementary. Huh. I know that name and it makes this building all the more intriguing. Mr. Outcault was a famous turn-of-the-century cartoonist from this region of Ohio.

"Do you want to hop off and go in?"

"Are we allowed?"

"I'm not sure. No one would ever know if we just went in."

I shake my head. Duke and rules have a certain type of working relationship. If a rule seems to make sense to him, he follows it. If not, he's game to bend or walk right over the lines it represents. I guess I'm more of a rule-follower than I thought I was.

"Not today. Maybe another time."

"I'll take you out here anytime you want."

With that, he starts the engine and we take off, leaving that unusual building taking up new acreage in my thoughts.

Duke drops me off and I walk away from him without a backward glance, the longing to kiss him consuming me, even though we just made out on his bike less than a half hour ago. The sound of his engine fades down the street behind me.

"I'm home!" I shout to Jayme.

She comes out of the kitchen juggling a bowl of popcorn and a tumbler.

"There's that smile again," she says, studying me. "Anything you want to tell me?"

"What are you talking about?" I ask.

Jayme sits on the couch and nods her head toward the chair in a silent invitation for me to sit. I stay standing, hoping I can dodge her inquisition.

Her eyes narrow just a little and then she says, "Last night, maybe a half hour after you left, I called your name to ask you something. I don't even remember what it was now. When I first went upstairs, I thought I'd go straight to sleep, but I sat up reading. Anyway, I called out to you and you didn't answer, so I went downstairs looking for you."

I move in front of the chair and drop into it as soon as I realize she's going to drag the details about Duke out of me. I may as well be comfortable while I'm being put in the hot seat.

Jayme pops a handful of popcorn in her mouth and holds the bowl out toward me. I shake my head.

"Since you didn't answer, I checked the basement, thinking you might be dancing. You weren't there–as you know. So, I went back up and knocked on the door to your room. You were gone, as you also know very well. But your car was parked out front. That only means one thing. Someone picked you up."

She punctuates that statement with this pointed look–her eyebrows raise and her head slightly tilts.

"Now. By my powers of deduction, your four closest friends were all in the house only an hour prior to you disappearing. Three of them left to go back to their husbands and children. So, I figure no one had come back to see you, which means you had a late night rendezvous with a man. And the only man I can think of would be Duke."

Jayme crosses her arms in front of her chest and raises one eyebrow. The gesture makes her look like an adorable little genie who could poof you into nothingness with a bob of her adorable little head.

"Why Duke?"

I'm stalling.

Of course it's Duke.

We both know it's Duke. The jig is up.

My life feels as though it's unraveling. You know when you yank on the wrong loose thread, and the whole garment starts to come apart, and no matter what you do, it's too late. It's going to be a mess and unwearable now. I'm going to have an unwearable, frayed life.

"After all that, all you can say is, 'Why Duke?'" Jayme asks with a flustered look. "It's obviously not RJ. I mean, you might have given him a second chance, but you would have mentioned it. Duke is the only man you'd have to sneak around with. Because of Chris. And I get that. What I don't understand is why you aren't telling your best friends."

She stares at me. I don't look away.

"You can tell me anything," she says softly. "I sat on the knowledge of your crush. Never told anyone."

I take a deep breath. She knows. I may as well come clean.

"You can't tell a soul–unless you want to break the fact that I'm unavailable to my secret admirer. I'm no longer interested in anyone but Duke anyway. Not that I ever was interested in anyone else."

At the mention of my secret admirer, Jayme's face flinches for the briefest moment. Maybe she's sick of keeping his identity a secret. Who knows. It doesn't matter anymore.

Once I start talking, the words flow like I took the lid off that boiling pot and let it spit, sizzle and steam all over the stovetop.

"You're right. I was with Duke. Thursday, when I showed up to party plan at his house, something snapped between us. I don't know what it was, but we kissed. And then we kissed and kissed. And then I found out I wasn't the only one with a crush. He thought his feelings were one-sided too. All these years. So, we kissed to celebrate that fun discovery. And then we ordered Chinese and watched a movie. And kissed. And then I fell asleep.

"Yesterday evening he asked if we could get together, but we had girls' night. And I really did want a girls' night. I also wanted to see Duke. So, when everyone left, and you were going to bed, I texted him and he came to pick me up and we hung out."

"And kissed," Jayme says with a goofy grin on her face.

"Yes. But so much more. We talked, laughed, cuddled–even thought about the future. He held me under the stars. It's all like a dream, only it's real. Then, today, after the game, he came to actually do some party planning, since we've been kissing instead of organizing this party that I do want to throw even though thoughts of my brother are driving me up a wall right now. It's not right that I'm jumping through all these hoops to make Chris happy, knowing he'll still be mad. But, I know it's not fair to spring a relationship with Duke on him at this point in his life either. And our yackity town will blow the whistle if any of them find out."

I blow out a breath.

"Once we finished planning this afternoon, Duke took me on a motorcycle ride down some back roads."

"And you kissed," Jayme says giggling.

"We did, but not only that. Gah! You make it sound like we're just sneaking around kissing."

"Aren't you?"

"A little." A smile splits my face. I can't help it.

"I'm so happy for you," Jayme says. "I still don't fully understand why you wouldn't just tell the girls. Or at least me."

"It's not personal. I was dying not telling you. It's just, things leak. No one may mean them to, but they do. And Em is married to Aiden. And Aiden is one of Chris' best friends. We are keeping everything quiet until Chris comes home and then we'll let him settle back in. We want him to be the first to know."

"You're really keeping everything between you two secret?"

"Yes."

"In Bordeaux?"

"I know. Do you think we're delusional?"

"Maybe a little. Even if you don't tell anyone, the way people watch one another here is beyond CIA level skilled. It's simultaneously sweet and annoying. Someone only has to say, 'Hey, Mabel, did you see Shannon and Duke together at Oh! Sugar …?' and the next thing you know the town's talking about how you're about to have his baby."

"I know!"

"But, I'll keep this locked up tight. I'm so happy for you. And for him. He got the prettiest and sweetest woman, with just the right dash of sass. He'd better know he's lucky."

"I'm lucky."

"You both are."

"Let's just hope our luck holds."

THIRTY-EIGHT

Shannon

I t's six a.m. As in six. In the morning. My phone buzzed on the nightstand so many times in rapid succession, it bounced off and fell on the ground. That clunk woke me. I drop my arm over the edge of my bed and clamber around patting the floor with my hand. Finally my fingers feel the edge of the case, and I pull it up and squint at the screen to see what kind of psychopath is texting or calling me at this hour of the night. It's still basically dark out, which means it's nighttime and I should be sleeping.

Duke: *Hey, beautiful.*
Duke: *Are you up yet?*
Duke: *Text me when you're up. I want to cook you breakfast before work.*
Duke: *Are you still not a morning person? I thought we all grew out of that after high school.*
Duke: *Is this excessive? Should I stop texting you? Do I seem needy? Because I'm needy in a manly way. Men have needs, Shannon. And right now, I need you.*

I throw my forearm over my face, letting my cell drop onto the bed beside me. Why am I smiling? I don't smile before morning soda, and I don't smile in the middle of the night just because a sexy, ridiculous man-child wants to cook me breakfast.

I moan. I'm going to pay for this. I don't do mornings. But, I'm about to do a morning.

Jayme must hear my groan because she stands right outside my doorway and asks, "Shannon, are you alright?"

"Uuunhhh."

"Shannon?"

"I'm alright. Just ahhhggghhh. Duke wants to fix me breakfast. Now. In the dark."

I hear her muffled giggles outside my door, so I throw my childhood stuffed ballerina gorilla at the doorway. I call her Gallerina. She misses the door and flops in an unsatisfactory lump on the floor. Because: morning.

"Are you going back to sleep?" Jayme stage whispers like Anna asking Elsa if she wants to build a snowman.

"No. I'm up."

I roll over and put the pillow over my head. "I'm really up," I mumble from under my pillow.

I hear my door open and Jayme padding across my floor. She partially lifts the pillow and peeks under it at me. Brave, brave woman. But, she is also the maker of my smoothies and the keeper of my secrets, so I only slightly snarl at her.

In one of her gentle voices, the one I imagine her using with her children if she ever had any, Jayme asks, "Do you want to have breakfast with the hot mechanic?"

"Mmhmm." I nod.

"Okay. Then let's start getting you vertical. What do you say?" I nod.

"Which involves you sitting up for starters. Can we do that?"

"I've got this," I say. Letting the pillow drop back over my head.

"How about I give you five minutes and I'll come back like a cheery little snooze button?"

"No cheery," I mumble from under the safety and cushiony goodness of my pillow.

"Okay. Grumpy wake-up coming your way in five." Jayme says in a super-cheery voice.

Five minutes later, or I assume it's five minutes, a very not-grumpy roomie is back. I'm sleeping. Really. Not dozing. I think I was already dreaming. Shirtless Duke was making me pancakes and licking syrup off his big fingers and holding a finger out to me and I was about to ...

I snap up. "Time for breakfast!"

"'Atta girl!" Jayme cheers.

I text Duke back.

Shannon: *Am I too late for breakfast?*
Duke: *Not at all.*
Shannon: *I don't do mornings.*
Duke: *You still don't, huh? Well, you don't have to come over. I just missed you and thought it would be nice to share breakfast before work.*
Shannon: *I start work at nine.*
Duke: *I take a lunch break at nine. (winking emoji)*
Shannon: *Ha ha. I'll be there in about 20 min.*
Duke: *Looking forward to it.*

I slide into some yoga pants and throw on a vintage T-shirt. Then I brush my teeth, throw my hair into a messy bun, and slip into flip-flops.

When I come downstairs, Jayme looks me over.

"Are you off work today?"

"Nope. I have time to eat breakfast and come back to get ready."

"Priorities," she says with a wink. "Did you brush your teeth?"

Only a true friend would ask this.

"Yep. And squished with mouthwash."

"Go get 'em tiger."

I laugh. It's not a full laugh. I'm still sleepwalking. But, I'm up, and I'm about to see Duke.

When I get to his house, the door is open, so I announce myself and walk right in. That's not completely uncommon around here. If the screen door is the only door shut, you can let yourself in if you know the person well enough—or if you're over sixty or under ten.

He's standing in the doorway of the kitchen when I come through the house, his arm extended overhead so he can casually lean against the frame.

"Well, good morning," he says. His voice still sounds a little gruff with the leftovers of sleep. It's as if brown sugar could talk. Yummy and gritty and sweet.

Duke leans into me. I tilt my chin up toward his face. He kisses my lips softly.

"You taste minty." He laughs.

"It was either that or kill you with morning breath."

"It would be a good way to go if it meant seeing you in the morning."

"It's too early for charm," I grumble, but I'm grinning despite my morning attitude.

"So, we've got pancakes and eggs. Does that sound good? I've got bacon or sausage in the fridge if you want meat with our meal. And fruit."

"Do you have Diet Dr Pepper?" I ask.

First things first, dad always said. Not sure he was thinking of soda for breakfast, but the principle applies.

Duke turns to the island and hands me a glass of ice and a can of unopened Diet Dr Pepper. I nearly weep.

"Marry me," I blurt out.

"Oh, I will. Remember I have to wine you and dine you first," he says as if saying he'll marry me is this given fact. Or a joke. But, deep down I think he's not really joking. It should freak me out. But it doesn't.

I sit at the island, pouring my carbonated glass-o-heaven and taking a delicious bubbly sip. And my view is stellar. You already know that. Duke moves through the kitchen with ease, grinning as he cooks, making the mere act of scrambling an egg feel like art and a study in the male form.

His forearm flexes as he flips pancakes. He hums a tune he may be making up as he goes. I study him shamelessly from over the rim of my glass, watching as his hair falls forward as it's prone to do. His ball cap isn't on. I love that thing, but Duke in the kitchen with a T-shirt and loose basketball shorts, and his hair slightly damp from his morning shower ... I'm all in. I sit here, thinking of how I wish I could reach out and brush that wayward lock away from his face, rub my palm on his stubbled jawline, kiss his lips ... And then I realize I can.

So I get up and walk over to him. I run my hand through his hair. He smiles down at me, but takes his free hand and moves me to the side.

"Let me plate the eggs and then we'll resume whatever you were starting there."

He slides a portion of eggs onto each of two plates next to our stacks of pancakes, then he sets the spatula down and turns toward me.

"You look good in the morning."

I laugh.

"I'm not joking. You look fresh-faced and so beautiful."

He strokes my face.

"You look pretty beautiful too."

"In a manly way, right?"

I chuckle. "Soooo manly."

Duke's face grows serious. "I want you, Shannon. I've wanted you for so long. And here you are." His words are a breath, a longing, a sigh that makes me lift my chin so he can see his yearning reflected in my eyes.

"You really do want me don't you?"

I'm still a little overwhelmed. I feel like someone is going to walk through and yell "Cut! That's a wrap!" and the scenery will be folded up and all this will end up being some play we were in, not my real life.

Instead of answering my question with words, Duke bites his bottom lip and I watch his pupils darken like an ink bottle spilling across paper. I loop my hands around his neck and tug him down toward me.

In the quiet stillness of Duke's kitchen, all I hear are the echoes of his words *I want you, Shannon.* And nothing matters beyond the way he wants me and the way I need him.

Duke bends in and wraps his arms behind me. We kiss in this homey, comfortable way. It's different from the feeling of our stolen kisses, or our first kisses where we were trying to make up for lost time and grab up what we could. This kiss feels like something so much more solid and lasting.

It's a kiss that hints at the future, what mornings could be like for years to come. Only those mornings will start much, much later in the day.

THIRTY-NINE

Duke

It's been a week of sneaking around, stealing time together, and indulging ourselves in the euphoria of our new relationship. I'm a combination of paranoid we'll get found out, irritated that we have to hide, and happier than I've ever been. But I'm also itching to hold Shannon's hand in public. Me. The guy who only does casual, out-of-town, short-term flings. I'm like a walking Beatles tune.

There's a car show in Columbus this coming Saturday and Sunday. The Fireflies don't have a ball game because it's the Fourth of July weekend. I'm hoping Shannon can come with me so we can be somewhere away from Bordeaux where I can take her out to eat, walk around among people with my arm around her shoulders, and pull her in for a kiss whenever I want.

Don't get me wrong, sneaking around has been its own form of fun, but it's already getting old and wearing on us both. I keep reminding myself and her it's only a few more weeks. By August this will all be behind us, and if I'm still living after we tell Chris, we'll have our whole lives ahead of us after that–together.

I take my cell out of my pocket and walk to the service drive out back of the garage so I can call Shannon without anyone overhearing me. I call her on her work phone just to mess with her.

"St. James Common Cents Accounting."

"Is this Miss Sent Jamess?" I ask with an accent that isn't quite British or German or really from any specifically identifiable country.

"Um. Yes. It is. May I help you?"

"Yasss. Yass you ken."

Silence. She doesn't know it's me. Or she knows and she's getting the upper hand.

I nearly chuckle, so I clear my throat.

"Miss Sent Jamess. I've had my eyeeee on you."

"Wha ...?"

She doesn't finish the sentence. Then she says, "Did you want to talk to Mr. St. James?"

"Meesture Sent Jamess? Actually, noh." My accent just slipped to something like an ancient camel herder in the Middle East—with a pack-a-day smoking habit and then ended with a very nasally French "no."

Shannon pauses and then resumes her professional tone. "Sir, we're an accounting firm. May I help you with something accounting-related?"

"Vell, as I said, I've had my eyeeeee on you. As an ahhdmirer. I vould like for us to haff an opportunity to meeet up."

I really hadn't planned this out. I thought I'd use that accent and she'd be on to me in a second. Then I'd leap right into my invitation for this weekend. But, I'm in this now.

"I don't even know who you are," Shannon says, keeping her tone professional, but also getting a little huffy. "And if you are the guy who sent me five bouquets of flowers, I should think you'd tell a woman your identity before you ask to meet up, as you so charmingly phrase it. Where are you from, anyway?"

My accent is from nowhere. Exactly no one speaks like this. At all, anywhere on the planet.

And five bouquets? What's up with that? I saw one. I had completely forgotten Jayme said Shannon has an admirer.

She's probably on the verge of hanging up on me, so I go all in. "Vell, if you saw my motorbike ahnd theeee vay I can plate an egg and peeek zeee best breakfast beverages, I zink you'd change your mind."

"Oh my gosh! Duke!"

She's laughing–hard. It's a combination of relief and being fully entertained by me. I love being the one to make her laugh like that.

"What even was that accent?" she asks through gasps of laughter.

"I don't even know," I admit.

"You're a dork."

"True. Just don't let that become common knowledge. I've got a reputation to uphold around here."

I can tell she's shaking her head.

"What did you really call me about?" she asks.

"I vant to meeeet up."

"Stop!" she starts laughing again.

"Okay. Okay. I actually have plans to go to the car show in Columbus this weekend. It might not be your cup of tea, but there are a few other things there I'd love to do together if you come with me. Think about it. We'd be able to walk around like a couple in public. I could take you out to eat."

She's quiet, so I'm quiet, holding my breath.

"I usually go overnight, but we could come back late Saturday. I know it's the holiday weekend, but we'd still be home for Monday's Red, White, and Blue, and Corn Too."

"Don't you think people would be suspicious if we both disappeared for the same weekend?"

"I already thought of that. We'll each take our own cars. You can meet me at the muni airport, park your car in the airport lot. I'll drive us from there. If enough people see us taking two cars, me driving away alone taking one road, and you driving off later down another, we won't look like a couple going on a weekend away together."

She only pauses for a moment before she shouts out, "I'd love to, yes!"

I hear her dad's voice in the background. Then Shannon covers the receiver so she can respond to him.

I hear her say, "Nothing, Mr. St. James. I'm just talking to a friend. I'll wrap the call up right now."

It's adorable how she calls her dad, Mr. St. James. I know she's keeping things professional at their workplace. I also know she'd want to kill me for calling her adorable. The way she says "Mister" reminds me of earlier this week when she called me Mr. Satterson at her dad's office. I liked it–a lot. I might have to ask her to call me Mr. Satterson one evening when we're alone in my home. We can play receptionist and ornery customer. And she can do that lip thing ...

Shannon snaps me out of my daydream.

"I've gotta run. Can't wait to meeeet up," she says, adding a little of my crazy accent to her voice.

"It vill be a weekhend to rememberrrr." I roll the R at the end because I can roll my Rs, and I want to hear Shannon laugh.

She's still giggling when we hang up.

I'm walking on sunshine thinking of a weekend, or even a full day, away with Shannon. The radio's blasting out *Blinded By the Light* by Manfred Mann's Earth Band. It could be my anthem, really. Aiden teases me about being born thirty or forty years past my time with my love for classic music and classic cars. But, you've gotta love a song where a man is singing an ode to his car and to street racing. Everyone thought he was singing about his girlfriend.

I glance toward where Shelb is parked out front. I love her. But she's no longer my number one girl. Not by a longshot. Good thing cars don't get jealous.

I meet Jayme at lunchtime at the library to study. She asked if

I wanted to meet at her house, but for some reason, I don't want to be there without Shannon knowing. And I haven't brought up my plans to take on teaching and coaching to Shannon yet. I don't know why. I probably ought to ask myself about that, but I'm too busy planning our weekend and getting my work done to give it much thought.

But now I'm thinking about it. Maybe I don't want to disappoint her if I don't end up nailing the exam. I want Shannon to be impressed with me. Besides, the more people I tell, the more real this becomes and the bigger load of guilt I'll be carrying on my back about how I'm letting Pops and this town down by pursuing my dreams.

Shannon and I talk after work. I try to talk her into coming over, but she's tired. When I ask about tomorrow night she said she and Laura are planning to grab pizza and catch up since they haven't seen one another for a while outside of their work at the salon and girls' night. I get that. I need my one-to-one with Brooks or Aiden. We might not sit around braiding one another's hair, but it's still needed.

Friday midmorning Pops calls me into the office. He only takes on smaller jobs these days. His hands are starting to ache and cramp if he does too much or when we're about to get a good rain. So, he spends more time sitting alone in this office or coming out to look over my shoulder while I work.

Our nurse practitioner told Pops he's got the signs of arthritis when he went to see her after Mabel and I nagged him to go get things checked out. He's stubborn, but not stupid. Eventually he knew we were right about him needing to have an actual medical professional assess him, and now he's on some supplements that seem to help a little. I'm thinking of him, his age and his health when I step into the office.

"Have a seat, Duke." Pops says.

There's something ominous in the air. I feel it.

I open the metal folding chair we stash in here in case a customer needs to sit. This place could use an overhaul to bring it into this century. It definitely screams single old man. But, we do good work, and we're local. I imagine what I'd do to fix the place up. Maybe even expand the office out a little to add a customer lounge. Nah. This is Bordeaux. We're not fancy. And this place isn't mine anymore.

I swallow a lump in my throat. Why do even the best decisions sometimes feel like someone's dying?

Dad steeples his fingers under his chin and gives me a look. His lips tighten and then he nods. "I'm fixing to start letting go of this place."

"I know. We've talked about that for the past few years."

"You're right, but I'm at a different place with things now. I've been planning on it for a while, but I need to stop planning and start doing."

I nod.

Pops takes a big breath and leans back in his chair. It's probably twenty or thirty years old, black, cushioned. It creaks a little when it moves. There's not a tear or a stain on the leather. The casters are worn down a bit, so are two spots on the armrests and a spot on the seat. But, his chair is like this place. Hanging in and faithfully serving people after all these years.

"I'm going to start taking Fridays off. And I want to bring in another mechanic."

I nod again and then I say, "Huh?"

"Another mechanic," Pops repeats. "If I back off, we'll need someone in here to take up the slack. And there's not a soul in this town who can do the job. There may be some young boy in high school I don't know who's got the knack–like you always had. But, I don't know of him, so I've been puttin' the word out around some outlying towns."

All I can do is stare at Pops. Someone who isn't family will come work here. It's never been that way as long as I can remember. This is Satterson's. We run it. Why am I feeling possessive over a place I'm about to abandon? I should be doing a jig.

"Okay," I say with a note of hesitation.

"I know it's hard to accept change, son. We all want to believe we're immortal. Even though we know that's not the case. Our family knows that truth more than some. It was forced on us. But, we still live like we've got forever. Something happens to a man when he sees the finish line coming closer."

Pops stares off out the door toward the service bay.

"Everything falls into place. That's what happens. I love this place. Always loved it. When my Pops opened it, I was young. But I grew up here. It's as much home as the house where your Ma and I raised you and your sisters. But, there comes a time when a man needs to ask himself if he wants to be sitting in an office most of his life, talking to townsfolk about their dead batteries and hearing them rant on about the cost of a catalytic converter. And my time for that is coming to a close. My backyard is calling to me. And so is my girl."

I'm usually not a quiet man, as you know. I'm silent right now. I'm sitting on a minefield of my own news and it doesn't feel right sharing it when Pops just laid his heart out.

"You've earned your retirement," I tell him.

"I might even take Mabel on a vacation somewhere. You know. Like Aruba."

"What makes you pick that place?"

Is it mere irony that Pops wants to go where Principal Barnes is headed? I feel my worlds colliding like a bad crash on a racetrack.

"Well, funny story. I bumped into Steven Barnes the other day. He said he and his wife were going there for two weeks and I thought, I've never been outside Ohio. All these years and my most exotic vacation has been going to see the Reds play and getting Skyline Chili in Cincinnati."

Does he know about my decision? He's not saying. Maybe he's waiting for me to say something. I need time. I want to tell him about my opportunity. But, now that he's planning to actually back off the business, I need to let him. I've got time. Well, I've got a few weeks at least.

Besides, I still need to pass the test. If I pass, I'll tell him. If not, no harm, no foul. I'll keep on overseeing Satterson's, leading the Fireflies to victory, and maybe I'll even add on a customer lounge one day.

I picture Cooter hanging out in there, scaring away other customers, giving commentary on my repair jobs, drinking up all my free coffee.

Nope.

No customer lounge. That's final.

FORTY

Shannon

Have I been avoiding my best friend for over a week?
Maaaybe.

Okay. Yes.

I've practically been jumping into the bushes if I see her anytime outside our unavoidable interactions at the salon. And, at the Dippity Do, I stay busy with clients, making small-talk, and asking Laura questions about herself so that she's distracted from prying into the reason I can't stop smiling.

And I can't stop smiling. For real.

I'm painting Mrs. Barnes' toes right now. She leaves tomorrow for Aruba with her husband.

"You look exceptionally happy today, Shannon. Not that you don't always," Mrs. Barnes says to me.

"She's been sickeningly happy for about a week now," Laura chimes in from where she's putting foil in Mrs. Milgarden's hair.

I smile at Laura with a toothy grin, showing both my top and bottom rows of teeth.

She shakes her head and mouths, *I'm getting to the bottom of this tonight.*

Great. She's going to dig and pry over pizza. And it's not like I don't want her to know. It's a fact that the more people you share a secret with, the less likely it will be that the secret stays hidden.

Mrs. Barnes carries on about what she's going to pack for Aruba. "We're swimming with actual stingrays. I still don't know if it's safe, but Steven assured me they wouldn't have it as an attraction if tourists got killed doing it. And, if I'm going to have a death by stingray, at least I'll have those darling pineapples on my toenails when I do!"

I chuckle. "You'll be coming back here in one healthy, tanned piece. Pineapple toes and all. I can't wait to hear all about it."

"Steven's so smart. That's why he's the principal. Well, that and the fact that the old principal retired to Florida and no one else wanted the position. But, that's neither here nor there. If he says we won't get hurt, I'm pretty sure he's right.

"Anyway ..." She goes on about ziplining, and how the resort has massages on the beach and won't that be a thing mixing sand and oil. And you'd think they'd have massages somewhere less sandy. Then she wonders out loud if those drinks with all the fruit in them will make her tipsy because she doesn't like being too tipsy–because she always rattles on without end and says ridiculous things when she drinks too much.

I'm just smiling.

It's getting obnoxious, I admit it.

But, every few minutes, I think of Duke, and I smile.

Laura keeps looking over at me like one of those cops in Blue Bloods when they corner the suspect in the room with the metal table. She's definitely the bad cop. She's giving me this, *you will crack or you will never see the light of day* glare whenever Mrs. Milgarden isn't looking.

I give her a *what are you even talking about* look in response.

We can have whole conversations with our eyes. It's a gift. Except when it isn't.

Laura has been my bestie since elementary school. She's like an artisan loaf of sourdough right out of the oven–a bit crusty on the outside, but all soft and warm under that tough exterior and so worth getting past the first crunch. Of the eight billion people in the world, Laura gets me–really, really gets me.

She's been aware of my crush on Duke for years. But I've never admitted it to her. If you think that makes me the lamest best friend in the world, I can't even argue with you. I probably am. I've actually flat-out denied feeling anything for him but brotherly love–or sisterly love–whatever siblings feel for one another.

It felt pointless to concede that I couldn't stop longing for him. Admitting my crush would not have helped my cause–which, at the time, was to be rid of my obsession with all things Duke Satterson. Somehow I convinced myself that denying it long enough would kill the feelings. We all see how well that worked out for me.

Last Thursday, when Duke stalked toward me through his kitchen and broke the tension between us with the kiss of my lifetime, everything changed. Now he and I are sitting on this secret for my brother's sake.

But, Jayme knows. And that makes me feel beyond disloyal to Laura.

When Laura finds out Jayme knew first–which she will find out; she always finds out–I'll be on her list. You never want to be on Laura's list. Rob was on her list for six long, excruciating years. But, now they're married. Maybe she'd forgive me too–in six long, excruciating years.

I think of Chris. As upset with him as I've been this past week, I know his heart is in the right place. He wants to see me happy and safe. And I love him. When he comes home I want to give him the gift of being able to focus on reintegration with his family and friends. He deserves to be celebrated and for everyone's eyes and thoughts to be on him and what he gave up to serve us.

I don't want to draw attention off Chris and onto me and Duke ... like when it came out that Sandra Bullock had been dating Ryan Gosling. Talk about distracting! Then again, anything about Ryan Gosling is distracting, am I right?

After two more manicures and a mani-pedi, my day wraps up. Laura's sweeping up the clippings from a cut she just gave. The other stylists are standing around chatting while they close up their stations.

Laura looks over at me, "Last chance to escape spending time with me tonight."

"What? Why would I want to escape time with you?"

"I've got a strong hunch, but let's be real here. You've gone just short of wearing a disguise and using a voice-changing device to avoid me for about seven days. So, you have an out right now. I'm going to get you to spill. If you're not ready to tell all, cancel our plans."

"Tell me how you really feel," I tease.

One thing I've always loved about Laura is her direct approach. You never wonder where you stand with her. You may sometimes wonder about her personal life because she keeps her cards tucked close, but she's never one to shield you from her thoughts or feelings about what you're doing or whatever's going on around us.

"I'm in," I say with more certainty than I feel.

Laura will get me to spill like a stool pigeon in a jail cell. I'm going to be singing the truth out in no time. She won't even need a bare bulb or threats to my loved ones. Maybe I want to spill to her. I really do.

She's my best friend. I love my brother, but I love Laura in a whole different way–like a sister, a sister I chose and who chose me back. And I trust her. I want to tell her.

I'll explain it to Duke later. He'll understand.

Laura smiles like the cat who ate the canary, minus any feathers sticking out the sides of her mouth. She's nearly rubbing her hands together in anticipation. Meanwhile, I feel sick to my stomach, and it's not the combination of an extra-large slushie from Dairyland and the bag of hot Cheetos I had for lunch inducing my queasiness either.

"Okay. Wrap up whatever you need to. I'll drive us over to Pops. I'll even let you pick the toppings."

"I don't know if I can eat," I mutter.

"You'll eat. It's just me. Whatever it is you're sitting on is meant to be shared with your best friend. I'm just doing you the favor of forcing it out in the open between us. I promise to be gentle."

I laugh. Not that she can't be gentle. She can be surprisingly protective and very careful. Loyalty is one of Laura's strongest traits. It's just the idea of me needing her to be gentle. I guess I do. I'm still so wobbly about Duke anyway. I go from complete, overwhelming ecstasy to wondering if he can make it past a six month milestone, to worrying about how my brother will take the news and what his reaction will do to us and our extended friend group.

I really do need to talk to Laura. I've been keeping all this inside too long.

We order my favorite pizza. No veggies. Pepperoni and sausage and garlic. Wait. Is garlic a veggie? Nevermind. It's not. It's a flavor-enhancing item. And I love it. Pops makes their crust with some magic combination of butter and garlic and spices brushed on and I could eat the crust alone.

Laura leaves hers on the plate sometimes, and I call them "pizza bones." I always snatch them up and eat them like breadsticks. That's one benefit of being a dancer who isn't trying to stay dancer-thin anymore. I can eat. And I do.

Once we're seated, Laura looks me straight in the eyes. We're at a booth separated from the tables in the center of the restaurant where some families are eating. It's not packed tonight. I'm grateful for the privacy.

"Spill."

"You aren't even going to lead up to it?"

"I'm not courting you, I'm getting you to finally tell me this secret you've got tucked away. No need to butter you up. I'm already taking you to pizza. And you'll notice I didn't bring Lexi and Jayme or Em into this. It's just the two of us. Spill."

"Wow. You really know how to woo a girl," I joke.

I take a huge gulp of my Diet Pepsi while Laura sits by doing her best impersonation of a patient woman. She wouldn't win any awards for this performance, to be sure.

I put my pop down on the table, take a big breath, and pull both hands up to my face to cover the ear-to-ear grin that will not subside when I think of Duke. I peer out through my fingers like that one emoji—you know, the peeking one.

"It's Duke," Laura says. "You and Duke. I knew it!"

She is not quiet. At least the *you and Duke* part was a little quiet. But the *I knew it* is loud enough for Pops to look over from behind the counter.

"Shhhhh," I say, from behind my mask of fingers.

"Drop your hands, missy," Laura says. "And, oh my gosh!"

I just nod. And blush. And grin like a dufus on laughing gas. I think my eyes are turning into little glitter factories. I feel them tingling with sparkles. That's how good it feels to be with Duke and to be sharing the news with my bestie.

"Oh my gosh!" Laura says again.

She shakes her head, bites into the pizza and says, "Oh my gosh," with her mouth full.

"I'm literally dying here," Laura says as she swallows her bite with a swig of root beer. "Did I call this or what?"

I told Duke she'd be so overcome with her rightness. Nothing makes Laura more happy than being right.

"You called it," I say, still beaming like some little forest sprite.

I could star in one of those gum commercials where everyone's falling in love and kissing with a little ding of a high-pitched bell going off each time they smile or kiss.

"Oh my gosh!" Laura shouts.

I give her time to assimilate the reality. Each *Oh my gosh* has a different inflection, *you're so busted, I'm so happy for you, I can't believe this* ... I think she's moving through some sort of stages of grief, only not grieving.

Finally, Laura simply looks at me with the sweetest smile. She shakes her head lightly and says, "Oh my gosh. You and Duke," like it's settled and a very good thing.

"Yep."

I smile some more. It's my new thing.

Then I say, "So, I guess your work here is done."

"Not even close, you. I need details. So many details. And why haven't you told me? Seriously! What was that about?"

Okay. Maybe this is her going through the stages of grief after all, and she's moving into anger from shock. I hope we skip past depression and bargaining right into acceptance from here.

"I never admitted my crush to you because I had this idea that not talking about it would make it go away."

"Yeah. That's not how it works."

"Obviously."

"How long have you been crushing on Duke?" she asks. Then she mumbles to herself more than me. "You and Duke. I knew it. But, wow."

"Um. A long time."

"Like a year? Since Chris left?"

"Probably forever."

She just laughs. "Yeah. That's about right. I always knew. I just kept trying to believe you when you said you didn't."

"Anyway, last Thursday I went to his place to plan Chris' homecoming, and well, one thing led to another. And we kissed."

I look down at my plate and cover my mouth with my napkin. I'm smiling so hard.

"You can smile about it. Stop hiding this happiness. I'll deal."

I look up.

She pretends to cover her eyes to protect from the glare of my radiant happiness.

"So, you kissed."

"Mmhmmm. He's perfect." My voice sounds airy, even to my

own ears. "I've liked Duke for so long. I built him up until his pedestal was so high. I've always known he was a goofball, man-boy with one toe over the line. But, this past week I've seen new sides to him. We've spent time talking and hanging out, just the two of us. Now I know him as a man, not just my high-school fantasy. And that should make things worse, but it doesn't. It's better. So much better. He's so careful with me, but he trusts me too. He treats me like a woman, not like Chris' little sister. He's smart, and thoughtful. And he kisses ..."

"Got it. He's a good kisser. No one ever questioned that. Look at the man. He oozes some sort of rare sensuality, and all that shameless flirting. He's just one of those people you're sure knows how to kiss."

I shake my head. He is a shameless flirt.

"It's something else having all that intensity of his laser focused on me. It's the sweetest thing and almost overwhelming."

"You deserve it. You know that right? You're such a catch. It's not like you hit the jackpot and you're the lucky one. More like the opposite is true."

"Trust me, he's a catch," I tell her.

"Trust me, you are." She points her slice of pizza at me to emphasize her words. "So, what's the deal with the secrecy?"

"Chris."

"Ahhh. Yeah. Makes sense. You want to tell him first. In person. But he's discharging. This timing stinks."

As usual, Laura sees through to the heart of a situation.

"It does."

"I get the reason you aren't letting this out now. But, you could have told me."

I look at her and reach my hand across the table to put my palm on top of her fingers. "I didn't mean to tell anyone. Jayme guessed. And I couldn't lie to her face. Then I felt so badly that she knew and you didn't. If I were going to tell anyone, it would be you."

She nods. Nothing else needs to be said.

"So, what's it like, secret-dating your life-long crush?" She shakes her head in disbelief again like she's going to have to repeat the truth to herself for days to come to really let it sink in. It's more that it's Duke, than anything, I think. She's picturing him and his playful ways and how he's so falsely arrogant for show. I know she's trying to figure out how a man like him finally settles down, even if he ends up with a girl like me. That's the way she'd see it.

"We lived for so long dancing at arm's length, it's like I don't know what to do with this new reality. Even the slightest touch of his hand on mine feels forbidden and risky and thrilling.

"I've made a living on whatever glimpses and innocuous conversations Duke and I shared over the years. We'd flirt or banter for fun and I'd tuck those interactions away and live off them.

"I want to allow myself to believe we can be more—to dare to hope we could have everything. But I know two things for certain. Chris will be coming home. And, like you said, we both want to honor Chris and all he gave up to serve. And honoring Chris means Duke and I may have an expiration date."

I feel my face fall a little. It hurts saying that out loud, and it makes it feel more real than when it was just a possibility I batted around in my own head.

"There's no way this ends with a happily ever after.

We're Johnny Depp and Winona, or Johnny Depp and Jennifer Grey ... or Johnny Depp and Kate Moss ... only without the same press coverage or scandalous rumors, and Duke won't have a *Shannon Forever* tattoo he'll have to alter to *non Forever* or something."

Laura chuckles.

"Actually, there will be rumors. What am I thinking? This is Bordeaux."

"You're not Johnny Depp and anyone. You're you and Duke. You don't have an inevitable expiration date."

Laura's face softens with compassion. "Do you want my opinion?"

"You're asking?"

"Not really. It's just polite to ask."

I laugh. "Go ahead. Lay it on me."

"Chris can suck a lemon. Bro code is dumb. This is your life. And Duke's."

Laura lets that truth-bomb sit on the table between us. She takes a breath and spears me with this look she's always given me when she wants me to take her seriously.

"Now, whether our boy, Duke, can commit to anyone is a huge unknown variable. He's never committed to anyone for longer than a half-year–if those were even commitments. Two seasons and he's out. There are the winter-spring girls and the summer-fall girls. And none of them have been local. This most recent one lasted longer. She got a whole year, but in the end, her fate was the same as the rest. I don't know if that's progress or not. But she still never crossed town lines.

"So, does he have commitment issues?" Laura hums like she's deliberating when we both know she's already fully settled on an answer. "Probably. But who doesn't when you think about it?

"Then again, he's always seemed to have this special thing for you, so it would make sense that he's finally settling down and he was just entertaining himself with companionship because he thought he couldn't have you. I'm not ruling out his capacity to commit. Just saying I want you to be careful. But I don't want you to miss this time. Early love. It's the best. If they could bottle it, we'd all walk around permanently smiling."

"True. It's the best I've ever felt, that's for sure."

I don't know if I can call this love yet. I do love Duke, but in the same way I love all my old friends. Do I love, love him? I'm not sure. I'm definitely falling for him.

I think of Laura's warning about Duke.

"So, what you're saying is to fully immerse myself in the

euphoria of new love while simultaneously keeping my guard up because Duke might hurt me at some point?"

"Right. Yeah. When you put it like that it's just wrong. So, you know what? Jump! Go! Run like it's March and you're in your skivvies and we're holding hands and leaping into the freezing Res water! I mean, I'm not jumping with you, but I'll be here on shore with a towel if he starts to drown you. And I'll kill him. Just sayin'. If he hurts you, he's never getting a haircut from me again."

"That's a death threat if I ever heard one."

"To him or Brooks it is."

We laugh.

"Those men and their hair," I say, rolling my eyes.

FORTY-ONE

Duke

This trip out of town may have been my best idea ever. Well, second best. The first was kissing Shannon that day in my kitchen.

I watch her from across the parking lot, pulling in and choosing her spot. When she sees me, she comes running over from her car toward me. I catch her midair and she wraps her arms around my neck and her legs around my torso.

This.

Her in my arms. In public.

It's everything.

Granted, we're on the secluded back lot of the airport with no prying local eyes, but still, we're not hiding. We're free of all that holds us back—even if it's only for a day.

"The things I want to do to you," I say at a near growl into her ear.

"Good things?" She teases me, still clinging, but leaning back to look in my eyes.

"Very good things."

I slowly let her slip down until her feet hit the pavement. Then I run the back of my hand down her arm, lean in and nip her earlobe lightly. I trail kisses down her neck.

"Those are good," she says in a breathy voice. "I mean, on a scale of good to great, I'd say you're okay."

She's barely able to use her voice without the telltale quaver.

I hum onto her neck, and feel the goosebumps raise on her skin under my lips. I love affecting her—love the way she responds to me.

"Okay, huh?" I ask.

"Yep," she says, popping the P for emphasis.

"Well, I'd better practice, you know, to improve my ranking."

Shannon tilts her head, intentionally exposing the column of her neck to me.

Batting her lashes and staring at me with a look that is a concoction made of one part challenge and one part longing, she says. "You better."

This girl. No. This woman.

I grumble or make some sort of noise that vibrates through my chest and reveals the rabid animal she always brings out in me. Then, with the restraint of a celibate monk, I slowly run my fingertips up her neck, following that path with my lips.

Right. Celibate monks don't do that. I'm just restraining myself from doing more.

I leave a trail of feather light kisses along the path to Shannon's mouth. When my lips find hers, I kiss her sweetly, showing her all the things I can never find words to adequately say to her. Shannon melts into me and I hold her as I run my hands up and down her biceps and our kiss deepens.

"I've got you," I murmur as we come up for a breath, our foreheads resting together like we're in the world's sweetest huddle. I want to shout about her from the rooftops–to go into town together, to have her with me in the open. Sure, sneaking around brings a certain element of intensity and intrigue, but I'm pretty much over all that. As far as I'm concerned, we've waited long enough for one another. I want to make this official. And I'm not a patient man when it comes to what I want.

Shannon looks into my eyes, cups my cheeks and in the most

affectionate tone of voice, whispers, "I've got you too, Duke. I do."

I'm not an emotional man, at least I don't think I am, but when she says those words, I feel tears pressing at the backs of my eyes.

I'm the baby brother. The only boy in a sea of slightly-overbearing women. I'm used to being coddled and directed. What I'm not used to is the reverent way Shannon seems to be telling me she'll do whatever it takes to stand by me and help me live out my dreams, face my fears, and fight my demons. In that simple phrase she said it all.

I have to tell her about my certification and the opportunity at the high school. She needs to know.

"We should hit the road," I say reluctantly.

"Let's get this party started!"

Shannon raises her arms overhead and does a little shimmy over to my Shelby.

Once we're buckled in and the sweet roar of the supercharged V-8 comes to life, I take off for the highway.

"So, what's new?"

"I offered to take on more classes at the Rec Center."

"We could use a little more dancing around here."

"Agreed. And more art in general. We're so good about supporting sports. We need more encouragement of the arts. I've got dreams. I just don't know if they're too lofty."

"I'm going out of my way to dream with you," I say, wagging my eyebrows.

"You dream of kissing me. That's different."

"Not going to deny that," I say with a look toward her mouth. "Can you blame me? I'm like a kid who finally got to eat ice cream."

She giggles.

"But seriously, I'm here for your dreams."

She gets real quiet and looks over at me through her lashes, "You are my dreams."

Whew. I don't even know what to say to that, so I just smile and loop our fingers together, keeping my left hand on the wheel and my eyes on the road.

Our road trip song list fills the car. It's a bizarre blend of sixties and seventies rock, modern hip-hop, and old school R&B. Like us, it doesn't make sense, but somehow it works.

An Al Green tune comes on and Shannon starts moving to the rhythm and singing the words softly, almost to herself.

I'm gone. Lost. At the point of no return.

And it's so much worse than I imagined.

And better. Infinitely better.

I had myself convinced I loved Shannon. That all these years she was it for me. And the few friends who suspected I wanted her assumed I'd break her with my cavalier, noncommittal ways.

I watch her while she's completely oblivious to the thoughts whirling through my head. She's lost in the music and letting herself be here, fully immersed in this moment.

They had it all wrong.

I won't break Shannon. She will decimate me. And I'm not going to stop her.

If all I have are stolen moments between now and when Chris comes home, I'm going to take each one.

No regrets. No hesitation. No holding back.

I bought Shannon something this week. It's not a ring. I'm crazy, but not clinically insane. We need time, even though we've known one another forever.

While I was picking up an engine in Dayton this past week, I passed this jewelry store. I parked the work truck and walked in. I started out looking at rings—thinking one day I'll be buying one for Shannon. Then this necklace caught my eye and nothing could have been more perfect. It's on a rose gold chain with a rose gold ballet shoe dangling down. There's a diamond on the toe of the shoe.

Giving Shannon this necklace is my way of showing her I want her to pursue her dreams, to remember them when she wears it, and to know that I plan to be there every step of the way, supporting her.

I'm going to wait to give the necklace to her at just the right time. In the meantime, this little black velvet bag is burning a hole in my pocket wherever I go.

Shannon looks over at me with a sheepish grin. "I have a confession."

My stomach clenches and my grip on the wheel gets a little tighter. I remind myself to breathe. Confession can mean lots of things.

As casually as I can, I ask, "Yeah? What's that?"

"I may have leaked the fact that we're seeing one another. I told Jayme when she guessed. And then Laura squeezed it out of me over pizza last night."

I look over at her. She's got this adorable guilty look on her face. Her head's tilted and her eyebrows are raised up toward the center of her forehead.

"I forgive you. It's really too good to keep quiet about it, isn't it?"

She smiles big.

"Anyway," I say with a shrug. "I told Brooks."

She smacks my arm playfully.

"You didn't!"

"He saw you in the bleachers at practice, so he kept ribbing me and poking at the truth. Finally, when we were working out yesterday, I let it out. He's going to keep it to himself. I trust him. I'm the person he's closest to in town anyway."

"I trust Jayme and Laura too."

"I'd tell Aiden, but I can't. He knows about the crush I had on you, but he made it clear if something's happening between us and he knew for sure, I'd be putting him between a rock and a hard place if it came down to keeping a secret from Chris."

"We stink at keeping secrets," Shannon says with a giggle.

"What do you expect? We're from a small town."

"It's the worst!"

"We've basically been raised on corn and gossip with a little lovin' in the mix for good measure."

Our laughter blends like the sweetest harmony, and all I can think about is the day ahead and then how perfect it will be when we finally get to tell everyone about us.

We park my car in one of the spaces where security guards are stationed to watch over the cars. I plan to walk around the show with Shannon, but I also cleaned Shelb up for a day of being the star she is. People love seeing a well-restored Shelby. I'll spend a little time hanging out, answering questions, or just letting people admire her in front of me later.

For now, I'm more interested in walking around the show with Shannon on my arm. I know a lot of the other drivers and car owners here. Most of them are from surrounding towns, so they're not about to spread news of me and Shannon into Bordeaux. Everyone here is used to me bringing a date. Even though Shannon's not just another girl on my arm, they won't know the difference.

We walk around admiring cars. Shannon's really into the automobiles from the twenties and thirties. She eyes the Roadsters and covers her open mouth when she sees this black Buick Y-Job. She's got taste. That car's mint.

She stops in front of this classic green pearl Madame X and gasps. "She's beautiful!"

The owner's probably in his seventies. He stands and wanders over from his folding chair under the canopy where his wife or girlfriend stays seated.

"Wanna hop in?" he offers.

"Oh! Could I?"

"This car was made for beauty. You should do me the honor of seeing you sitting in the driver's seat."

Ah. He's my breed of man: a smooth-talker. Good thing he's old enough to be our grandpa. He looks over at me with a wink. I nod to him as he opens the door and Shannon slides right in. She looks up at him and he says, "Go ahead, put your hands on the wheel like you're about to take 'er for a spin."

She does and she bounces just a little when her hands meet the polished wood. I had no idea Shannon would light up like this over cars. As if she weren't already perfect, she's got me deeper than ever. There's nothing more appealing than a woman with an appreciation for a good car.

I take my phone out and capture a few shots of Shannon behind the wheel. She hams it up, waving out the window, blowing me a kiss, leaning her arm on the door panel with one hand on the wheel.

She relinquishes her spot eventually and we thank the owner of the car. We're only a few steps away when I sweep her into my arms.

She squeals at the unexpected move.

I turn her so she's facing me. "You're amazing. Do you know that?"

"You're not so bad yourself," she says, smiling up at me.

People file by us, moving from car to car or whatever they're doing. We're in our own world in the middle of it all.

I weave my hand into Shannon's hair, tilting her face toward mine. I study her before I lean in to claim her mouth in a kiss.

She loops her arms over my shoulders and stands on her tiptoes to reach me, and I pull her in closer. Our lips meet and we're falling together. We've kissed in private, but we're out here in a crowd, kissing for everyone to see and there's something about it that makes this connection between us all the more intimate and intense.

We pull apart. Shannon glances around shyly and then looks back up at me. My eyes rove across her face, taking her in like I'm standing with my toes dangling over the edge of the Grand Canyon. She's beyond description, layers and depth, vast and awe-inspiring.

When I kiss those pouty lips again, I move slowly, tenderly. Our connection tugs me deeper into sweetness and need.

When I pull away, she tucks her bottom lip into her mouth and lets it pop back out. Then her thumb comes up and she rubs across my bottom lip.

"You had my lipstick ... smeared ..."

She holds her now-reddened thumb up like exhibit A, and I resist taking it to my lips to kiss it or playfully nip and suck it. I've never wanted to kiss a woman's thumb before. Is it weird? Probably.

Shannon giggles this bashful laugh. I try my best to diffuse her nerves by puckering and pursing my lips. "Was it in my shade?"

She looks up at me through her lashes and nods while she laughs this melodic laugh.

Then she says, "I'm sort of giddy."

She coyly turns her head downward. I barely see the blush rising up her neck toward her cheeks from this angle.

"It's not natural. Is it?" she asks. "To feel this way about another person?"

She's asking me? How would I know? I just know there's no one else like her. And she's mine. And this is my moment.

I reach in my pocket and pull out the black bag. A look of confusion passes over Shannon's face.

"I don't know what's normal, Hollywood. I just know how you make me feel and what you mean to me."

I take her hand and turn it palm up in my hand, and then I place the bag into her hand.

"What's this?" Shannon asks.

"Open it and see."

She gently pulls the drawstring and shakes the necklace out into her cupped hand. Then she gasps.

"Duke! It's beautiful."

She holds the necklace up from the clasp so the ballet shoe dangles out in front of her face.

"When did you ...? How did you ...? This is so thoughtful."

I step behind her and take the necklace out of her hand. Then I sweep her hair out of the way and lift the necklace around her neck and clasp it in place, letting my fingers graze along the chain before I walk around her to admire her.

Shannon lightly pinches the charm between her thumb and pointer finger, rubbing it as if it's her most prized possession, and then she lets it drop onto her chest where she places her hand over it for a moment.

The smile on her face says it all.

FORTY-TWO

Shannon

This necklace. It's so unexpected.

It feels like an anchor and a set of wings all at once. My fingers keep returning to the ballet slipper charm. I might be reading into what this gift means. I want to believe Duke is telling me he heard my heart. He wants to support me as I go after my crazy, impractical dreams. And he knows what matters most to me.

On top of all that, this necklace reminds me of Bridgette, but in a happy way. We shared dance. I think I'm finally ready to dance for the two of us.

Duke and I walk through the car show holding hands as though it's the most natural thing in the world. Whenever we stop, he'll bend down and place a kiss on my forehead, or he'll lift our enjoined hands and place a kiss on my knuckles. He gazes into my eyes at times, and I feel like all my worries about him were unfounded. He makes me feel like nothing matters but us.

I am one hundred percent addicted to everything about Duke, including his red hot kisses—yes, he tastes like the candy he indulges in from time to time, but face it, our kisses are all kinds of red hot.

I find myself waiting for the playful glances he sends my direction, the way he studies me, his soft touches that send chills skittering across my skin. I relish the feel of his abs under my hands when I'm on the back of his bike, and the words he says to me about us and feelings he has for me.

I have never felt so wanted, noticed and special in my life.

When we make our way back to the Shelby, someone has put up a couple of lawn chairs for us. I take a seat in one and Duke sits in the other. He hands me a pop from a cooler sitting between us and the couple next to us who have a vintage T-Bird sitting out with the hood open. You could eat dinner off the engine, it's so shiny and clean.

"Thanks, Jack," Duke hollers over to the man.

"No problem, Duke. You know that. I come prepared."

"Well, you know me," Duke says. "I don't."

They laugh like old friends. I wait for Duke to introduce me, but someone comes up to Jack and starts asking car questions.

Duke winks at me and takes a sip of his soda.

A little annoying voice in my head says Duke is like this with everyone. He's flirty and warm. I'm no different to him than the rest of the world. I touch the necklace for assurance while I tell the voice in my head to kindly shush up. She doesn't listen. Instead there's this residual quiet whisper taunting me that I won't get to keep what we have because nothing this good lasts.

It's like when you're on vacation and you hit that certain deep level of relaxation. You can't maintain that kind of chill vibe in your real life because you'll come home to bills and laundry and responsibilities. Duke and I will hit reality at some point too. The question is, what will happen then?

"Hey," Duke says, looking at me with his puppy dog eyes. "Where'd you go?" He taps my temple lightly with his finger.

How does he know me so well?

He's Duke. That's how.

We grew up together. He's been around me as much or more than anyone else in my life. It makes sense he'd be aware of shifts in my thoughts and moods.

"I just ..." I don't get to finish that sentence because someone shouts Duke's name. It's a female voice that sounds very happy to see him. She comes running to where we're sitting, wearing a pair of very short cut-off jean shorts and a red polka dot bikini top. She has an old, but fashionable cowgirl hat on with two long, blond curly pigtails sticking out from the back. Her calves are covered by a pair of well-worn cowboy boots. She doesn't see me, or if she does, she couldn't care less that I'm here.

"Duke, Duke, Duke!" She shouts with a big smile as she bends down toward him and throws her arms around his neck in a big hug. He pats her back once and gently pushes her shoulders so she detaches from him.

Whew. I thought we were going to need some spirit gum to get her off him. Clingy much?

She still hasn't looked at me–at all.

"Hi," I say, leaning in across Duke a little. "I'm Shannon."

Oh yes. I guess I am territorial after all. And I'm about to hop into Duke's lap, wrap my arms around his neck and start petting him like he's my own grizzly bear. Or something like that. A declawed, domesticated bear, who only has eyes for me.

But first I need to find a cardigan to cover up Betty Boop and all her boopiness. Land's sakes.

"Oh," Miss Pinup says to me. "Hi."

I smile. I promise it's a smile and not a snarl. Well, maybe it's a smarl, or a snile. I'm somewhere on the spectrum between friendly and feeling the tiny hairs on my skin raise like a feline arching for a catfight. I put my arm on Duke's and set my hand on top of his. He smirks.

This is so not funny, mister. Stop your smirkity smirking right now. Duke does not get to think I'm cute when I'm jealous–because I'm not. Not jealous and not cute at it.

I'm just setting clear, healthy boundaries. Ones that say, "Mine," It's like a *No Trespassing* sign. Betty Boop needs to watch for my barbed wire fence, that's all. Wouldn't want her to snag her shorts on the spiky things.

"It's so good to see you, Duke," Elly May Clampett says to him. "How long has it been?"

Duke shrugs.

Little Miss Daisy Duke knows he's mine. She's just trying to spark something. So far he's behaving like a well-trained pet bear. Good Duke.

"Oh, goodness. Let's see." Boopity Boop Boop says with a bend at the waist that is completely unnecessary unless she's trying to dislodge something. "We were here together two years ago, wasn't it? Do you remember when we ..."

"Amber," Duke growls.

Oh, my. The bear has been poked.

"Sorry. Sorry. I was just walking down memory lane. Good memories." She licks her lips slowly while she runs her finger along her clavicle.

A man walks up beside Rosie the Riveter and asks Duke, "Is this your Shelby?"

Duke nearly hurdles over Amber to get to the man. They start talking, and Amber notices me now. Oh, yes she does. As a matter of fact, she turns to me with a very purposeful look in her eyes, honing in on me like she's C-3PO in denim cut-offs and an immodest swim top and she's here to deliver R2-D2's holographic message to save the galaxy.

Her voice isn't exactly quiet, but she's talking so only I can hear her.

"Good luck," She glances wistfully at Duke.

"He'll make you want him like you've never wanted anyone. And then poof! He'll disappear. He's not built for longevity, but the ride is nice while it lasts. Take it from one who's been there. Enjoy these moments while you have them. He makes you feel like no one else exists outside your little bubble. It's a gift, or a curse. A gift while you're with him, a curse when he decides time's up.

"Right now, you're the sun in his solar system, but he's too much of a free spirit to really settle down. You'll find out he's holding back big pieces of his life from you. That's when you know. You're not what you thought you were. But like I say, enjoy the ride. You'll never find another like him. It'll be the best six months of your life."

I want to tell her that it's different between me and Duke, that I grew up with him, that we've been pining for one another all these years. But, something about how she described how he made her feel sounded way too on the money.

At least she doesn't wait for me to answer. She turns and walks away. She passes by Duke, running a hand down his arm as she leaves.

"Good to see you, big guy."

I have never wanted to scratch someone's eyes out before. It's not a feeling I ever thought I could experience. I need air–even though we're outdoors.

I walk toward Duke, who is turning toward me anyway like a nervous, guilty man, even though he's really done nothing wrong–yet.

Before he can say anything, I say, "I'm going to use the restroom. I'll be right back." I walk toward the row of porta-potties and try to shake off the slime of that encounter.

I can't seem to get over the way some of the things Amber said line up with what I know. And she's not wrong. I've felt like I was the only one who mattered, like our world consists of the two of us and we mean more to one another than anything or anyone else. It's obvious Duke doesn't feel anything for Amber now. He was kind, but put up good limits.

But, did he ever treat her differently? Did she matter to him in the past? I'd say the answer to both those questions is a resounding yes.

FORTY-THREE

Duke

Amber.

Well, that sure threw a wrench in today's plans.

Yes. She and I had fun. I never led her on. We had "the talk" before we started going out. I told her I don't do serious, and I'd love to meet up sometime and hang out. If the first date went well with any woman before Shannon, I'd always reiterate the fact that I'm not looking for anything serious or long-term–just having fun for a few months or so.

Amber's not the first to try to push me for more. I hated it when she went there. I felt responsible, even though I'd been so clear up front.

Aiden met Amber once. I had invited him to a car show when Amber and I were first hanging out. He shook his head and said, "When are you going to stop picking women like that?"

A man ought to listen to his best friends. They always have his back. At the time I thought he was jealous, or he'd sniffed too much goat manure and it warped his brain–the part that was supposed to be out dating and having fun at our age.

Amber's beautiful, but in a way that says she's working hard at displaying the merchandise, not in the natural and alluring way Shannon is. I can't even compare the two women, even though

I'm sure that's what Shannon's doing while she's locked in a porta-potty. No one stays in those things longer than they need to, and she's been there at least five minutes.

I tell the guy talking my ear off about the Shelby that I need to check on my girlfriend.

"Oh. Yeah. Fine," he says. "How much would you sell her for?"

"My girlfriend?"

I look at the guy like he's nuts.

He laughs. "No, no. The car. Your Shelby."

"Ohhh. Okay. She's not for sale. She's worth over one hundred sixty five. But she's not for sale." I laugh. "Neither of them are."

He laughs with me. "Welp. If you ever change your mind, here's my number."

He hands me a business card.

"Not changing my mind, but thanks," I say as I pocket his card and walk toward the porta-potties.

I don't know which stall Shannon went into, so I avoid the staring patrons while I pace up and down in front of the row of potties saying, "Shannon, It's me Duke," over and over until I hear a voice from one.

"I'm in here."

"Are you coming out?"

"Maybe."

"It can't smell good in there."

"It doesn't."

"Come on out. We can leave or stay. We can do whatever you want—or need."

"Stop being nice, please."

"Okay?"

What's that supposed to mean?

"And stop treating me like I'm special."

Aha. Amber. I could hang her upside down from one of the belt loops on those cut offs and force her to eat those cowboy boots of hers one bite at a time. I won't. I'd never lay a finger on a woman.

"You got it," I say. "No more treating you special. Especially when you spend enough time in there to smell just like whatever's down in that hole. I'll be treating you super-unspecial then. Might even have you ride home on the roof."

The door flies open.

Shannon takes a big gulp of air.

I chuckle.

She looks up at me with doe eyes.

"You," I say, tilting her chin up toward me. "Are so very unspecial. You are just like everyone else I've ever met. Nothing special here. Same ol', same ol', that's what you are. Blah. Bland. Average. One among many ..."

"Shut it, Satterson," she says, bumping me with her hip.

I wink at her.

"And no winking either."

I salute her. "Aye, aye, very-average captain, ma'am."

"You could talk your way out of a jail sentence."

"It's a gift," I say, almost winking. I stop myself mid-wink, so it ends up looking like a bug flew into my eye instead.

I want to put my arm around her, to comfort her. Amber dug in and got under her skin. I'm not sure what was said when I was talking to that Shelby fanatic. I should have never left the two women alone. There's a life lesson for you.

I stop in my tracks and turn. Shannon stops and faces me. "You know me, Shannon. This ..." I wave my finger between us. "This is different. I've never felt like this for anyone but you. Not even close."

Those are the only words I have for her. The pure truth. She'll either believe me now, or I'll have to work to prove them.

I look down at her. She's staring up at me with her hands on her hips. Finally she nods her head.

"You dated her?"

It's not a question and I'm no dummy. I see a trap when it's set. Shannon's not trying to trap me, but if I answer, I'll be snared and we'll both be hurting. Shannon doesn't want an answer. She wants to get this out of her system.

I just nod the slightest bob of my head.

"What were you thinking?" she huffs. "Nevermind. I know what you were thinking. I saw all that you would be thinking about."

I think I blush. My face feels hot and tingly. I take it. I'm not going to argue with Shannon right now. This is about her bleeding the wound so we can get back to us.

She huffs again. "She's so ..." Shannon moves her hands in an hourglass figure. "And so ..." she shakes her head. "And so ..." She grunts out this frustrated noise.

I'm feeling this with her, but also can't help but think how adorable she is right now, all flustered and worked up about Amber, who doesn't matter to me any more than that man who wants my Shelby. Amber never had a chance with me. And why was that? Because of this fiery woman to my right.

Shannon always had me. She just didn't know it. I need her to know it now, though.

We get to the lawn chairs and Shannon plops into one. Her boiling emotions seem to be simmering. She's muttering half sentences and phrases to herself like, "polka dotted man-stealer," and "I'll show her something special," and "my grizzly bear."

I love her.

I. Love. Her.

There's this whoosh like a gale-force wind went right through me from my toes out through my head.

I love Shannon Leigh St. James.

I actually love her, love her.

It's not this small thing, my love for her. It's like a tsunami married an earthquake and they decided to dance on the surface of the sun for their honeymoon.

I look over at the love of my life, muttering away like she's five minutes from being taken off by some guys in white scrubs.

I love her.

Not the time to tell her, obviously, but I'm going to kiss her. I have to.

I bend over her, getting right up in her face. She stops talking and gasps this short intake of air.

In my mind I'm thinking, *I love you. I'll always love you. I'm going to be good for you. I'll do whatever it takes to be worthy of you because I love you.*

I bend in a little more. Shannon grabs the front of my shirt like she's drowning and my shirt is the life ring. This is good. Very good.

She pulls me down toward her and our lips don't meet as much as they crash together. She kisses me like she's branding me. I'm good with that. Totally good. I want to say, "Brand me, baby," but that probably wouldn't go over so well considering the past hour we've had, so I just show her. I stroke her hair, cup her face, run my hands up and down her arms.

She pulls back, lips swollen, hair a little mussed. She looks to the side where Jack's watching us like all he's missing is a bucket of buttered popcorn. He nods at me like *'atta boy* and looks away.

Shannon runs her hand down the front of her shirt and looks down. Then she tilts her head up to me.

"We're different," she says. "We've got something different."

"We are. We do." I say. "Night and Day."

"Okay."

"Okay."

"I kinda lost my mind there for a minute."

"I kinda like you losing your mind," I say with a wink.

She doesn't stop me from winking.

"You ready to go?" I ask her.

It seems like we've had enough of the car show for one day.

"Yeah."

I say goodbye to Jack, let the security guards know I'm taking off. They wave the crowd out of the way once Shannon and I are buckled up. We take off in silence.

REO Speedwagon's *Keep On Loving You* comes on from our song list. I'm not big on fate, but I have to say, the timing was more than providential on that one. I squeeze Shannon's hand. I'm gonna keep on loving her. How could I not? I only hope she's going to do the same–fall for me and then keep on falling.

When Kool & The Gang's *Get Down On It* comes on, Shannon starts singing the question, "What you gonna do?" I sing back "Get down on it," and we belt out the rest of the lyrics together.

Amber's fading far into the distant dust behind my rear bumper and Shannon and I are driving into our future. I can't help but think we're stronger for having endured a little hardship. But, I'm no philosopher, so I just keep singing old-school funk with my girl.

FORTY-FOUR

Shannon

"How was your day away with you-know-who?" Jayme asks when I come in the door.

I told her where I was going for the day since she already knows everything anyway.

"Crazy."

Jayme looks up from her computer. I plop onto the floor so Groucho can walk over and set his big fat head in my lap and drool on me. Nothing says welcome home like a lap full of slobber. I scrub his head and he makes this weird moaning noise.

"What was crazy?"

"Some girl Duke used to date was there. She came up to me all watch-out-you're-not-special, we-all-think-we're-special. And I took a drink of that Kool-Aid for about an hour. But, we got through it."

"You are so special," Jayme says.

"To Duke?" I hate that I still feel so insecure, but today rocked something big. Maybe it was like an earthquake, whatever's reinforced holds up. What was already rickety crashes down. I've obviously got some rickety spots where Duke and I are concerned.

"To Duke. You're special to Duke and to so many other people. But, you're extra special to him."

"How do you know?"

"I'm a romance author."

She giggles and winks at me. It's her stock answer, but also one she pulls out when she means it.

"And ..."

"And you two are hashtag relationship goals. You have the je ne sais quoi everyone dreams of having with that special someone. You're the 'it factor' of romance."

"Okay. Okay." I giggle. "If you say so."

"I know Duke. He's a flirt, but when he comes to tuck you in with sunflowers and a bag of mom-approved home remedies, or he sits out in the drizzle just to watch you come home from dating another man, he's got it bad, girl. And that's good."

I smile remembering those moments that were so easily erased by Betty Boop in her polka dotted, frayed short-ed Vulcan mind-meld. I should say that sentence out loud. Jayme would love it. But, I'm too worn out.

"I'm going up to bed. I'm beat. Fighting for your man is exhausting."

I stand up and Groucho's head flops down. He lets out a grumbly noise.

"I bet," Jayme says with a chuckle. "But, remember, you didn't really have to fight. You already won. Trust me."

"Thanks," I say as I climb the stairs.

My phone buzzes in my purse. When I get to my room, I fall back onto the mattress and take my cell out to check who messaged me.

Duke: *Hey. You holding up?*
Shannon: *Barely. I'm good though. You?*
Duke: *If you're good, I'm good. Thanks for coming with me. Besides the unmentionable who won't be mentioned, I had a great day with you.*

I finger my charm, rotating it on the chain and rubbing my thumb across it.

Shannon: *I had a good day too. Really good. I like that thing you do with your lips.*
Duke: *Talking?*
Shannon: *That, but the other thing.*
Duke: *Smiling?*
Shannon: *You've got a great smile, but no.*
Duke: *Eating?*
Shannon: *Not so much.*
Duke: *Running my lips up your neck and nibbling your ear.*
Shannon: *Yep. That's the one.*
Duke: *I can come over right now. I'm not busy at all. Wide awake all of a sudden too.*
Shannon: *I'm already in bread. Let's take a rain check.*
Shannon: *gah. *bed*, not bread.*
Duke: *A raincheck? So not fair.*
Shannon: *I'm worth the wait.*
Duke: *You are beyond worth the wait. Sleep tight, Hollywood.*
Shannon: *Yoda too.*
Shannon: *Gah. You. You too. Tight you sleep, Yoda.*
Duke: *The force be with you, Princess Shannon*

I drop the phone on the bed and smile. We're good. It was our first official bump in the road and we survived it.

Our town makes a big deal of the Fourth of July. The day-long street festival pauses for the parade featuring that year's Miss Corn Husk–who has been the same person since I turned sixteen, but we all pretend to act surprised when Ella Mae wins, again. We close out the celebration of our nation's independence with fireworks at night.

It's been two days since Duke and I snuck away to the car show. I didn't see him yesterday–I just needed some space to be me. I danced for over two hours in the basement in front of the wall of full-length mirrors Jayme and I hung down there. As always, dancing got me out of my head and into my body where everything seems to flow and release without effort.

While I danced, I thought about Duke. It dawned on me he's the only man who's ever had the power to break my heart–because he's owned it for as long as I can remember.

If he breaks me, I'll be like Humpty Dumpty. No one will be able to put me back together again. Maybe that's what happened to Jayme. When her ex cheated, it was the one thing that ended her capacity to let men into her beautiful, carefree heart.

I twirled in place, spinning once, then pushing to spin twice. Back in the day I could pirouette en dehors five to seven rotations. I might be able to work up to that level again, with dedicated practice.

I had stopped dancing long enough to look my reflection in the eyes in the cheap mirrors as I leaned on the portable barre I bought at a garage sale in Columbus last year.

Right then and there, in the solitude of my basement, I decided I will let myself fall for Duke and believe the best of him. I'll let him have all of my heart—not that I really have a choice. I'm going to stop thinking of Beth or Amber or any other women in his past and allow myself to fully experience being the complete focus of Duke's passion and attention.

As soon as I resolved to open my heart, I twirled and easily made three rotations. Maybe our relationship won't end in heartbreak. Maybe we'll finally get a chance at forever.

I'm still feeling the benefits of such a long dance session yesterday during the drive over to the Fireworks show with Jayme. My mind is clearer and my body feels sore, but relaxed. Jayme parks her car and spots Laura and Lexi across the way.

"I'm going to say hi," she says, turning to me.

"I'll meet you in just a bit," I say as my eyes scan the crowd.

She knows I'm going to look for Duke.

It's dusky out, so I don't see him sneak up behind me. I jump when I hear his voice.

"Hey, gorgeous."

"You scared me," I say, barely turning toward him. People are everywhere, and no one seems to be watching us, but I'm hyper-aware how it could be construed if our body language looks too friendly.

"I'm going to walk over behind the hardware store," Duke says. "Meet me back there in a few minutes."

I should stay right where I am, or go hang out with Laura, Lexi and Jayme. Everyone and their brother is out here. Not *my* brother, thanks be, but you know what I'm saying. Duke and I can be discreet, but people still might notice. Duke's like catnip to me, so I take off after him.

When I turn into the vacant parking lot, I see him leaned back against the brick wall. No one's on this block because the fireworks are the next block over and people are grabbing spots on the sidewalk and in the city square park to lay out blankets and chairs so they can watch the show.

I walk over to Duke and lean back against the wall next to him.

"Are you having a good day?" he asks in a low voice.

"I am. Are you?"

"Could be better."

I look over at him and smile. He grabs my hand and runs his fingers across the back of my knuckles. His eyes go to my neckline. Then he reaches out and holds the ballet slipper charm between two fingers.

"You wore it."

"Of course. I love it."

"I love ... it too."

"Thanks again."

307

He smiles that smile of his. The deep one.

"You know what I love about you?" I ask.

"Everything?" he laughs at his own ridiculousness.

I want to say, "Yes. I love everything about you." But I can't right now. Not after my heart was put through a paper shredder yesterday. Instead, I tell him what I was thinking.

"I love ..." I place my finger next to his mouth and trace the line. "... this dimple right here."

"Just that dimple?"

"Yes. I mean, I love them all, but that one is like a bonus."

He shakes his head lightly and half his dimples disappear, but the ones on the left side of his face remain pronounced. He's wearing this sexy half-smile as he turns and steps in front of me, placing his hands flat on the wall on either side of my arms. My heart rate kicks up. We're basically in public in Bordeaux. Yes, it's nearly dark out now. And if anyone saw us, they'd see him, caging someone in. You couldn't clearly see it's me. But, still.

Duke's voice goes down into a register that would make a jazz singer jealous.

"I want to kiss you," he says.

"Please."

He leans in and brushes the softest kiss across my lips. It's feather light and warm, gentle and meaningful. This isn't the kiss of a man out to have a good time. This is a kiss of something more.

A hum rises up my throat. He makes me feel so languid and half-drowsy, just by the way he looks at me with those marbled eyes of his, half-open when he gently ends our kiss with another tender caress of his lips across mine.

Duke's gaze is heavy and soft. "Did you just purr at me?" he asks with a chuckle.

"I think you like me purring," I say.

Who am I?

He answers with so much gravel in his voice he could open a small quarry.

"The things you do to me, Hollywood. But, now I'm going to do that thing you like."

"Talk?" I ask in a breathy whisper.

"Nope," he says, brushing a kiss along my jawline.

"Smile?" I giggle, but it comes out muffled.

His eyes crinkle in the corners and he looks down at me with a mixture of playfulness and want. It's a heady combination.

"Already doing that," He touches the tip of his nose to mine and then places a kiss there.

"Eat?"

"Also wrong," he says, kissing from my temple across my eyelids to the other temple.

My knees are going weak. I may slide down the wall any second.

Duke nibbles his way up my neck to that spot on my earlobe.

"That," he says with satisfaction, wrapping one of his arms around behind me just in time to stabilize me. "That thing that makes you melt like putty in my arms."

I should be embarrassed by the way I sway toward him a little. But Duke makes me feel safe and bold.

"We have to stop," he whispers across the shell of my ear.

"Stop?" I ask. I hear my own voice. It feels separate from me.

"Yep," he says, leaning me back onto the wall and pushing himself so there's more distance between us. "I'll end up losing the very miniscule thread of self control that's holding me together right now."

I feel the flush of the skin around my neckline. I place my hand on my throat and steady my breathing. Everything between us feels taut and electric.

Duke steps back and clears his throat.

"You know what I want right now?" he asks.

"Corn?"

It's a valid question. This is Red, White, and Blue, and Corn Too, after all. We've got popcorn, street corn, corn nuts, corn pone, caramel corn, corn chowder, not to mention the corn crafts and corn memorabilia ... If it's made with corn, you can get it at one of the vendors today.

"No, not corn," he says. "I want you. But, we need to show up to the fireworks, separately. Too many people can do math in this town, and they'll start adding things up and talking if we both are gone together for too long."

"We should fire the math teachers," I say.

"I'm all for that."

I almost pout, but he's right.

He leans in and kisses me one more time. "Come over to watch movies with me tomorrow night. We can just hang out. Eat dinner. Whatever you want."

"It's a date."

I see it in his eyes. We both want more. As exciting as it is to sneak away behind buildings, or into the back of a truck at night, or out of town in the Shelby or on the Harley, we both want to be free of this need to hide.

"It won't be long," I assure him.

We agree I'll walk out first, Duke will wait two minutes and take a different route back to the park where our friends are gathering to claim a spot for the fireworks show. It's the same spot every year. We've got our traditions.

As I'm walking away he says, "Next year I'm your lawn chair for the fireworks show."

"Next year," I say as I turn the corner.

FORTY-FIVE

Shannon

Tuesday my afternoon nail appointments cancel. It's after lunch when I walk into our house and blink.

Duke is sitting at our dining table with these dark rimmed glasses on, making him look all sexy Clark Kent-ish.

"Hey," I say, unable to wipe the confused look off my face.

"Oh, hey," Duke says, looking up from a pile of papers and books spread across the dining table.

"What are you doing here?" I ask as Jayme comes out of the kitchen looking like she just robbed a bank, cheated on her taxes, and ran over the neighbor's rose bushes.

"Oh, Shannon, hi. I thought you were doing nails this afternoon at the Dippity Do."

This keeps getting weirder.

I look between sexy Clark Kent Duke and my bank robber, rose-killing roomie.

"Um, yeah. I was. My last two appointments cancelled, so ..."

Why do I feel like I need to excuse myself for being in my own home?

Why is Duke here if he thought I was working?

And when did he start wearing glasses?

Duke stands and walks over to me.

"Why don't you sit down?"

"Are you going to tell me what's going on?"

"Yes. I should have told you a while ago."

I stiffen. Duke takes my bag off my shoulder and calmly hangs it on one of the hooks near the door.

I sit on the couch and Duke sits next to me. I tell myself not to cross my arms, but they go up anyway. I feel like I need armor to keep me from touching him or falling apart.

"I'll just be in the kitchen if you need me," Jayme says.

Duke takes a breath and turns toward me. "I got this call earlier this summer from Principal Barnes. He wants me to coach at the high school."

I can't find words to congratulate him. What does that have to do with him being here with Jayme? And why didn't he tell me this sooner? We've literally had at least ten conversations about goals and the future–mostly my goals, but still.

"In order to coach, I need to teach. And the history teacher isn't coming back, so Principal Barnes asked me to teach history. I'll be getting my certification if I pass this exam. Well, I'll be entering a cert program. But I'll start teaching right away in the fall."

My jaw drops open. I'm not just saying that. I feel my mouth form this giant O. I'm pretty sure it looks like I'm at the dentist with that tiny mirror on a stick shoved way back toward my molars.

I search for something to say.

"Why?"

"Why am I going to teach?"

"No. Why didn't you tell me?"

He huffs out a long breath. Then he drops his head into his hands. His elbows are resting on his knees so I only see the top of his head.

"It's hard to explain. I've got the garage. Pops wants to retire. I want to support him. He deserves that from me. But Aiden said go for it. And I think he's right. I still don't know what's going to happen to Satterson's and I'm not even sure I'll pass this test, or if I'll be a good teacher. What if I mess those kids up and they can't get jobs down the road because I took this job I shouldn't have taken? And none of this explains why I didn't tell you. I guess I'm just not used to having someone on my team."

His head is still aimed so he's talking at the floor.

"Duke."

He looks up.

"That makes sense."

"It does?"

"Yeah. I mean, I don't like that you held this back from me. But I understand why you were hesitant to talk about everything. It's not solid yet."

Amber's words roll through my mind: *You'll find out he's holding back big pieces of his life from you. That's when you know. You're not what you thought you were.*

"I want you to know about it—about everything in my life. I almost told you twice yesterday, but then the moment slipped away."

I try to force myself to believe him. This is Duke. Amber was obviously jealous and full of sour grapes, not that she had room in that outfit to be full of much. Even a few grapes could have resulted in a major wardrobe malfunction.

"And why are you here? I mean I get the whole thing about being uncertain and feeling responsible. Why are you in my home today looking like sexy Clark Kent?"

"You like these, huh?"

He waggles his eyebrows and pinches the stem of his glasses so he can slide them down about an inch and make eyes at me from over the top of the glasses.

"I like them. Okay? Why are you here?"

"Jayme's helping me study. Don't get mad at her. I swore her to secrecy."

He pauses and then he gets this beseeching look on his face. "Give me a chance, Shannon. I want to let you in. There's no part of my life I don't want to share with you. I just need to get used to being a part of something more."

I nod. "I want to give you a chance."

I do want that. I just don't know how many more blindsides I can endure in one week.

"Do you have any other secret surprises hidden from me?"

"Nope. Not a one."

"Okay. I'm going up to change into my yoga pants. Carry on."

I shout to Jayme that the coast is clear and then I go up to my room and lay on my bed with my kindle. I pull up one of Jayme's books. Sometimes you need to lose yourself in something so unlike reality just to get a breather from all the curve balls life seems to be lobbing your way. *Charming My Undead Boss* seems like it will do the job nicely.

When Duke and Jayme are finished studying for his exam, I come downstairs and hug Duke goodbye. I step out onto the porch with him so we can give Jayme the respect of not feeling like the awkward third wheel. This afternoon has been awkward enough already. Groucho has his head on Duke's shoe, but Duke gives him a little shove and then he shuts the door so we're alone out here.

Duke pulls me in toward himself and breathes this deep sigh into my hair while he tucks me in closer. I look up and put my palm on his cheek. We don't kiss, but we wordlessly smooth over the rough edges–at least most of them.

Jayme has this look on her face after Duke leaves.

"I'm okay," I tell her. "It just surprised me. I sort of understand why he'd hide everything from me, but also, it throws me for a loop. If we're as serious as he says we are, why isn't he coming to me with his goals and opportunities? When was he going to tell me all this?"

"I just feel bad that I was a part of keeping his news from you. I want you to trust me."

"I do. We're good."

"Wellll ... there's this thing."

"Well? What thing?" I sit down. I've got a feeling I need to be sitting down.

"So, you remember the flowers you had been getting?"

"From the admirer?"

"Yeah. Those."

"Of course."

She clears her throat. "I was him."

"You were ..." I pause while the reality sinks in. "Oh. Why?"

"The flowers that started it all, well, they were cast offs, but as I made them into a bouquet, I thought, I'm bringing these home to Shannon. And not just like I usually do. She needs to know she's special. You'd just been in a dating slump and I thought you needed encouragement."

"So you wrote the card."

"On a whim. I thought it would be a one-time thing. I'd be like, 'Surprise! I'm your admirer!' But when I saw your reaction, it seemed harmless to let you think some random guy was into you. I knew many guys probably were–are. I just wanted you to see what I see. You kept finding the RJs of the world. Not knocking him, but he wasn't the one for you. I figured you'd open your eyes to the fact that men watch you everywhere you go. Maybe if you broadened your horizons, you'd find someone who fit."

Jayme's eyebrows are drawn up and her eyes are watery.

"I never meant to let things get out of hand. With each bouquet you'd have this sweet reaction, and it was fun. I wasn't thinking. I'm really sorry. And then when Duke saw the arrangement on the table and got a little jealous, I decided the deception was worth it." Jayme pulls her mouth tight and shakes her head. "Have you ever started something innocently and then it got out of hand without your permission?"

"Yeah. I'm pretty sure keeping this secret about Duke, or maybe even dating him at all before Chris gets home is going to be just that."

Jayme shakes her head. "Your brother might get mad, it's true. But, I don't think you two could have kept from going for one

315

another much longer. It was time. You've been holding back all these years. I don't want you to regret that—you deserve to be happy with a man who literally falls over himself to be with you. I'd never have guessed Duke had it in him. But he's so in love with you."

"Love? Are you sure?"

"It's love. Trust the romance author."

"So far, that line has never panned out for me with you."

"Hasn't it though?"

"Maybe you're right."

"I'm right. And I'm really sorry about being your secret admirer. I didn't mean to trick you. I do admire you, but that's no secret."

"No harm. Well, a little harm. But I'm actually relieved there's not some cowardly man skulking around town with an anonymous crush on me. I'm glad I just have a friend who wants to see me happy instead."

"And a man who is madly in love with you. Trust me."

Maybe she's right.

Maybe I should trust the romance author.

FORTY-SIX

Duke

P ops used to always end our discipline with a question: *What did that teach you?* As old-school as he is, he had a forward-thinking approach to parenting. Or maybe that was old-school too. Either way, he wanted us to grow from our mistakes.

I pick up my guitar and cradle it in my lap. I'm not really playing, just strumming chords absentmindedly while my mind rolls through the mistakes I've made with Shannon. I had taken the afternoon off work to study with Jayme since I'm taking the test in the morning.

Now I'm just sitting here alone in my house feeling remorse for messing things up, and for ever dating anyone who wasn't Shannon, also for being the type of guy who leaps before he looks.

After hurricane Amber descended on our otherwise perfect day Saturday, I wanted to rebuild Shannon's confidence in my feelings for her. I ended up making things worse by not including her in my struggle about taking the position at the high school.

Pops' voice nudges me: *What did that teach you?*

I need to let her in. Shannon needs to be the one I go to when I'm struggling, not just Aiden. No secrets.

That dog, too. Groucho looked at me as I was leaving Jayme and Shannon's house with a look that said, "Dude ... you messed that up so big. I mean, I'm only a dog, but you are going to have to do something huge to make up for this. Like buy her a big steak bone." Then he drooled a little on my shoe for emphasis.

Maybe he didn't say that steak bone thing. Maybe he just called me a bonehead. He wouldn't be wrong.

I'll be the first to admit I'm not good at this relationship stuff. But I want to be–for her. I've been so swept up in the sweet relief of finally having Shannon, I forgot the real reasons we might not work—the biggest one being that I'm not good enough for her.

I'm just about to start singing when there's a soft knock on the doorframe. I set the guitar down and stand.

"Hey there," Shannon says.

She's got a plate of what looks like freshly-baked cookies in her hands. She's showered, and just the slightest bit hesitant. I want to erase that feeling between us and restore the ease and comfort we've always had.

"Did you bake those?"

I open the door and she steps through. I get a whiff of her– peaches, sunshine, gardens in the summer. My girl.

"You're kidding, right?"

"Okay. So, you brought me cookies that you didn't bake?"

"And for that you should be grateful. If I baked these, you might not live to take the exam tomorrow."

"So these are unpoisoned cookies?"

"Definitely. They're I-want-to-always-work-things-out-with-you cookies and also I-wanted-to-say-good-luck cookies."

"They're very talkative cookies, packing all that into a few sweet bites."

"Cookies can do that."

"They sure can."

She smiles up at me, pulls the saran back and pushes the plate my way. I pluck one off the pile of what appears to be an even dozen.

"I'm sorry, Shannon. I should have told you. I'm not good at this stuff."

I lean back on the back of the living room chair. Shannon sets the plate of cookies on the coffee table behind me. Then she walks back toward the doorway, facing me.

"What stuff aren't you good at?"

"The relationship stuff. I act before I think. I put my foot in my mouth, and I don't consider you the way I should."

She steps toward me, placing her hand on my forearm.

"I don't think that's exactly accurate. You've been thinking of me plenty. You just need time to adjust to having someone you want to share things with. You've essentially been single your whole life. You can't expect to get this right without a little practice."

She's too good for me. But, I can't let her go, even if she'd be better with someone who got this stuff right. There's no way I want her with any other guy. The mere thought of another man makes me buzz with some sort of caveman-like urge to drag her away from all men ever. She's mine, and I'll do what it takes to be more for her.

She leans up and places a soft kiss on my cheek. As much as I want to kiss her, that's not what this moment is about. I wrap my arms around her and we stand in my living room, holding onto one another while things fall back into place between us.

We seem to know when we've patched things up as much as we're able, because we both break the hug at the same time. Shannon's got a soft look in her eyes– contentment, I think.

"I'd better go so you can have a restful night before your exam. Are you nervous?"

"I'm nervous I'll pass. Nervous I won't. I still haven't told Pops about all this. See, it's not only you I botch things with."

"You need to tell him."

"I almost did the other day, but then he brought up retirement. Actual plans. He's trying to bring in a mechanic from another city. I couldn't drop this bomb on him that day. Then you and I went to Columbus, and there was the Fourth, and now I'm off for this afternoon and tomorrow morning. I told him I had a few things to take care of. He never pries. Well, he does. But he also doesn't."

She just nods.

"I'll tell him."

"I know you will. Make it sooner than later. Oh! Laura called after you left. She wants us all to meet up at Dixie's Diner for supper tomorrow. Can we take a raincheck on dinner here and join them?"

"Sure. No one called me yet. Are you sure it's not a girls-only thing?"

"No. Rob or Aiden will probably be sending you a text."

"Everything good for next Saturday?"

Chris comes home in a little over a week. The welcome home party is a few days after he gets back. Shannon and I are probably two weeks away from being able to go public with our relationship. Honestly, I'm beyond over the stress of hiding and keeping secrets.

"We're all set. I think it's going to be great."

"Me too. You're a good sister. And an even better girlfriend."

"Is that what I am?"

"Haven't I said it out loud?"

"I think I'd remember the day Duke Satterson called me his girlfriend." Shannon's hand pops onto her hip in that stubborn, sassy pose of hers.

"Well, then, go home and put hearts all over this day in your calendar. Because you are definitely my girlfriend."

You know what I said about this not being the time for kissing? Times change.

I pull Shannon to me and lean onto the back of the chair. She nestles between my legs and wraps her arms over my shoulders. I run my hand down her hair and look into her eyes. She pulls my ball cap off, tosses it onto the sofa and rakes her hands through my hair. There's this playfulness to the way she's taking charge right now and a glint of mischief in her eyes.

She runs her hand along my jawline. I love when she does

that. Shannon's touch sends warm shivers across my face. My eyes shut as the power of what I feel for her nearly blows me over.

I don't think I was made for such an intense connection, or maybe I was. It's like taking a Bugatti Chiron turbo on the highway after it's been sitting idle too long. At first you wonder if it's going to give out on you, but if you're lucky, it surprises you and roars to life. Before you know it, you're cruising at top speed down an open road.

Shannon's lips brush mine. I grasp the back of her head and pull her in. Our mouths fuse and she lets out those sweet noises that always seem to ripple through me.

This kiss is an apology and a restoration. It's a promise and a declaration. And it's sheer longing for so much more. I want everything with Shannon. Everything.

I almost tell her I love her when we separate, she's still in my arms, lightly brushing the back of her knuckles from my neck to my chin, tracing across the stubble on my jaw.

It's not a secret—my love for her—but the way I first say the words to her needs to be special. Not on a night when we're still patching up the places that got ripped wide open by my carelessness and inexperience.

Shannon's squeal can probably be heard from the front office of her dad's accounting firm to the outskirts of town.

"You passed!" she yells again, as if I didn't hear her the first three times she shouted those words in succession.

"I did."

Her dad's voice comes through from behind her. "Who passed what?" That's followed by another accountant in the office shouting, "Everything okay out there?"

"Sorry, Daddy. A friend. A test thing."

Then she shouts, "Yes. A-okay!" to the accountant.

I can tell she's flustered. She never calls Mr. St. James Daddy at work. Her attention returns to me, but she's back in receptionist mode.

"Thank you for informing me. I'm thrilled for you."

"I could tell," I tease. "And thanks."

"So, are you going to tell that very important man about this development?"

Pops. Yep. That's the plan.

"I'm planning to go tell him right now. I just wanted to call you first."

"I like being first."

"You're definitely first. So far ahead of everyone else it's not even a contest anymore."

There.

I didn't say those three important, life-altering words, but I said as much.

And I will say them. Just not over the phone.

Shannon and I hang up. I call Principal Barnes. He's still in Aruba, but he'll get the message that I passed the exam and I want to talk about officially accepting the offer when he's home and ready to connect.

I drive to the garage. As soon as I walk in the office, Pops brings me up to date on the jobs that came in this morning, and then says he's got an errand to run. I tell him I need to talk to him about something important. He asks if it can wait til tomorrow. I've waited this long. What's one more day?

Pops doesn't come back all afternoon. The garage feels a little vacant without him. It's not like he's here every waking moment, but then again, he sort of is. I get a glimpse of what life would be like for me if I didn't take the coaching and teaching position.

I'd be here alone, or with some mechanic I barely know, working on cars in this garage, and helping customers at the gas pumps. And I'd miss out on a life I think I might be cut out to live. I'm not sure what the future of Satterson's is going to look like, but it's clear my time here is coming to a close.

After work I run home for a quick shower and then I drive

over to Dixie's to meet my friends. Besides the fireworks show, where I intentionally sat near Aiden and Em to put distance between Shannon and me, we haven't been in the middle of our friend group since we've been dating. This should be interesting.

The waitress seats the nine of us in a big back booth. Three couples, me, Jayme and Shannon. Somehow the two of us get positioned next to one another squished between Jayme and Rob. We put in our order, and the conversation flows like it always does when we're together. Our food comes, but that doesn't quiet us down much.

I keep stealing glances at Shannon and she gives me furtive smiles when we think no one's looking. It feels dangerous and electrifying, and mildly stupid. Sort of the story of how I've lived most of my life. Only, with Shannon, I want to be more careful since she got blindsided by my carelessness twice already this week.

Shannon's hand rests between us on the booth where no one else can see it. I slowly move my hand over and interlace our fingers giving her hand a conspiratorial squeeze. Shannon gasps and then turns her gasp into a fake cough. I swallow back my smile.

I shouldn't enjoy this, the illicit sneaking around, but somehow it heightens everything between us. It's not as if the charge constantly tugging us together needed any jumper cables. We'll be out in the open in no time, so we might as well grab a few last thrills from our covert situation while we can.

I run my thumb in lazy circles across Shannon's skin, savoring this chance to touch her. She gives me a coy smile, one just for me. Jayme looks down at our hands and smiles like only a romance author would. Jayme's the only one at the table with a direct line of sight to that spot on the bench seat. I'm grateful for her solidarity with us.

Laura says something to Shannon. I don't hear what it is. My mind has one channel right now, and it's completely tuned into Shannon and the secret clasp of our enjoined hands. I'm as blissed out as I've been in years—maybe ever.

And then, like the sound of a key scratch across the paint of a mint Camaro, I look up and see him, strolling—no, striding—across the diner, straight for our table with a smile stretched across his face.

Chris.

He's home.

Early.

And I'm sitting here holding his sister's hand under the table like the lovesick fool who made out with her last night. The next few moments go by in a slow-motion blur and I can't tell whether I lift my hand away from Shannon's, though the thought is there to separate myself from her before he sees us. I think I end up clinging to her instead.

Chris approaches our table and his smile flickers like a candle in the wind. Shannon obviously sees him at this point, drops my hand and jumps up to greet her brother.

Did he see us?

Did I want him to?

And what will happen to me and Shannon now that he's back?

"You're back early!" Shannon shouts as she wraps her arms around him.

Chris' face assumes a neutral expression. Military neutral. Something he probably trained hard to learn. It's not his relaxed, hey-guys-surprise-I'm-home-early face. That's all I know.

"Yeah," Chris says, pulling Shannon in tight for a hug and bending his head down to hold her to himself. His eyes meet mine and I have very little doubt as to what he just saw.

Our friends start clambering out of the booth to greet Chris. Everyone crowds him for hugs and greetings. Shannon doesn't look at me, not even one stolen glance. I try to get her attention, but she seems determined to avoid me. I can't blame her. My heart is in my throat and my mind feels like a firework launch pad, rapid-fire explosions shooting off in every direction.

"I wanted to surprise all of you," Chris says.

"You did," I half mumble to myself as I stand and give Chris a full hug. We clap one another's backs and my momentary melancholy lifts like a mist.

My best friend is home, safe and solid. And I am glad. I really am. Looking at him, and the man he's become, I'm proud. Something about my world just clicked back into place with his return. I've missed him more than I let myself remember, especially since I started dating Shannon. As soon as she and I decided to pursue one another, Chris became this ominous presence between us. I lost sight of him as he really is.

He backs off our hug, giving me a look that chills me, even though there's no overt malice in his expression.

FORTY-SEVEN
Shannon

We're in so much trouble.

FORTY-EIGHT

Duke

W e're in so much trouble.

"Duke, could I have a word with you outside?"
Chris' voice is commanding, like the officer he is.

"Um, sure."

I can't help but glance at Shannon before I turn to follow
Chris. She avoids eye contact with me, her face showing every
emotion rolling through her. I'm half-tempted to tell Chris to
wait so I can talk to Shannon, but he's already heading toward the
door.

Aiden shoots me a questioning glance. Laura and Jayme look
sympathetic.

Our friends part so I can walk through the little cluster we've
formed in front of the booth. I follow behind Chris, allowing my
eyes to travel back to our friends one more time before stepping
into the muggy summer evening.

It's obvious to me that Chris wants to talk to me about what
he just witnessed. I thought he might not have seen it, but I know
now I was wrong.

"Welcome home! Early!" I say in as unaffected and enthusi-
astic a voice as I can muster.

"What was that?" Chris asks, ignoring my welcome.

"What?"

"What is going on between you and my sister? And how long has this been going on? And why hasn't anyone told me?"

I clear my throat. I'm not ready for this. We planned Chris' party, we even had some thoughts about letting things settle in the week after the party and then we were going to find a time to sit together to carefully break the news to him.

But, he's here now, so here I go.

"We just started seeing one another."

Chris shakes his head. "You and Shannon? When?"

"Last week."

He turns away from me, so I can't see his face. His hand scrubs down his jaw. He begins pacing six steps in one direction, six in the other. It's measured and controlled. I'm not getting punched yet, so that's a win.

When he finally turns to face me again, he says, "You went for my sister? What part of that decision feels like a good idea?"

It's not so much a question as a statement of disbelief.

Chris' jaw is tight, and his arms are crossed, showing off biceps twice the size of mine. Freaking Army workouts. He's a beast now.

"It's not like you think."

"What's it like, exactly?"

"We didn't plan on it. It just happened."

That didn't sound as good coming out it as it sounded in my head. I start to say more–to clarify–but I'm interrupted when the door behind us opens and Shannon walks toward us. Her arms are crossed over her chest, her eyes trained on her brother.

I look at her, wanting to make some sort of connection, to assure her we're still good even if Chris needs time to swallow this pill. She looks at me for the briefest moment, sadness etched across her face.

"It just happened?" Chris says with increased intensity, not even acknowledging Shannon.

Shannon's eyebrows lift. A look of confusion passes over her face.

Chris looks between me and Shannon. He runs his hand across his cropped cut.

Shannon starts to say something, but Chris barrels forward. "I trusted you, man. I trusted you. I didn't ask Aiden or Rob or anyone else in town to keep an eye out. I asked you. So, maybe I'm the idiot. But I thought you cared about her enough to keep her safe. Instead, you're adding her to your rotating list of flings!"

Shannon flinches.

"Chris," she says, her tone a mixture of annoyance and pleading.

He spears her with a look. "I'm not holding you accountable here. But, you know him. He's like a brother to me, but I'd never wish him on a woman. He's not relationship material."

Wow. He didn't punch me, but I think I'd rather he did.

I stand stock still, the wind knocked out of me in a way no fight ever managed to do.

The more I let his words sink in, the more I feel the truth in Chris' statement. His delivery may have been harsh. He's in shock, and he's angry, but he's not wrong.

Chris is dead wrong about Shannon being one more name on a list, but yes, you could make a list. A list of mistakes. A list of regrets. A list of me trying to redirect my feelings for Shannon so I could toe the line. But still it's a list that clearly highlights my inability to form a relationship that lasts. I've never demonstrated to anyone, not even myself, that I have what it takes to be in a serious relationship.

Not relationship material.

Isn't that what I showed Shannon this week? She had to deal with Amber, and even in the back of the truck, she was distracted by her concern about my past with Beth and other women. Then I failed to include Shannon in the biggest decision of my life. Instead, I went to Jayme in secret and hid everything from Shannon. Maybe all I'm good for is flirting and having a fun time.

We've only been together a little over a week and Shannon's already had to deal with too much.

Do I really have what it takes to be in a healthy relationship long term?

I thought I could do things differently with Shannon. After all, she was always the one I really wanted. But maybe Chris is right. I may not be the man for her.

She definitely deserves better.

Shannon's face crumples as she processes her brother's assessment of me.

"I can't believe this," Chris mutters.

He's shaking his head, no longer looking at me or Shannon.

"I'm standing right here," Shannon finally says. "You don't need to talk as if I'm not here."

I want to send her a reassuring smile, but my confidence has been deflated. What would I assure her of, anyway?

I can't stop hearing the words: *Not relationship material.*

Shannon glances at me and then she looks away.

This is a high-speed collision without brake pedals. I don't know what to say or do. No matter which way I steer things, no one's walking away from this unscathed. And maybe that's for the best. Maybe we were doomed from the start. I was self-indulgent, going for her when I didn't know if I had what it takes to be the man she needs. Chris has every right to be upset when I look at it from his standpoint.

"We would have told you eventually," Shannon says. "We were trying to protect you."

"Protect me?" His tone is incredulous. "I didn't ask him to protect me. I asked him to protect you."

"Again," Shannon says with a pointed stare at her brother. "Duke's standing right here. Also, I'm not a child. You don't need to protect me."

She said my name, but she never looked my way. I want to reach out, pull her to me, face this as a unified front, show Chris he's wrong. But, that voice in my head keeps repeating this bitter truth: *Not relationship material.*

All I can do is shake my head and look at the ground.

I knew this was coming.

It doesn't matter whether I anticipated it. Now I'm in it and it's way worse than I thought it could be.

It reminds me of the time in sixth grade when I was riding down this steep hill on my bicycle approaching a corner at the cemetery. I let my bike pick up speed and then my hand grasped the wrong brake. When I hit the front brake, my bike flipped end over end. I flew like superman over the handlebars. I saw that coming too. But seeing it coming didn't prepare me for the feeling of eating asphalt and scraping every exposed piece of skin on the gritty surface of that road.

This stings way worse.

"I'm not taking advantage of her," I try to explain.

I may not be good enough for her, but I've never wanted to hurt her. I tried to be more than I am. For her sake, I wanted to be able to do this differently than I ever had.

I look over at Shannon, but she still won't look at me. She knows I'm not taking advantage of her, doesn't she? She's definitely not another fling.

"And, if anything," Chris says to Shannon. "I think you would know better than dating Duke. You've always had a good friendship with him and it should have stayed that way."

He mutters the next words, but we all hear them as if he shouted them. "I don't know what's wrong with your man-picker. You never picked anyone good enough for you."

It's a sideways compliment, but dressed in such an insult. And Chris' words light something in Shannon. I see her shoring herself up.

She still avoids looking at me, but she's staring down her brother like she always did when she fought with him over the years, with her sassy, spirited attitude, trying to make herself appear physically larger than she is. Her shoulders puff. Her chin juts. Her eyes lock with his.

"I have a fine man-picker, Chris. And it's always picked Duke. Always."

Shannon doesn't look my way.

Chris shakes his head. He doesn't even bother to answer her challenging statement.

I stand frozen. Only for one reason: *Not relationship material.* She just declared her feelings for me, bravely, boldly and without hesitation. I can't return the favor because when I do, I'll be telling her we're meant to be. After what Chris just said about both of us, I'm not so sure anymore. Maybe her picker is broken. She's been dead set on being with a man who isn't relationship material.

All I have are feelings for her—so many feelings. But, can I be the man she needs? I've always wondered that.

Chris isn't a jerk. But, the way he's acting—I barely recognize him. Still, under all the hurtful comments and arrogance, he's the guy I always knew him to be. He's protecting his sister from a man who isn't good for her and he's livid that I ever crossed that line—behind his back.

A palpable tension fills the space between the three of us. No one breaks the silence. Shannon stands tall, wordlessly daring her brother to say one more thing. I probably look like a puppy who got kicked and sent out to sleep in the rain. Chris remains neutral but steely in his resolve.

"I can't do this right now," Chris finally says. "When I heard all my friends were hanging out tonight, I thought I'd surprise everyone at once by showing up here.

"Instead, I walk in on this spit-show. You both betrayed me—especially you, Duke. I just need time to process everything. Give me time. I don't know how we get past this, but I've heard enough from both of you tonight."

I feel like asking him who he thinks he is. And under any other circumstance I would.

My face feels heavy. I feel the droop of my shoulders. My lips form a tight line. I pull my keys out of my pocket and look toward Shannon once more. My mind is a jumble. I want to sweep her away and try to salvage our relationship. But as soon as that thought hits, I wonder if that's the best thing for her–if I'm the best thing for her. I don't know what to do. She's not giving me a clue. If I go by her body language, she's shutting me out.

Chris turns away, his back toward us. He's not walking off yet, but it's obvious he's finished talking. And now, I'm getting mad. I don't get angry easily. My head is like the debris cloud of a tornado, carrying random bits of broken impressions and feelings, everything swirling too fast for me to nail any one thought or emotion down. It's on a sure path for destruction if I stay here.

Shannon's standing no more than six feet from me, but it feels like a chasm separates us. Her arms remain folded across her chest. She's simultaneously defending herself and holding herself together. And she still won't look at me.

"I'm going to get my purse." She finally mumbles without glancing in my direction.

A tear slips out of her eye and makes a slow trail down her cheek.

"Shannon?"

"Not now, Duke."

"Okay."

Okay? A voice in my head instantly starts screaming at me to say more, to touch her, to pull her to me.

But I know I can't. No words will be enough. To touch her would not be fair to her–not while I'm questioning everything.

Instead, I'm frozen in place, watching her retreating back until the diner door closes behind her with a thunk. I walk toward my car. figuring Shannon won't want to have to face me when she comes out, and honestly, she shouldn't have to considering the state I'm in.

It's better if I go.

I sit in the driver's seat, my head resting on the steering wheel. I rear back and bang my head a few times. It doesn't help.

"Sorry, Shelb." I mutter.

I pull my phone out and shoot Shannon a text before I drive away.

Duke: *Sorry.*
Shannon: *It was awful. Way worse than I expected. For many reasons.*
Duke: *Yeah. Can we talk? Maybe tomorrow?*
Shannon: *Sorry, Duke. I'm not sure. I need space.*
Duke: *Okay.*

I want to tell her I'll be here when she's ready, but I don't know if I will be. I need to take some time to figure out what I have to offer Shannon before I go rushing back to her with promises I can't be sure I'll keep.

FORTY-NINE

Shannon

I walk inside the house with the clattering of the screen door at my back. I don't look over my shoulder. I don't stop walking until I'm up the stairs, in my room and face down on my bed with my pillow stuffed under my head so I can really and truly cry. And I do.

The tears flow enough to soak my pillow, so I lift it, rearrange to find a dry spot and continue my spot-by-spot effort to drench my bedding. It's going well. At this rate, I'll have it soaked in less than an hour.

Jayme comes in. Of course she does. I love her and her motherly ways, but this is one problem that can't be fixed–especially not by a romance author.

The mattress dips with her weight. She silently rubs light circles on my back like my mom did when I was little, before Bridgette left us. Before the world turned my mom into a shell of a human being, eaten alive by grief.

I understand Mom more than ever now. If anything nonphysical could have the power to kill a person, it's grief.

I try to talk. "I think ... I think ... I think it's ooooover." I cry harder. "But ... buh buh but ... I ... I ... I ... I ... luh ... luh ..." I gasp between sobs. "... luh ... love ... him."

"I loooooove himmmmm!" I wail.

My cries get louder and then I take a deep breath. In a weary voice, I beg Jayme to tell me. "I really love him. Why? Why does it hurt so much if it's love?"

I'm bawling uncontrollably, gasping for air between wails, and Jayme's still drawing on my back like a monk with a sand table. It's unexpectedly soothing. Snot is coming from my nose. I can feel the redness of my face. The splotching. The puffing. I've never been a pretty crier.

I sit up, intent on aborting the my-bedding-is-my-kleenex program. I need real tissues, or more like a few rolls of toilet paper.

Jayme looks at me with the sweetest look of compassion on her face. "You know how I said you could never be ugly?"

I start laughing. It's more of a hysterical laugh.

She laughs too. My laughter spurs hers and then hers spurs mine. Jayme falls backward flat onto my bed and I'm standing, holding my stomach, cracking up while I'm still crying. I never even knew I was capable of emotional multitasking until this moment.

All this shared laughter feels like the thinnest ray of hope in a pitch black dungeon.

"I've never been so glad to be wrong," she sputters out between laughs. "You look awful."

"This is supposed to make me feel better?" I laugh harder, running to my bathroom to grab the roll of TP.

I won't describe what's coming out my nose. I know you don't want to hear about it.

Breakups, my friends. They are ugly, snotty, drippy, puffy, splotchy nightmares.

Who's got a sponge for a pillow, a face that would serve as a Halloween costume, the sweetest housemate, and might just make it through losing the love of her life? Maybe not this splotchy ballerina. That's who.

But, maybe I will.

While I blow my nose and run cold water on a face cloth to lay across my swollen eyes, Jayme draws a bath. Seriously, people. That woman needs to be loved by a man. Not me. I'm not that woman. Jayme is. She's such a treasure. If I thought she didn't secretly pine away for romance, I'd cosign her spinster-for-life program. But, I don't believe she really wants to be alone forever. Even at the height of my own personal heartbreak, I believe in love. Just not for me.

After my bath, and a change into a pair of soft pj shorts and matching camisole top, I'm snuggled on the couch while Jayme brings me a bowl of ice cream with toppings.

"It's the go-to dinner for heartbreak," Jayme announces. "I'm pretty sure eighty percent of romance novels have the ice cream wallow moment. Not my novels, of course. Vampires and ice cream, or aliens and ice cream ... It doesn't work."

"It works for this human," I tell her around a spoonful.

"I'm so glad."

My eyes are still puffy, hours after I did the speed walk to my room to lose my marbles over the loss of Duke. I feel like I took prednisone. I've got this permanent moon face.

"Duke is awesome," I say with a shuddering breath.

"He is," Jayme agrees.

I love that she's not all, "He's a jerk. Let's egg the Shelby." Besides the fact that I don't look great in orange, I don't want anyone to hate him on my behalf. I don't even hate him. Because he is awesome. He's the most awesome person I know.

But he didn't tell Chris he loved me, or even that he wants me. He didn't do anything but say "It just happened," as if I were some mistake–like he accidentally started kissing me and couldn't stop. And he never corrected Chris about me being one more fling. He stood there, taking in Chris' words as if they were some revelatory truth.

"Unfortunately," I sigh. "Duke's not cut out for the long-term. I need a man who will stand up for me when times get tough, not turn tail and take the easy road while shoving me into oncoming traffic. And maybe that man doesn't exist. In which case, I'll be an old cat lady with you for the rest of my life. Minus the muumuus and crazy look in my eyes."

"I do not intend to ever allow a muumuu past that doorway. And if I have a crazed look, it will only be over a writing deadline. It will be temporary and will pass once I submit the manuscript. Understood?"

Jayme has very specific plans for her extended-singleness, including rocking her status as favorite honorary aunt to all the kids in our friend group. I'll vie with her for that if I never date again.

Jayme's flopped sideways over the stuffed side chair across from me, her legs dangling over one armrest and her head leaning on the other. She lifts her head so she can make eye contact with me.

"I think Duke meant well. It's his first rodeo. He's never been in a committed relationship that required him to step up."

She pauses for a moment and then gives me an unexpected whiplash with her next statement.

"I vote for a second chance."

I feel like someone put me on a merry-go-round at the park, spun it incessantly and then jerked it to a sudden stop.

"You vote for a second chance?"

"Not in an et tu Brute way. I'm not turning on you and going all team Duke over here. I just believe he didn't mean to leave you hanging. I was in the restaurant when he went outside with Chris. You were averting your eyes on purpose. I saw the way Duke looked at you before he walked out. Then he looked back again before he went out the door. It was a blindside. Your brother said some pretty harsh things. Who knows where Duke's head's at after being caught off guard and cut down so severely. I'll tell you one thing."

Jayme pauses and almost mumbles the next phrase, "From the romance author's perspective."

She holds my eyes. "Misunderstandings kill romance. People need to talk things out, not hide from situations and assume."

"Did he mess up?" She asks.

She doesn't answer–because she's a writer and she takes rhetorical questions at face value.

"And will he mess up again?"

Again, she doesn't answer herself and doesn't wait for me to answer. I kind of geek out over her literary self for a minute before my mind drifts back to the fact that my housemate thinks I need to unwrap this precious, tender organ that is my heart and see if it can go for another spin around the food processor that is a relationship with Duke.

Okay. You're right. That's a bit dramatic.

"I don't know if I can."

I scrape the sad dregs of my bowl of frozen comfort food. My voice sounds small, even to me.

"You don't know if you can crawl back into those arms again, let him kiss you again, hear him say all those sweet things to you again, laugh at his amazing sense of humor and his ridiculous fake bravado again? Or you don't know if you have it in you to give him a chance to mess up, even if he wants to keep trying to make things right?"

I'm stunned into silence.

I start doodling in my melted ice cream puddle with the tip of my spoon. When I look down, I've written his name.

It occurs to me right then. I can't get a Dukecersism. It's nothing I can do for myself. I couldn't before we were together, and I can't now. I love him. And I want him. It might take me a little while to recover from this last blow, but I want to give him a second chance.

There's a knock at the door. Groucho makes a funky noise. My heart does too. The noise inside my heart sounds a lot like Duke's name. Is it him? Did he come back? If he did, should I tell him about the second chance and just ask for a few days to recover from what we went through at the diner? Will I let him hold me?

That last one's not even a question. If Duke Satterson is on my porch right now, I'm going to let him hold me. We won't kiss, but I'd fall into his arms for a moment. Or an hour. Or the rest of the night.

I feel this warmth of hope and a swell of gratitude for my wise and gentle roomie. If it weren't for her, I might have let the best person I've ever loved walk away for good.

Jayme stands up, giving me a questioning look. I nod to let her know he can come in.

She opens the door and her breath hitches for a moment. What's that about? Groucho's walking over toward her, you know, at the pace of a pregnant tortoise in winter, but he's getting there.

Heaven help us if we ever need him to protect us from danger. Oddball would pitch in, though.

"Chris."

Jayme's tone is not mean, but she's a little feisty on my behalf. If you could see her right now, you'd bite your lip to keep from smiling at the adorableness. She's five foot two and has a rounded figure. Her hands are on her hips. She's wearing jeans and a graphic T-shirt that says *I'm in my write mind*. My brother is six one and burly. Even more beefy after all his time in the service.

Jayme's stance says, "Don't mess with me." Her tone of voice does too. She looks like Sister Smurf taking on the Hulk, and my money's on Smurfette for this one.

Chris is here.

It's not Duke.

"Shannon," Jayme calls as if I'm in another room. "Someone called the militia. Should I let him in, or should we exercise our second amendment rights?"

I chuckle. "Let him in."

Chris walks past Jayme, sizing her up and lightly shaking his head. She didn't grow up around here and he left before she moved in, so he hasn't spent much time with her. She's making a heck of a first impression.

"Could we have a moment alone?" he asks me.

"That didn't go so well last time," I say.

340

"I'll leave you two alone," Jayme offers. "And I'll be right up there if you need me. You know the safe word."

I chuckle and thank her.

"Safe word?" Chris asks.

"She's joking. Humor. You know? You used to have some. Did they march it out of you?"

I regret my words as soon as I say them. I have no idea what Chris endured in the Army. He went overseas. Yes, he mostly organized, directed, and took responsibility for his company, but still, I'm sure I'll never know the depth of what he experienced.

"Sorry."

"It's okay. I deserved that."

"Yeah. You did. And a whole lot more."

"Aiden took me out to the farm after everyone left the diner."

"And."

"And he read me the riot act."

"Good."

I cross my arms over my chest. I love Chris, but what he pulled at the restaurant was uncalled for. I get him wanting what's best for me, but saying Duke's not relationship material and calling me one of his flings ... Well, I never thought I'd hear words like that from my brother. Not to mention criticizing all my past relationships and dating choices in one fell swoop.

He's silent. I guess we both changed while he was gone. He left a baby sister, just out of high-school. He came home to a grown woman who speaks her mind and doesn't need bodyguards.

"I was shocked. I felt betrayed," Chris explains.

"I get that. We anticipated it. If you had come home on schedule, we would have been able to ease you into the reality."

"And what is that reality?"

"That I'm in love with Duke."

He shakes his head.

"Is he not your best friend?"

"That's so different. A man can be a great bro, and not

someone you'd want dating any of your sisters or any woman you know."

"Wow."

"He's great with guys. Loyal. Funny. Even has hidden wisdom. And he always had my back until this."

"Newsflash, Chris. This isn't about you. Duke and I found out we've had feelings for one another for years. Years, Chris. And you know what he did with those feelings? He sat on them. He tried to date other women. He watched out for me, even though it killed him to see me date other guys. I wasted time dating those other guys. All the while we each stayed on our side of the line. The line you drew. And one night, it all snapped. We couldn't stay away from one another anymore."

"Okay. That's plenty."

"Is it though? You act like Duke did this to hurt you. Or I did. But in reality, we both robbed ourselves of years of happiness. And we spent the last two weeks sneaking around town like criminals, hiding our relationship from this town. From this town, Chris! You can't hide here. And we did. Mostly. Anyway, we did all that for you. It sure wasn't for our health."

"Why did you do this behind my back, Boogs?"

It's short for Bugaloo and he's digging deep using that term of endearment right now.

"We were only thinking of you. We wanted you to have time to come home, have the hero's welcome we thought you deserved and to adjust."

Chris leans back onto the sofa. He probably didn't even realize how perfectly postured he had been sitting before this. When he slouches back, I see him–my brother. He's the guy I grew up with, the one who goofed around with me. The one I looked up to.

"I get why you're like this–all overprotective of me," I tell him. "No one gets it more than I do. But Chris, I'm twenty-six. I have a brain. And you know what? I'll make mistakes. And I'll get hurt. But I can navigate my way through those things."

He looks over at me. "So, I'm pretty much fired."

"You were never hired. You're my brother. And I need a brother. I don't need a bodyguard or some sort of supervisor or chaperone."

"I'm sorry, Boogs.".

"No. None of that Boogs stuff. Seriously? Are you trying to make me give you a wet willy? Because I will."

He chuckles. "I'm sorry."

He looks down and then he looks back up at me. "I really messed up."

"You did."

"It's hard coming home after being gone so long. People have changed. Half my friends are married. Trevor has a baby! Aiden has two kids. It's like I've been Rip Van Winkle, only I've been overseas and experienced so much. It wasn't fair to you and Duke the way I acted."

"Nope."

"Do you forgive me for being a stubborn, overprotective brother?"

"I'll get there. I'm working on it. You were such a jerk, Chris. And, you owe Duke an apology too–big time."

"I know. Believe me. I know. And you're right. Have you talked to him?"

"No. I came home and cried. Then Jayme talked some sense into me. I plan to talk to him. I only hope you didn't ruin things between us. I've never seen him so downcast and reserved. The things you said ..."

He shakes his head, obviously still making an effort to wrap his brain around me and Duke being together, and probably trying to come to terms with how he acted. At least, I hope he is.

"Do you know how he feels about you?"

"We haven't said the big three words yet. It's all new in one way, but so old in another. Duke has looked out for me while you were gone. Brought me medicine when I was sick, showed up to ruin my dates in the name of watching out for me, and made me feel more special than anyone else ever has. He listens to my dreams and believes in me."

My fingers absently travel to the ballet slipper charm on my necklace.

I hear myself recounting Duke's actions and I chide myself for getting mad at him for not stepping up when Chris called us out. Hasn't Duke consistently shown me his heart? I'm pretty sure I know how he feels, even though he hasn't told me yet. Jayme's right. It's his first rodeo. I only hope he gives us a chance after tonight.

"I'm an idiot," Chris says.

"Yep," I say, with a small smile. I will eventually forgive Chris, but I'm still mad.

"Can I have a do-over?" Chris asks in that way he always did when we were younger.

"You get a do-over and you'd better use it to make things right with my boyfriend."

Chris nods. His face takes on a serious expression that's new to me. He looks more official and reserved, but still like himself.

"Your boyfriend," he mutters. "Wow."

FIFTY

Duke

I can't feel anything but a fluctuation between excruciating pain and a sad numbness. I'm in my house hiding out. I told Pops I don't feel well. He muttered something about back in his day a man never let a woman keep him from going to work. Of course, news of Chris' confrontation at the diner had already spread around town.

Before we hung up, I told Pops about the exam and my plans to leave the garage and start teaching. Last night put a lot of things in perspective. Surprisingly, Pops wants to see me do what makes me happy. He says he can bring in some other mechanics and we'll train them up. I'll work some odd hours until things are stable.

I've put together a new spotify playlist set to replay on a continuous loop. I call it "The Saddest Songs of the Seventies."

I'm laying on my couch crying and staring at the ceiling. Anyone who wants to can come grab my man card and throw it in the dumpster. I don't need it anymore anyway. The only reason I wanted to be a man was for Shannon. And I blew it like I'm blowing my nose, only worse.

I should have stood up to Chris. I should have spoken up

when Shannon did. I left too much unsaid. And now she wants space, which I'm pretty sure means she doesn't want me.

I haven't even bothered to get dressed, so I'm in an old T-shirt and thin plaid pajama bottoms. My hair is a mess and I'm pretty sure my eyes are red. I didn't even cry when I was in little league and we lost the championship game. But, I'm crying now.

I hear animated chatter coming up the driveway.

There's a knock at the door and an unmistakable voice says, "Open up, Duke. We know you're in there and we're too old to stand out here in this heat."

Pulling the age card. That's low.

"I'm coming," I growl.

Don't get me wrong. I love our seniors. Just not when they show up the day after a breakup. Because I know what's coming and I'm not strong enough to withstand it.

I open the door.

Memaw, Mable and Esther enter my home like the three fairy godmothers in Sleeping Beauty, only they don't float in, they march. And I'm pretty sure they don't have any magical powers to help me win back my princess.

That's the corniest thing I've probably ever thought. Someone should shoot me and put me out of this misery. I've started hanging my hopes on Disney movies. It's a new low.

"Stop moping," Memaw says with a single nod of her head.

"And goodness, Duke," Esther says. "It smells in here. You only broke up yesterday. How did it get so stinky so fast?"

I take a sniff. It doesn't smell. But, when I inhale a second time, I smell it. Vinegar? Dill? It's not super-strong, but I do smell it.

"That's Mabel," Memaw says. "She started watching those TikTok videos that tell you to use pickles for deodorant."

"It's limes," Esther says. "You're supposed to use limes. Don't tell me you've been rubbing pickles all over that aging body of yours. I'd think you're pickled enough!"

Mable looks horrified. "Are you sure it was limes?"

Memaw shrugs. Esther nods.

"Gimme your phone, Duke," Esther says, holding her hand out to me. "I need to show her. She'll never take my word for a thing. This'll be no different."

I hand Esther my phone.

"Put that down, Esther," Memaw says. "We're not here about Mabel's personal care habits. We'll tend to that later. We're here to fix Duke and get him back with Shannon."

I'm not sure how they plan on fixing me, but the idea of getting back with Shannon has me feeling the slightest bit of hope, no matter how irrational it seems.

"Can I get any of you a drink?" I ask.

"Why, yes please," Mabel says, at the same time Esther says, "We're not here on a social call, Duke. We're here on business."

I don't know which one I should listen to. Mabel's dating Pops. But, Esther always seems to be in charge.

Memaw settles it. "I'll get drinks. You sit. I can always shout from the kitchen with my opinion."

"Good," Esther says, sitting on my sofa.

Mabel sits too.

Memaw walks through to the kitchen and opens my fridge. "He's got beer, iced tea, and some sportsy thing that says energy on it. It's watermelon flavored."

"Oooh. I'll take one of those," Mabel says.

"No you won't," Esther scolds. "You'll be up all night having to go to the bathroom, unable to sleep, probably fall and break your hip trying to paint the ceiling off the energy that thing'll give you. No sir. You stick to tea or water."

Mabel pouts for a moment. I stifle a chuckle.

"I'll take a glass of water," she finally says.

Esther pats Mabel's knee and Mabel smiles at her.

Right then and there I determine a very real fact. I will never understand females and I really shouldn't try.

Memaw comes out with a tray that I've never seen or used

before. I wonder where she found that. And she's got a glass of water for each of us.

"Okay. Let's get down to business," she says, sitting down on the other side of Mabel. "You know we're here to help you with Shannon."

"I knew you fancied her," Esther says. "The way you showed up at dance class. And the way the two of you eyed one another." She fans her face. "It was hashtag relationship goals, as my grand-kids say."

"We wish you didn't try and sneak, though. That just never works out." Mabel says.

Memaw chimes in. "Remember when we were in high school and Bonnie and Bert thought they'd sneak around."

"Whewee. She got it good from her parents." Mabel says.

"And his." Esther adds.

"Anyway," Memaw says. "We want to help you plan your grand gesture."

"My what?"

"It's the thing men do to win a woman's heart after they've been foolish and done what they always do."

"What do we always do?" I can't help but ask.

"You know how men are. They just don't think. Then they do or say something that upsets us."

Esther chimes in, "Or they don't do or think what we think they should."

Mabel and Memaw nod effusively.

"Well, that's the time for the grand gesture." Memaw says.

"Oh." I say. "Like a dinner out, or chocolates and flowers."

"Bigger," Mabel says.

"Much bigger," Esther adds.

"If you mess up big, you've got to make up big," Memaw says.

Esther adds, "Kinda like how the punishment fits the crime. Except the gesture fits how much of an idiot you made of yourself."

Then Memaw says, "Trust me, Duke. This is age-old wisdom. It'll save you a lot of pain."

Mabel says, "Just name some children after us for all the help we're giving you."

Esther shakes her head. "As if he wants children named Virginia, Mabel and Esther. Please. We've had a hard enough time with these names. Why carry that burden on in another generation? You name your kids what you want to, Duke."

"Thank you. I appreciate it."

"Okay," Memaw says. "You need a grand gesture. Something that won't leave any doubt in her mind about how you feel about her. Make it big, Duke."

A thought starts to build, which means the pickle juice or the grief is really getting to me. Am I honestly taking relationship advice from three seniors who bicker and watch TikTok for personal care advice? I guess I might be.

My three godmothers fade into a conversation about dentures and something that happened at the Seed-N-Feed while I think about Shannon. Somehow them coming over made me feel a little better. After a bit of gossiping, they seem to remember I'm in the room.

"We've taken up enough of your day, Duke," Memaw says, standing. The other two follow her example and stand up too.

"Get dressed and take action," Esther says. "That's what you do now. Moping won't help you. It's fine to mope a little. It's natural. But then you aren't gonna win your girl back with that. You've got to fight for her."

Mabel just smiles at me and pats my arm as she follows the others out the door. "She'll come back. Don't you worry. You two are in love. Love overcomes all the smaller things."

I smile back at Mabel and walk with her to the door. When they leave I collapse into my chair and start thinking about grand gestures. Something in me feels bigger, like I actually have a chance of making a relationship work with Shannon.

I take the advice of my guests and shower. I also take my trash out to the curb because I'm not a complete cretin, but I look to make sure none of the neighbors are out before I go.

I'm walking back toward my house, when a car pulls up to the curb. I pick up my pace, but I'm not fast enough. The driver exits the vehicle and calls my name.

Chris.

I keep my back toward him. I'm ready to try to make up with Shannon for being indecisive and silent last night, but I'm not sure I want to see Chris now, or for the foreseeable future. Much of my restless night was spent rehashing his attitude and words and as much as I see where he was coming from, I can't get behind how he handled himself—or us.

"Duke," he calls out again.

I stop and turn, crossing my arms over my chest.

I tip my chin to him. He remains by his car, obviously uncertain about whether he's welcome any further onto my property.

"May I come in?" he asks. "I want to apologize and make things right—if you'll let me."

I nod and turn toward my door. I'll hear him out.

Chris follows me into the house. I gesture to the couch like the third ghost in the Christmas Carol. I only hope my silence has the same effect on Chris as that ghost had on Scrooge.

Chris sits. "I'm sorry."

I stare. It feels unfamiliar not to be the talkative, bubbly guy, always lifting others out of their seriousness, but right now, this quiet feels right. I'll listen. He can talk. We'll see where this goes from here.

"I said things last night ..." he shakes his head. "I can't believe what I said. I was in shock, but that's no excuse. I'm sorry."

My lips tighten. He's sorry, but I'm still hurting. Shannon's still taking space and I don't know what that means. And all I know is that I've got a big project ahead of me if I am going to win her back and give us a chance at forever together.

Chris runs his hand over the top of his hair. Then he looks up at me. I'm still leaning on the edge of my chair, standing, not sitting. It's a power position, and I know it. But after the fiasco in the parking lot, I feel like I need the upper hand with this guy who always had my back until last night.

Chris' eyes take on a pleading expression. "I know the way I handled being blindsided was way out of line. I hurt Shannon. I said things about both of you I shouldn't have said. You're one of my best friends. I just want you to know I've always respected you."

"Except when it comes to relationships, or your sister," I challenge him. I had to speak up. Silence has a limit.

"You always dated casually. Shannon ... I just didn't want her to be another ..."

He struggles to find words and I let him squirm.

"I should have let you two explain to me. You're grown ups. Even if she is another fling to you, or she's after you and you don't care about her the way she does for you ... bottom line, it's not my business."

Now we're talking.

"I love her."

I let those words hang in the air between us.

Chris does a spit-take. His head literally snaps up.

"You love her?"

"I do. So much. She's it for me."

He might not believe me. He might try to block me. I'm over the doubt of last night. It's amazing what a sleepless night will do for a man's sense of resolution. I'm sure of one thing. Walking away from Shannon isn't an option.

"I'm going to pursue her. I have to apologize for not standing up for us last night. And then I'm going to show her what she means to me. Whether you like it or not."

Chris nods. "So, what do you need from me?"

FIFTY-ONE

Shannon

"It will be okay," Jayme assures me.

I'm tossing the entire contents of my closet onto my bed and floor like a caucasian Marie Kondo with a not-so-secret espresso addiction.

Jayme walks up to me and places both palms on my shoulders. She has to reach up a little to do it since I'm nearly five ten and she's eight inches shorter, but she's got the whole small-but-mighty thing down to a science.

"Stop," she says in her sweetly commanding voice. "You're making me dizzy. Plus you're making a mess—more of a mess."

I throw my arms overhead.

"I can't go! I can't."

"Sit." Jayme steers me toward the bed and physically lowers me so I'm sitting on the edge—several shirts are under me, so I scootch them around to make room for myself before I resettle. Not that I'm settled, let's not get confused here. I'm so unsettled, I could give a shaken pop bottle a run for its money.

"You'll make it through this. It's just a ball game. Besides, Duke will be busy with the players on his team."

"Being adorable with them. Being all compassionate and encouraging and funny."

"And why haven't you talked to him yet?"

"I don't know. I want to. I keep meaning to. But a part of me is waiting for him to make the first move. Do you think that's wrong?"

"I don't, actually. He messed up. He didn't mean to, but it was a triple whammy–running into Amber at the car show, keeping the job opportunity under wraps, and then the way he handled the night Chris came home. It's like his boat sprung three leaks in a row. He needs to patch the holes. I get it."

"Thanks."

I drop my head into my hands. "Maybe I'll just approach him. This waiting is excruciating. I told him I wanted space. Maybe he's just waiting for me to make the first move."

Duke and I haven't talked all week. We weren't going to deal with the difficult aspect of being together until after Chris had been properly welcomed home. His party is this evening after the afternoon ball game. I've thought of calling Duke or popping by all week, but then I'd get these thoughts that kept me from reaching out.

What if he realized he's not as serious as he thought he was about me?

Did he take Chris' words at face value?

Why shouldn't he?

Should I let him know I want to give him a second chance?

The more days that have passed, the harder it has been to think of bridging this distance between us. I know we need to.

I keep picturing him, not speaking up when Chris confronted him about me being a casual fling.

I throw myself backward onto my bed, hitting the back of my head on a sandal when I land. I really did go through my closet like a class five typhoon.

"Aaaagggggghhhhh!"

"Okay," Jayme says. "Let it out."

"Gaaaaahhhhh!"

"Good. Good. Just let all that out too."

She's like this midwife for my emotions.

"I'm so dumb!"

"You're not dumb. But you are in your underwear and the game starts in an hour, so if you need to shout any more, now's the time. Then we have to get you dressed and clear a path out through this jungle of your discarded wardrobe so we can get ourselves over to the ballfield."

"Blllaaaahhhhgggghhh!"

"That was great! Okay." Jayme claps her hands like a bossy little sprite. "Now we get up and get dressed. What do you say?"

She's talking to me like I'm a preschooler who missed her nap and needs to get ready for a birthday party.

"Remind me why I have to go to this game."

"You suit up and show up to life. You face this situation head on. We live in Bordeaux. You can't hide out forever."

"But, maybe I can hide out for a little bit. Like today."

And tomorrow. And next week.

If I knew how Duke felt—really how he felt, I'd be so much more motivated. I had convinced myself he cares when Chris came to apologize, but then I went back to asking myself why he didn't speak up. Why didn't he reach out since Friday at the diner? And now, it's just awkward. Time has passed and we haven't talked. I'm scared to risk and find out he really doesn't want to pursue something serious with me.

"Is that what you want?"

"No."

Jayme takes a seat next to me on my bed. "What do you want?"

It's this gentle question, asked in her careful voice. I could cry, but I've cried myself out for now.

"I want him. I've always wanted him. Isn't that pathetic?"

"It's so far from pathetic, I don't think we even have a view of pathetic from here. It's beautiful. And you aren't going to get him by hunkering down in a bedroom, surrounded by enough clothes to dress a small country. So, let's put your game face on and show up. It won't get easier. Trust me. It's time."

I look her in the eyes. She's got this look that says I'm not staying home today no matter what I do or say. I wouldn't put it past her to drug me and drag me. That would be interesting–it could be a whole *Weekend at Bernie's* thing where she props me up and makes my arm wave while I'm passed out. Of course, that guy was dead. Lucky him.

"Chop chop," Jayme says, jumping up off the bed and holding up a top. "This is great. It brings out the color of your eyes."

"Which I would want to do because?"

"Because you aren't a quitter. And because you love this man. And he's good for you, despite the huge learning curve he has ahead of him in terms of how to do long-term, committed relationships. And you are going to look back on this day and say, that was the day I wouldn't have changed if I could have."

She has this odd look in her eyes.

"What do you know that I don't?"

"Nothing," she says, turning away and busying herself picking up my castoffs.

"Which jeans are you going to wear? Or do you think a skirt or shorts?"

She still hasn't looked me in the eye. She's talking to me from over her shoulder.

If I didn't know better, I'd say Jayme was hiding her face from me. If she is, she's obviously not going to tell me whatever she's hiding. And I don't have the emotional energy to figure her out and grieve the love of my life on the same day, so I pick up the top she handed me. It does make my eyes pop.

I step over a few articles of clothing and pull out a pair of cut off jeans shorts from my shorts drawer. They are nothing compared to Amber's shorts. No. Correction. They're something compared to hers. There's actual fabric involved. But, they do show off my legs. And I happen to know Duke likes my legs. His eyes have traveled there on many a vacation.

I smile thinking of Duke looking at my legs. Maybe we do have a chance. Okay, legs, I'm leaving this in your hands. Not that you have hands. You're legs.

I may be officially losing it.

I hold up my selections to Jayme. "I've got an outfit."

Jayme does jazz hands. "She's got an outfit, ladies and gentlemen! I'll just give you space to get that adorable outfit on your adorable self and we'll tackle this mess later. You need time for hair and makeup."

She is acting odd. It's not just my imagination. Maybe living around my grief is getting to her too.

Once I'm dressed and have done my hair and makeup, Jayme insists on driving. Fine. She often drives us anyway. Her driving doesn't mean anything is strange. But something feels strange. Maybe it's the nerves prickling my entire body and making me unable to sit still.

I've got my hair in wavy low pigtails sticking out from under a ballcap. I put on two extra coats of waterproof mascara–since I never know when I'm going to spring a leak these days. My lips are a color called Slay. It's this cherry red I barely ever use, but something about it makes me feel like I've got a handle on life. It works for Gwen Stefani and Christina Aguilera, so it's bound to work for me.

Red lips, girlfriends. Don't ever underestimate the power of a well-applied power shade of lipstick.

We easily find parking at the Rec Center and walk toward the ballfield. My stomach is doing some sort of Olympic routine, and it's definitely not going to win any medals.

I see him.

Duke.

He's talking with Brooks, his hands propped on those perfect hips, a smile in his eyes as they talk about strategy or whatever coaches talk about before games.

He looks up and smiles in my direction as if he knew the moment when I walked onto the bleachers. He's smiling the smile he always gave me, the one before everything went to Hades in a flaming handbasket.

I smile back.

He waves. It's this super-cool wave. Some guys couldn't pull it off. They'd look like they were trying to stop traffic. Not Duke. He's got all the moves. Oh, yes, everything in me remembers those moves. And him. And I just want to run and wrap my arms and legs around him and cling to him for a minute—or the rest of our lives.

Instead I give him that finger wave Cherry gave him at the fair. Whatever. It was all I could think to do on the spur of the moment. I probably should have spent less time deconstructing my closet and more time thinking about what I'd do when faced with Duke Satterson in person. He seems to like my little finger wave because all his dimples come out to say, "Hey there."

Maybe if we never talk again, we could get back together. It seems like talking is what messes us up. We could have the love affair of a pair of mimes. Just waving and winking and smiling. And kissing. Do mimes kiss, or do they just stand apart from one another puckering?

Oh, yes. I've lost it. There's no doubt about it.

Brooks gets Duke's attention and Duke looks away from me to answer Brooks, but he glances back at me one more time and winks. Yep. Mime love. I'm all about this.

The umpire says it's time to start the game. I watch Duke the whole time. It's somewhere at the bottom of the third inning when the Firefly mascot comes marching in front of our bleachers with a sign that says *I'm so sorry, Shannon.*

I do a double take. People look at me and smile like this happens all the time. No one but me seems shocked.

I look over at Jayme. She's bouncing in her seat and grinning.

"What is going on?" I ask her.

She shrugs. As if she doesn't know. She knows.

I look over at Duke. He's smiling. His eyebrows are raised like he's waiting to see how I react.

"He's sorry," Mabel says from a few rows behind us.

"He wants you back," Esther says.

I turn around. Mable's holding a sign that says, *I messed up (me being Duke, not Mabel).* And Esther has a sign that says, *Can you forgive me? (me being Duke, not Esther).*

When I turn around, the high school marching band has taken the field. Mid-game. They aren't wearing their uniforms. They're all in summer clothes. But, they have their instruments.

All the ballplayers are lined up in front of the dugout like they knew this was coming and cleared the field for whatever's going on. Did they know? Were they a part of this?

The high school cheerleading squad runs out in front of the marching band. The percussionists start playing this drum beat and the cheerleaders shout out,

"Duke and Shannon!"

"We all agree!"

"Duke and Shannon!"

"They're meant to be!"

The band starts to part. The cheerleaders do a jump formation, and my brother walks right through the middle of it all with a sign that says, *Duke + Shannon.* Just that. There are hearts all over the poster board. It's so not my brother. He doesn't do pink poster board signs with hearts. And he doesn't approve of me and Duke. Only, maybe he does. He looks across the field at me and gives me a small nod and a thumbs up–his seal of approval.

Duke's striding toward me. He looks nervous, but so very Duke. I'd stand up, but my knees feel like they'd betray me.

"Hi," he says when he reaches the half-wall dividing the bleachers from the field. Every eye is on us. I can feel them staring, but I only see him.

"Hi."

"Could I talk you into giving us a second chance?"

"You never had to talk me into it. I'm yours."

In this agile move that makes me want to do all sorts of things to him, Duke places one hand on the half wall and hurdles over it in a single movement so he's standing right in front of me. I stand up. We just look at one another, smiling like big dorks in love. Sort of like mimes, but much less creepy, and without the white stage makeup or striped shirts.

"I like that lipstick," Duke says quietly.

"Want some?"

"I thought you'd never ask."

"Kiss her already," someone shouts.

The crowd starts stomping their feet and the drums catch on to the beat as our whole town chants, "Kiss her, Kiss her!"

I should be embarrassed, but I'm too swept up in the way Duke's looking at me. He looks around at the crowd, ever the ham, and asks, "Her? I should kiss her?"

People shout and whistle. I blush until he moves in and places his arms behind me, tugs me close and brings his lips to mine. I wrap my arms behind his neck and kiss him back.

He pulls away and says, "I love you, Shannon Leigh St. James."

It takes me a moment to process what he said.

He loves me. Oh my gosh! Duke loves me!

"I love you too, Duke Andrew Satterson"

He kisses me deeply, and I can feel his smile through the kiss. Then he leans back and shouts, "She loves me!"

He suddenly braces his arms behind my back and dips me, laying a kiss on me that makes me glad he's holding me up.

People go nuts. It's a lot to take in. Really, it's too much. But I can't bring myself to care because Duke hasn't let me go. And I've decided I won't ever let him go either.

The End

~

... but wait! There's an epilogue!

DUKE

"I'm taking this off!" Shannon says playfully.

She's in the passenger seat of my Shelby. It's early, even for me. She threatened me when I showed up at her home before sunrise.

When Shannon answered the door, she mumbled, "If you're coming over in the middle of the night, you need to bring a case of soda or we're not even talking."

I promptly handed her the giant tumbler of Diet Dr Pepper on ice I had brought with me.

Shannon took the drink from me, cradled it near her chest, and stood on tiptoe to kiss my scruffy cheek.

"You're the best."

"I just know how to woo you. Caffeine and chemicals are the way to my girl's heart."

She giggled after taking a huge sip of that disgusting beverage.

Despite the pop, it still took Jayme's persuasive ways to get Shannon dressed and into my car.

The sun still hasn't started to peek over the horizon. Timing is everything.

"Leave it on," I tell her. "I'll tell you when to take it off."

"Where are you taking me?" she asks, grasping at the blindfold.

"Nowhere if you take that off."

"Mean."

"We'll see."

"Bossy."

"When I need to be."

"Too bad you're adorable."

"Yeah. That's a real bummer."

"Good thing I'm so adorable."

"Agreed."

"You're infuriating, Satterson."

"Hold that thought," I say, as I turn the steering wheel to aim us down an unpaved road.

"Okay," I tell her. "Take it off."

"That's what he said," she jokes while she lifts the bandana off her face.

Shannon peers around, squinting as her eyes adjust to the dusky pre-dawn light. She looks around at the nearly empty field with a quizzical look and then she looks further into the distance.

"Is that a ...?"

"Hot air balloon? Yep. Wanna go for a ride?"

She starts bopping around in her seat. "Yes! You remembered my bucket list."

"I remember everything about you, Hollywood. Now let's go before we miss our launch time."

Shannon and I walk over to the man who is taking us up this morning. His name is Jacob and he runs this whole hot air balloon experience. We load into his jeep and he drives us to where the balloon is tethered to the ground. A few men whom he tells us are his ground crew follow behind us.

Shannon and I hold the sides of the balloon while this huge fan inflates it. One of the ground crew captures our picture. Once the balloon's full of air, the pilot lights the burner and we watch as the fire brings the balloon upright.

Jacob says, "It's time to load the gondola," so I help Shannon into the basket and then I climb in behind her. I'm not a small guy. I look around realizing how much I really do love her to be willing to go up in this bread basket with nothing but a piece of nylon between me and my splatted death onto the surface of the earth.

Yep. I love her that much. Not even a question.

We start to lift when Jacob twists the nozzle controlling the flame. The roar of the fire is louder than I expected, and hot, but I barely have time to think about all that because we're lifting off the ground and Shannon is beaming. The sun crests over the horizon at just this moment. I couldn't have ordered up a better sunrise.

I put my arm around Shannon's shoulders and she leans into me as we soar over farms and rivers, woods, and small clusters of buildings below. Every so often Jacob squirts some shaving cream overboard to determine which way the winds are blowing.

We float along for a while and then I see my cue.

"Look down there," I say, pointing at a group of people gathered in a field below us.

Shannon looks. "I see people."

"Do you see the sign?"

"What sign?" She leans a little, which is fine because the edge of the basket comes up almost to her shoulders. "Are they holding a sign? I see a white thing. How can you tell it's a sign?"

I don't answer, because I'm down on one knee behind her. But the basket is way smaller than I had imagined when I booked a private flight, so my face is nearly planted in her butt.

"Duke?" Shannon says, turning slightly so I'm now nose-level with her hip.

She looks down at me.

"What are you doing down there? Oh! ..."

She tapers off as the pieces fall into place and she obviously makes sense of why I'd be kneeling in a wicker basket, suspended over the planet, nearly sweating from the heat of the flame overhead.

"I love you, Hollywood. I've loved you for longer than I can remember."

Both her hands fly up to her mouth and she gasps. Her eyes go wide.

"You're it for me. Honestly, you always were. I can't promise you I'll always get it right. As a matter of fact, I can promise I'll mess up, even when I try to get it right. But I promise to make you laugh, to stand by you, to love you well, to kiss you until you're breathless, and to never let you forget how special you are to me. That is, if you'll be my wife."

Shannon squeals. She jumps a little, which makes the basket wobble. I hold out the black box with her ring in it. The lid is open to show off the rose gold band with a marquise cut diamond to match the ballerina necklace I bought her last summer.

I just found out the name of that diamond shape. You learn all sorts of things when you want to get serious with the woman who keeps rocking your world in the best of ways.

So much has passed between the day Shannon forgave me in the middle of our little league game and now. Shannon's teaching two more dance classes every week at the Rec Center. The town council approved the purchase of the country elementary school and plans are in the works to restore it and turn it into a community arts center where Shannon will teach dance in an actual studio and other artists will teach classes, hold exhibits, and sell their art. Surrounding towns are showing interest in the project.

I've been teaching and coaching for nearly a year at Bordeaux High. Pops hired two mechanics, Fritz and another guy named Pete. I drop by when I want to, but it's not my job anymore. Pops says he's still going to leave the business to me when the time comes, but I'll keep a lead mechanic on to run things.

I look up into Shannon's eyes, thinking about how I almost lost her and how far we've come.

She's shouting "Yes! ... Yes! Yes! Yes!"

A tear travels down her cheek. "I love you Duke. You are my favorite part of every day, the one who makes me laugh the hardest of anyone I know. You're my safe place to land. The thing I want most in this world is to be your wife."

I'm her safe place to land. That sentence nearly knocks the wind out of me.

I slip the ring on Shannon's finger. She holds her hand out to look at it and then she cups my cheek and looks down at me.

"You want to be my wife *and* bear my adorable babies," I add.

"Slow down, big guy." She giggles and shakes her head at me like I'm the most incorrigible person she's ever met. I probably am.

She will bear my adorable babies.

She and I both know it.

I stand up and cup her cheeks. We don't kiss right away. We simply stand there, staring at one another, so much being said in unspoken ways. And then I lean in and claim her lips in a kiss. She runs her hands through my hair. I left the ball cap at home. She's mine. I don't need to wear it every day now. But I'll always be working to be worthy of a woman like Shannon.

Jacob clears his throat and I look over. He's smiling.

"Congratulations."

"Thank you," Shannon and I say at the same time.

She looks up at me, beaming. I loop my arm around her shoulder and pull her toward me.

"It's time to land," Jacob informs us. "I've got a spot targeted, but the winds have turned a little unpredictable right now, so we may have to adapt. Nothing to worry about. Hot air balloons don't have steering wheels, so I use the wind to our advantage. We'll be fine."

Shannon looks up at me. I feel her grip tighten at my side. I mouth, "I'm sure it's fine," to her.

She holds up her hand so her ring glistens in the sun and quietly whispers, "We're engaged!"

Shannon's my fiance. A smile breaks across my face.

I look down beneath the balloon, trying to figure out the

logical trajectory of our landing. "Jacob? Are we aiming a little close to that pond by those cattle?"

"We should be fine," he says.

He cranks the flame and we lift a little, but then a wind catches us and he lowers the flame again.

"Bend your knees, lean against the back there. Make sure you are standing next to one another,"

Jacob's voice has less of a *hey, welcome to your romantic engagement balloon ride* tone and more of a *guys, we better batten down the hatches* tone.

We do as he says. Shannon grips my hand until my knuckles start to turn white.

"We're fine. It's just prep for landing," I assure her.

She loosens her grip a little, but she's not saying a word. Her wide eyes are trained on the pond that seems to be moving toward us from below.

Cattle graze in the field as if it's any other morning in Ohio, completely unaware of the fact that we may be about to crash in on their breakfast in a big way.

"Bend your knees! Keep 'em bent," Jacob says quickly. "We're going down."

The balloon heads toward the pond and the gondola just barely avoids skimming over the top of the water. I'm about to breathe a sigh of relief when the basket bounces along the ground on the other side of the pond and tips sideways during the landing. Shannon and I fall backward with the basket. But, we made it.

We're laughing, full of adrenaline and the happiness of having just gotten engaged—and the added bonus of being back on solid ground.

I roll over to help Shannon out. I look down just in time to see the huge cow pie under my elbow—the cow pie I just leaned into with all my weight. Shannon starts laughing hysterically as I crawl out of the basket and extend her my other arm, the one not coated in cow dung.

The cattle around us continue to graze without even flinching.

I strip off my jacket, leaving me in a T-shirt that doesn't smell like manure. The ground crew drives up with our friends caravaning behind them. The crew sets up a folding table with fruit, croissants, muffins, juice and champagne while our friends gather around us.

"Did you see the sign?" Jayme asks right away when she bounds out of the car towards us.

"I couldn't even tell that was you!" Shannon says, holding her hand in front of her to show off her ring.

"She said yes!" Jayme shouts.

"What did the sign say?" Shannon asks.

I walk over and put my arm around Shannon. "It said, Marry Me, Hollywood."

Shannon turns to me and smiles. "I'm gonna marry the heck out of you Duke Satterson."

I pick her up and spin her around. When her feet hit the ground, I pull her in for a kiss.

"You know what you're getting into here, right?" I ask her, my mouth close enough to her ear she's the only one able to hear my words.

"Oh, I know alright," she whispers back at me. "I'm marrying the biggest flirt in Montgomery County."

"And I'll be spending all that flirt on you, future Mrs. Satterson."

"I'll be counting on it."

Bonus Epilogue

SHANNON

"Hey!" Duke's enthusiasm carries through the phone.

Even though he's not right in front of me, I can picture his boyish grin and the sparkle in his eyes. And, as usual, I feel a smile pull at my cheeks at the sound of his voice.

I take one last glance around the classroom turned dance studio and flick off the lights.

"Whatcha up to?" Duke asks.

"Just closing up from my last class at the Center, but you already know that."

"Yeah. I do. How'd my baby do dancing today?"

"She's great."

"He. He's great."

"I feel like she's a girl."

My hips don't lie. Boys ride up front like basketballs. A mom carrying a boy is all belly. At least that's what Memaw said. And this baby is making my backside wide and full. It's a girl. I just know it.

We'll know for sure in a month, when we have our baby shower. We decided to do a gender reveal just before the shower so guests can plan their gifts accordingly. My girlfriends convinced

369

me to do things that way. At first I thought I wanted to be surprised, but now I'm itching to know.

"And I know he's a boy," Duke says, his warm, deep voice wrapping around me like the best of hugs. "You know how I know?"

He's boyish and giddy. I can't help but play along.

"No. But I know you're going to tell me."

I hoist my duffle up on my shoulder and push through the double doors of the refurbished country elementary school we've reclaimed as a center for the arts. A student from my class waves to me as she runs out toward the van where her mom sits waiting for her.

"He's a boy because God knows I couldn't handle any more beauty and cuteness than I already have in my life. I'd die of cuteness overload." The way he laughs at his own joke makes me giggle.

"So you're saying our son won't be cute?"

"I'm saying our son will be manly. I can handle that. Another girl? One as beautiful as you?" He makes a choking sound, exaggerating the noises as if he's gasping for air, and then goes silent. "That was me dying of cuteness overload."

I giggle again. "You're ridiculous. We're guaranteed to have ridiculous children."

"Maybe we'll have practical children like you."

"I'm not always practical." I throw my duffle in my back seat and walk around to the driver's side.

"You're definitely not ridiculous," Duke nearly pouts. "... unless you count your texts."

"Ha ha."

"Meet me at home?" Duke asks. I can almost picture him wagging his eyebrows suggestively.

"For what?"

"Dinner. I want to feed you dinner. What sounds good?"

"Hmmm. Burgers." My mouth waters. Cravings are so real.

"And melon. And bananas. Fruit salad. Fruit salad sounds good. And sherbet. Oh! Fruit salad on sherbet."

Duke chuckles. "I'll get all that. Onion rings?"

"No!" I shake my head even though he can't see me. Then I turn the key and head out of the lot onto the country road leading back into Bordeaux. "Sorry. I mean, no thanks. Onion rings don't sound good."

"They sounded good last week."

"I know. Sorry. Every day is new when it comes to what the little dictator wants. She doesn't want onion rings. She wants fruit salad."

"It's one hundred percent okay with me. What my wife wants, my wife gets."

"Can I get that in writing?"

"I'll write it on a takeout napkin from Mad River Burgers." Duke pauses, his voice shifting to something more seductive. "And then I'll whisper it in your ear after dinner."

"Okay, okay. Slow your roll or we won't even get through dinner."

"And that would be bad because? ..." He chuckles softly.

"You're incorrigible."

"You love my incorrigibleness."

"I do."

"Still saying *I do*. See that, folks? She still says *I do*."

I smile. "I definitely still say *I do*."

"Me too, Hollywood. Every day. Now get home and get cozy while I pick up all the items on your dinner wishlist."

"Thank you."

"I live to please you."

I laugh.

"What? I do," Duke protests.

"I'll see you when you get home."

I thought I'd get over this man and his flirty ways. I imagined he'd get used to me and tone it down a bit. I should have known better. Duke Satterson is on like a stadium light. Full-glare halogen. He doesn't have a dimmer switch, and I'm beyond grateful. He hasn't stopped letting me know what I mean to him ever since we started dating.

We say our goodbyes and I drive the rest of the way to our house. It used to be Duke's house, but I moved in after we married. And now the spare bedroom is set up as a nursery—at least the furniture is all in place. We're waiting on the gender reveal to put the finishing touches on the decor.

I park my car in the driveway, grab my duffle and head inside through the back door. By the time I've changed into my favorite maternity sweats, Duke is home with bags of food.

"Dinner is served!" he announces while he sets the bags on the counter.

I get down the plates and set them on the counter and then I reach for the paper bag labeled *Mad River Burgers*.

"Uh uh uh," Duke playfully scolds. "You didn't tip the driver yet."

"Oh? And what did the driver have in mind?"

Duke grabs my hips and pivots me toward him. He settles onto a kitchen stool, spreads his legs, and pulls me close.

"Let's see," his eyes meet mine.

Today those familiar eyes are more green than usual. The brown flecks look like chocolate chips scattered in the green. He's studying me, like a bull behind the gate at a rodeo, ready to let loose, but temporarily contained.

I suddenly remember how much I perspired during dance class.

"You do not want to hug me. I'm a sweaty mess right now."

Duke secures his arms around me. There's a glimmer of mischief in his eyes. "I want to hug you. Sweaty or not doesn't matter to me."

I wriggle like I'm trying to avoid his hug, but ultimately, I collapse into him and he smiles with the victory.

"That's more like it. How long has it been since I've seen you?" his voice rumbles through his chest where my head is tucked in under his chin.

"Eight hours?" I guess.

"Eight long hours. You're trying to kill me, woman."

I laugh, but it's muffled in his shirt.

Duke kisses the top of my head. "Man, Shannon! You stink!"

I push against his chest. "I warned you!"

He laughs and tugs me close. "I'm kidding, babe. I don't smell anything." He pulls back so he's looking in my eyes again, but he holds me in place. "Now, as I was saying, this driver ..." Duke kisses the tip of my nose. "Drove to two stores." He kisses my cheek and then drags his stubble gently down my jawline until he's kissing my chin. He looks up at me through his lashes. "And at one store, he had to wait for them to refill the fruit salad from the back of the deli—because what his wife wants ..." He lifts his face and moves upward. My eyes flutter shut and he places a soft kiss on each eyelid. "What his wife wants, she gets."

I hum, my eyes still closed, and lean in toward my husband, wrapping my arms around him. Burger, schmurger. Food can wait.

"Shannon." Duke says on a whisper.

"Mm hmm?"

"I love you, babe." His voice is tender with emotion.

I love that about him. He's so fun and loud and crazy. But then he can be so sweet and heartfelt and sincere.

"I love you too, Duke."

He leans in and kisses me, his palm flat on my back and his other hand smoothing my hair. His lips are full and warm and he kisses like we're not waiting to eat, like I'm not shaped like a baby manatee, like we're just now seeing one another after a month apart.

It's always like this with him. Sure, we argue and disagree. We drive one another crazy. But Duke never lets those things last.

He's always quick with a joke or a kind word to turn things around. We promised early on that we would stay on the same team and never take life out on one another, and so far, we've kept that promise.

I grab Duke's cheeks, stand on my tiptoes and kiss my husband. He holds me tight and kisses me with the same toe-curling intensity he always does. Sometimes it's soft and heartfelt. Other times it's playful. And most of the time our kisses are laced with a desire for more. But it's always intense with Duke. That's just how he moves through life, and it's definitely how he loves— all in, no holding back, and full of passion.

We don't have to hide our relationship anymore, but sometimes I pretend we do just because I love feeling like he's completely mine and I get to keep him all to myself.

My stomach growls and the baby moves just a little, readjusting or something.

"He moved!" Duke pulls away from our kiss and puts his hand on my belly.

"She did," I say with a wink.

Duke lowers his head and says, "I tried to get you onion rings, but mom wasn't having it. Sorry, little man."

"Woman," I say.

Neither of us is super-serious about our attachment to the gender of the baby. We've just started this back and forth like a game. And we get to play for one more month. Then we'll know for certain.

"Go get comfy on the couch," Duke says. "I'll serve the burgers and fries and put the sherbet in the freezer for dessert."

I kiss his cheek and head into the living room, letting out a contented sigh along the way. It feels good to have a night at home, just the two of us. Between a late dance class once a week, Duke's little league practices, and after school events he has to participate in for his job, we sometimes go two or three nights without having dinner together. I'll cancel my evening class once the baby arrives. Duke's baseball season will be over soon. Then we'll be here most evenings—the three of us.

I'm scrolling my phone when Duke comes in with two plates in hand. He sets them on the coffee table and takes a seat at the end of the couch, lifting my feet to place them in his lap.

"We could eat at the table like civilized people," I say.

"Where's the fun in that?"

Duke hands me my plate.

"I like eating like this," he says. "We can eat at the table tomorrow night."

"I just don't want to eat on the couches when the baby's here." I tell Duke.

"I'm pretty sure he won't know where he's eating for a while."

"I just want to set up good habits."

"Okay," he squeezes my foot reassuringly. "We'll eat at the table. Later. Tonight, let's just watch a movie while we eat."

"Sounds good."

Duke starts scrolling channels while I dig into my burger.

His phone vibrates with a text right after he hits play and picks up his plate to start eating. He reads the text and looks up at me.

"Hey, Hollywood?" He looks concerned.

"What is it? Your mom?"

"No. Aiden"

He's about to say more when my phone rings.

I look over at Duke. "It's Em."

"Answer it," he says.

I press the green icon to take her call. "Hey, Em. What's up?"

"Shannon! Hi!" Em's voice sounds overly happy, maybe even forced.

"Are you okay?" I ask.

"I'm okay. Of course, I'm okay. Why wouldn't I be okay? I'm totally okay. Yep. Okie dokie. Super good."

I look over at Duke. He's eating and watching me. I shrug my shoulders and give him a look that says I don't know what's up.

"Okaaaay." I say to Em.

If anything screams *not okay*, it's someone repeatedly assuring you how okay they are.

"What's up?" I ask.

"Well, I'm fine. Good. As I said, "But I do need something.""

I wait. Em's quiet. I hear voices behind her, but they are muffled.

Duke gives me a questioning look. I shrug again.

Em stammers out her next sentence. "I ... uh. Well ... I need ... I mean I want ... um ... actually ... I have Lexi here. She's going to ... Here. Here's Lexi."

Wow. That was bizarre.

"Hey, Shannon!" Lexi's voice is also extra-peppy.

"Hi?"

"Yeah. So. We're having a spontaneous girls' night and we want you to come. Here at Em's. Can you come over here ... like in a half hour?" There's muttering and then Lexi gets back on the line. "Make that forty-five minutes. Can you?"

"I'd love to, but Duke just brought home burgers from Mad River and we're going to have a night in together. I just got out of dance. I'm sweaty and gross. You wouldn't want me there anyway."

"Oh, but we do. We really do. We actually ..."

Lexi's voice is cut off and Laura grabs the phone. "Shannon. This isn't optional. We need you out here. It's girls' night with a twist and ... well .. Em needs you here. Don't you, Em?"

Em's voice comes through in the background. "Yes. Yes. I need you Shannon."

"You guys are acting really weird."

"We are! Aren't we?" Laura says.

Then Em's back on the phone. "Uh. Yes. Oh my gosh. So weird." She ends with a nervous laugh and then adds, "So, will you come?"

"I don't know. Duke had practice late last night with the Fireflies. And I was too tired to stay up and hang out the night before. We're due for a night at home together. And I really want this burger."

I look over at Duke. He's nodding with agreement.

"We'll get you burgers!" Laura's back on the phone.

"Lots of burgers! With bacon!" Lexi shouts in the background. "And cheese! And no onions."

"Duke's going out with the guys, I think," Laura adds.

"He is?"

Duke's face scrunches in confusion.

"Yeah. Aiden just texted him." Laura says.

"He did?" I cover the mouthpiece and say, "The girls say you're going out with the guys."

Duke whispers back. "Aiden said Rob needs me. He's got something going on. It's sort of an impromptu gathering to handle whatever's up with him."

"Okay," I say, cloaking my disappointment. If Rob needs him, I don't want to be selfish.

"We'll pick this up where we left off when I get home," Duke says. "Okay?"

"Yes. That'll be good."

I still don't really want to go to girls' night. Maybe I can explain to the girls that I'm worn out. Then I could just watch a movie in my cozy sweats until Duke gets back.

Duke stands up, taking his plate with him. He leans over me and kisses my forehead. "Tomorrow night the whole town could burn down and I'll stay here with you, okay?"

I chuckle. So dramatic. "Yes. You've got a deal."

Laura must think I'm talking to her. I nearly forgot she was still on the line.

"Great. See you in forty-five. Go shower." Laura says in that bossy tone of hers that leaves no room for argument or dissension.

"I think I might just call it a night and stay in."

"Nope. You're not. It's still early. You've got time to hang with us and still relax at home and get all your beauty sleep. Get showered, Shannon. Trust me."

"You're still acting super-weird."

"That I am. Now go."

I hang up. Duke's got his keys in his hand and he's headed toward the front door.

"Laura told me to shower and come over to the farm."

"You don't have to," Duke says. "She's not the boss of you."

"I know. I'm not that tired, though. I'd just be sitting here waiting for you to come back."

"I like the sound of that."

I smile up at him. "I'll just go hang out with them for an hour or so and come home after that."

"Sounds good. I'll see you when I'm done helping Rob." Duke bends in and kisses me softly.

"Save some of that for dessert," he winks. Then he adds, "Raincheck on all the things,"

"We really are married, aren't we?" I stand and grab my plate to take it into the kitchen.

Duke chuckles. "You're just figuring that out?"

"I mean, we're scheduling time together. We never did this when we were dating. Back then you'd drive by in the middle of the night and pick me up in the pickup or on your motorcycle."

"I'll still drive by in the middle of the night. Want me to take you out to the old Clawson place tonight at midnight? We could make out in the back of my truck like old times, look for shooting stars. I'll even let you have the blankets if it gets chilly."

I smile. I don't think I could even climb up into the bed of the truck as big as I am right now. Dancing is one thing, climbing into trucks is another entirely.

"I hate to tell you, but I think I'll be dead asleep in one of your old shirts before midnight."

"And I'll have my arm wrapped around you and our son in our bed. Sounds like a raincheck on having a midnight date in the back of my truck too."

"Sorry."

"Don't be sorry, Shannon. I've got you in my bed at night, in my kitchen in the morning, and in my heart whenever we're not together. I couldn't ask for more."

"Okay," I actually blush. "Well, rain checks all around then."

"I'll take all those rain checks," Duke says. "And I'll cash them in before the baby comes. And I'll see you when I get home."

"Sounds good."

"I love you, Hollywood." He steps closer and kisses me again, then he pulls me in for a hug.

"I love you more."

"That's up for debate." He smiles down at me. "But I'm the luckiest man alive. That's a fact."

He pulls back, placing one more kiss on my lips, then he leans down and says something to our baby. He cups his hand like it's a secret, but I hear him.

"If you're cooking up a body in there, don't forget the boy parts, mkay, little man?"

"You really don't want a girl?" I ask.

I know we joke, but sometimes I just want to be sure.

"I want a girl. Or a boy. Or whatever we have." Duke's tone is serious as he runs a hand along my cheek, his other hand resting protectively on my protruding belly.

"Me too," I tell him.

I set my hand on Duke's shoulder and look him in the eyes.

"You'll love having a little girl, Duke. You'll spoil her to bits, and she'll be madly in love with you. And if we have a boy, I don't know what I'll do." I smile up at him. "Two Dukes? I don't think the world is quite ready for that."

"I'm ready," he says quietly. "I'm so ready, Shannon."

We stand there, smiling at one another and then I say, "I'd better shower. I'll see you later tonight."

Duke leans in and kisses me one more time. "See you tonight."

I carry my plate into the kitchen and then I head to the

shower. I'm just finishing getting dressed when there's a knock at the door. I wrap my hair up into a messy bun. and walk into the front room. Of all things, Laura is on our porch.

"Laura?"

"No backing out. Glad you showered. You'll be glad too. Let's go."

"I was coming over, you know."

"I know. I'm just here in case you changed your mind."

"So, you're kidnapping me."

"Technically, it's not kidnapping if the person is a grownup and they come willingly."

"For the record, I'm not coming willingly."

"Trust me. I wouldn't be making you do this if I didn't think you really deep down want it.."

"That's some twisted logic."

"Mm hmm."

Laura jingles her keys in the air.

"I need to dry my hair."

"Make it snappy."

"Remind me why you're my best friend," I tease.

"I won't have to remind you when you're surrounded by the girls tonight."

As much as I hate to admit it, the idea of hanging out with my girlfriends sounds better than it did when Duke was still home. We haven't had a girls' night in a while. I'm not admitting that to Laura, though. She's the best gloater I know.

I dry my hair, put on a light touch of mascara and lip gloss, grab my purse and follow Laura out the front door.

"I'm not staying super-late," I tell her.

"Fine. I'll take you home anytime you want. You just say the word."

"Really?"

"Yep. Whenever you've had enough time with your four closest friends, say uncle, and I'll bring you right back here."

"Okay."

Something's fishy. I can't tell what yet.

Laura drives us out of our neighborhood to the country road that runs in front of The Old Finch Place where Lexi and Trevor live, past farmland and ranches until we arrive at Aiden's. She's quiet the whole drive and I actually appreciate having a little time to be the passenger. The baby kicks again and I rub my hand over my belly.

"Is she wiggling?" Laura asks, glancing over at me.

"She's more active at night."

"Little Laura likes to move."

I giggle. Laura's been joking about us naming the baby after her ever since she found out I was pregnant.

I'm still giggling when we pull up the driveway.

My mouth drops open.

Cars fill the gravel driveway and the paved area just beyond the house. It almost looks like it does when Aiden and Em host a barbecue.

This is not girls' night.

"What is going on?" I ask Laura.

I glance in the rearview mirror.

I could call our town delivery guy, Decker, and ask him to pick me up and drive me home. Then I could change back into my maternity sweats, one of Duke's T-shirts, and watch reruns of *Friends*. I'm about to share my plan with Laura when Aiden's truck pulls in the driveway behind us. Duke is sandwiched in the front seat between Aiden and Rob.

This just keeps getting weirder.

"What are they doing here?"

More cars follow Aiden's truck, parking along the fenceline.

"What is this?" I look over at Laura.

"Well ..." she starts to say.

I glance in the rearview mirror again. Rob's hopping out of Aiden's truck and Duke's right behind him. As soon as his boots hit the ground, Duke starts walking straight toward Laura's car—toward me.

I open the passenger door and climb out.

"What's going on?" I ask Duke.

"I have no idea. I got to Rob's and the guys told me they needed me to look at something. Next thing I know we're driving to Aiden's. It's all very cryptic. What did the girls say?"

"I haven't seen them yet."

The words aren't out of my mouth for a second before my best friends come bursting out of the farmhouse and onto the driveway.

"You're here!" Lexi shouts.

"I am."

"Oh, good. I thought you were going to bail on us," Lexi says. "We couldn't have that."

"What exactly is going on here?" I ask Laura, who's now out of her car standing next to the driver's door.

Laura walks toward me. Duke. Lexi, Jayme, and Em are right on her heels.

I stare at my four closest friends. Looking at each one in turn. Their faces don't reveal anything. Em looks nervous.

"Surprise!" Lexi shouts.

Aiden echoes Lexi in a very loud voice. "Surprise!"

Duke and I share a look. At least he's as confused as I am.

All of a sudden, the barn doors open and people pour out. Other people come toward the driveway from around the other side of the house.

Everyone's shouting "Surprise!" And each guest is either wearing a pink or blue shirt.

"What ...?" I start to ask, but Laura cuts me off.

"It's your early baby shower. Even though it's not that early. After all, we're only eight weeks from your due date."

"Our ... baby shower?" I ask, looking at Duke.

"And gender reveal!" Rob shouts.

"Gender reveal?" Duke asks. "How do you know the gender when we don't even know the gender?"

Grant speaks up from the small crowd of people now gathering around us in the driveway. "We might happen to know the nurse who did the ultrasound. She technically works part-time for me, so I had access to the records as your doctor. It may have involved a dozen of Memaw's cupcakes as a small bribe in exchange for the ultrasound images."

"We aren't suing!" Duke shouts. "Let's get this party started!"

The crowd of our friends and townspeople erupts into whooping, shouting and cheering. We follow Laura and Rob out to the barn which has been decorated with strings of twinkle lights and tables. Up front are two chairs and a stack of gifts.

Laura takes charge and divides the crowd into teams. We play games like diaper change relay and blindfolded name-that-baby-food. After we eat a meal of barbecue and side dishes, Rob gets everyone's attention.

"Okay, everyone! We're about to have you start heading to the back of the barn out to the pasture, we'll have the main event."

He turns his attention to me and Duke. We're sitting side by side at a table at the front near the massive stack of gifts.

"You might have noticed our shirts," Aiden says, using what I call his YouTuber voice.

Duke and I nod.

"Each guest made a guess as to what gender baby Satterson will be."

Duke and I look around the barn where friends and family are gathered around tables. Children run outside the barn doors playing what might be a game of tag or hide and seek, I can't tell. My heart swells. This is better than any shower I could have planned. Mine would have been all women. It would have been sweet, but Duke and I would have missed sharing this, being surrounded by the people we've grown up around.

Duke whispers into my ear. "There's about a fifty-fifty divide between pink and blue."

Aidens raises his voice and says, ""So, let's see who's right and who's got to wait for your next baby to get a chance at being accurate."

The crowd laughs. Duke wraps his arm around my shoulders and gives me a squeeze.

Duke constantly teases me about us having our own baseball team made up of Satterson children. I sometimes wonder if he's joking. I keep telling him to let me get through this first one before we get too carried away with family planning. I'm sure we'll have more, though. Maybe four? We'll see. I want a house filled with Duke's children, that much I'm sure of.

"So, without further ado," Rob says. "Everyone ready?"

Mabel's voice rings out above the rest of the crowd when everyone shouts, "We're ready!"

She adds on, "I don't have all day!"

Esther whisper-shouts, "What's so important that you can't spare an hour to find out what kind of baby Duke's having? You used to change that boy's diapers."

I look at Duke and giggle.

"I didn't wear diapers," he whispers to me. "I came out potty trained. Just like our child will. You wait and see."

He pushes his chair out and stands to help me up. Everyone starts heading out the barn doors and gathering in the pasture.

I look up at Duke. He has the most innocent, serious look on his face.

"Duke."

He smiles down at me and extends his hand. We walk around the back of the barn where the crowd in pink and blue are gathered.

"Are we ready?" Aiden shouts.

"YES!" everyone shouts.

"Ready Rob?" Aiden yells over to Rob.

"I'm ready!" Rob turns and presses a button or something. It's hard to see from where I'm standing.

Duke's arm is wrapped around my shoulder, he's squeezing me to himself, and my hands are balled into nervous, excited fists. We're about to find out what we're having, joined by our friends and family. We'll all find out together.

"Okay!" Rob shouts. "Count down with me!"

The whole crowd starts counting backward from ten to one. "Ten ... Nine ... Eight ..." Duke and I join in. "Seven ... Six ... Five ... Four ... Three ... Two ... One!"

At the sound of the word, "One," everyone around us pulls the string to their hand-held popper. Bursts of colored streamers fill the air. Then ten smoke cannons fire off plumes of pink smoke in a show that puts the Fourth of July pyrotechnics to shame.

"It's a girl!" People are shouting all around us. "It's a girl! They're having a girl!"

Duke spins me so that I'm facing him. He grips my upper arms and looks me in the eyes. Tears are streaming down his cheeks. "Did you hear that?" He brings his hands up and cups my face. "It's a girl, Shannon. We're having a girl."

I nod, my own tears streaming down my face.

"She's going to be a ballerina," Duke says in the most reverent tone I've ever heard him use. "And I'm going to teach her to play ball and change the oil on a car. But not right away."

"Yeah," I giggle through my tears. "Not right away."

"Shannon," he nearly whispers. "We're having a girl."

I nod, unable to form words.

I've been carrying this baby for over seven months. She's fluttered and kicked, given me morning sickness, made me wake more times than I can count so I can pee in the middle of the night. I already feel this inexplicable connection to her. And now I know for certain what I only felt as a hunch: she's a girl.

The crowd is bustling with excitement around us, but all I see is Duke. His smile. His kind eyes looking into mine. And then his words. I'll never forget the words he says next.

"I want to name her."

"Now?"

"Yes, Shannon. Now. I want to name her after your sister. I want to name our daughter Bridgette."

I choke out a sob and fall into Duke's arms. He holds me, running his hand down my back. People are starting to say things to us, but I hold onto Duke a few moments longer.

I pull away and look up into his eyes. "Yes. Let's name her Bridgette."

Duke holds my chin and leans in to place a kiss on my lips.

"She's going to be amazing," he whispers. "Just like her mother."

If you want *MORE* of the sweet, funny, heartwarming Bordeaux stories, read Jayme's story in *Doctorshipped* next.

Grant   Jayme

He's tall, dark, handsome ...
and oh-so grumpy.

Share the book love ...
Something you can do really quickly:
If you loved **Censorshipped**, you can help other readers find this
story by leaving a review on Amazon.

Never miss another Savannah Scott sweet romcom

Get connected ...

I send out a weekly Sweet Reader email full of fun, behind-the-scenes sneak peeks at my writing and life, deals on books, and book recommendations. Want to look forward to something in your inbox? Sign up for *Savannah's Sweet Reads email*.

Go to SavannahScottBooks.com to find all the links you need to free books, bonus chapters, and all things Savannah Scott!

You can also follow Savannah on Amazon, BookBub, or Goodreads.

A little note from me to you

I grew up in a small college town in southwest Ohio with farmland all around the outskirts, rivers and gorges to play in, and plenty of woods to hike in.

People stopped to chat when they ran into one another in the grocery (while impatient kids watched the ice cream melt in the cart). Neighbor children ran in and out of one another's homes all day long until supper time.

We caught fireflies on summer nights, sledded down snowy hills on campus, chatted around bonfires on our friends' farms, and drove tractors before we ever legally drove cars. (*Shhh. Don't tell.*)

I adore the small-town Ohio culture. My memories are filled with down-home goodness set in a beautiful landscape with rich history.

I love writing books that make people laugh, with a little life lesson or two tucked away in them somewhere. I always end with a happily ever after that gives us all a smile in our hearts.

Thank you for letting me share my stories with you.

All the Thanks

A story is birthed in one imagination, but it is raised by many hands and hearts.

I want to thank **Gila Santos, Tricia Anson and Charity Henico** for reading the bonus epilogue and giving me such solid feedback. A special thank you to **Tricia Anson** for helping me pull together the launch of the Third Anniversary Getting Shipped Celebration.

And to my **Awesome Advanced Readers** and the **AMAZING Bookstagram and Bookish Community** on Instagram and Facebook. You people bless my socks off—as evidenced by my nearly-constant bare feet.

Thank you to my oh-so-talented sister, **Mary Hessler Goad** for the redesigning of this cover and all the covers in the Getting Shipped series.

Laura Cohen, you are a delight. Thank you for taking my hand-drawn sketches, my doodles, my cut-and-paste representations and making us all such a beautiful map of Bordeaux. I adore it, and I know readers do too.

Jessica Gobble, My first and best cheerleader, my ride-or-die, my pie-hoarding secret-keeper, the one I laugh most with and cry first with. You are the sister of my heart and my soft place to land.

Jessie, I love you. You are my favorite. Thank you for being along for this wild ride. I would NOT be here without your love and belief in me. My readers owe you big.

Jon, my not-book boyfriend, Thank you for believing in me and supporting me. And thanks for all the private stand-up comedy I get to have on the daily with you. Ours is my favorite friends-to-lovers story.

And the biggest thanks to **God** for making me a storyteller and giving me the gifts I've received on this journey.

A story of stories

In December 2021, I published my first romcom—*Friendshipped*. Over the following year and a half, I wrote the rest of the Getting Shipped series, and this town, Bordeaux, came to life.

In the fall of 2023, I had an idea. I decided to overhaul this well-loved series for the third anniversary of *Friendshipped*.

I pulled together a team ...

I commissioned an artist to create a map of Bordeaux based on the way I imagine the town.

I worked with my designer to reimagine all the covers to bring them up a notch. I revised the manuscript for *Friendshipped* to elevate it to the level of the rest of the series while still retaining the original tone and essence of the story.

I wrote bonus chapters and epilogues for all the books. I hired audio narrators to help me produce the audiobook of *Courtshipped*, the prequel to this series.

The Getting Shipped series was the catalyst for my career shift. This series and its success helped me "quit my day job" to fulfill my dream of becoming a full-time author.

I have readers like you to thank for helping me make that dream come true.

One final thought. If you happen to know a billionaire who

falls in love with this series and decides to recreate the town of Bordeaux, send them my way. There are a whole lot of us who want to meet for coffee at Bean There Done That, stop into the Dippity Do to get a haircut and hear the latest gossip, and attend a bonfire at Aiden's farm.

Until then, I'll meet you in the next book.

Savannah

Made in United States
Cleveland, OH
13 June 2025

17717111R00239